TRUE IMMORTALS

TRUE IMMORTALS

Steven Bratman

**SPONTANEOUS
ORDER PUBLICATIONS**

Spontaneous Order Publications
Albany, NY. USA
Copyright © 2023 by Steven Bratman

Cover illustration by Juan Kantor
Printed in the United States of America
Print ISBN: 9798393653156
Library of Congress number on record.

1 2 3 4 5 6 7 8 9

CHAPTER 1

THE TRUE IMMORTAL

"Not the intense moment isolated, with no before and
after, but a lifetime burning in every moment."

T.S. ELIOT, *EAST COKER*

Try living in a house made of heroin and see if you don't get
addicted. They're shallow, narcissistic, fearful, overcautious,
grandiose and out of touch. But so good-looking.

THE CHRONICLER

BLAIR

IN THE LIGHT of his headlights, the clumps of dead grass by the sides of the road stood out like gray bristles, coarse as the hairs on his pursuer's neck. Wooden slats tottered beneath old barbed wire. In the distance, the red lights of a refinery or fertilizer factory hung in the clear winter sky like artificial constellations.

Blair's rational mind told him he must have lost Menniss 100s of miles ago, but he didn't feel safe. His insatiable, bred-in-the-bone caution impelled him to burrow deeper, to burrow ceaselessly, to escape even the possibility of a possibility that his pursuer might find him again.

But this was getting absurd. He'd outwitted the man once already, at the restaurant that morning. Richard Menniss was only a mortal. He had no superhuman powers, just determination and a ridiculous assumed name.

A cattle guard vibrated the Volvo's tires, and the road descended to follow the slow turns of a wash. Blair drove for miles beside barren rocks dusted with snow. The road ascended again and crossed the wash on a narrow aluminum bridge out into open country.

Blair slowed for a fox crossing the road. The creature stopped halfway and turned to gaze at him, its eyes red in the Volvo's headlights. More than the eyes were red: the fox had a bloody gash across its face. Blair closed his eyes, horrified. When he looked again, the fox was gone.

A coyote must have done it. The plains were full of them. And coyotes could track you by scent, not just by sight; the fox was lucky to have survived.

Blair pulled off the asphalt and stopped the car. Listening to distant howling, he sat in the dark and thought: *this is wrong. I'm forever, the Crown Jewel of Creation. I shouldn't have to play the hunted animal, always running and hiding.*

But this perfect body gave him no choice.

RICHARD MENNISS HAD entered Blair's life 36 hours earlier in the form of a FedEx letter package delivered by a woman in her late 30s, full of life within her heavy uniform. When she handed Blair the cardboard envelope, he pretended to think it was a letter bomb. Not because he had any premonition; he was just flirting.

"A letter bomb?" she asked archly. She had lovely black hair. "Do you have serious enemies?"

"I was rude to a telemarketer once."

"That *is* serious. Telemarketers frequently send letter bombs." She moved her hands delicately over the cardboard. "I don't feel any wires."

"Let me check." He imitated her movements but more sensually. "What else should I look for?"

"Well …" She glanced at her watch. She pushed on the edges of the thin cardboard package to make the sides pouch out and shook it. "It feels like a regular-size envelope floating around in there. I think you're okay."

Blair said he wanted to try for himself. He squeezed the package several times and found the expansion erotic, like a heaving chest.

He began a flow of patter he meant to sound like patter. Maybe, he suggested, he should wrap his arms around his recliner and open the envelope on its far side so the solid piece of furniture would shield him from the blast. Obviously, he should wear heavy gloves. But what should he wrap around his arms to protect them?

"Good question." She looked at her watch again. "I wish I could help. I do so hate it when my customers get blown up. But I have to go."

"Perhaps you could stop by later to see if I've survived?"

"I'd be glad to," she said.

He read the name off the tag on her uniform. "Well then, see you later, Lisa."

"Goodbye, Alan," she said and departed his story.

How had she known? But of course—the name on the package.

In his mind, he referred to himself as "Blair" because that was the name Saul had given him. He'd only used it during a single frame, that precious 12 years he'd spent with Kathryn. In his current Texas frame, he was Alan Davidsen.

Blair shook the package again and listened to the standard-sized envelope rattle around inside. He peeled back the cardboard strip to open the package and reached inside to take out the inner envelope. When he read the words written across its face, his heart clanged.

To Blair Oliver.

Kathryn had been Mrs. Blair Oliver. Was it from her?

The letters were too blocky. But perhaps Kathryn's hands had grown so arthritic she could no longer form her famous feminine loops.

He ransacked drawers for a letter opener, couldn't find one, and grabbed a paring knife from the kitchen. He slit open the envelope and drew out the single sheet of heavy, cream-colored paper. Though Kathryn always used flowery stationery, this was a naked page. Kathryn's lovely cursive always slanted downwards, but these words marched upright, like soldiers in formation.

To The Honorable Blair Oliver:

Please forgive me if this isn't the proper salutation. I've never spoken to one such as yourself, and I don't know the appropriate formalities. Be assured, sir, that I intend you no disrespect. Quite the contrary. I am in awe.

I have discovered your nature, sir, and I am staggered. Please, sir, I respectfully beg of you, would you be so kind as to

meet with me—in a place of your choosing—and tell me how
it works? I'm normally a practical, down-to-earth man, but I
would entertain any explanation, no matter how supernatural.
The discovery of your existence has filled me with amazement
and wonder.

Please call me at the number below and we can arrange a
meeting.

Sincerely,
Richard Menniss

Blair bunched up the paper and gripped it hard, as if to squeeze the intruder out of his life.

He heard Saul's voice in his mind.

There is nothing more dangerous than a man or woman who
has discovered your immortality.

Mortals may, in time, resign themselves to aging and death,
but this is a resignation forced by circumstance rather than
freely embraced. Once he glimpses in you the possibility of escape
from age and death, he will—even if he is the most respectable
of men—become rapacious. His humanity will be overwhelmed
by lust for what he believes you can give him. He will grasp at
you with a strength that surpasses sanity, grip you like the old
man in the fable who sits on the Brahmin's shoulders. These
tragic and dangerous creatures have been called Peiniea (the
Hungry Ones) and Rasmeosi (Those Who Grip), or Luefelloto
Lofelli (Seekers of Lifeblood). In English, they are often referred
to as hangers-on.

By no means will such a being accept the bare truth, that
immortality is an irreducible fact of nature, incapable of being
gifted or conveyed. Rather, he will know to a certainty that you
possess an herb, a spell, a sacred spring, a mysterious power in
the blood that, once consumed, provides the gift of eternity. He
will demand access to this gift and will countenance no denial.

An alchemical gentleman once came to believe I possessed the
Philosopher's Stone, lodged, peculiarly enough, in my liver. He

wished, therefore, to possess my liver. My flight encompassed three continents before I escaped his voracious reach.

He is a terribly dangerous thing, your hanger-on, more dangerous than war, famine or weather. You must at all times strive to avoid being discovered by such a being, and if, by ill chance, that disaster befalls you, you must flee instantly, letting nothing dear delay you.

MORE THAN A century had passed since Blair last received this admonition, and he'd never been called upon to act on it. But Saul had delivered the lecture so many times and with so many vivid variations that it remained top of mind. In one oft-told tale, a hanger-on imprisoned an Immortal behind a wall, *Cask of Amontillado* style, refusing to release him until he gave up the secret of immortality. This continued for decades until the mortal finally died, and the True Immortal, dependent on him for food and water, did too. How did Saul know? The Immortal had been given a quill, ink bottle and paper to write down the formula or charm, and he kept a diary until his miserable end.

With stories like that to motivate him, Blair instantly remembered and obeyed. He grabbed his escape bag and fled. He drove on small country roads, using various tricks he'd seen in movies: doubling back, making sudden turns, periodically pausing out of sight of the road to check for pursuers. When he felt confident no one could be following him, he took to the freeway. He drove all night, with no fixed destination other than leaving Texas behind.

At dawn, he found himself on the outskirts of Kansas City. The geographic circle of his possible overnight travel now covered thousands of square miles. Menniss couldn't possibly find him. He was anonymous again, hidden and safe.

BLAIR STOPPED AT the first restaurant he came to, a Denny's at the southern edge of town. The air was cold, and he put on his heavy coat. He patted the gun in its deep inner pocket, then walked up a curving cement path that led to the restaurant's door.

Inside, the air was humid and warm and smelled like pancake

syrup. Pleasant, warm restaurant noises comforted him: the clatter from the kitchen, the high and low notes of conversation at the tables, the squabbles of children and admonitions of parents. But when the hostess greeted him, he became acutely aware of how travel-stained he must look. He set his coat on a chair to mark his place and hurried to the restroom. Finding a splash of ketchup on his tailored black pants, he hastily rubbed it away, flushing with embarrassment. In the restroom, he dampened his hair and restored the black waves. He shaved and admired the darkness the blade left behind; a gift of his Hungarian ancestry, his fast-growing beard made him look deep and brooding. Not that he possessed depth or spent much time brooding, but he looked the part.

He came out of the restroom in a cheerful and flirtatious mood and watched an elegant, dark-haired waitress on the far side of the restaurant set out dishes for a table full of businessmen. Lost in this imaginary love affair, he didn't notice the man who had taken a seat opposite his coat until it was too late.

The hanger-on—for it had to be him—was massive and muscular. He wore his hair cut short, military style. He must have been at least 60, maybe a bit older. Although he was clean-shaven, unpleasant stubble covered much of his neck. He had a heavy, coarse face with sprawling, blond eyebrows, large jowls and a nose that looked as if it had been broken more than once. But he had intelligent, sensitive eyes—an unnerving contrast.

Rising, the man introduced himself as Richard Menniss. He moved with a powerful physicality that also expressed deference, like a military officer greeting a superior. Menniss held out his thick, hairy hand, and despite himself, Blair shook it. The hanger-on's grip was strong but not aggressive, and neither lingered too long nor broke off too quickly. Gesturing at the table, Menniss said, "May I buy you breakfast, sir?"

The tall waitress, the one Blair had admired, hurried past, holding a tray. Blair longed to talk to her; he had a *right* to talk to her, but Menniss made him unfree.

"I hope I haven't offended you by offering a meal." Menniss sounded uneasy. "As I wrote in my letter, I don't know your customs.

I had hoped—at least, it's been my experience and education—that, in all cultures and all times, breaking bread together is an accepted way to establish connection."

"Perhaps I do not wish to create such a connection," Blair said.

Menniss had been standing at a slight angle to Blair, but now he faced him directly. "Sir, I'm a student of your life. I know everything important you've done since you first appeared in Australia. I know where you've lived since then, too, except for a period of 12 years when I lost your trail. Just now, I followed you from Dallas to Kansas City. May we agree that the connection already exists?"

People were beginning to look at them.

Assuming an acquiescence Blair had not yet given, Menniss nodded and let himself down in his chair, sealing the deal by spreading a red napkin across his lap.

Blair felt the heavy coat behind him on the chair and thought with some comfort of the gun packed into its inner pocket. But he needed time to arrange matters properly. "You have impressive tracking skills," Blair said.

"I've had a lot of practice," Menniss said. "I've worked as a freelance bounty hunter slash detective slash spy for the last 10 years."

To gain at least some edge, Blair raised the level of his diction. "And by whom, exactly, have you been employed?"

Menniss effortlessly matched the change. "I am engaged exclusively by clients who require a high level of discretion. Men of considerable wealth. Men of distinction as well, perhaps, but that is supposition; for security reasons, my clients and I do not meet in person."

"And your real name is?"

The hanger-on frowned slightly. "Yeah, I suppose 'Menniss' is too cute. But I'm used to it now. And all your names are made up, too, so we're even."

Their waitress arrived, not the elegant, tall one, but a nurse-like woman, the type that makes one feel nurtured and cared for. Though he knew he should be calculating an escape, Blair let himself speculate on how best to seduce her. He would begin by appreciating her professional kindness, knowing that this would bring out her personal kindness. And then probe still further: why are you so kind?

Because you're lonely? Of course you are. And I am, too, lonelier than you can imagine.

But the hanger-on's heavy, depriving presence crushed all possibility of flirtation.

Menniss ordered breakfast. Blair followed suit, and the waitress left.

"And what did you do before you went freelance?" Blair asked.

"I worked for the CIA," Menniss said.

Blair half-rose from his chair. The CIA? If they were after him, he couldn't possibly escape.

Menniss reached across the table and patted Blair's shoulder with a cupped hand. "No need to jump out of your skin. I said I *used* to work for the CIA. I don't work for them now. I hate the government, and I would never sic it on anyone. How about I fill you in on my background? I think that might help."

It isn't right, Blair thought, that this evaporating creature should dominate me so entirely. But he does.

"I BEGAN AS a patriotic idiot," Menniss said. "My motto was, 'America has enemies, and someone has to kill them, so why not me?' I went to a school for commandos—Special Forces, they call them now—where the toughest of the tough go to learn how to kill bad guys. Or so I thought. We spent much more time studying history than learning how to make people dead. We listened to lectures on local customs and did so much role-playing it was almost touchy-feelie. The plan was to bond with the natives and get *them* to do the killing. Enlightened thinking, wouldn't you agree?"

Without giving Blair a chance to reply, Menniss went on. "We trained for half a year, and then they sent us out to live with a bunch of kick-ass Laotians right there in their villages. They were natural fighters and braver than shit, and we got along great. We got along so great that a month into it, my best native buddy took me out in the jungle to meet his Sensei. Sensei was the real thing, a white-bearded wisp who could beat the crap out of any three young guys without breaking a sweat. He introduced himself by beating the crap out of *me*, just like in the movies. And when I was lying on the floor sucking air, what does he do? He gives me a lecture on Buddhism.

"I'd met plenty of priests and gurus before, but they were all ass-holes. Sensei was *spiritual.* Before I met Sensei, I didn't believe there was such a thing as 'spiritual.' He was kind and wise and full of power all at the same time. Have you ever met anyone like that, sir?"

That should be me, Blair thought. After 300fr years, I should have wisdom and personal power. But I don't have much of anything.

Again, Menniss didn't wait for an answer. "I'd spent six months with Sensei when the choppers came and pulled us out. Change of plan—surprise, surprise. They dropped us in a new part of Laos, among a different bunch of natives. These new natives were great too, but they hated the other natives. And our job was to help our new friends kill our old friends, which we could do well because we'd just spent half a year learning everything that could be learned about the guys we were now supposed to help get killed. See, the higher-ups had lied to us on purpose. If we'd known from the beginning that we were infiltrating rather than making allies, we wouldn't have infil-trated half so well. Enlightened thinking."

Pausing to wipe his mouth, he added, "And that's what we did. We went in with native group number two and helped them slaugh-ter the shit out of native group number one." He said this in an offhand way, as if he didn't care, but his eyes gave him away. "And what about Sensei? Sensei wasn't one of those martial arts idiots who thinks he can stop bullets with his bare hands. He finds a reporter, douses himself with gasoline and burns himself to death while the guy takes pictures. He wasn't the only one who did that, but he was the only one I knew. Peaceful from beginning to end. Sir, could you sit still and quiet while your body burned up? I don't think I could."

Now's the moment, Blair thought. I should grab my coat and run while he's distracted by his memories.

But he couldn't move. Menniss was compelling, an oncoming train.

"As for myself," Menniss said, "I couldn't deal with it. Betraying people isn't my thing. I'd impressed the professorish wonk-wonks who gave us our history lessons, and I got myself transferred to the CIA. My idea was that I wouldn't have to betray anyone in person; I'd only set up things so other people did it. But, as it turned out, I couldn't stand that either, and I quit. So don't worry—I don't work for the CIA. I don't love my country either. I don't love anything much. I to freelance my skills, and that's how—but look, here's breakfast."

There had been a shift change, and a new waitress brought them their food. She had a face from a fashion magazine: olive skin, a narrow, delicate nose and thin eyebrows. Blair found her physically appealing, but what most appealed to him was her effect on Menniss. Those bare shoulders, those beautiful legs, those delicate fingers: Menniss couldn't bear so much sexiness close up. It was written all over him.

So close and entirely out of reach. They used to come after *you*, Richard Menniss, didn't they? Beautiful girls—a commando's perquisite. They hung on to you, leaned against you, and took off their clothes for you. But that was when you were young. Now, your skin is lumpy—your face sags—you're an old, old man, and women smell death on you.

But not me. So far as she can tell, I'm about 24. And I've had 300 years to practice. Watch me work.

All Blair did was smile at the waitress. But it was a calibrated smile, laced with undertones and overtones, designed to highlight his brooding face, deep-set eyes, soft hair and his cheeks with their ever-visible shadow. The smile said, "I've known anguish, but at this moment, looking at you, I'm happy. I'm free." It would have come off ridiculous if spoken aloud, but unspoken, it slipped beneath her defenses.

Was she blushing? The dark tone of her skin made it difficult to tell, but she fumbled his dishes. She set them in the wrong places and, while rearranging them, knocked over a ketchup bottle; she dropped a spoon, and it teetered on the table's edge; she reached for the spoon, and so did he. Their fingers touched and she melted.

So trivially arranged.

But when she turned to serve Menniss, she found her balance again. She catered to him kindly, treated him like a senior citizen, and all but offered to spoon-feed him his waffles and wipe off his drool.

As she left, she gave Blair a parting smile like a signed work of art. Lovely.

But that wasn't the point. The point was that she'd broken the spell. He was free now, and it was time to escape.

ACROSS THE RESTAURANT, a server moved among the tables, refilling coffees. He was large and heavy-boned, possibly Samoan. If that server were to stand on the one side of their table rather than the other, he'd block Menniss perfectly. How much longer till he arrived? Ten minutes, perhaps less.

Menniss had made no move toward the huge plate of waffles beneath his chin but sat motionless, uneasy.

"Is something wrong?" Blair asked solicitously. "Don't you feel well?"

"No, no, I'm fine," Menniss said. "It's just that I thought perhaps … coming from long ago, as you do … perhaps you might want to say some kind of grace before we eat. I don't want to offend."

"Not at all, not at all," Blair said. "Dig in."

Menniss grunted, cut off a large slice of waffle and ate as if he were starving.

Blair ate lightly, a little of this, a little of that. As if to shift his bowl of fruit salad to a more convenient position, he adjusted his dish of eggs-over-easy to make room. In the process, he pushed his coffee cup to the edge of the table. He rescued the cup and moved it to a vacant space opposite Menniss' coffee, on the side of the table where he hoped the Samoan would stand.

But the server still had half a dozen tables to attend before theirs. To buy time, Blair said, "I take many precautions to hide my … unusual characteristics. And yet you found me. How did you pull it off?"

Menniss spoke with largesse. "One of my clients—well, practically my only client these days—takes an interest in disappearances. Not the famous disappearances but the unimportant domestic cases nobody else cares about. He pays me to study them. A few years ago, he flew me to Australia to investigate the story of a man who'd disappeared in the early 1960s. I could tell right off the story was fishy."

"In what way?" Blair asked with genuine interest. "How was it fishy?"

Menniss waved a fork full of waffle at him. "Because the way the man died didn't fit the way he lived. Up until that last trip, he's Mr. Cautious. When seatbelts get invented, he's one of the first Aussies to buy a car that offers them: a Volvo. When he goes scuba diving with friends, he calls it quits when his air tank reaches half full. If he goes off for an afternoon ramble in the bush, he takes a short-wave radio."

Menniss shoved the waffle slices in his mouth and kept on talking. "On that last ramble, though, he didn't have a working radio; it broke the day before and was in the shop. But he goes on that ramble anyway. He drives off and never comes back. Tragic." Menniss took a long drink of water. "But, in my experience, people don't change their habits like that. My theory is that he went off without his radio because he *meant* to disappear."

The Samoan server was lingering too long at another table. Blair lifted his nearly drained coffee cup and tried to get his attention. No luck. "Maybe he was having a midlife crisis," Blair said. "Your Mr. Caution. Maybe he'd gotten sick of being so careful and wanted to loosen up."

"A midlife crisis at age 35? I don't think so. I tracked down a police detective who remembered the case, and he told me that at first, he'd thought the same thing—that it was a staged disappearance. But one compelling detail threw him off that track. A brilliant touch, a magnificent detail, the work of a master."

Blair found this third-person analysis of his life inordinately pleasurable; it had been more than a century since he'd spoken with anyone who knew he was an Immortal. "And what detail was that?" he asked.

Menniss stuffed his mouth with another wad of waffle and, rather indistinctly, said, "The dog."

"Pardon?" Blair's tone suggested he couldn't understand the word, but he'd made out the word just fine; it was its significance that eluded him.

"Mr. Caution took his dog with him on the day he disappeared. A great big shepherd mix he'd owned for five, six years. Name of Aslan. By all accounts, he loved that dog. And since your average normal human doesn't deliberately abandon his dog in the outback, even when he means to disappear from his wife, the police backed off from the deliberate-disappearance theory."

The server was moving again, though with an agonizing absence of hurry.

"But what if it was an outdoors kind of dog?" Blair asked. "The kind that has to be persuaded to stop eating the neighbor's sheep? And what if it so happened that the place where this man abandoned the dog had plenty of water nearby and things to hunt? No, in my opinion, the dog part doesn't prove anything at all."

Menniss folded his hands on the table and tipped them slightly to the right, a meditative pose. "In his *opinion*," he murmured. "That's funny." His expression changed, and his voice turned harsh. "You never checked to see how it turned out, did you? I can see you didn't. You don't know."

Once more—it was ridiculous—Blair felt caught fast. "Know what?"

Instead of answering, Menniss dug around in his jacket pockets. He had the kind of jacket that's full of pockets, and the search took some time. Finally, he found what he was looking for: a set of photographs. He held them fanned out in one hand like playing cards, their backs to Blair. After studying them briefly, he pulled one out and set it face up on the table.

A terrible image. A horror. His poor dog's head, with its tongue stuck out and rigid.

"They found him curled up on the driver's seat," Menniss said, his tone chummy. "It seems he died from dehydration, waiting for you to come back."

Blair stared numbly at the photo. But it made no sense.

They'd waited together on that high rock, Aslan sitting patiently beside him. When the helicopter came, he gave Aslan a command, one of many that the intelligent dog understood. "Aslan, run to the lake! Run! Go now!" As the helicopter rose, he watched the dog race toward the water, joyously scattering the birds, a lovely last image.

But after that, Aslan returned to the hot car? He'd jumped back in through the open window and stayed there?

Why? The lake was so close.

"Since no normal human being would deliberately abandon his dog in the desert," Menniss went on, "the police gave up on the possibility of deliberate disappearance. But I drew a different conclusion. I figured he wasn't a human being; he was an Immortal. And Immortals don't take mortal beings seriously. For instance, me sitting here. I'm a big guy. Stick a carrot on me for a nose and dress me in white, and I'm a snowman on your lawn. In a day or two, I've melted away. Nobody misses a snowman once it's gone. And that's how you feel about mortals. Dogs, people, all the same. You don't care about any of us flash-in-the-pans, do you, sir?"

You don't understand me at all, Blair thought. Not at all.

But if you meant that speech to tie me down with guilt, it didn't work. You've reminded me of who I am: the Crown Jewel of Creation. No mortal being shall have dominion over me.

The server had disappeared, but now he came out of the kitchen holding two fresh pots of coffee. Blair shifted his weight and prepared.

Menniss set two more photos on the table. "One from Australia and the other from Brazil."

Blair gave them a vague glance. "Interesting," he said. "And how did you connect the first to the second?"

"Fingerprints."

Fingerprints. So simple. He remembered when those first came out but had temporarily forgotten about them. Saul had warned him that Immortals (and hafeems) typically lagged the modern by a century or more. He would have to be more careful.

"The man's poor widow … she turned a bit delusional. She couldn't believe her husband was dead. Her idea was that he came down with amnesia, and he was still wandering the bush. So she circulates photos and fingerprints to everyone she knows. I get my hands on some, and I use my CIA connections to crosscheck, and lo and behold, the same prints show up 25 years later in the case of a man who went missing in Brazil. Amazingly well preserved, don't you think? He's still quite the good looking *young* man, in my opinion."

With a fingertip, Blair idly shifted the photos around. There was no denying it.

Menniss still held one more photo in his hand. He gave it a last lingering look, then held it out for Blair to see. "She still misses you," Menniss said. "After half a century. Isn't that pathetic? Here, take it."

Blair cradled the photo in his hands and stared at the image: a terribly old woman. A woman dying of age. Wrinkles had swallowed her face, grew like moss around her lips and half covered her eyes. But beneath the ruin, he could still make out Kathryn. And he still loved her.

In his mind, he reversed time's destroying marks. He saw Kathryn as she'd looked that last time he saw her, framed by the doorway of their house, her face made even more beautiful by the first light sketches of age. Turning time back another 12 years to the moment they'd first met in a coffeehouse in Sydney.

"It must be hard on you, staying so perfect while they shrivel," Menniss said. "They wear out awfully fast, getting their wrinkles and all. What I wonder is, why did you pick someone *older* than you? In apparent age, I mean. I'd expect you to go for the young ones, the 18-year-olds. That way, they'd last a little while before you had to throw them away."

You don't understand anything, Blair thought. "What do you expect me to do? Stick around till my wife looks like my grandmother and my son could be my father? Until the whole world knows what I am?"

Menniss gave him an encouraging nod.

"Think about it," Blair went on. "If you look the same at 36 as you do at 24, maybe that's believable. But much beyond that, people will notice. I have to move on every 12 years or so and start a new life. And I have to keep each new life separated from the others, like a new painting in a new frame. My lives stack on each other, but they don't connect. Maybe that's why I never get anywhere."

The photo of Kathryn was a typical posed shot, with the subject angled slightly to the side. But it seemed that at any moment, she might turn her head in the photo, look straight at him, and realize his betrayal. "You didn't die," she'd say. "You didn't suffer amnesia. You abandoned me."

Blair turned the photo facedown on the table so she couldn't do it.

He'd made the resolution many times before and always broken it, but he made it again: no more relationships. No wives, no lovers, no friends, no children. He would live entirely alone, keep company with no one but the one companion he never had to betray, never needed to abandon: his perfect, timeless body.

And it was ready. It overflowed with readiness.

Hold on just a few more minutes, he thought. The server is on his way.

"I'm supposed to turn you over," Menniss said.

"To whom?" Blair asked.

"To my client, the one who set me onto you. I call him the I-H. Short for Immortal Hunter. He pays well for hafeems, but he has a jackpot on offer for True Immortals." Menniss leaned over the table, his heavy face like a fist. "Should I call him and tell him to come collect you? God only knows what he'll do once he's got you." He licked his lips and swallowed. "But I *haven't* told him. And I won't. All I want is for you to tell me the secret. Just tell me, me personally, and I'll help you hide again. Hide so well no one will ever find you, not the I-H, not anyone."

At last, they'd gotten to the point. Saul's words came back again.

Hangers-on will never believe that immortality is an irreducible fact of nature, incapable of being gifted or conveyed. Rather, they will know to a certainty that you possess an herb, a spell, a sacred spring, a mysterious power in the blood that, once consumed, will provide the gift of eternity. And in their hunger for this gift, they will credit no denial.

"Just tell me," Menniss urged. "Tell me right now."

Should he make up a story? Tell Menniss the Philosopher's Stone was hidden in the Great Pyramid at Giza? Saul had done that once. But Menniss was too intelligent.

Despite Saul's warnings that it never worked, Blair tried the truth. "I don't *know* why I live forever. I really don't." He did his best to look as innocent as he was and wished he had cherubic blond hair and blue eyes instead of that damn brooding look stamped onto his features. "I don't know any more than you do. You said you've met hafeems. Do they have any idea why they live so long?"

Menniss sat back again, his eyes distant. "It's not the same thing," he said. "They do age. They're trapped, same as me." He licked his lips again.

The coffee server was only three tables away now, smiling at a little boy and talking to his parents. "So you don't believe in life after death?" Blair said. "I mean, if you believe in that, you're not trapped, are you?"

"Maybe I believe in it," Menniss said, his voice bitter. "But I don't want to go there yet. I've fucked up this life. I want to try again."

Blair lifted his empty coffee cup. The server acknowledged him with a motion of the head. But there were still two more tables to go.

"I wish I could help you," Blair said. "I mean it. But I don't know how." He set down the coffee cup and tapped on it nervously. Still tapping, he moved his fingers to the saucer's rim and then to the table's edge. "Anyway, what makes you so certain I'm a True Immortal? I wish I were, but a hafeem doesn't begin to visibly age until he's about eight or nine hundred years old, and I'm nowhere near that."

Viciously, Menniss said, "Don't you dare lie to me, sir. I've had the honor of speaking with hafeems. They don't grow back body parts. Only True Immortals do that." He gestured to Blair's hands, now spread out on the table's edge, all 10 fingers whole. "When you lived in Greece, you lost one of those. As I say, don't lie to me."

The server positioned himself exactly where Blair had hoped he would, his bulk blocking the hanger-on's way. "Would you like yours refilled too?"

"Yes, please do," Menniss said.

To his body, Blair said, *Go!*

His arms shoved the table forward, driving it deep into Menniss' belly. He grabbed the photo of Kathryn and his coat and ran toward the exit. As he passed the hostess, he tossed her a 50-dollar bill so she wouldn't call the police; he couldn't deal with the police. Weaving his way through a family entering the lobby, he pushed open the door and leaped out into the freedom of the wide morning world.

His body flew over the lawn, aglow with perfection. Jumping over a bright green hedge, it pivoted to the right and sprinted down the sidewalk. His body wanted to keep sprinting for the pure joy of it, but he'd reached the Volvo. On command, his body vaulted the hood and, in a single sweet motion, opened the door and climbed inside. Blair looked back at the restaurant and saw Menniss making his way out. He was fast for an old man. Blair started the car and pulled away. In his rear-view mirror, he saw Menniss windmill and skid as he reached the sidewalk.

Blair drove to the end of the street and turned right at the first intersection. He came to an alley and turned left. The alley came out onto a street, and Blair gunned across to the continuation of the same alley. He made five more turns, putting distance behind him.

But not enough distance. Tires screeched as a black Mercedes hopped the curb just ahead and roared toward him.

Blair wanted to floor the Volvo, to use all its power the same way his body had shown its full power in that short race to the car. But he didn't dare. The police might get him. He was terrified of the police: mortals with guns, mortals with the power of imprisonment, infinitesimal in themselves but backed up by the worldwide warren of mortals.

Menniss had no such fear. Though Blair had a substantial lead as he turned into another alley, the Mercedes closed the distance, skidding and knocking aside trashcans. Blair reached a busy road just ahead of his pursuer and slid into a traffic hole. Menniss missed the hole by a fraction of a second and entered the flow five cars back. A light turned yellow. Blair slowed, then drove through it at the last legal instant, leaving Menniss stuck on the other side of the intersection.

Except Menniss refused to stay stuck. Blair watched with horror as the Mercedes drove onto the wrong side of the street, hooked around the stopped cars and pushed through the intersection despite the red light. A highway on-ramp appeared, and Blair turned onto it. The ramp had two lanes at its entrance, and there were three semis in the right lane, slowly accelerating up to freeway speed. Blair passed them just before the lanes merged into one, and now he had a trio of 18-wheelers protecting his rear. But Menniss roared up the shoulder and passed the semis, setting off deep, outraged horns like those on great ships at sea.

But there were other trucks on the freeway, and they were loyal to their kind. They let Blair through, for he'd committed no insult; they closed up behind him to block all lanes of traffic against Menniss because he had. When Menniss again tried the shoulder, they drifted over and wouldn't let him pass.

They traveled together in convoy, the Volvo ahead, several semis behind him, and a frustrated Mercedes in the rear. Blair ignored several off-ramps and then turned sharply to take one. As he'd hoped, Menniss didn't see the maneuver until it was too late for him to imitate it.

Missing the ramp, Menniss humped the Mercedes over a dirt barrier, half-sliding, half-driving down to the frontage road. He spun around at the bottom and accelerated. Blair felt a terrible thud as Menniss rammed him. Another thud and the even more terrible sensation of losing control: he couldn't steer. Menniss had hooked onto him from behind, bumper caught onto bumper.

Bondage to a mortal through the medium of metal. Perishable eternal life hitched to a man who has nothing to lose. Because what does a mortal risk when he risks his life? A brief flash of years, no more.

Not like me. I have infinity to lose.

No transient dying man shall disturb the line of my life. And the universe shall smile on me, its most perfect creation.

Power and giftedness came to his hands. He braked, accelerated and braked again. He gave a violent twist to the steering wheel and broke free. He braked hard and felt the Mercedes strike him again. This time Menniss hadn't planned the collision, and he bounced, fishtailing, onto the dirt shoulder. Blair accepted the jolt and took its speed into himself. Another on-ramp appeared ahead, and he climbed up it, remaining within the legal speed.

A highway patrolman on a motorcycle appeared, a tiny slip of a being. Blair took up position to hide him from Menniss. As Blair hoped, the Mercedes came roaring up the on-ramp at 100 miles an hour or more. The policeman dropped back; lights flashed red, blue and white; a siren tapped twice. The Mercedes pulled over.

Blair, adhering precisely to the speed limit, kept driving.

MENNISS WOULD BE trapped for 10 minutes at least; with luck, he might be detained longer. Plenty of time to escape.

At the first exit, Blair left the freeway and dove into a maze of rural roads. He turned and turned again. He passed a broken-down farmhouse surrounded by machinery in an advanced state of rust and a brightly painted barn advertising dressage and show jumping lessons. Turning and turning. Now into emptiness—vast fields dotted with snow. The smell of cows—beef cows, not dairy—standing at fence lines with the dead-eye stare of animals raised to be eaten. Constant turns and doubling backs. Racing up dirt tracks. Getting on and off highways for 100s of miles.

In the distance, the red lights of a refinery or fertilizer factory hung in the sky like false constellations. A cattle guard beat its tattoo against the Volvo's tires, and the road descended to follow the slow turns of a wash. The road climbed over the wash on an aluminum bridge into open country. A fox crossed the road, its gashed face glinting red in the headlight's glare. Coyotes must have attacked it.

Blair braked to a halt and closed his eyes. When he opened them again, the fox was gone. He pulled off the asphalt, stopped the car, and listened to their distant howls. Aslan could have taken on a whole pack of coyotes. Aslan was a dog's dog, strong and wily. He could have survived on his own anywhere, here on the plains of western Colorado or there in the Australian outback. Instead, he'd returned to the car and died.

Why?

Blair opened the glove compartment and took out Kathryn's photo. He switched on the overhead light and stared at her dying face.

He'd taken her hand in marriage, knowing that he'd abandon her in 12 years. Seeming to give himself when he could only loan.

He thought again of Aslan, trusting unto death. He thought of

Saul, standing alone next to that rock on the sand. He thought of other women he'd married and deserted.

Slumping sideways onto the passenger seat, he began to cry.

THE STICK SHIFT pushed uncomfortably into Blair's flank, and he sat up.

He imagined his body speaking to him: you're safe now, and that's what matters. It's time to start your life over as you've done so many times.

He opened the window. Icy air filled the car, but he wrapped loneliness around himself like a blanket and held out the photo of time-ruined Kathryn. A wind came up, and he let the photo flutter away in the dark. He let go of Kathryn. He let go of everything. He took refuge in the one companion he'd never have to abandon, this marvelous creation, this perfect body: immortal, forever renewed, forever made whole.

He started the car again and drove on. The road improved, and he pushed the Volvo to a fast but safe 60. He reached a long straight-away heading west. Ahead, he saw a city's yellow glow in the night sky. It was time to go somewhere rather than flee.

THE STREETLIGHTS OF Fort Collins, Colorado, illuminated Blair's hands on the wheel. He couldn't help but admire their beauty— slim yet strong, flawless, the fingers long and graceful. Looking at his face in the rear-view mirror, he admired the depth of brooding emotion it seemed to show. But he had no brooding emotion. He was empty and free.

He passed a shop whose pink, green and blue lights spelled out "Madam Linda, Psychic and Palmistry Consultant, Futures Told, Lost Loves Found, Career Counseling and Tarot Cards." What would she make of me, he wondered? The blocky form of a bowling alley pushed its yellow shoulders out toward the street, and he imagined the thunder of the hurled bowling balls, the friendly clatter of pins. Perhaps he'd go bowling. But not tonight. He passed used car lots, all-night liquor stores, thrift shops, pawnshops, downscale strip malls, tattoo parlors, the typical flora at the edge of a city. He loved places like these, so full of gaps, of broken areas to hide in.

He pulled into The Appaloosa, a fleabag motel whose only obvious virtue was a deeply recessed parking lot. Parking at the lot's darkest corner, he shut off the ignition. He stared into a large open field that stretched out ahead. Exhausted, he might have fallen asleep in his car, but the cold seeped in and made him shiver. He roused himself and heaved open the door. Stepping out into a freezing wind, he threw open the trunk and put on his heavy coat and a black woolen watch cap. He locked the car, adjusted the gun in the coat's inner pocket and set off toward the motel's office.

He passed a swimming pool loaded with leaves and surrounded by fractured particle board furniture. Detouring around a couch that oozed foam rubber through cracks in its vinyl, he reached a covered walkway.

A door opened ahead of him, and a pot-bellied, middle-aged man walked out. Despite the cold, he wore a sleeveless undershirt, and his arms were covered with white blotches like stubby amoebas. "Hey, kid," he whispered. "You want to buy anything?"

Blair said, "No, thank you," and hurried on, nearly colliding with a young woman as she left her room. She wore a short skirt despite the cold and was all business, already on her cell phone taking down directions.

Surely the Crown Jewel of Creation deserves better than this, Blair thought. I should go back to the car and drive on. This town must have a Marriot or a Hilton.

But he was too tired to drive any further and, anyway, he'd reached the office. A plastic sign pasted on the door read, "We cooperate with the Larimer County Stamp Out Crime at Inns Initiative." Blair pushed the door open and stepped inside.

In one corner, a soft-drink machine rattled to itself; in another, a plastic tree grew out of a wooden barrel repurposed as a planter. The only light was a single incandescent bulb that hung naked from the ceiling on red and white wires. A high counter of white vinyl ran the length of the room. It was piled with stacks of old magazines, dirty cups and legal notices held in clear plastic stands. The desk behind the counter held a writing pad and a few boxes of filed three-by-five cards. There was a chair at the desk but no attendant. A door beyond the counter stood partly open.

Blair saw the usual silver bell on the counter. He tapped its weighted nipple. So tiny a bell, yet so piercing a sound. Its coruscating ring summoned memories: the same bell in stables, inns, law courts. In mansions for calling the servants. At the windows of civil service offices, where he waited to file a false birth certificate with a duly bribed civil servant. On the bakery counter where, at the end of each week, he would buy himself and his first wife a cake. This bell had accompanied him his whole life as a type, if not an object, and he found this consoling. He caressed the shiny chrome steel and was still caressing it when a young woman came in through the door behind the counter.

She wore shapeless, black trousers made for men and a baggy, black, flannel hoody whose folds made her breastless. She had gray eyes that hinted at violet when the light struck them at a certain angle. Judging by her smooth skin and the equally smooth distribution of the fat layer beneath her skin, she couldn't be more than 26 or 27. Her hair was short and arranged in greasy, pyramidal spikes, and a heavy, metallic stud glinted in one nostril of a delicate nose. She was beautiful.

There was a seat at the desk behind the counter, but she didn't sit there. "Yes?" she said tonelessly.

"I'd like a room," he said. "Are there any vacancies?"

Neither moving her feet nor turning at the waist, she reached out sideways and flicked open a beige plastic box. She plucked a card out of the box and held it out to him.

He took it and asked for a pen. She held one out with the same casual lack of interest. He asked if they had a room far in the back, explaining that he liked to be totally alone.

"We used to have a kennel out back," she said.

Hoping it would amuse her, he wrote his address as *The Appaloosa Motel, room to be decided*, but she didn't read it. When he paid with his credit card, she didn't look at his signature. She filled out her part of the check-in card with similar negligence.

Her fingers were slim and elegant. She brushed those feminine fingers through her unfeminine hair and yawned without excusing herself. In the musical voice that typically followed a yawn, she asked, "Wake-up call?"

"A wake-up call, madam? Never in life." He gave her a formal bow, flourishing his watch cap. He had no particular intentions toward her; this was ritual, random flirtation, nothing more. He rose from his bow and added, "You have been most obliging indeed, and I thank you for it."

A hint of a smile appeared on her face, like that of a child who'd been sent to bed early peeking around a hall corner. He turned to go.

When he pulled open the glass door leading out of the office, he saw her face in its reflection and watched a series of mysterious moods pass over it: Amazement? Disbelief? Fear?

Her unreadable reactions traveled with him as he hurried out into obscurity.

A REDWOOD ENCLOSURE near his car held a dumpster, and he tossed his road trash into it, raising a sweet odor like rotting bananas. He stepped into the open field behind the enclosure to breathe fresh air.

The field stretched for a good half-mile before him and equally far to his right. On his left, not more than 20 feet away, a line of trees bounded the field. In the dim light, he could make out dozens of prairie dog mounds rising like small volcanoes. An underground city. If he returned in five years, every prairie dog now alive would have died, but the prairie dog city would live on. Mortals survive only in aggregate; he'd been a fool to love one singly.

There was no moon yet, but thousands of stars shone through the clear, high-desert air. The ancient stars. One day mortals would learn how to go safely into interstellar space, and he'd use their technology to escape this petty Earth. He knew it would take centuries to reach even the nearest star, but that didn't matter. Not to him. He had endless centuries, an infinity of centuries—provided, of course, he wasn't killed.

He wasn't supernatural; he just lacked sickness and the ticking clock. A bullet in the heart, a knife to the jugular or a skull-breaking blow would kill him as surely as it would kill a mortal.

I can live forever, he thought, but I could die tonight. I have to protect not a life guaranteed to end but one potentially eternal, an endless, exhausting privilege.

He brought his suitcase to his room and set all the locks. He pushed a table against the door and lugged over a heavy bureau to block the window. He put a bedside stand on top of the bureau. Anyone trying to get in would at least make a lot of noise.

He took his gun out of his coat and set it on the toilet tank, within easy reach of the shower. He turned on the water and adjusted the temperature. There was a full-length mirror in the bathroom. Though he tried not to look, he couldn't help catching a glimpse, and now he was caught, too exhausted to fight off the narcotic draw.

He faced the mirror directly and stared at the reflection—this perfect, flawless object, inviolate despite the accidents of three centuries. His left knee, once shattered by a musket ball, but now pristine. His right forearm had been burned badly but was unscarred and radiant. His body, as a body, achieved in each moment an effortless perfection that the person Blair would never match.

He tore his eyes away from the mirror and stepped into the shower. The downpour of hot water washed away the stink and the dirt, the superficial accretions of time, restoring his body to perfection.

His mind wandered to the girl in the office. He'd played the 19th-century gentleman, and she'd responded with … with what? Fear? Horror? Perhaps nothing at all. Perhaps what he'd seen was no more than the distorting effect of a moving mirror.

Perhaps neither fear nor horror, but desperate desire, a longing for something she knew she would never find but longed for anyway. The same thing he longed for: another Immortal.

No, the true explanation was perfectly obvious. She was a slumming intellectual who curled up in her bare bed with Jane Austen and the Bronte sisters. At this sleazy motel, she wouldn't encounter many visitors who shared her interests. He'd affected the language of a character in one of her books, and she'd felt intrigued and lonely, no more than that.

He shut off the water, dried himself, brushed his teeth and shaved his stubbly beard.

He could go back to the office to charm her. She would open to him and flower in that wonderful way a woman flowers when she decides to trust you. He'd bring her back to his room, and they'd make love beneath these sanitary white sheets, mortality meeting immortality, a burning moment touching infinite time.

If only he weren't so tired.

HE AWOKE SUDDENLY, senses alert. He listened but heard nothing. He slid his hand under the pillow and released the safety catch on the gun. Holding the gun in his hand, he switched on a bedside lamp, expecting to see Menniss looming before him. But there was no one in the room. It was a quarter to 12; he'd only slept an hour.

He closed his eyes and saw lights in his mind: a trail from Kansas City to Fort Collins lit at the places he'd stopped for gas and paid with his credit card. He'd paid for the room by credit card too.

Did Menniss have friends who could break into the credit card system and track him? He had no idea. If there was even a chance the hanger-on could do so, he had to leave instantly.

There was always a chance.

He heaved himself out of bed, rummaged through his suitcase and pulled on fresh clothes. Working with extreme care, he silently pulled back the furniture from the door and window. He lifted the hem of the dirty curtains and peered into the lot.

No new cars.

He put on his coat and set the gun back in its inner pocket. Easing open the door, he looked out and still saw nothing. Ragged lines of windblown snow across the asphalt reminded him of the lines across Kathryn's aged face. He hurried to the Volvo, put his bags in the trunk, and squeezed the lid until it latched. He had his hand on the driver's door when a sound from the road sent him running for the deeper shadows behind the dumpster.

He looked around desperately for a way to escape. Beyond the prairie dog field, he made out low-lying houses and, further on, a tall darkness that might be the back of an office building or a supermarket.

But he couldn't run across the field; the moon had come up, and the white glow that highlighted the prairie dog mounds would highlight him too. He had to get across under cover of the tree line 20 feet away.

He ran for it.

The Mercedes turned into the parking lot, its diesel engine all the louder since the motel's stucco wall reflected the sound.

Blair threw himself forward and reached the first of the trees before the headlights could touch him. Crouching beneath a white pine, he watched the Mercedes drive by. It was muddy, and Blair could barely make out Menniss behind the dirty glass. Blair squeezed deeper into the undergrowth. The Mercedes glided to a halt behind the Volvo, and Menniss stepped out, not more than a dozen yards away, his bulk silhouetted against the lights at the back of the motel.

The hanger-on was taking a terrible risk. A single shot … but Blair couldn't shoot him. He didn't dare draw the attention of the police.

He watched Menniss make his way toward the office. When he disappeared around the far edge of the motel, Blair ran.

He scraped his way through dense branches, afraid Menniss would hear him. He happened on a deer trail and broke into a run, shielding his eyes with one arm. Though his eyes would heal if he punctured them, it wasn't a good time to go blind.

Far off, a heavy truck thumped over a bridge, and a nearer motorcycle whined, but no feet came thudding after him. Still, he didn't have much time. Menniss would find the room empty, and this line of trees was the obvious way to escape.

The trees abruptly vanished as the deer trail reached the end of the greenbelt and opened onto a sidewalk beside a wide road. Blair stood inside the last of the cover and considered where to go.

There was a warren of corrugated aluminum warehouses on the far side of the road; Blair could make out a body shop, a battery store and a welding-supply outlet. He could hide among the warehouses and hitch a ride in the morning with one of the customers.

But he'd have to cross the road to get there, and it was unspeakably wide, perhaps 100 feet. If Menniss stuck his nose into the street, he'd spot Blair, a fox in the headlights. He didn't dare cross.

Directly ahead, the sidewalk passed five slovenly backyards on its way to the rear end of a shopping center. There were sheds in the backyards, alongside cars on blocks and piles of trash. Should he consider making for one of the sheds? He should not. Houses like these had pit bulls and owners with shotguns.

He had no time. What about the shopping center? That was his best chance. He darted forward.

Blair passed three backyards, then a fourth, and still no diesel engine. He passed the last house and came to a sloping, grassy lot littered with beer cans and cigarette packs and shaded from the moonlight by a large weeping willow. A footpath in the grass led up to a broken concrete curb and, beyond that, the supermarket's asphalt apron.

He climbed the path. The supermarket rose high ahead of him, its rear face built of fake red and gray brick. Off to the left, after a gap, he saw the back of a strip mall that stretched for 100s of yards, a long wall neatly divided by blue, slatted pull-down doors. Each door had its own dumpster illuminated by a bright yellow insect light. No cover there.

A large cinderblock enclosure struck out from the wall, and Blair sprinted toward it. Inside, he found a double-size, blue dumpster, brown scissor-jack loaders and gray pallets stacked high. The floor inside was concrete. He looked around wildly for a metal door on the ground, one of those entrances used by merchants to carry supplies directly down to their cellars. No metal door.

He crouched behind the pallets, kneeling on cold concrete and frozen scum. He waited for the sound of a diesel engine. He heard rhythmic tapping, but it was only a dumpster lid banging in the wind.

The Crown Jewel of Creation. How lovely to know dumpsters so intimately. How pleasant to skulk like this at the backside of the world.

TEN MINUTES PASSED, and still no Mercedes. He couldn't stay here all night or he'd freeze. He edged forward to the limit of the cinderblock wall. The space that separated the supermarket from the strip mall was 100 feet ahead and to his right. He considered running for it, but before he made up his mind, he caught sight of a figure walking toward the gap from the far left. The figure was too slight for Richard Menniss, and it walked like a woman, though a woman wearing a shapeless green-yellow overcoat and a khaki stocking cap. She vanished into the space between the supermarket and the strip mall, but not before Blair caught the glint of a nose stud in the overhead lights. It was the clerk from the motel.

So much for his vow of solitude. She was his best chance. He left his hiding place and started after her.

There was a sizable concrete square between the supermarket and the strip mall, a space that in a European city would have been decorated with something attractive, but here remained bare. Blair missed Europe and its buildings that predated him.

He glimpsed the clerk again just before she disappeared into an all-night liquor store at the end of the gap. If he followed her inside, would he be visible to the world's eye? He would not. The windows were screened off to make display cases: pyramids of cans and bottles outlined by white, green and red Christmas tree lights.

He pushed open the door and entered the gaudy, warm, hidden space, its vivid labels and brightly colored bottles, a crow's idea of paradise. A florid man behind the cash register looked up doubtfully; he wore a button that read, *Ten Years Sobriety*. Blair gave him a thumbs-up and walked deeper into the store.

The young woman was examining a shelf of liqueurs. He approached her via a perpendicular row of wines, toying with a few bottles along the way. Coming close, he said, "Wouldn't you know? There's a 2000 and a 1998, but no 1999."

"Good God, a liquor snob at midnight." She'd taken off her stocking cap and held it in one hand. The greased spikes in her hair were now mostly flattened.

White cards dangled here and there on the shelves, quoting reviews or recounting awards. He flipped one up and read, "Accents of manzanita and apple."

"Sounds like Bakersfield's best four-dollar merlot," she said.

"An 11-dollar merlot from Chile," he said.

She turned, recognized him, and turned away again. "What,

can't you sleep without getting drunk on Chilean merlot?" A dramatic pause. "*Chilean*, for all love."

She'd remembered his archaic phrasing in the office and returned it. A charming flirtation.

"I can never sleep," he said. "I stare at the ceiling and think about my sins."

"And which sins are these?"

"All the women I've loved and left."

He'd meant it as a seductive shave off the truth, but she took him seriously. She looked at him over her shoulder, then turned her body too, a movement that seemed coarse under the green tweed coat but might have been graceful. "So what do you do? Cheat on them? Screw the whole block?"

"No, never. One woman at a time. It's just that I always leave."

She tossed her head as if she had long hair; perhaps she'd worn it long until recently. "That's all? Then what are you going off on yourself about? Serial monogamy is what everyone does these days."

"And you think it's okay?"

She came to join him at the wine shelf. "As much as anything is okay."

He found this surprisingly comforting.

She stroked the label on a bottle of pinot noir, its flowers stylishly crafted in bas-relief. "Unless," she added, "you're always the one who leaves. In that case, you're just a narcissistic asshole."

"I don't mean to be," he said. Feeling that genuflection was called for, he knelt to look at the bottom row of wines. "I'm Blair, by the way."

"I'm Janice." She reached down to shake his hand. Her fingers were cold. The ugly coat retreated and showed a delicate white space between the tendons of her neck.

Blair watched her struggle. He watched her give up the struggle in self-pity and perhaps spite. "I'm drinking alone," she said. "You want to keep me company?"

"I'd be honored."

"Honored?" Ironic but also fragile.

"Yes," he said. "Have you ever tried Ethiopian merlot?"

She kneeled beside him, and they studied the bottle together.

When Blair paid, the man at the cash register smiled with beneficent approval. No doubt he knew Janice; perhaps he preferred that she drank with a lover rather than alone, thinking it closer to sobriety.

BUT WHEN THEY reached the door, Blair worried that Menniss might have staked out the area. As they left the liquor store, he lagged behind Janice to keep her body between his face and the parking lot. When they turned the corner, the angle of view required him to walk a little ahead, and he did that, too. He condemned himself as an unchivalrous bastard, and as soon as they'd made it far enough into the gap, he took her hand.

She'd put on black cotton gloves with a weave of gold thread, and the extra thickness made her fingers feel especially delicate. In his other hand, the bag of wine bottles clanked. She led him through a break in the concrete curb and down onto a path that led into the sleazy neighborhood whose backyards he'd seen earlier.

Pausing at an opening in a battered chain link fence, she said, "You will be honored to know that you're about to gain admittance to the gated community of Fuckedupville."

"My old hometown," he said.

"You're from Fort Collins?"

"No, Fuckedupville. It's an international franchise."

She laughed, a sparkling, happy sound. She squeezed through a break in the fence, and he followed. Turning up his collar against the wind, he said, "It looks like a good place to hide."

"What are you hiding from?" she asked.

"I meant you."

"I asked first."

"No, you didn't. I asked by implication," he said.

"Doesn't count," she said.

"I'm hiding from people. People in general, and certain people more than others."

"Me too," she said. "I've been doing it forever."

"You're not old enough to have done anything forever."

"Trust me, it's been forever."

A casual remark, but it sparked the absurd, urgent fantasy.

"Everything I've done," she said, "I've done forever. Except get well. That's new. But it's happening. I'm getting healthy."

"That's wonderful," he said.

Janice stopped and looked up at him. She had at least six metal poles and three studs in each ear, and her face was hard. "Taking a guy home I've just met, a guy who says he always does the leaving? Doesn't that sound healthy?" But she hooked a gloved finger on the top button of his coat and pulled him toward her.

The hardness evaporated, and she laughed. "Don't worry. I'm not *that* healthy yet. I make exceptions. I hurt myself so no one will hurt me. I'm obsessed with death so I don't have to live. And what I just said is magazine wisdom. If you take it seriously, I'll shove you."

She shoved him.

She took his hand, and they began walking again. The street had no sidewalk. They came to a large pile of Quaker State oil cans and stretched out their arms to pass around it. At an even larger obstacle, this one made of old newspapers in orange plastic wrappers, they had to extend their arms so far only the fingertips touched.

They passed a mobile home pumping heavy bass notes through drawn blinds. After another mobile home, this one set up on red jacks, they stopped at a rundown wood-frame cottage. Its windows were sealed against the wind with sheets of plastic held in place by uneven two-by-fours. For a front lawn, it had bare dirt littered with trash and a prone refrigerator. A pile of moldering paperback books on the steps leading to the door oozed a whitish substance not unlike steel-cut oats. Her house.

They climbed the steps. Janice took out her keys, hesitated, and bounced on her toes as if ready to jump. "In case you mean to go all psychotic on me," she said, "I should let you know I have guns in there." She curtsied, unlocked the door and let him in.

Trash was everywhere: magazines, envelopes, yellow *final notice* bills, plastic bags from Wal-Mart, underwear that had been walked on and books. Lots of books. Books tossed on the floor, heaped in corners, piled on the battered green couch; books stacked on the peeling teak-veneer coffee table and the kitchen table with its mismatched chairs. Books on the television, the windowsills and every available counter too.

Art-quality prints covered all the windows. One print showed soft clouds above the circular turrets of a fantasy castle; another, nude Japanese ladies bathing behind a screen of soldiers with sharpened bamboo stakes; a third, an image of woman's back made up like a tennis shoe with white laces crisscrossing through metal eyelets inserted in her skin. He couldn't take his eyes off that one; it was a photo, not a painting.

Janice said she'd be back and disappeared down a corridor. He made his way to the kitchen and set his coat on the back of a cast-iron chair. To clear a space on the kitchen counter for the wine, he pushed aside cups, burnt toast and a roll of paper towels. The roll must have been dipped in coffee or tea because one of its edges was brownish and swollen. He took the bottles out of the bag and arranged them neatly. Looking for somewhere to throw the bag away, he opened a white-painted cabinet door beneath the sink and found an overflowing trash can topped with orange peels growing blue mold.

He wanted to run. He never dated women like Janice, only nice women who wanted to raise a family and didn't live in a house of chaos on a street made for crack houses. Once again, he found himself staring at the photo of the pierced female back: seven eyeholes on each side, about right for a boot. But it was a human back. And Janice had said she had guns.

Yet he didn't dare leave. Menniss was roaming around outside, ex-Special Forces, ex-CIA, professional bounty hunter turned hanger-on.

Janice was coming back. While looking for a corkscrew to use on the wine, his eyes lit on an old-fashioned coffee grinder, half hidden behind a blender. It wasn't just old-fashioned; it was *old*, an antique, a cherry-wood coffee grinder like the one he'd grown up with. Trash everywhere, and also an antique like this. Janice was a strange mixture of people.

Instead of a black hoody, she now had on a black cotton shirt that a man could have worn but was unbuttoned far enough to show the top of a lacy black bra. Around her neck, she wore a thin strip of leather like an evaporated dog collar. She'd ruffled her hair, and it showed a hint of curl. Though rounded, she wasn't heavy. She now had a ring through her lower lip that matched the nose stud and the bars in her ears. She wore red pants that reached a few inches beneath the knees, and a long tattoo in the shape of a whale extended down one calf to her ankle. Her feet were naked in brown sandals. He thought she might be wearing clear lipstick.

Janice touched his lips with hers, just a touch, and then moved him aside to get at a drawer. "Go sit," she said, and he did. She found a straight corkscrew and pulled out the cork with enough strength to make it look effortless. She searched her upper cabinets, stretching so high that her shirt pulled out from her pants, and brought down two wine glasses. Setting the glasses by the bottles, she studied her cluttered kitchen table. With a slow sweep of one forearm, she tumbled books, magazines, a box of checks and numerous envelopes over the table's edge and onto the floor. She looked at him for his reaction.

"That was cute, wasn't it?" she said. "I'm flirting."

"Just be yourself," he said.

"Oh? And which self do you have in mind?" She poured the wine from high above, a steady stream expertly cut off with a quick lifting turn. Sliding gracefully into the chair beside him, she said, "At the moment, I'm a young woman seducing a young man. Not that you need a lot of seducing. Tomorrow morning, I'll turn into magical morning-after girl, the kind who refuses to let the guy promise he'll come back. That Janice will make you breakfast, say a few interesting things and kick you out.

"After you leave, I'll turn into sad-morning-after Janice, all hurt and abandoned. She'll remember something she wanted to say or something you said that she wanted to answer, but oh well. She'll empty the trash, see used condoms and get depressed. She'll turn on music, and when it doesn't help, she'll call her sponsor. Spiritual Janice to the rescue. Self-honesty, all that crap. Later, she'll talk some shit with her neighbor Maurice—'Buzz-up,' he calls himself, a great friend who never tries to fuck her. What I mean is he doesn't *try*. He does ask politely sometimes."

Knowing what he was supposed to say and meaning it vaguely, Blair said, "I don't *want* you to feel hurt and abandoned."

"Shush. You're making me forget my point. Which was? Oh, yeah. You told me to be myself, and I said, 'Which one?' Because there are a lot of Janices. You could put each one in its own little picture frame and admire it. Each one is a whole life. I advise you to enjoy the Janice you have now. She's pretty hot." She raised her wineglass.

If she were immortal and hoped against hope that he might be too, wouldn't she hint at it exactly like this?

"Raise your glass too, silly," she said. "I want to propose a toast. And stop looking at me so seriously. I'm just putting on an act to make you think I'm deep. Please don't fall for it, because I'm not."

He managed to hold up his glass, but the strength of the fantasy made his hand shake.

Pitching her voice in an artificial toasting tone, she said, "To the brightly painted picture between now and morning. To the frame's sharp edge that crops time off at dawn. Cheers, dear." She clinked his glass. Taking a sip, she added, "I still need to frame those damn prints in my windows."

Though he did get out his own "cheers," he was reeling. Every word she said sounded like a clue.

Janice looked at him suspiciously. "You're taking me seriously, aren't you? Don't you get it? I have to prove to you I'm not only a lowlife. That's all."

Of course she would pretend she didn't mean it; in her place, he would too. He had to encourage her, meet her halfway, and then see what happened.

He refilled their glasses and raised his to hers. "To moments that go on past all limits," he said. "To time that has no end but goes on and on."

Her eyes opened wide. "Wow," she said. "That's *really* good sex." She clinked his glass and downed hers in an unbroken series of swallows. "But are you up to it? Don't raise hopes you can't fulfill."

She'd said the words with overplayed seduction. But was there another layer, a double entendre reversed? A pretense at talking about sex while meaning something else? Begging him not to raise impossible hopes for love free from the 12-year guillotine?

She put her thumbs on her temples, fingers partly covering her eyes. "I have a headache," she said. She turned giddy. "But not that kind of headache, don't worry." Refilling her glass, she raised it and said, "Cheers to one-night stands. To morning farewells. To true love that lasts exactly as long as you're in bed."

It was a deliberate crudity, a test. "That's not what you want, is it?" he said, testing back. "It's not what I want. I hate the leaving. I feel abandoned even when I'm the one who goes."

"Three cheers for abandonment." Half-shrieking, she sloshed wine down her arm.

"But it hurts you." He wanted to match the famous brooding moodiness of his face with equally brooding words, but he was too exhausted. "Even if you say it doesn't."

"Five cheers to hurting myself!" She convulsed with hilarity. She refilled their glasses and tried to drink hers but laughed too hard and sputtered. She clapped a hand over her mouth until she finished coughing; she drew her middle finger across the length of her lips and licked the wine off it.

They'd emptied a bottle. She opened a second and brought it to the table. Pushing it away, she turned serious. "I have a question for you. If I ask you, will you answer honestly?"

Was she about to give him another clue? He hoped he could catch it despite being so drunk. "I will answer as honestly as I can."

She nodded to herself. "No matter what a woman says she wants, what she actually wants is marriage for life, at least according to the magazines, and they know everything. When a woman beds a man she doesn't know, she pretends to herself that this is just the beginning. Sometimes she even believes what she's pretending, especially when the sex is hot. The only exception is when it's too obvious the guy's a loser, and in that case, what she's doing is using sex to violate herself. Like a piercing. That's what the magazines say. Do you agree?"

"I do not agree," he said. "Every woman is unique, and—"

She cut him off. "And blah, blah, blah. I've already said we're going to do it, so you can quit seducing me and answer the question."

"You're funny." He smiled. Parts of himself that he couldn't see smiled too.

"So what do you think?" she insisted.

"Honestly? I'd say I think it's probably true for most women."

"I agree with you. And I'm not immune myself. But listen closely."

"I'm listening." Listening for the clue.

"It's not *exactly* the same for me. I do dream about staying together for a while. I'm drunk enough to admit it. But I don't dream of marrying for life. Do you want to know why? Because that's a suicide pact. Think about it. If you ask that kind of woman what she likes about marriage, she'll say, 'growing old together.' It's like skipping through the novel to the last three pages where the sweet, almost-dead couple sit in their rocking chairs sharing memories, and then one drops dead, and the other does too, and that's what makes it all perfect. In other words, marriage isn't about life. It's about dying together. For that kind of woman, anyway. It's how they deal with the idea of death. It doesn't work for me, though." She paused. "For various reasons."

How more direct could she get?

"I understand," he said. But he hadn't put enough feeling into it. He was exhausted, terrified, running from a madman and turned inside out by that photo of Kathryn. What were the chances he'd meet another True Immortal by chance? Zero. He was making the whole thing up.

"I saw a movie once ..." she began.

"So did I." He stroked her arm.

"Wait. Listen. It was an IMAX. There were these two skydivers, a man and a woman, doing tricks in the air. You know what I mean: somersaults, holding hands, spinning. Of course, they can't do it forever, or they'll go splat. The man lets out his parachute first, all bright and billowy above him. But the camera is with the woman, and she hasn't let out her parachute. So you know what it looks like? It looks like the man is yanked up and away, really fast, torn out of the picture. Really, he's just slowed down, and she's the one who's moving. One moment he's in her world, skydancing with her, then the air grabs him, and he's gone." She filled their glasses. "The air.

It's so light and thin. How can it do that? Grab someone and take them away."

It wasn't a hallucination; she'd described exactly what it feels like to be an Immortal. It had to be real. Quoting Saul, he said, "Time is even lighter than air. Time is the lightest thing there is. And yet it grabs people and takes them away. Every one of them."

Her eyelids reddened, and red circles appeared on the ends of her nostrils. "It takes them all away," she said. "They disappear. They die of one thing or another. Or they go away. Day, after day, after day, after day ..." Nodding her head with each repetition. "... after day, after day, after day ..."

"Year after year," he said. Then, probing, "Decade after decade."

"Century after century," she said. "Millennium after millennium. Forever. You want it to stop. It's so painful you sleep with someone to stretch out the moment, to make the future disappear. But the future hits you anyway, and it's all over. I can't stand it."

"Unless you meet someone who's the same as you." He fought back tears. "Unless you meet someone who understands because he's gone through the same thing."

She glared up at him, her eyes red-rimmed and wet. "A chance meeting in a shitty motel? Is that how it happens? A guy asks for a room in the back, and he's so brooding and beautiful you're half in love with him already, and then you see him again, and it turns out just by accident he's able to understand?" She rocked in her chair like a child rocks to console herself.

She was on his lap now, straddling him; she was hitting him lightly on the chest. "It's too damn random, and it pisses me off."

He stroked her face.

She took his hands, put them on her cheeks, and held them there. Pushing his arms aside, she dropped forward against him, her lips on his neck.

He could feel her heart pounding. "How many centuries?"

She was breathing fast now. "Ten. I've been waiting 10 centuries for you."

"For me, it's only been three."

"Lightweight." She kissed his ear. She slid her arms down around his waist and pulled her hips against his.

"Where were you born?" he asked. "What happened along the way?"

"Shush," she said.

"Just tell me ..."

She put a finger on his lips. "Not now. It's time to stop talking. It's time to dissolve."

BUT THEY DIDN'T dissolve right away. She hid behind mere physical sexuality, letting her heart and mind shut down. He barricaded himself a different way, by getting stuck in ideas. He wanted to talk to her, ask a thousand questions, but each time he tried, she put her lips over his mouth and bit his tongue. They made an unspoken agreement: if he wouldn't think, she wouldn't hide.

He tried to show all of himself, but he couldn't. Kathryn owned too much of him. And there was so much shame and guilt. He'd never shown his shame to anyone, and now that he tried, he understood why he hadn't before: whatever he showed to someone else, he had to see himself.

Was he crying? There was water on his cheek.

Dissolving.

Afterward, she said, "I've never felt so immortal."

He pulled her close to him, for once in his life holding a treasure that wasn't himself.

BLAIR WOKE SUDDENLY, his heart pounding. The spidery red numerals on the bedside clock read 5:00 a.m. He heard Janice breathing, deeply asleep, her naked shoulder facing him.

The whole house took a breath.

A hinge squeaked; someone had opened an outside door.

And the gun was in his coat in the kitchen.

He felt the floorboards shift as the house adjusted to a heavy presence. He was paralyzed with fear, and then he wasn't. He slipped out of bed, scooped up his clothes and dressed silently. He put his hand on the sill at the window and found the curved, metal latch.

He would run and run again. He would escape Menniss and keep running.

Janice mumbled in her sleep. He couldn't understand what she said, but he remembered the last words he'd heard from her: "I've never felt so immortal."

For the first time in his life, he couldn't run.

The floorboards creaked again. Menniss had reached the living room. Janice sighed and fluttered her eyes but did not wake. The creaking came closer and entered the hallway.

Blair looked at Janice, a pale, dim form cradling a pillow. He didn't have any actual proof she was immortal. They'd never gone beyond hints and innuendo. At first, she wouldn't let him ask direct questions, and then they'd had sex so intense he couldn't remember anything like it, and after that, he fell asleep holding her.

The floorboards paused. Menniss was at the room Janice called her library, the first door along the hallway. Janice tossed over in bed, facing the empty half where he'd been sleeping.

Blair pulled up the window sash, but no chilly outside air came rushing in. He remembered the plastic sheeting and pressed his fingers against it. The plastic was tough. He looked around in the moonlit room for a pair of scissors or a nail file, anything sharp, but couldn't find anything.

The floorboards moved again, Menniss abandoning the library, coming toward them. Janice had mentioned a gun. Where did she keep it? Under her bed?

She was lying with one arm flopped over the edge of the mattress. Should he wake her and ask where it was? But she might cry out, and Menniss would come thundering in like a bull or a boar. Blair reached around her arm and found stray clothes, ChapStick, and a shoe. No gun.

No time left.

He crossed silently to the door, leaped out and rushed the blocky form silhouetted against the greater light of the living room. Was this how mortals did it? Blinded themselves at the moment of crisis? Let themselves forget for a moment?

The hanger-on felt as massive as his Mercedes, but he toppled, and they fell together. A metal object clunked against the floor. Blair reached for it and grabbed the barrel of a gun. An overwhelming force took hold of his hair, lifted his head high and slammed his face onto the floor. Pain shot from his nose deep into his head. Before Menniss could take it, Blair tossed the gun, and it clattered down the hallway.

Blair rose on all fours, but a heavy elbow knocked him down. He grabbed the elbow, twisted it and bent it back. Menniss went with the motion, broke loose, got to his feet, and tried to kick Blair in the stomach. By reflex, Blair evaded the kick, grabbed the foot and toppled his attacker.

Then came a sound that made them both freeze, the *ch-chunk!* of a pump shotgun.

Hallway lights switched on, intensely bright. Janice, naked except for black underpants, her body covered with tattoos, gestured with the gun. Menniss rose, stepped back and raised his hands.

In the bright lights, he saw Janice's body more clearly than he had the night before. He hadn't realized she had so much ink: a Japanese-style full sleeve, a row of red and black stars on one thigh and grapevines twining between her breasts and down her belly.

And she had a scar on one knee. An ordinary thing. Most people have them. Except True Immortals don't get scars.

Menniss held up a placating hand. "It's not what you think. He knows me."

She was furious, bouncing from one bare foot to the other, the gun pointed at Menniss' belly. "He knows you? This guy a friend of yours, Blair?"

She wasn't his partner, his equal. He'd imagined it all.

Forlornly, he wondered if she could be a hafeem. But she'd said, "ten centuries." By then, a hafeem would show age. He'd made it all up because he wanted it to be true.

"Blair," she said. "Is he a friend of yours? Or should I shoot him?"

"Don't shoot him," Blair said. "He's not a friend, but I do know who he is. Remember I told you I was hiding from people? I meant him specifically. He's some kind of lunatic stalker."

"Fucking wonderful," she said. "You couldn't just give me HIV? Instead, you give me a stalker?"

"Lady, listen ..." Meniss took half a step toward her, but she gestured with the gun, and he stopped. "Listen to what I have to tell you. Your cute young boyfriend here, he's at least 90 years old. Did he tell you that? Maybe a thousand years old, I don't know. But I can prove to you he's at least 90. He married a woman in Australia in 1947. He's still married to her since he never divorced her, only ran away. And he's had three wives since then."

"Turn around," Janice ordered. "Turn around and face the living room. *Now.* And keep your hands like that. Colorado has one of those 'make my day' laws. Did you know that? You broke into my house. So I can shoot you whenever I want. I can shoot you in the back if I feel like it. Should I shoot him, Blair?"

"No," Blair said. "Don't shoot him."

"Take a step back, stalker guy," she said. "And another. Okay, that's good. Stay away from the couch. Stay right there. I said *stop.* Blair, call the goddamn police, okay?" She pointed to a pile of clothes in a corner and said, "The phone's under those."

"How does it work?" Menniss asked. "A special breathing practice? A forest tree fungus? A mental concentration?"

"I swear to you, sir," Blair said, "I have no more idea how it works than you do."

"But that doesn't make sense," Menniss said. "How can you not know why you live forever?"

"They're discussing this," she said. "Christ. I don't believe it."

"I was just born this way," Blair said. "That's the truth."

"Blair, you're scaring me. Will you call the fucking police or not?"

"He doesn't dare," Menniss said. "He doesn't dare call the police because he can't chance being noticed. When you're immortal, you reinvent your life every 12 years. Otherwise, people begin to notice. Your boyfriend has a clever method. What he does is raise a crop of imaginary children. He gets them birth certificates and social security numbers and even graduates them from school. Only, somehow, they don't get their picture taken. Not until he needs to move on. Then he steps into the shoes of the one that suits him best and gets a passport photo and a driver's license. It works fine so long as no one looks into it too closely."

"The police won't care about any of that," Blair said. "You're a housebreaker. They won't look into my identity."

"I have friends in the CIA, remember? One call, and Homeland Security's on it."

Janice looked away from Menniss just long enough to give Blair a wild-eyed glare. "You're taking him seriously?"

"And Homeland Security will find you quite interesting, won't they?" Menniss said. "Who are your parents? Oh, you're an orphan? And no history of gainful employment. But you're loaded with money. So who's behind you, Mr. Terrorist?"

"Terrorist?" Janice said. "Blair's a terrorist?"

"No, of course I'm not," Blair said.

"No, he's not. But will Homeland Security agree? I don't think so. And when you're in one of their secret prisons, hidden in Romania, maybe, or Poland, do you know who will stop the waterboarding? The Immortal Hunter. The I-H. The guy who set me on to you and who wants to know all about you. He'll take you away somewhere. And then—well, I don't know what'll happen. Maybe he'll dissect you and try to figure out why you don't get old."

"What the fuck?" She was no longer dancing from foot to foot. "What are you trying to tell me? Blair's some kind of mutant? Like he's got an immortality gene and lives forever?"

It came to Blair in a sudden revelation; it was an unraveling of preconceptions, a realization of the obvious, no less stunning than if it had announced itself with hammer blows.

AND SO, BLAIR thought, *I never did sell my soul to the Devil; I'm not tainted by Satan. Genes. That's all. I live forever because of some sterile, clinical fact.* He felt a certain disappointment.

Menniss was trying to talk but interrupted himself, sputtering. "What an idiot! Blind ... going all starry-eyed and supernatura l ... Why the fuck did I ...? But I've always had a bit of a superstitious streak. Still, I've met hafeems before. I figured it was like tall stature.

I figured they were just … Why didn't I see that True Immortals are the same? It's so obvious now. Something in the *genes*."

"I told you I couldn't help you," Blair said.

"I see that now." Menniss looked suddenly older, worn out. His hope was gone. "Just in your genes. Are your children immortal, too, then?"

"No," Blair said. "I guess you'd say it doesn't breed true."

Janice let the shotgun droop toward the floor. "Well, I guess I'm breaking my pattern," she said. "I usually go for total losers. But immortal mutants—that's a change. I'll have to tell my Narcotics Anonymous group. They'll be proud of me." She reached for a sheet that lay wrinkled on the floor.

As she wrapped it around herself, Menniss sprang. He threw a massive arm around Blair's neck and shoved the Immortal's head down.

Blair felt a searing pain, then Menniss let go. Blair clapped his hand to the pain and found only a ragged hole where his left ear had been.

Menniss stood holding bloody flesh in one hand, a knife in the other.

Janice shook the gun violently. "Drop the knife," she screamed. "Drop the goddamn knife!"

Menniss tossed the knife onto the kitchen floor and cradled Blair's ear in both his hands.

"I'm going to shoot him now." Bouncing from foot to foot again, her naked breasts shaking. "Fucking shoot him in the gut."

"No, Janice," Blair said. "Don't. It's over. It's okay."

"It's okay? What the fuck's okay about it?"

"Because he has what he wants. He doesn't care about me anymore. He's just going to leave. Isn't that right, Menniss? You're just going to leave?"

"The hell he is," Janice said. "He just cut off your ear. And why the fuck aren't you writhing in pain?"

Blair wanted to reassure her by touching her, but her finger was too twitchy on the trigger to risk it. "Please, Janice," he said. "Listen to me. Don't worry about my ear. It'll grow back. And if you shoot him, the police will come, and he's right about what that could lead to. Anyway, just now, I need some help. I don't feel as much pain as you would, but it still hurts some."

He released the pressure on his ear and let blood stream down his neck and arm. He let his knees buckle as if he were feeling faint, but faintness from pain grows out of fear of permanent injury, and he had no worries there. "Could you get me something to stop the bleeding? A washcloth would do." He found a chair and sank into it. "Please?"

Giving him a ferocious glare, Janice shoved the gun into Blair's free hand and marched down the hallway.

Menniss was already rifling the kitchen drawers. Finding a clean sandwich bag, he dropped the ear into it. "Thank you," he said. "Thank you very much. I owe you." He opened the freezer, took out an ice tray, and slammed it on the counter to free the cubes. After adding a handful of ice cubes into the sandwich bag, he shoved the bag into his pocket. "By the way, before I walked into the Denny's, I attached a GPS tracker to the underside of your car. That's how I followed you. Look for a black metal oval about three inches across. And there's also one in your coat. I inserted it at the restaurant. That one's not so great—it transmits only every four hours to save batteries. But I'd get rid of it if I were you."

GPS. What was the matter with him that he didn't think of that? His mind was always stuck in the past. Saul was right—he needed to hire a security consultant every few years to update his contingency plans.

Menniss put the plastic bag in his coat pocket and buttoned the pocket. "I told you that because I owe you. And let me tell you another thing: run."

"Why?"

"Because there are other interested parties. The I-H himself, for example. But I've seen hints of at least one, maybe two others looking for you, too." He moved toward the utility room and its door to the outside.

"Wait," Blair said. "Please." He hesitated. "If you learn how to make it work ... if you figure it out ... would you ... ?" He couldn't let out what his heart wanted to say. *If you figure out how it works, would you tell me so I can bring Kathryn back?* He managed to get out one word: "Kathryn."

"I'm sorry," Menniss said. He stepped toward Blair and cupped his shoulder, not patting it as he had at Denny's, just holding him. "I am truly sorry. She died a year ago, my friend. It's too late for her."

A year ago. A year. Such an infinitesimal sliver of time. If she had lived till now, till a little past now, she might have lived forever. But now she was nothing. She was erased.

Because of an infinitesimal sliver of time.

They heard heavy footsteps—Janice returning. Menniss hurried out.

JANICE HAD HANDED him a washcloth, and he'd applied pressure to his wound while she spread towels over the couch. Her blue terry-cloth robe was covered with dark patches of blood, and a trail of blood led from the couch to the kitchen, but he wasn't bleeding anymore.

"Do you want me to drive you to the hospital?" She was standing over him, more annoyed than sympathetic. "Or should I call an ambulance?"

"I don't need to go to the hospital," he said. "I'm fine."

"You pour out buckets of blood, and you're fine?"

"I'll be okay. I only need some water and something salty."

"I'm calling 911."

"Don't." He reached to touch her, but she made a face and pulled back from his bloody hand. "I heal incredibly fast," he said. "Unless something kills me right away, I'm fine. It goes along with immortality. Do you have pretzels? Or salty potato chips?"

Janice brought him a glass of water and threw a bag of pretzels on his lap. She tightened her robe and surveyed her kitchen. "Blood everywhere," she said. "Like someone slit their wrists. Or popped out a baby."

She brought out a mop and a bucket and mopped violently. After she finished the kitchen, she got to work on the trail of blood to the couch. She straightened, leaned on the mop handle and wiped her nose with the back of her hand. "That thing you said last night while we were making love? About how you'd never let me go, not for 100 years, not for 1000, not for ten thousand? That wasn't just lovemaking talk?"

"I meant every word of it," he said.

Janice bent down and viciously pinched his chin. "I'm not asking you to pretend you still love me. I'm asking about the numbers. Those numbers in particular. A thousand years? Did you mean that literally?"

"I did," he said. "I thought you were an Immortal. I thought we could spend centuries together."

She let go of his chin. "You thought I'm *immortal?* And when did you figure out I'm just a regular fucked up person?"

"When I saw that." He pulled aside the hem of her robe and touched the scar on her left knee. "Immortals don't have scars."

She crossed her left leg over her right and ran her fingers along the scar. "I got it rollerblading. I think. Or maybe when I fell off my bike as a kid. What the fuck gave you the idea I'm immortal?"

"I've been trying to work it out," he said. "It was some of the things you said. And a whole lot of wishful thinking. I was scared and exhausted and you rescued me. My mind seems to have filled in the rest."

She leaned forward to look at his ear and dabbed it with the clean edge of a towel. "It's not bleeding anymore. Eat some more pretzels."

He did. She brought him another glass of water. "What things that I said?"

He found it difficult to focus. "Right before we fell asleep, you said, 'I've never felt so immortal.' What did you mean?"

She turned to the side as if she had a lascivious, sweet secret to share with her shoulder. Flipping the long hair she didn't have, she looked at him again. "We just fucked each other's brains out, remember? Doesn't everyone feel immortal while they're making love? Biological urges, the species continuing itself." She squeezed her hands against her temples. "But maybe you don't feel that way since you're *actually* immortal. It makes my head hurt trying to figure it out."

He understood. He always sensed the immortality of his body, but he didn't very often feel that *he* was immortal. Maybe while making love was the only time.

He tried to explain, but she put her thumbs to her eyes and said her head hurt too much. "Not enough sleep. But go on. Tell me something else I said that made you think I was immortal."

"What about that parachute story? That's exactly what it feels like to be immortal. You go on and on, but everyone you know is yanked away by time." Like Kathryn, shriveled into an old woman and taken away forever.

She seemed amused. "The skydivers? I was flirting, you dumbshit. I was trying to act profound. I even told you that. Besides, that happens to us mortals, too. People die. What else?"

He had to search his mind this time. "We were talking about the feeling of loss. You said, 'century after century, millennium after millennium.'"

Now she got angry. "I've had a shitty life, and my life *feels* like 10 centuries of shit."

"What kind of shitty things?"

"Why do you care?"

"I care." More than he wanted to admit.

She sat back and crossed her arms. "We did skip the personal history phase of the relationship, didn't we? Hard to fit into a one-night stand. Anyway, I'm bored of telling it."

"How about the short version?"

"Eat your pretzels."

Though he'd finished the bag, there was plenty of salt left behind. He sat up and used a wet fingertip to get at it.

She picked at her fingers, her thumb visiting each one in turn. "My father was a professor of history, and he wrote a lot of books. They're real books, not pop trash, but they sold okay, and we had enough money. I grew up upper middle class: Montessori schools, private lessons, and summer art camp. Then one day, I was sitting in my dad's lap, arguing with him about something, and he dropped dead. A heart attack."

"That's terrible," he said.

"And it goes on. My mom gets a boyfriend who molests me. I don't tell anyone, but luckily, she dumps him. I'm just starting to get it together when a drunk driver kills her."

So much loss for someone so young. Maybe she really does understand. But he knew he shouldn't let himself care.

"You still listening? It goes on. I go to live with an uncle who gropes me, but now I'm older, and I blackmail him. I promise never to mention what he did if he rents me an apartment, buys me a car and sends me to prep school. And so, he does. My life starts to make sense, and I even get into Bennington College, my idea of heaven. Only then, my uncle dies, and it turns out he has kids somewhere, and they get all the money. What happens next is a big, long fuckup. But I've been getting healthier lately. I still take home strangers, but they're a better sort of stranger. Immortals, you know, that sort of thing. And I haven't taken drugs for two years, though I still drink too much."

She left the coffee table and squeezed next to him on the couch. In an entirely new voice, this one sweet, even childlike, she said, "So you're 90 years old?"

"About 300," he said.

She lifted a handful of his hair and examined it critically. "If you got your hair streaked silver, you'd make more sense." Affection in her voice. "You've been married before. That's what Menniss said. It's true? How many times?"

"Too many."

"Tell me." She didn't sound affectionate anymore.

"I can only stay with someone for about 12 years. After that, I have to leave. Otherwise, people can figure out that I don't age." It was a plea.

She moved her lips, mentally calculating. "About 15 wives, then?"

"Depending on who you count as a wife. It tears me apart, leaving them. But I have no choice."

"But you don't so much feel sorry for them as you do for your-self. Isn't that right? Let's face it, you're about as typical a narcissist as they get."

Again, he found it strangely pleasurable to be seen and criticized.

"And you've had a lot of children," she said.

"I try not to. They die, you see. Immortality doesn't pass on."

"And so, when you have children, you abandon them." She was speaking to herself, not to him. "Everyone. You leave everyone." She slapped herself on the knees, a masculine gesture of finality. "Well, I haven't changed my pattern after all. I'm still sleeping with narcissistic assholes." She stood and held out her hand to help him up. "Come on, then. If I'm not taking you to the hospital, I can at least clean you up. Get that 300-year-old ass off my couch and into my bathtub."

He found it embarrassing to get undressed in front of her, but she insisted. She stuffed his blood-soaked clothes into a black plastic trash bag and steadied him as he climbed into the tub. Using a wet washcloth, she rubbed the blood off his cheeks, shoulder and back so professionally that he remarked on it.

"I was a nurse's aide for a while," she explained. "Great work if you can deal with minimum wage. Should I use peroxide so it doesn't get infected?"

"I can't get infected. It goes along with the immortality."

"Oh, fuck you." She went back to work, gently cleaning away the blood near where his ear had been. "Twelve years? That's not so short. I don't know anyone who's been in a relationship for 12 years. Unless it's a bad relationship." Very gently, she cleaned the raw area itself. "So, all of those wives you had? They're dead, except maybe the last few. Do you ever think about them? Do you miss them?"

He knew he was supposed to say that he missed them all terribly, but he only missed Kathryn.

"Shut up," she said though he hadn't said anything yet. "New question: did you ever tell any of your wives the truth? I mean that you're immortal?"

"No, never. You're the first."

"I don't remember us getting married."

"You're the first *woman* I've told. Or any mortal. Saul warned me never to talk about it. He said it was always a huge mistake."

"Saul?"

"Saul's a hafeem. That's short for 'half-immortal.' Hafeems age, but slowly. Saul rescued me from the people in my village before they could burn me at the stake."

"They thought you'd sold your soul to the Devil? Well, that's only reasonable. So this Saul guy got you out of there?"

"Just in time. Then he stayed with me and taught me things. He kept me safe from hangers-on. That's what he called people like Menniss."

"And after that?"

Blair felt a peculiar desire for the contemptible in him to be recognized and condemned. "I let him help me for almost 200 years. And then I sent him away. My New Year's resolution. New Year's Day, 1900. I got cocky. I thought I didn't need him and told him so."

"Thanks for all the help, and now go fuck yourself."

"More politely."

"That was pretty fucked up. Wouldn't you miss him? Didn't you want someone you could be honest with?"

"I was full of myself. I wanted to be on my own. But, yes, I missed him almost immediately, only I was too proud to go back."

"Happens to me too," she said. She filled up a cup with lukewarm water and poured it over his hair. She refilled the cup and poured it repeatedly until the water stopped running pink. "You thought I was immortal?"

"I did," he said.

"That's funny." She gave him a big green bath towel and leaned against the bathroom's door jamb to watch as he dried himself. "You look terrible."

"My ear will grow back. My body restores itself to the way it was before."

"That's cool. I don't get one part: why did Saul have to save you? Even if they burned you at the stake, wouldn't you have grown yourself back?"

"No, it's not like that. It's not magic. I need time to heal."

"Like a starfish."

"What do you mean?"

"They grow back their arms. But it takes some time."

She made him leave the bathroom while she took a quick shower.

When she came back out, she said, "So it's all bullshit."

"What's bullshit?"

"The idea that you're immortal. You're not."

"What do you mean I'm not immortal?"

"Oh, come on. You're doomed to die someday, guaranteed. The odds will add up, and a grand piano will fall out of a window and smash you. An earthquake. A tornado, a terrorist, whatever. The only difference is that I know the maximum time I have to live, and you don't. And you'll die looking perfect. Though I guess if I die soon enough, so will I."

It was almost morning. She had some men's clothes in her closet and told him to pick through them for something that fit. But she didn't have gauze bandages, so she left to buy some at a nearby Walmart.

JANICE HAD A remarkable selection of men's clothing stuffed into the big U-haul box at the back of her closet. Blair found black pants that fit him and an elegant white dress shirt. He shaved his face with one of her razors. Except for the bloody hole where his ear had been and a small dent in his nose, he looked pretty good.

His coat was still hanging on the chair. Blair checked all its pockets and found a piece of rubber about an inch long and as thick as his finger. He bent it back and forth with all his strength, but it wouldn't break. He tried to cut it with scissors but couldn't. He found a heavy Chinese-style cleaver and slammed it clear through. The edges glimmered brightly with copper. Continuing to chop until only tiny pieces remained, Blair gathered them into a cup and flushed them down the toilet.

Was he doomed to die, as Janice said? He couldn't believe it. Not with a body like his, overflowing with power and life. He was the beloved of the universe, the Crown Jewel of Creation. He would be careful and lucky and would live forever.

Live forever alone, himself with himself, because it was the only safe way.

He had his hand on the doorknob when it turned of its own accord.

HE STEPPED BACK to let Janice in.

"You found the clothes." She ripped open a package and bandaged his missing ear. "You look awful."

"It'll get better soon."

"No, it won't. Nothing is getting better. I have a bad headache, and you're going away. Goodbye." She waved her fingers upwards, shooing him. "Get out of here. Go already."

He didn't move.

Janice shoved past him and strode to her kitchen. She scrubbed the counter with a yellow sponge, poured Ajax into the sink and scrubbed that too. She stopped scrubbing and glowered at him. "You're still here."

Though she'd spiked her hair again and put on shapeless black clothes, hiding her beauty only made her more beautiful.

She turned her back to him and scrubbed her stovetop. "It's none of my business, but I think you should get in touch with that friend of yours. That Saul guy, the one who's only sort of immortal."

"Why?"

"Why? Because you're clueless."

"Saul probably hates me."

"He should. But I bet he doesn't. Now please, will you get the fuck out of here?"

The print that had fascinated him last night captured his gaze again: white cotton laces zigzagging through eyeholes in a woman's back. "Come with me."

She still had her back to him. "Why in hell should I come with you?"

"I met Jane Austen once. I can tell you some great stories."

She turned around, washed her hands at the sink and dried them on a paper towel. "You don't want me with you. I'm just a mortal."

"I want you," he said.

She sighed and rested her head on the long metal faucet. "The cold feels good."

The faucet bent alarmingly, as if it might break.

It broke, and she jerked up her head. "No woman has ever touched your heart, not in 300 years. So naturally, I'm positive that I'm different, that I'm so wonderful I can break your pattern. It's so predictable and so stupid."

"One of them did touch me," he said.

"Oh, fuck you," she said. "Fuck you." She lifted the broken faucet arm and said, "Shit." She dropped it. "So what happened to her? The one who touched you. Is she still alive?"

"She died last year. Menniss told me."

"What did she die of?"

"Of age," he said.

"Oh," she said.

Shaking, she rested her head on the counter.

She stood up, wiped tears from her face, and headed down the hallway. "Come tell me stories while I pack."

CHAPTER 2

THE HAFEEM

To the Elves, Iluvitar granted eternal life,
but to Men he gave the gift of death,
a cause of great suffering for mortal and immortal alike.
And for what purpose he gave this strange gift,
not even the wisest know.

J.R.R. TOLKIEN (PARAPHRASED)

Flashing back 50 years. The pace slows because he's the wisest of hafeems.
Listen to what he has to say and be patient; it will pick up again.

THE CHRONICLER

SAUL

~~~~~~~~~~~~~~~~~~~~~~~~~~~~~~~~~~~~~~

1975

MOSCOW UNDER BREZHNEV. He would miss the city terribly. Even in miserable Johannesburg, brightly colored soda cans adorned the tarpaper hovels, but here among the heaped hills of concrete apartments, there were no decorations beyond the occasional drooping plastic plant: what other place could so perfectly reflect the state of his soul? But he'd lived here 15 years, and it was past time to leave.

It was early afternoon in late autumn. Saul meandered the windy streets in a state of nostalgic farewell. He strolled through a park where aged pensioners sat dull-eyed among monumental statues of Lenin, Marx and other heroes of the Worker's Paradise. One old man broke into a fit of coughing so violent and prolonged that Saul turned back to ask whether he needed help. The man shook his head and offered Saul a cigarette.

They sat together on a bare wooden bench and shared a smoke. Soviet cigarettes were said to be made from shredded bureaucratic documents rather than tobacco, and Saul found nothing in the experience to disprove this rumor.

Saul had sufficient funds to purchase far superior cigarettes from Western Europe, but while he did occasionally burn such luxuries and inhale their smoke, the act gave him little pleasure. He'd never possessed the gift of easy pleasure, an unfortunate quality in a man likely to live several thousand years. His character was such that it required a focus, a goal, a sense that his efforts furthered some purpose.

But he'd outlived so many purposes.

For example (Saul reflected), he'd studied medicine with Galen, mastering all the medical knowledge of the Greco-Roman world in hopes of healing the sick. Three decades later, he maintained respect for the goal but not the practice. For, as he observed, patients recovered or worsened, lived or died, quite independent of his ministrations. Nonetheless, he was expected to accept a substantial fee.

During a subsequent interval of apprenticeship with physicians in China, he discovered the reason for this failure: the accumulated wisdom of Greco-Roman medicine was miserable superstition. He mastered the more subtle methods of Chinese herbal medicine and found them satisfactorily profound. But when he turned to practice, he again experienced the painful juxtaposition of high fees and questionable benefits delivered.

For the next thousand years, he rejected the entire profession of medicine as fundamentally parasitic and fraudulent. In the 18th century, however, he was impressed by the discoveries of "scientific" medicine and took it up again. He studied under the greatest physicians of the time and learned to discard ineffective herbal remedies in favor of mercury and arsenic.

Mercury and arsenic! Not merely ineffective but positively poisonous. Lucky the patient who avoided the ministrations of *any* doctor during that period.

But (as Saul further reflected) the problem wasn't medicine alone; all his other efforts in pursuit of the good had turned out badly.

In the 17th century, he'd risked his life among those he had then called "savages" to provide them the benefits of Christianity, an effort now characterized by history as the arrogant, colonialist oppression of primal peoples.

Then there was his fourth century moralistic phase: whipping women for adultery, stoning men for homosexuality, and slaughtering Mithraists and Manicheans for heresy. He had, at the time, seen his actions as just, even merciful; he'd meant to serve God. But as subsequent centuries passed and his moral compass changed, he came to view that epoch of his life with profound loathing.

And then there was his most recent idealistic goal, less monstrous but just as failed: his attempt to mentor a young and impressionable True Immortal.

Like the citizens of Moscow under Brezhnev, he now knew that he lacked sufficient wisdom to properly construe a higher purpose, much less serve one. Only, lacking a higher purpose, what was there to live for?

SAUL WANDERED THE streets of Moscow in a state of abstraction, drawn inward by these gnawing thoughts. When his mind exhausted itself and the physical world returned to awareness, he found himself in a dark and shabby quarter. His left leg, troubled recently by problematic veins, ached and throbbed. The sun had set long ago, and the few streetlights that functioned offered no more than flickering illumination. He had no idea where he was.

A young woman stepped out of the shadows between two brutalist-style apartments. She wore a tight, orange dress that appeared ready to burst open as much from the poor quality of the fabric as the size of her bosom. In the tone of simulated lust favored by prostitutes, she asked him if he would like "a quick one," gesturing toward the long, narrow passage behind her as an ideal spot for the transaction.

Still somewhat abstracted, Saul didn't immediately reply, and the woman varied her approach. "I bet you're the kind of man who'd like to treat a girl right," she said. "My place is nearby. And I don't charge much."

Saul recovered himself and his manners. "You are without doubt a lovely young woman," he said. "And you most certainly deserve to be treated well. But, alas, I've come to this district in error—I'm lost, you see. I wonder whether you'd be so kind as to help me with directions back to my quarter." He described the general location, near enough to where he actually lived.

She popped a stick of gum in her mouth. "Do I look like I work for the tourist bureau?"

"My apologies," Saul said. "No offense intended. Perhaps I could pay you your usual fee merely for the privilege of having seen your beauty?"

She popped a second stick of gum in her mouth and, with a sudden movement, pulled open her dress to show him her breasts.

Again taken by surprise, he managed to get out, "Very well-formed, indeed."

She lifted one breast from below and aimed its nipple at his face. "You think?"

"Beyond doubt. And I'm truly gratified. Thank you. And I'd thank you again for directions."

But she wasn't done. She placed her hands beneath her breasts and caused them to undergo various gyrations, a procedure Saul endured with an expression of interest. When she returned her breasts to her dress, Saul opened his wallet and offered her a 50 Deutschmark bill (marks were hard currency).

Far too much, but she took it and indifferently gave him instructions.

Saul set off at a determined pace. As he walked, his mind offered up images of his apartment: its coziness and safety, its music, its consoling works of philosophy. He would take a hot bath and read Seneca.

But as he hurried on, the atmosphere of his surroundings worsened rather than improved. He grew distinctly uneasy. It dawned on him that the prostitute, having glimpsed the contents of his wallet, might have directed him not toward safety but toward thieves of her acquaintance from whom she might get a share.

He smelled industrial fumes. There were no pedestrians on the littered street or cars on the road; the only sign of life was the occasional glance from behind a drawn curtain. A battered black Lada turned a corner ahead of him and pulled over to the wrong side of the street to park by his side.

Should he run? He should not. Thieves were generally youthful, and he would certainly fail to escape; the safest course was to offer no resistance. After all, he was a middle-aged man with graying hair. If he gave over his money upon request, why would they harm him?

He stood submissively as the driver and two young men from the backseat climbed out. They were large and muscular and wore suits. They arrayed themselves around him in such a disciplined manner that Saul thought for a moment they might be KGB, except that KGB agents wore suits of higher-quality material.

A fourth man now emerged from the car. He wore a ski mask, and for the first time in many decades, Saul experienced fear. If all they meant to do was rob him, why the mask?

This man, obviously the leader, was taller than the others but less muscular. He didn't move in their blocky manner but with an insolent slouch. Was he an official who might be recognized (hence the mask)? A man with power but no happiness who might enjoy beating someone to death?

Saul felt a certain abstract camaraderie with this hypothetical bureaucrat. To kill a man, to pummel him, wouldn't this be an appropriate external equivalent to the internal pummeling he'd given himself these several hours?

He considered whether he was willing to die. Surely, he cared little for life, or else he would not have been so careless as to fall into this situation.

If there were only two of them, Saul might have attempted to fight. He wasn't the helpless middle-aged man he appeared; over two and a half millennia, he'd learned many methods of hand-to-hand combat. But against four, and three so large, there was little chance of success.

On balance, Saul decided, he'd prefer to live. His only hope lay in analyzing the character of this smaller man, the leader. But eyes fail to reveal the soul when a mask hides the surrounding face.

What about this man's posture? He leans back on one hip. With contempt? Rather with irony.

Seen as isolated flesh against the black cotton of the mask, the man's lips resembled thick mobile worms. "Old man," he said, "have you come here to be robbed and beaten?" His voice tilted toward the gutter but hinted at refinement, even education. And the sense of irony was without question.

I can use this, Saul thought. Perhaps. But it's my best chance. "It would be an honor to be robbed and beaten by one such as you," Saul said.

The nearest of the two young thugs took the words for mockery and seized Saul by the collar. He drew back a heavy fist and looked to his leader for direction.

A brief silent tableau, and then the man in the ski mask broke into rolling laughter. "No, Grigor," he said. "Do not hurt this man. We cannot rob him. We cannot harm a hair of his graying head. Why not? Because he wishes us to. Only those who prefer to live their lives unmolested may we rob and beat. Is that not Marxist-Leninism?"

Grigor appeared uncertain about whether to take these words seriously; he didn't release Saul's collar until the leader touched his hand. A single light tap and Grigor stepped back.

"I am Alexei," the man in the mask said.

"And I'm Saul. May I take it that you have no intention of robbing me despite my expressed wish?"

Alexei brushed down Saul's clothes as if to straighten out the damage Grigor might have caused if events had proceeded differently. "No, my friend, we shall not rob you. Nor beat you, either. But you must not continue walking this way. They are not all good Soviets ahead. You will meet Azers and Chechens, people with indifferent concepts of morality. Men who rob even those who wish to be robbed."

Having finally caught the joke, young Grigor roared with laughter.

"We cannot take his money unless he beats us senseless, can we, Alexei? He must force us to take it. Then it shall be an unrobbery."

"An unrobbery!" Alexei exclaimed. "You are brilliant." He put one arm around Grigor and the other around Saul. "But, alas, we have no time to be beaten senseless. We have other business to attend to."

Alexei gave Saul clear directions to his quarter, but the mask stayed on.

THE DANGER HAVING passed, Saul's skin broke out in a clammy sweat, and his heart concurred via periodic thumps. He no longer had any doubts that he wished to live. There's nothing like physical fear, Saul thought, to suppress the philosopher and re-animate the primal man.

But Alexei's directions had been precise, and Saul soon saw landmarks of central Moscow. He made his way to one of the bridges that cross the Moscow River and joined a stream of people walking along its pedestrian bridge: young men and women returning home

from the newly available western "discos," married women and old
grandmothers going even at this hour to stand in line for some new
product arriving next morning from the West, factory workers of
both sexes in identical smocks, older men drinking from bottles.

A barge approached, and Saul paused to appreciate the echoes
set in motion by its great diesel engine. He listened to the sounds
change as the barge passed beneath the walkway. When the sound
died to a splashing wake, Saul noticed that the human chatter around
him had similarly dissipated. He looked around with anxiety and discovered that the bridge had grown empty. Those few pedestrians who
remained were hurrying away from a set of silent new arrivals, men
as large as Alexei's thugs and far better dressed.

Had there been a coup? Would he find tanks at the other end of
the bridge? He attempted to follow the others and flee, but guards
blocked his way. For a second time that evening, Saul had no choice
but to stand his ground.

He stood and waited. A solitary old woman entered the bridge
from the opposite end and made her troubled way toward him. She
leaned on a cane and wore innumerable shawls and scarves to protect her from the cold wind blowing up the river's channel. Saul
flattened against the guardrail to give her more room to pass. She
looked up at him in gratitude, and it was then that he saw her face.

She wasn't elderly at all—she was merely ancient. Ancient
beyond imagining.

He'd successfully managed his encounter with the thieves, but no
strategizing could alter the result of this encounter. She was impervi-
ous to all stratagems, having seen each one enacted a thousand times.
The Eldest would do what she willed.

What she willed, apparently, was to shade her eyes and watch a
cloud pass over the moon from left to right. Perhaps, if the cloud had
traveled right to left, she would have walked on without speaking; if
it hadn't moved at all, she might have had Saul thrown into the river.

She abandoned all pretense of decrepitude. She stood at her
full height, her face deceptively young, her black eyes feral and wise.

Her Russian mixed all accents and hinted at all the grammars of the world. "I, Yavànna," she said, "I ask the help of Saul. I ask that you ponder a question and advise me. I do not command. I ask."

"Whatever you ask of me," Saul said, "with all my heart, I will seek to answer truly. But I cannot imagine any question to which I know the answer while you do not."

"*I* can imagine such a question. And *I* say you can answer. Else why should Yavànna ask? For you are a thing I am not. You are mortal."

"I am mortal, certainly," Saul said.

"Yes. And that is why you may know what I do not. My question touches sickness, injury, aging and death. Of these, I ask: be they curse alone or in any manner gift?"

He struggled to understand. "You're asking whether mortality is a gift or curse? That is a terribly difficult question."

"If it were not difficult, why would Yavànna ask? I have asked others, and I will ask still others, some whom I have known for centuries and others whom I will, by chance, someday meet. Difficult to answer, and yet you have not long to contemplate. Twenty years will I allow, 50 years at most before I require your wisdom. Will you help me?"

"I will do my best, Eldest," he said.

"Yes." She leaned against the guardrail and turned her young/old face to the water. "There are two groups," she said. "One is strong, the other less so. One is grave and wise; the other, wise and capricious. To the group capricious and weaker, I have given my protection."

"As you would," Saul said. He felt an upwelling of human affection for her. "You have always taken the side most given to accident."

"Yes. And I may, by chance, withdraw my protection. As you know. You will try to answer?"

"With all my ability, Eldest."

Yavànna drew her shawls and scarves back in place. She bent and became an aged woman once more. But only for a moment. She straightened; she fully unveiled her face. She spoke not in Russian but in the ancient Greek of Saul's childhood. "Listen," she said.

"I listen, Eldest," he said.

"Listen, yes. For this, I *command*." She held him with her prime-val stare. "Saul has reached faith's death. But the end of faith is the beginning of forgiveness. This I command: you shall cease your pen-ance and live again. Do you hear?"

"I hear, Eldest," he said.

"You shall live, yes," she said. "And I command where you shall come back to life, and where you will begin to ponder the question I asked you."

He knew the place before she spoke its name, and his whole being ached, but he didn't protest. "Yes, Eldest," he said, "I shall return to Santa Cruz, I shall cease to do penance, and I shall live again."

Pedestrians were beginning to come from the far sides of the bridge. She folded herself into the image of age, bent over and hob-bling on her cane. Ordinary noises of people surrounded them as the bridge filled again, and she was gone.

HE'D PRACTICED THESE transitions for millennia, but each period and circumstance presented new challenges. Winding up his affairs in Moscow was a simple task of bribing the appropriate officials to erase all records he'd ever existed and bribing a second group to ensure the first had done so properly. The task of creating a secure new identity presented greater challenges.

Through certain contacts judiciously nourished, he learned of a certain Lee Salal, a US citizen aged 55 possessing independent means and given to solitary travel. Mr. Salal had no living relatives and lacked close friends or other intimate associates. While visiting Jakarta, the unfortunate Mr. Salal had stumbled in untimely fash-ion over a crack in the sidewalk and received into his skull a bullet intended for another. Neither of the warring criminal syndicates involved in the assassination had any quarrel with the United States, nor did they wish to provoke one. They were, therefore, nothing but grateful when Saul offered to take the accidentally assassinated man off their hands.

He did so by becoming him.

Saul flew to Jakarta and from there to New York City using a false passport of the highest quality in the name of Lee Salal. From New York, he traveled by bus to a sparsely populated region of Kansas and established residency by purchasing land. In the remote and rather disorganized courthouse that held jurisdiction over that piece of property, Saul recorded a legal change of name to Saul Velis.

This name change would make it more difficult for anyone to track him, but his primary motivation was sentimental: he'd been named Saul the last time he'd lived in Santa Cruz. He considered taking additional steps to muddy the trail, but experience told him there was no need and that he had no further excuse to delay. With a heavy heart, Saul boarded a Greyhound bus headed for Santa Cruz, the one place in the world he'd hoped never to visit again.

THE BUS TRAVELED for two days and two nights. On the third morning, it crossed the Bay Bridge, a construction of riveted steel girders whose heaviness and crudity would have pleased Stalin himself. But this was San Francisco Bay, not Moscow, and on the far side of the water, Saul could see the Golden Gate Bridge half shrouded in fog.

The Golden Gate Bridge. Truly a wonder of the world. The Great Pyramid asserted the hard fist of human power, and the Parthenon raised a lofty marker of human artistry, but both those wonders looked backward in time; they signified how far humanity had come. The Golden Gate Bridge looked forward, signifying, in that much-ridiculed but nonetheless real American manner, that the way ahead was open wide.

Open, for example, to a stroll on the moon. American mortals had indeed set foot on the surface of that celestial body. Surely this was one of the greatest accomplishments in all human history, even if it accomplished little more than the creation of a peculiarly enduring series of boot prints. There were more than a dozen living men—very dull men, alas, not apparently transformed by the experience—of whom it could be truthfully said, "He has traveled to the moon and back." Saul had met shamans who claimed this ability, but he felt comfortably sure they had been lying.

The bus descended on a swooping curve into San Francisco and entered a forest of bright advertisements. One frequently repeated image showed a woman who had been struck in the face at some point in the past and was shown developing that form of hematoma known colloquially as a "black eye." To Saul's astonishment, words printed across her forehead suggested a pugilistic spirit unusual among women—some obscure matter of loyalty was involved, and she would "rather fight than switch." The cause of this relished combat was, oddly, a brand of cigarettes named Tareyton.

Another billboard displayed a woman standing beside a cigarette that rose to the level of her shoulders. The diameter of this particular product was unusually small relative to its length, and the same could be said of the woman. The caption for these companions in slimness stated, "You've come a long way, baby."

A novel message, all in all. Females were now being encouraged to shorten their already-brief lifespans by imitating the behavior of males: consuming poisonous intoxicants and engaging in combat. Truly an advance toward equality.

It had been little more than a century since he'd ceased to regard the subjugation of women as natural. And it had not been very much longer than that since he'd learned to reject literal enslavement. Even so great a man as Socrates had never considered that slavery might be unjust, much less that a woman might be fully human. In a few centuries, the mortal world had as far transcended its ancient ethical limits as its technological.

Which of his current beliefs would he in future come to condemn? He couldn't know.

The bus stopped briefly in San Francisco before heading south toward Santa Cruz.

Taking on a reddish-brown tint at the city of San Jose, the sky became blue again as they drove toward a modestly sized mountain range. They ascended via an ambitious highway that cut through the mountains in bracing hairpin turns. Tall redwoods rose in increasing density behind the smaller vegetation at the edge of the asphalt, and once the bus ascended to sufficient altitude, they stood sentinel alongside the road. The bus achieved the summit, and the Pacific Ocean stretched out for an extended moment before they descended back into the forest. Here redwoods entirely dominated, enshrouding masses of trees that extended for miles, canopies so thick and vast they could conceal entire cities within their darkness.

The road flattened. The bus navigated a freeway interchange. It stopped at one intersection and then another. Then it glided to a halt at the dingy Greyhound Bus station of Santa Cruz.

SANTA CRUZ, CALIFORNIA. An earthly paradise. A college town on the beach, a city of colors, a soft world whose climate fostered lush gardens, itinerant street performers and public semi-nudity. Saul sighed and set off to explore the city on foot.

He walked along the levy of the San Lorenzo River, watching seagulls investigate stones at the limits of the flowing water. He passed under a street whose concrete bridge was enlivened by a bright mural that depicted people of many races encountering such enlivening creatures as dolphins, caribou and unicorns. A great blue heron drew in its flapping wings and landed on a large rock in the river ahead. To avoid frightening it back into flight, Saul deviated from the river and climbed a steep stairway that zigzagged up the side of a hill. He reached the top and looked at a city he hadn't seen for 75 years.

Whether by design or accident, Santa Cruz had grown in a manner that greatly pleased the eye. Streets flowed in harmony with the curves of the San Lorenzo River and inlets of the sea, and the neighborhoods showed pleasing variations in style, shape and color.

He turned around to look at the neighborhood where he was currently standing, the one at the top of the hill. It was a dazzling panoply of Victorians and Queen Annes. As is typical for homes built in those architectural styles, they were embellished with colorful, fanciful shingles and courses, finials, bosses, crockets and crestings, brackets and breadwork, bay windows, cone-topped turrets, balconies and gables, and acres of stained glass. But what he'd never seen before, and what overwhelmed him, was the intensity with which color had been used to amplify these standard features. Each shingle, each finial, each cresting, all the elaborate details of these homes were individually hued in a loving and subtle palette. One large Queen Anne wore earth tones—clay red, burnt yellow, ochre, umber, and gray-green, each varied into 100 hues, making the house a type of landscape. Another home cried out playfully in clashing turquoise against brick, yellow against lime, orange against magenta. And yet another, perhaps his favorite, restricted its palette to shades of gray and gray-blue, but only to offset a garden wild with color: flowers climbing ramps, overflowing arches, outlining paths and rising up walls.

Saul discovered in subsequent weeks that Santa Cruz's population was equally colorful, especially that youthful portion on display in the open-air Pacific Garden Mall. Young men and women gathered there, swathed in brightly colored clothes imported from Afghanistan, India and their own imaginations. They gathered in groups to sing Gregorian chants, in ensembles to play the recorder and in troupes to juggle sickles and torches. Some created complex rhythms by beating spoons; others produced melody through the application of a violin bow to a hand saw. On Thursday nights, three monks who composed a monastery fully compliant with the rules of St. Benedict descended from the mountains to play conga drums in an outdoor space set aside by a local ale house. When they were finished, people with shaved heads and dressed in profoundly orange attire worshipped Krishna with bells, metal clappers, chants and dance.

In all this, the city's youth sought to return to a bygone era in which life had been lived to its fullest, a vaguely conceived epoch that combined the Middle Ages, the Renaissance and vaudeville. The theoreticians of this imaginary, syncretic period gathered at a café known as Pergolesi, and in time, Saul came to spend the greater part of his days there. He did so in part to study contemporary language, an essential effort for one who had last spoken English in Victorian-era Britain. But he found that he enjoyed the intellectual discourse that went on in the café as well; though often puerile, he found it nonetheless enlivening.

And here at Café Pergolesi, sipping tea and listening, Saul overheard a tale that set the train of his life in new motion.

THE PATIO OF Café Pergolesi was a beautiful setting for intellectual discourse. At the edge of the redwood deck, trellises of wisteria, hollyhock and passionflower stirred slightly in the breeze. A solitary redwood tree pierced the deck's center, holding in its lower branches shelves stacked with multi-grain scones, wheat-germ muffins, carob croissants, and other highly fibrous foods said to be "natural" and "organic."

On the day Saul first heard of Bonnie Akers, he was sitting at a table close to this central redwood tree and listening to the conversation of a young couple nearby. The man, who sported a handlebar mustache and goatee, held a silver-handled cane. His name was Howard. The woman styled herself Beatrice and dressed in black-and-yellow striped clothes that gave her the appearance of a voluptuous wasp. In addition, she possessed a quantity of reddish hair so radiant and vast as to temporarily blind the eyes of passing servers. She combined these two qualities in an intelligence that was both radiant and waspish.

Howard evidently had it in his mind to sleep with Beatrice at the earliest practical occasion, and toward this end, he engaged in a practice esteemed by young men of all ages—namely, showing off. Saul might have saved Howard the trouble, for he perceived that Beatrice was fully willing to seize the young man in her arms at once, proximate prelude to the rest. Indeed, she seemed irked by her suitor's flights of self-promotion. However, launched into them with such rapidity that she had little choice but to play along.

It developed that young Howard felt it necessary to justify the nature of his gainful employment. He was a CNA, a certified nurse assistant, and worked at a nursing home called Cedar Manor. The problem lay in his remuneration: he received no more than the lowest allowed by law. Even in the lofty intellectual world of Café Pergolesi, this was a potential embarrassment.

"For me," Howard said, "working as a nurse's aide is a philosophical exercise. I'm using my time at Cedar Manor to study how the imminent approach of death affects people."

Beatrice leaned toward him over the table. "Do tell what great insights this philosophical exercise has given you?"

The young man adjusted his handlebar mustache and smoothed his goatee. Speaking in a manner that seemed overly formal even to Saul, but that Howard must have thought would impress the girl, he said, "It is my theory that extreme old age distills people to their essential selves. For example, one of our patients, Campbell, was once quite the dashing military officer. According to his relatives, women would fall for him right and left; in fact, he usually had one woman on his right and another on the left. Now, he's a disgusting old man and a raving maniac, but you know what his ravings show? Loneliness. He clutches at you. He tries to pull you close. So here's my point: I think he's showing his essential nature. He wanted all those women because he felt so lonely."

"Interesting," Beatrice mused. "I wonder how I'll turn out when I'm demented. A vicious harpy bitch, betcha. Tell me more."

Young Howard boldly raised a creamer above his cup of coffee; he poured from a sufficient height as to risk spillage, yet not a drop spilled, not then or even when he stirred it with a spoon. This confident gesture reminded Saul of one of his rare children, a young man about Howard's age who'd perfected a similar display. What a dashing, gallant lad he'd been, and to what splendid effect his dress uniform had shown against the backdrop of his black coffin.

Having lightened his coffee to his taste, Howard set it aside without taking a sip. "I have a patient named Bonnie Akers. She's boiled her whole life down to a single sentence. I believe that if I could discover what she means by it, I would learn something enormously profound."

"And what was this cryptic nugget?" Beatrice asked.

Howard rubbed his goatee. Perhaps he hadn't thought to the end of this anecdote and now doubted its reception. "Her endlessly repeated phrase—her bon mot—her maxim—her epigram and epitaph—the summation of her life—" He stopped speaking and set to work twisting the ends of his handlebar mustache.

"Yes, yes, and yes," Beatrice said. "Go on."

"I'm trying to get the delivery right." He displayed symptoms of inward concentration. He delivered five words in a voice pitched several notes higher than his usual: "Goddamn son of a bitch."

The phrase hung in the air for a doubtful moment, and then the young woman burst out laughing. Saul silently blessed them for their connection. They would soon enough wither and die, but for the moment, they'd found companionship.

"She's a very peculiar woman," Howard went on. "She's a private patient, which means she has money, but no one ever comes to visit her. That's odd when people have money. And though her chart says she's 85, she doesn't look more than 50. You want to hear my theory?"

"Yes, Howard, I want to hear your theory."

"I think she's one of the great ancient sages of the world, living in disguise."

"And her wisdom," cried the young woman, laughing, "consists of 'goddamn son of a bitch?'"

Saul didn't laugh. He pushed forcefully away from his table, threw down far too much money and hurried out of the café, his thoughts whirling.

A woman in a nursing home who appeared 50 but whose chart said she was 85? A hafeem? A disabled hafeem living in a nursing home? One of his kind subject to the impertinences of mortals, steeped in her own urine, swaddled and bound in humiliation?

A century of apathy evaporated. He would investigate, and if she turned out to be a hafeem, he would rescue her.

Never mind that it could be a trap, that this benevolent interest could get him killed. It was his moral duty.

THE NURSING HOME sat on a coastal cliff several miles north of Santa Cruz. Three windblown cedars at the edge of the parking lot provided the excuse for the name *Cedar Manor*. A field of blue-green Brussels sprouts stretched from there to the cliff, surrounded by bright yellow, flowering mustard.

Saul guessed that the beautiful setting somewhat assuaged the guilt of those who abandoned their relatives here, but the home itself was a brute stucco prison. On that first visit, Saul gathered only vague impressions of bizarre individuals in tall-backed chairs accompanied by a general howling and calling out. No one came to help him, so he found his way by following small arrow-shaped signs pasted on the walls. Since the office appeared unoccupied, he completed one of the application forms and turned to go, expecting to receive a phone call some days later. Before he could depart, an older man stepped out of an inner office, introduced himself as Mr. Lackman, the nursing home administrator, and proposed to conduct the interview at once.

Lackman had a bureaucrat's face, obscure with gray fatigue, but Saul sensed a certain buried cunning. Lackman seemed the right age to be a hanger-on, and his position would allow him to easily set the type of trap Saul feared. The accumulated prudence of 25 centuries urged him to abandon the project, but he would not. He'd sickened of prudence.

Lackman gave the application a sour glance. "Saul Velis. Age 55. Most of our nurse assistants are much younger."

"I keep myself fit," Saul said. "I'm certain I can handle it."

Lackman glanced at Saul's compact, strong-looking body and nodded disagreeably. "But there is the tedium to consider," he added. "The demeaning nature of much of the work. With your education and experience, you must have other options. Why work here?"

"As a moral exercise," Saul said. "I've lived selfishly for many years, and I want to give back to society."

Lackman did not exactly snort; rather, he emitted an unconsummated sound resembling a snort. "How laudable. To serve the elderly, the helpless, and the dying. Very virtuous. Our physician, Dr. Pierce, that's why he works here. But Pierce earns considerably more than a nurse assistant. I could perhaps stretch slightly for someone of your age and experience ..."

Saul demurred. "Not at all. I wouldn't want to cause friction between myself and the others. Please start me at your usual rate."

Lackman produced a ghostly smile, no doubt pleased by the thought of having saved a few pennies. He searched in a drawer—"fished around," to rehearse the current idiom—and brought out a stack of orientation materials, which he handed to Saul. Lackman pointed out various papers in the stack containing information Saul should study, particularly the subject of uniforms. He

mentioned the necessity of obtaining state nurse assistant certifica-
tion within 30 days and how this could best be done, then returned
to the subject of uniforms.

Lackman underlined passages in the handout that addressed this
essential topic and added commentary of his own: the moral value
of pure whiteness in uniforms, especially in the eyes of visiting relatives; the various types of stains that might occur and the optimum
means for their removal; the fundamental distinction, despite the
superficial similarity, between stains caused by blood and by spa-
ghetti sauce; the temptation of bleach was always to be resisted; the
hideous color changes when said temptation was not resisted. Lackman continued waxing eloquent on this topic until a complaining
relative called. Saul, slated to start the next day, was left to find his
own way out.

IF LACKMAN HAD entered his career with idealism and, after losing
most of it, had settled his remaining stock upon uniforms, he was
not wrong to have done so. Saul had worn many forms of clothing
in his two-and-one-half millennia, but none possessed the spiritual
qualities of translucent white nylon.

Having arrived a few minutes early, Saul sat in his car and ran
his hands along the sleeves of his jacket. His fingertips detected a
texture of parallel lines so finely embossed that his less discerning
palm felt no texture at all. He lifted the bottom of his jacket and
noticed it appeared vaguely beige, transmitting the tint of the car's
leather seats. When Saul stepped out of the car, sea and sky tinted
the uniform pale blue, except toward the bottom of his pant legs,
where the asphalt contributed a darkening effect.

A sensitive uniform and a confident one, too. It seemed as if it
were the uniform and not he who strode across the parking lot and
advanced up the broad path to Cedar Manor's entrance. It was
the uniform that vigorously seized hold of the nursing home's door
and pulled it open. Once inside the vestibule, however, the uniform
encountered a difficulty that it lacked the skills to resolve, and it
called on Saul, the person, to solve the problem.

The vestibule served as an airlock, protecting the motionless air of the nursing home from the strong winds that might otherwise blow in from the sea. Saul had passed through the outer door, but to reach the nursing home proper, he would have to open a second set of doors. Unfortunately, his progress toward them was blocked by the presence of an individual lacking somewhat in the matter of sanity.

This obstacle was an aged man with a reddened face, sizable on his own account and incarcerated in a large, padded chair that extended his dimensions. From the orientation materials, Saul recognized this confining device as a "Geri chair." It was reminiscent of a 19th-century elementary school desk, but its seat and back were composed of padded vinyl rather than wood, and the swing-over arm served as a restraint rather than a writing surface.

The geriatric personage confined in this chair reached out toward Saul's face with dirty, yellowed fingers. "I saw them melting like wet soap," he said. "Soaping into ghosts. Arrested, roasted, frosted, frighted."

The words did not, strictly speaking, convey anything at all, but Saul couldn't fail to perceive the emotion behind them. "I can scarcely imagine the torment, sir," Saul said. "A horror no man should have to face."

The skin around the patient's eyes contorted strangely, and Saul hoped that whatever nightmare the man had once experienced might now express itself. But the patient's attention fell upon the fingers of his right hand; he stared at them as if they belonged to another. He wiggled them, disproving that theory; the hand rose and laboriously attempted to take hold of an invisible object floating in the air. Saul took the opportunity of this distraction to ease his way around the Geri chair, but the patient's plucking fingers abandoned their pursuit of the nonexistent and seized Saul's arm.

"No sneaking away from Campbell. He'll eat the living daylight savings out of you. He'll slit your frigging underfig, your bellyfig, your jello belly. Abandon me, soldier? Never."

So this was the Campbell young Howard had mentioned, a former womanizer distilled by senility to his essential loneliness. Howard's description had indeed been apt. "Pleased to meet you, Mr. Campbell," Saul said.

"*Mr.* Campbell? You insolent son of a dog. Shockling's too good for you. I'll have you shattled and sacked. *Lieutenant* Campbell of His Majesty's Horse Guards."

"Of course. Please pardon my ignorance, for I'm only a civilian."

Campbell gently patted Saul's arm. "There are no civilians in civil wars. Livid gores. Gorgeous girls. Oh, so gorgeous."

"Indeed, sir, and you shall have many more conquests soon enough. And now, with your permission, may I pass?"

"Pass? You'll pass pissing pus before you leave me."

The inner door opened, and a tall woman in her late 40s entered the vestibule. She wore the classic nurse's uniform of starched, white cotton, modified only in that she'd substituted a black Ché Guevara beret for the more common starched white hat. Her name badge read, "Carol Denning, RN. Charge Nurse."

"May I introduce myself?" Saul asked. "I'm Saul Velis, a new nurse's aide."

"Lucky you," she said.

DENNING TOOK FIRM hold of the Geri chair's handles and tipped it backward. Campbell threw out his arms and cried, "Whoa there!" as if to an unruly horse.

"We let him get psychotic twice a week because it wards off pneumonia," she explained. "But enough is enough. It's time for his Haldol."

"My lushy, my slush," Campbell said. He reached behind to touch Ms. Denning, but she easily evaded him. Pushing open the inner door with an expert foot, she navigated the Geri chair into the hallway and motioned Saul to follow. He had to walk quickly to keep up. They traversed a corridor lined with sitting residents. Most were silent and slumped as far as their restraints would allow. A few beckoned; several raved.

One woman sat in an ordinary wheelchair, unrestrained, with a small square rug across her lap. She possessed the most deeply wrinkled face Saul had ever seen, but the way she watched as they approached suggested that her mind was clear. When they came abreast of her, she said, "I believe you're new here."

"Yes, I am. My name is Saul. Saul Velis."

"My name is Leyla. Good luck to you. It's a hard job. Now hurry and catch up with Carol."

Ms. Denning had gone a good way down the corridor. Saul jogged until he was once again beside her. They passed a room designated "Recreation." Saul glimpsed a woman standing in the center of a circle of Geri chairs. She was bouncing an inflated beach ball off the skeletal, semi-conscious figures surrounding her.

"Our recreation director," Denning explained. "Poor thing."

They turned a corner, now entering an even longer corridor lined at intervals with occupied Geri chairs. A young man, his arms loaded with pungent bedding, backed out of a room and nearly walked into them. He proved to be Howard, the young man from the café. His goatee and mustache fit well with the white nylon uniform.

"Howard," Denning said, "meet Saul. Saul, meet Howard." She didn't slow her motion. Over her shoulder, she added, "Please show him around, will you?"

Howard dropped the soiled linen in a hamper and held out a hand to Saul, but before Saul could reach for it, he withdrew the hand, brought it to his nose and made an elaborate expression of disgust. He rubbed both palms on his white nylon pants. "Howdy," he said. "Why do I think I recognize you?"

"We might have seen each other downtown. Perhaps at one of the cafes or bookshops?"

"Maybe Bookshop Santa Cruz. My single favorite place in all the world. Along with several others."

From somewhere down the hallway, a thin voice with a distinctly English accent called out, "Help me! Won't someone please help me? It would be a great kindness if someone would help me."

"I guess someone needs help," Saul said.

Howard's eyebrows knitted in confusion.

"That woman calling out," Saul explained.

Howard tipped his head to the side and stroked his goatee, his blue eyes blank.

"When someone has a free moment," the woman said, "would they be so kind as to help me? I need help."

Saul said, "I mean her."

Enlightenment dawned on Howard's face. "Oh! You mean Elea-nor. She's always asking for help. But no one's ever been able to discover what kind of help she wants. In time, you stop hearing her."

A staccato male voice shouted, "Hurry, quick, I need help! Hurry! Come quick!"

Another voice shouted, "Betsy, my glasses, damn it."

"I would so much appreciate a spot of help."

"Hurry! Hurry! Come quick!"

"Please? Please? Please?"

And from far away, a very faint "Goddamn son of a bitch."

SAUL DIDN'T DARE show specific interest; he would have to wait until the ordinary motions of work brought him in contact with her.

"It creates a moral risk, of course," Howard said.

"What does?" Saul asked.

"Accustoming oneself to ignoring cries for help. If carried too far, it might breed insensitivity. And that would be a Bad Thing. Which would be a shame because Cedar Manor is one of the few places in the world where it's actually possible to do Good Things."

"Please elaborate further," Saul said.

Howard's face puckered in concentration. Using his fingers to indicate quotation marks, he said, "In the real world, the concept of 'doing good' is fraught. If you look at history, it's obvious that 'good' acts often have 'bad' effects. That's why people like to say, 'all that matters is good intentions.' Because then you can say, 'I am a Good Person who does Good Things,' and feel warm inside. But what if those Good Things may lead to Awful Consequences?"

"Please," Saul said, "go on."

The young man's nylon-clad chest swelled at the praise. "Here inside, though, it's possible to achieve unambiguous good. Our job is to help people accomplish unambiguously legitimate goals they can no longer achieve alone—basically, to avoid not pissing or shit-ting themselves."

"A highly simplified moral universe," Saul said.

"A moral paradise."

"At least, so long as you're not the recreation director."

Howard chuckled, a pleasant sound that both congratulated Saul on his insight and fully endorsed it. He took a list from his jacket pocket and carefully unfolded it. "We have eight patients to take care of. Believe me, that's nothing. I've worked in other places where the norm is 14 or 15. With a workload like that, you can't take care of everyone, so you triage the pissing. It's terrible. Well, shall we launch ourselves?"

They set off down the hall at a fast pace, but they'd progressed no more than a dozen feet when Howard came to a sudden halt, clapped his palms to his cheeks and stared through an open door. A man lay prone on the bare linoleum floor in the room beyond, making swimming motions.

"Change of plans," Howard said. "We start with Mr. Bates." In a low voice, he added, "Mr. Bates may not look it, but he's aware of everything. Keep that in mind."

The room was adorned in a surprisingly respectable fashion. A fine antique dresser, a brass standing lamp and a massive leather recliner were arrayed about the room and paintings of excellent quality were secured to the walls with heavy metal brackets. In one corner, a locked museum-style case of thick Plexiglas displayed four samurai swords. The only items of an institutional nature were a waiting Geri chair and a hospital bed with metal side rails.

"Are you all right, Mr. Bates?" Howard asked.

Mr. Bates stopped swimming and nodded.

They examined him together. Aside from a small scrape on the toe, Mr. Bates appeared to have survived his fall without significant harm.

Howard pointed to the hospital bed, where a white-and-yellow restraint vest remained in place just below the pillow. "He wriggled out of his vest. And then he climbed over the rails. He doesn't do that often. I wonder if he has a fever. Let's check the vitals sheet."

They left Mr. Bates face down on the floor and examined this "vitals sheet," which turned out to be the facing page of a small stack of papers held fast in a clipboard attached to the foot of the bed. Notes written in various hands recorded periodic measurements of his temperature, breathing rate and blood pressure. A laminated, three-by-five card tied to the bed rail near the clipboard displayed his name, age, illnesses and medications. But, to Saul's amazement, there was no mention of the man's tongue. Could current medical practice have dispensed with the examination of the tongue? It seemed impossible.

"No fever or anything," Howard said. "Hmm. Maybe he needs his medications adjusted. I'll tell Dr. Pierce."

The aides kneeled on opposite sides of the patient, held him by the arms, and, on Howard's "Hup, hup, ho," lifted. But the outcome was far from satisfactory. In theory, Mr. Bates was supposed to rise limply until fully upright; instead, he kept his body rigid and swiveled rather than rose, his feet the fulcrum.

"Uh-oh," Howard said.

Once they'd brought him to an angle of about 45 degrees, Mr. Bates began spasmodic walking attempts, and his feet, clad in socks, slipped on the linoleum floor.

"Please don't be embarrassed, Mr. Bates," Howard said. "We're going to have to turn you over."

Howard and Saul caused Mr. Bates to undergo a full rotation so that now he stared up at the ceiling. In this new position, his heels slid easily along the floor as they dragged him toward the toilet. Mr. Bates remained motionless throughout, possibly enjoying his unusual vantage.

The bathroom was too small for three, and Howard sent Saul out to complete various tasks involving bedding. When all was ready, they took Mr. Bates to his Geri chair, found clothing in the dresser, and threaded his arms and legs through the proper apertures.

"Most nursing homes," Howard said, "don't even bother to keep people's clothes straight. Everyone wears everyone else's things. It looks like an orphan asylum, all the inmates ragtag in clothes too long or too short. Some of the patients don't know, of course, but the ones who do—it's humiliating. It's terrible." A new note of intensity had appeared in Howard's voice, but he lapsed into internal feelings and said no more on the subject.

Working together, they settled Mr. Bates in the Geri chair, locked its swinging arm and tied a vest restraint around him.

Howard brushed his palms together in the manner of one who has accomplished something satisfactory. "Well, that's that. Ready for the day's program of sitting and staring?"

It came across to Saul as surprisingly callous, but Mr. Bates arranged his lips in a manner that resembled a smile.

"It's a standing joke between us," Howard said. "The thing is, we have to get all of our patients out of bed and up in a chair because otherwise, they get pneumonia. But it's not as bad as it seems. Isn't that true, Mr. Bates? He explained it to me one day when it was easier for him to talk. Even though he's just sitting there, he's not bored. He's very busy reexamining all his memories. He says it's like living his life over, but this time without the rush."

"An excellent form of contemplation," Saul said.

The old man said something so quietly it seemed more outline than sound. Saul tipped his head close and made out the words, "I'm cold."

Saul found a quilted cotton comforter and set it over the old man's lap. Mr. Bates clutched the comforter in both hands, rubbing it mechanically between a thumb and two fingers. He was breathing oddly. Not breathing, but speaking. "Thank you."

"My pleasure, sir," Saul said. He repeated, "My pleasure," and the words came out choked, so great was the flood of happiness that overtook him.

THEY PLUNGED BACK into the corridor and, by 11:30 a.m., had raised from bed to chair their entire allotment of patients. It was now time to take a quick lunch.

Saul followed Howard to the "breakroom," a cherished haven behind the nurse's station. They walked gingerly past the desk where Ms. Denning, martial in her Ché Guevara beret, engaged in mortal combat with a stack of charts. Some distance beyond her, an aged man in a dark tweed jacket worked rapidly at a stack of charts. Presumably, this was the staff physician, Dr. Pierce.

Saul felt an immediate loathing, not for the man, but for his profession: ethically deranged, arrogant, parasitical, self-inflating, useless, worse than useless, a career that privileged its practitioners to receive great sums of money in exchange for harming their clients.

But perhaps he was being ungenerous. It was certainly possible that today's physicians more often benefited their patients than harmed them. Yet he thought of lobotomies, thalidomide and cancer chemotherapy, and remained skeptical.

The breakroom was a fluorescently lit grotto swimming with white nylon uniforms. Most of the nurse's aides were young and female, radiating a sweetness Saul heartily enjoyed. The older aides possessed a kindly, if more jaundiced, manner. Saul had begun to relax into the general warmth of the room when one of the rare male aides gave him an icy stare. This reawakened him to the danger of his position. He dared not let down his guard.

Howard took a frozen slab out of a freezer and inserted it into one of those peculiar new devices that heat foods with invisible rays. As for himself, Saul had brought a cold sandwich. He took a seat at an empty table and devoted himself to eating. He'd scarcely begun, though, when, to his surprise, Dr. Pierce entered the room. In all the eras when Saul had been a physician, no colleague would consider mingling at table with those so far beneath him. The elderly physician went so far as to stand beside Howard and, while utilizing another oven, converse with him. Highly concerning. As the staff physician, Pierce was in a prime position to operate Cedar Manor as a trap.

The young man and the old extracted their melted slabs and came to join Saul at his table. Howard promptly engrossed himself in conversation with an attractive young aide at the next table. The doctor introduced himself with a friendly handshake. "Is this your first day here?"

"Indeed it is," Saul said.

"Have you worked at any of the other homes in the area?" Pierce asked. "No, probably not, or I would have seen you."

"You work at more than one?"

"At several. I consider it a kind of missionary work. I'm a lay minister, you see. I believe one should demonstrate Christ's love rather than talk about it." He paused and displayed the simultaneously vulnerable and superior manner a sincerely religious man adopts when unsure whether an audience of unknown religious temperament will appreciate, humor or mock him.

"I couldn't agree more," Saul said.

The doctor's face brightened. "I spent most of my life working as a missionary overseas. When I retired, I didn't know what to do with myself and looked around for some way to keep busy. I was both grieved and pleasantly surprised to find that there are people just as needy as anyone in the Third World living right at my door-step." He hesitated again. "Are you a Christian? Pardon me, I know that's none of my business, but from what you said earlier..."

Saul suppressed an urge to smile. Was he a Christian? Not so simple a question. He'd grown up worshipping the gray-eyed god-dess Athena. Later, he'd become a Marcionist, an adherent to a form of Christianity considered acceptable until several bishops gathered at Nicea and voted it a heresy. He'd subsequently studied with Nestorius, Apollinaris, Pelagius, Augustine, St. Symeon and Martin Luther, men of unquestionable spiritual genius who, unfor-tunately, tended to despise all the others. He'd also tasted Tibetan Buddhism and Advaita Vedanta and found these religions no less compatible with Christianity than the various forms of Christian-ity were with one another. And he still retained a definite fondness for Athena.

"I'm Christian but non-denominational," Saul said.

"I'm glad to hear it," Dr. Pierce said. "Non-denominational is an excellent denomination. May I make a suggestion?"

"I'd greatly appreciate it if you would," Saul said.

"Most of our patients are too lost in their minds to find Christ, and even basic kindness is mostly wasted because, in a few minutes, they forget you were ever there. It's pretty grim. So I recommend considering everything one does here as a sacrifice to God. It fends off depression."

Lackman had entered unobserved and taken a seat at a nearby table. "But doctor," he said, "When we imitate Christ, surely it is the love we give that matters, not the results?"

"He likes to bait me," Dr. Pierce said in a reedy voice.

"Bait you?" Lackman said. "Not at all. It's just that I can't imagine a better way to imitate Christ than to spend a lifetime in unappreciated, useless service. One might even say that a true Christian should wish never to die so that instead of going to Heaven and enjoying himself, he could stay at Cedar Manor forever."

This reference to physical immortality sent Saul's heart racing. Who but hangers-on spoke of such things? And yet, perhaps such conversation was only natural at this house of death.

"Much as it might appeal to one's Christian sense of duty to live and serve forever," Pierce said, "the Lord hasn't given us eternal life on Earth but only three score and ten."

"But Dr. Pierce, haven't you already gone a wee bit past that?" Lackman said.

Ms. Denning poked her head in the door. "Speaking of going a little past, look at the time. There are hungry people out there."

"Righty-oh," Howard said. "Let's go, Saul. Time for your initiation."

The word brought terrible images to Saul's mind, rites torturous if not fatal. With some trepidation, he asked, "What initiation?"

"Time to feed Bonnie Akers," Howard said.

"You'll live," Carol Denning said.

THEY LEFT THE breakroom and immediately encountered a new tribe of employees. The members of the kitchen staff wore street clothes rather than priestly white, but being possessed of elastic blue hairnets, they were not entirely abstinent of nylon. They pushed tall metal carts loaded with lunch trays to strategic locations and scurried away. Howard led Saul to one of these carts and pulled out a tray labeled "Bonnie Akers." Saul offered to carry the tray, but Howard held it possessively.

Bonnie Akers' room was situated at the far end of the nursing home's longest corridor. Howard opened a door, and together they stepped into a storage closet. The walls were no more than eight feet apart, and the deep shelves on each side were filled with handheld urinals, sheets, incontinence pads, bedspreads, jugs of cleaning fluid, pillowcases, rolls of toilet paper and the like. However, the far wall of this apparent closet was not a wall but something like a stage curtain, with heavy, pleated drapes hanging from ceiling to floor. Howard relinquished the tray to Saul and parted the curtains to reveal a large room beyond.

Light streamed through a sliding glass door at the room's far end and illuminated a hospital bed. A tiny woman lay in the bed facing them. As they approached, she gripped the rails and thrashed her legs rhythmically, creating a sound like a washing machine out of balance.

"Hello, Bonnie," Howard said.

"Goddamn son of a bitch," she replied.

Saul found the scene profoundly disturbing. "Why isn't she in a chair? I thought we were to get everyone up."

"She's the exception to the rule. Dr. Pierce says she doesn't need to. Isn't that right, Bonnie? The way you thrash and scream, you'll never get pneumonia. You do your aerobic exercises so vigorously that you're probably the fittest patient in the place. Saul, could you set the food tray on that bedside stand and check her vitals?"

Here at last was a chance to verify the claim that had brought him here, but he hid his eagerness and scanned the notes while he recorded the patient's pulse rate, blood pressure and respiration. A glance at the laminated three-by-five card next to the clipboard verified what Howard had said at Café Pergolesi: Bonnie Akers was supposedly 85 years old, but that wasn't believable. To Saul's experienced eye, the elasticity of her skin, the state of her subcutaneous fat, her veins and the small number of red and brown spots limited her age to mid-50s at the highest.

If she were mortal.

But if she proved to be a hafeem, as Saul suspected, she could be perhaps 2000 years old. She would continue to visibly age, of course, but at a rate 20 times more slowly than other mortals. How long before the discrepancy became so obvious that the authorities discovered it? What new humiliations would she be put through? She might live another millennium or more, helpless and demented, enduring needle stabs and electric jolts delivered by baffled scientists attempting to penetrate the mystery.

"Why are there so many gaps in her vitals?" he asked. "No one seems to have taken her temperature since the day before yesterday."

"She's a little difficult at times." Howard was busily rearranging items in the room. He pushed a Geri chair beside the hospital bed and set two ordinary chairs near the bedside stand that held the food tray. He laid out two dry washcloths on the stand beside the food and wetted a third at the room's small sink.

As if he'd just noticed the recorded statement about Bonnie's age, Saul said, "She's 85? Is that possible?"

"That's what the records say. But she doesn't look it, does she?"

They gazed at her together.

Perhaps annoyed by the attention, she rolled onto her back and proceeded to strike the mattress violently, each kick raising her body inches above the bed.

"Perhaps the exercise keeps her youthful looking as well as healthy," Saul suggested.

"Maybe." Howard further adjusted the Geri chair at the side of the bed. "It's time to eat, Bonnie."

"Goddamn son of a bitch," she replied.

"Watch closely how I do it," Howard said.

He unwrapped Bonnie's fingers from first one rail and then the other. As each hand left its purchase, it gripped Howard's forearm, proffered for the purpose. With his free hand, he lowered the rail and pulled Bonnie's still-kicking legs over the edge of the bed. He then used her iron grip on his arm to rotate her into a sitting position.

She ceased kicking and drew her legs up to her chest; her face grew progressively more distorted with anger until it ceased to appear entirely human but took on the character of a Noh mask.

"My God," Saul said. "What happened to her?"

"No one knows." Howard put his free arm under Bonnie's knees, lifted her body and with a pivot, set her into the pre-positioned Geri chair. "But Doctor Pierce thinks it might be mercury poisoning."

A frisson of apprehension rose up Saul's spine.

"In the old days," Howard went on, "they used mercury to treat certain infections. I guess it worked sometimes. Only it also causes permanent brain damage."

Saul felt himself breaking into a cold sweat. "Mercury? Didn't they quit using that long ago?"

"In most places. But Pierce says that some doctors kept giving their patients mercury through the 1920s. To treat certain infections."

Saul knew perfectly well this was a euphemism, for, by the 20th century, the previously broad applications for mercury had declined to one, that of treating syphilis. If one took her recorded age of 85 as correct, she could have come down with syphilis anywhere from birth to age 30 and received mercury treatment just as it was going out of fashion.

When he'd been a Harley Street physician in 19th-century London, more than half of his male practice consisted of patients with advanced syphilis. Primarily, these were wealthy gentlemen who had been infected through intimate association with prostitutes, as was common for their class and time.

The gentlemen came but not their wives, for the prejudices of the time attributed syphilis in females to infidelity rather than conjugal transmission. Women were too ashamed to present themselves at Harley Street and instead sought help from unlicensed female herbalists whose treatments did nothing. Even back then, Saul had found the practice unacceptable. To require fidelity of women but not of men, to accuse ill women of infidelity when they'd acquired the disease from their husbands—Saul felt it was deeply offensive. He was moved by a sense of justice to seek out the wives of his gentleman patients and provide them the same modern treatment that their husbands received: mercury.

And when his patients went mad, he attributed their insanity to advanced syphilis itself rather than the treatment. Several decades would pass before medicine discovered it had made a grievous error and that mercury treatment, too, was filling the wards of Bedlam.

Bonnie Akers might have been one of his patients.

He might have turned a hafeem into *this*.

BONNIE AKERS RAISED herself in the Geri chair with venomous dignity, her lips tightly pursed, her arms at her sides. Her gown came up, exposing her naked crotch, and Saul pulled it down. Howard rolled the Geri chair up beside the food tray and sat in one of the two chairs he'd previously placed in position. Saul sat in the other.

Howard removed the metal plate cover and exposed three white porcelain bowls, each half full of liquid substances of varied colors. He dipped a teaspoon into a bowl of green liquid and held it up. "Green glop," he announced. "Highly nutritious." To Saul, he said, "Pureed spinach."

In deadly silence, Bonnie opened her mouth wide enough to allow Howard to insert the spoon. She closed her lips on it, and he removed it gently. The process was repeated with spoonfuls taken from each bowl in series. He achieved six dollops, at which point she clamped her mouth shut and refused to accept a seventh.

"You have to eat more chicken, at least," Howard said. "It's protein."

She squeezed her lips so tightly shut that the muscles of her face bulged. Her eyes grew wide and vicious; the whites showed above and below the iris.

"Bonnie," Howard said, "you need protein. The doctor says so. Because, according to your blood tests, you're low on it."

"Goddamn son of a bitch," she said.

"Bonnie, dear," Howard said, "We don't want you to starve."

"GODDAMN SON OF A BITCH. GODDAMN SON OF A BITCH! GODDA—"

Howard took advantage of a vowel to pop in the spoon. Bonnie jerked her head away, pulling away the utensil and leaving it dangling from her mouth. She raised herself further in the chair, her eyes red with outrage. With a practiced hand, Howard maneuvered the spoon from her mouth, turning it to scrape off most of the food against her upper teeth.

Once it was gone, she continued explosively. "Goddamn Son Of A Bitch!! GODDAMN SON OF A BITCH!!!! **GODDAMN SON OF A GODDAMN GODDAMN BITCH!!!**"

Howard continued to insert the spoon at one vowel or another, but she began to successfully thwart him with her tongue, forcing out most of the food he managed to insert. Saul watched with great unhappiness as a stream fell from Bonnie's chin onto her lap. "Why not just stop feeding her?"

The question appeared to unnerve young Howard; his speech

became interrupted and blocked. "But she'll ... She has to get enough ... I think it's protein especially ... or maybe vitamins ... In any case, otherwise, she'll starve."

"**GODDAMN SON OF A BITCH**!!!!!" Bonnie said.

"As you've correctly pointed out," Saul said, "our role here is to facilitate the will of the patients. If she doesn't wish to eat and would rather we go away, shouldn't we oblige her in this instance as much as in any other?"

In an utterly normal voice, Bonnie said, "Go away."

They stared at her in astonishment.

"Even if she starves?" Howard asked.

"Isn't that her prerogative? Aren't we her servants?"

"For legitimate desires, yes. Is starving herself legitimate?"

"What other escape does she have but to refuse to eat? One might disagree with the choice, but one can't call it illegitimate."

Bonnie watched attentively as Howard adjusted his mustache, groomed his goatee and rubbed his eyes. He ran his hands through his hair. "I guess you have a point. But are you sure, Bonnie? Do you want to starve?"

She opened her mouth wide and shut it so fast her teeth clicked.

Howard said, "Well, then." His movements, usually sharp and precise, became vague; he tried to wipe Bonnie's mouth with a dry washcloth when he meant to use a wet one and, upon discovering this error, dropped the wet cloth on the floor. Saul prepared him another, and Howard applied it in an odd patting manner, more affectionate than effective.

Throughout this process, Bonnie neither resisted nor cursed. She watched silently as they changed her bed, removing the double layer of soiled incontinence pads and the sheets that were wet beneath them. When they discovered feces, Saul hid them with his body to spare her indignity. Saul did most of the work, for Howard seemed stricken.

"I'll transfer her back to her bed," Saul said.

"Are you sure?"

"No question."

"Well then. Okay. I suppose I might as well get rid of this soiled linen while you do it. Unless you need me to help."

"Not at all," Saul said. "Go ahead."

Saul waited until Howard had passed entirely through the curtain before he unlatched the Geri chair's restraint and swung it out of the way. He put one arm under Bonnie's knees and the other behind her back and lifted. She grabbed his left forearm with a tight grip that tipped her head against his shoulder and assaulted him with the rank odor of her hair and body. In a voice so quiet Howard couldn't have heard even if he'd been lurking just behind the curtains, he whispered, "Hafeem, my dear? Half-immortal?"

Her eyes, inches away, had been deflected, but now they swiveled toward him. He saw tears, though whether of anger, sadness or insanity, he didn't know. He gently set her down on the bed and pulled the fresh covers over her. He leaned over to adjust her pillow and whispered. "I'll help you. I'll do whatever it takes to help you."

The words began as a shout and climbed to a shriek. "God damn son of a bitch. GOD DAMN SON OF A BITCH! **GOD-DAMN SON OF A BITCH!**" She whipped her body with utter abandon. "**GOD! DAMN! SON! OF! A! BITCH!**"

Her ability to thrash did not decline, but her vocal cords gradually gave out. Her voice became progressively hoarse and breathy. She lost the ability to emit pitches, but even the wheezes she forced out conveyed violence.

"Don't take it personally," Howard said, coming up from behind him. "She gets like that sometimes."

AT THE END of his shift, he left Cedar Manor in a state of physical exhaustion, his mind a welter of partially coherent thoughts.

He would have to grant at least this much to the current powers of medicine: at no other time in history could so many people have been kept alive in such an advanced state of decay. Cedar Manor was mortality distilled. Or, perhaps, pickled.

He felt the ache in his troubled left leg, an ache no True Immortal would feel, and sensed his fundamental kinship with Mr. Bates, with Leyla, with the other failing patients he'd cared for all day. He touched the ache in his heart that could not be satisfied and felt a kinship with those patients whose cries for help had no known satiation.

It seemed to him—influenced by the unwarranted certainty of grief—that his hand had certainly been the one to poison Bonnie Akers. Yet another of the unspeakable atrocities he'd carried out trying to do good.

But the Eldest had commanded him to cease penance.

He wondered whether self-forgiveness came more easily at the edge of death, those last moments when no possible word or deed could rectify one's sins.

But the Eldest had commanded him to live. And he'd placed himself in a house of death.

Lost in thought, he failed for some time to realize that he'd reached his home and parked in the driveway. He shut off the car and listened to the sound of the surf, the healing crash of water on sand. He got out of his car and crossed the street to where a sidewalk led along the top of the cliff. It was late afternoon. The sun low in the sky turned the ocean's face black, except where small waves caught the light and flickered orange, making shapes like low-flying flocks of birds.

The cliff sent out arms into the sea in various places, creating isolated beaches. On one such beach, a young couple lay under blankets in a state of affection. Saul enjoyed the sight of their mutual fondness and only belatedly averted his eyes when he realized they were engaged in an intimate activity ordinarily reserved for more private circumstances. During his moralistic phase in the fourth century, he would have had them beaten or worse. What a vile being he'd been.

But the Eldest had commanded him to cease his penance, and he walked on.

Though ideal in many ways, the location of his home possessed one grave shortcoming: it lay only a short walk from the beach where Blair had dismissed him.

It was still twilight when he arrived there. Saul stared at the solitary rock below on which Blair had stood theatrically and sent him away. As he always did when he stood there, he ached to climb down. But he hadn't given in to temptation before and would not do so now.

Over time, he had come to understand the cause of his grief. Like all ordinary mortals, he desired an heir; unlike ordinary mortals, he'd been doomed to watch his children die of old age. This had left him with a deep, unfulfilled yearning. Upon encountering Blair, this yearning fastened on the young Immortal and performed an adoption. Saul, however, had remained entirely unaware of this private arrangement made by his subconscious; he'd believed his interest in Blair to be entirely altruistic. When Blair summarily dismissed him, the pain had been all the more overwhelming for being uncomprehended.

His grief was like that of a parent whose only child had cut him off. A legitimate sorrow, to be sure. He should allow himself to feel it.

Saul carried out an interior process rather like yoga postures performed in the presence of spears, allowing sorrow to pierce every portion of his soul. He removed all protective layers from his heart so that nothing could impede the violence of his grief. He permitted the sense of loss to have its way with him.

And then he walked back home.

SAUL STUDIED THE glowing, red letters on the face of a small panel beside his front door. This so-called "security system" gave forth a confident claim that no one had entered his home in his absence. He entered the alarm code, turned the deadbolt and stepped inside. As he reached toward the light switch, he sensed the presence of men—too late. Numerous strong arms seized him. In silence, they competently tied him to a chair, gagged him and departed.

He sat alone in a state of physical and mental immobility for perhaps half an hour. Then an exterior door opened, and a low-voiced conversation ensued. The conversation ended, and Lackman stepped into the room.

He was Lackman and yet no longer Lackman. His gray fatigue had given way to enthusiasm and energy, extending so far as to manifest itself in pacing. His voice, previously American, now hinted at an archaic British accent. But that was a typical ruse of hangers-on.

"Please accept our apologies in advance," Lackman said. "If things work out as we hope, you will certainly forgive a fellow half-immortal his precautions. A 'hafeem' as you said to poor Bonnie, and as we heard quite clearly through the microphone."

A hidden microphone! Of course he knew of such things, but he hadn't expected to be under quite such comprehensive surveillance in a nursing home. Still, he should have expected it.

"Shall we get down to business?" Lackman said. "We currently find ourselves in a situation fraught with complexity, as I'm sure you understand. Shall I give you a moment to consider?"

Wearily, Saul considered. If (to begin) Lackman was a hafeem as he claimed, then the onus was on Saul to prove himself a hafeem too. Otherwise, Lackman would conclude that Saul was a hanger-on and take decisive action.

However (on the other hand), if Lackman was a hanger-on posing as a hafeem, the requirements were reversed. Saul would have to falsely prove himself no hafeem but a fellow hanger-on. Otherwise, Lackman would engage in the usual ridiculous efforts to extort from Saul the "secret" of prolonged life.

Yet (to continue deeper into the logical maze), if Lackman were truly a hafeem, that second strategy was the worst possible option. Saul would have just proved himself a hanger-on to a hafeem.

"I have your attention, yes?" Lackman said. "If I remove the gag, can I trust you not to call out?"

Lackman removed the gag, but Saul didn't call out. He did, however, speak at once, hoping to seize the initiative. "You spoke of 'our' apologies. Were you using the royal we, or do you represent a group?"

Lackman busied himself with the fireplace. He worked methodically and with a maddening slowness. It was only when the logs burst into flames and he could stand back and warm his hands that he answered the question. "We are members of an organization headed by a hafeem named Baehl," he said. "Perhaps you have heard of us?"

Saul had never heard of a hafeem named Baehl. Furthermore, as the name sounded suspiciously like that of a Mesopotamian god, the choice seemed suspiciously theatrical. He ignored the question and said, "All the residents of Cedar Manor, are they hafeems?"

"All but a handful," Lackman said. "And all the staff."

"Shame on you, sir," Saul said. "Shame on all of you. How can you sleep at night? How can you live with yourself, subjecting your fellow beings to such miserable indignities?"

Lackman had not left the fire nor ceased to warm his hands. "Calm yourself," he said. "Surely you recognize that Cedar Manor is not as sterile or so uncomfortable as you imply. Those few of our patients who are cognitively capable have made the deliberate choice to live there. The ancient hafeem Leyla, whom I believe you have met, is a prime example. I will concede that our patients who have lost their minds deserve more dignity than we seem to allow them. However, being unconscious, they lose nothing in the present, and their presence aids a noble endeavor that might benefit them greatly in the future."

"And what noble endeavor is that?" Saul asked, then immediately regretted having done so.

"To speak of it only in part," Lackman said, "we seek to gather together all the hafeems of the world."

But Saul had no patience for grand endeavors or speeches on their behalf. "Perhaps we will discuss it later," he interrupted. "As for now, I have a question. Have you read the works of Ruth ben-Avraham?" In the second century BC, this worthy Hebrew had written what he considered the world's first novel, an excellent work that had fallen out of history.

"No, I don't know of this Ruth ben-Avraham," Lackman said. "But if we are firing shots at random, do you recall the True Immortal who was considered a saint in his lifetime, counterfeited his death, and came back to worship at his own shrine? And that at this shrine, a century later, he became custodian, the better to observe his devotees?"

"And no doubt to join in their devotions." Saul thought of Blair's youthful narcissism and smiled. "I say this not from knowledge of the man in question; I'm merely speculating from the natural character of a True Immortal. To return, I believe I detect a hint of an Elizabethan accent in your English. I've always maintained that Edward de Vere, the Earl of Oxford, is the true author of Shakespeare's plays. I'm not alone in this supposition. The *Encyclopedia Britannica* informs us that he is the most likely candidate after the Stratford man. But there is a mystery. I see from your expression that you're aware of the mystery."

Lackman's face had indeed brightened.

"One can easily explain," Saul continued, "why Oxford would maintain the deception during his lifetime. But the perplexing question remains: how, and why, did the secret remain concealed after his death? That is, in my opinion, the sole meaningful argument Stratfordians raise against the advocates of de Vere."

Lackman rubbed his hands heartily. "Shall I provide half the answer and allow you to complete the other half?"

"Indeed you may, sir," Saul said. "But choose your words carefully. If you say too little or too much, the opportunity to conclude our situation will have been squandered."

Lackman agreed and, after an indecently long interval, stated a few essential facts. Saul responded with certain other facts, and the situation substantially resolved.

And then Saul placed him.

They'd never seen each other except from a distance and in the dark, but he knew. "You traitorous, heretical bastard," Saul said affectionately. "You were so vastly younger then, Sir Charles. Not so wrinkled—so bald—so shriveled as you are today."

Puzzlement, and then a dawning light. "Doctor Nichols? You double-dealing, crude, conniving swine. You traitorous deceiver." His face glowed with friendly pleasure.

"Indeed," Saul said.

"I once had a commission from Her Majesty's Secret Service to assassinate you."

"And I, you, from poor Mary. Back when I thought I could affect the course of history for the better."

"Have you also entirely given up on that activity?" Lackman asked, as he released Saul from his bonds.

"I'm a fool, sir," Saul replied, "and find it impossible to choose my efforts wisely. Knowing so, I no longer attempt to do good except in the most minor of ways."

"I KNOW HOW to solve that," Howard said. "Consider all matters slight." He'd entered the room from the direction of the kitchen, carrying an ornate walking stick and wearing a white long-tail tuxedo. Except for a silver lamé bowtie, he was all in white.

"A whimsical philosophy, to be sure," Saul said. "And under many circumstances, an appropriate, even a spiritual one. But doesn't such a humorous approach fail when confronted with great pain or power?"

"It depends on how funny you are." Howard crossed to one of Saul's antique armchairs and attempted to hang the hook of his cane on the wooden knob at the back of the chair. This difficult process required him to bend forward, study the knob closely, and make multiple attempts. When the cane rested stably in place, he drew his palms apart in a voilà gesture and settled comfortably in the chair, at which point the cane clattered to the floor. Acting as if he were pretending to ignore the sound, a multi-layered pretense, he said, "I believe it to be a fundamental mathematical truth that for every tragedy, there exists a joke capable of turning it back. The problem lies in finding the right gag fast enough."

Saul bowed. He said he agreed with the theory but doubted that anyone possessed so great a store of humor as to succeed in practice.

"That may be true," Howard replied, "but one can try."

Howard's verbal sparring partner at Pergolesi, red-haired Beatrice, entered the room. She was followed by Dr. Pierce, Carol Denning and Leyla, maneuvering herself in a motorized wheelchair.

"Are you okay?" Denning asked him.

"I seem to be," Saul said.

She examined his recently bound arms and legs. Her touch was entirely professional, but, to his surprise, he was suddenly aroused. She pronounced Saul well but choked slightly on the words and gave him a meaningful look as she stepped away.

For his part, he remembered his responsibilities as a host. He hastily rearranged couches and chairs in a circle so the guests could sit comfortably and face one another. He brought out glasses from an antique French armoire and offered them a beverage; he suggested that of the options available, they might particularly enjoy a certain cognac of remarkable vintage.

They all chose the cognac.

He served each one in turn. Howard insisted that Saul keep pouring until the cognac reached the brim; he balanced the overfull glass on the tip of his finger and moved it in a vertical circle without spilling any.

When Saul filled Denning's glass, she thanked him, but she appeared disturbed, even angry. "It was all so disrespectful and so unnecessary."

"What was?" Saul asked.

Denning directed a ferocious glare at Lackman, who did not respond. "To treat you like we did," she said.

"Well," Saul said, "someone did have to identify me as a true hafeem."

"But we already knew. We knew even before you came to Cedar Manor."

Outrage alternated with astonishment. "You already knew I was a hafeem?" He looked at them all and settled on Lackman. "Then why, sir, did you treat me so?"

Lackman responded in the settled manner of one who has had great experience regarding the issue at hand. "We had to calibrate the event with great care. Suppose, for example, that I'd lightly introduced myself as hafeem during our initial interview. Would you have waited patiently for further discussion? Or would you have taken your first chance to escape, assuming I was a hanger-on? Someone in your position might even resort to violence. Recalling certain actions taken by yourself in the guise of Dr. Nichols, I am now all the more certain that you would not have shied from violence. What better way to avoid such unpleasantness than by employing an overwhelming force of professionals? And what quicker way to bring about a state of full acceptance than to set up the typical logical conundrum and allow you to break the deadlock on your initiative? Would anything less have satisfied you?"

"You do make good points." Saul rubbed his minimally sore wrists. "Indeed, I might otherwise have behaved precipitously. Very well. Moreover, I see that I forget my manners." He raised his glass to Leyla. "A toast you, madam, for you are the eldest among us. I wish you all honor, respect and health."

"Wishing, wishing, wishing," Leyla said. "What good does it do to wish me health? It will take more than words to give me that."

"I express only the wish, for I cannot make the gift."

"What you lack is imagination. I won't toast to words wishing me health. I will raise my glass toward success in reality." Her hand shook badly, but she held her glass high. "To Baehl and his project."

"To Baehl and his project," the others said.

Saul joined in, though he had no idea what they were talking about.

"Pepper away," Howard said.

"Pardon?" Saul asked.

"Don't stand on ceremony. Live a little; slake your curiosity. Pepper, salt or whatever projectile seasoning you prefer. Ask your questions. You must be overflowing with them."

He was overflowing indeed. "Well, for one, how did you discover I was a hafeem? Before my arrival here, that is? And why didn't you merely Shanghai me the moment I arrived?"

"I'll take that," Howard said. "To answer your second question first, Lachman remained fearful that you might be a hanger-on, and insisted on this complicated method of verifying your character. But I'd already identified you in Moscow to my own satisfaction, in the usual way ... detectives ... photos ... etc." He waved a hand about. "We were at the very point of seizing you out there, in fact, seconds away from the grab itself when you did something so remarkable that we couldn't see it through."

"Remarkable? When did I, in Moscow, do anything remarkable?"

"Quite recently. It was brilliantly played! Hysterically funny. My good man, your timing, your delivery, your manner, the way you read your audience even though you couldn't see my face—it was one of the great privileges of my life to witness such an improvisation of genius. Faced with humor of that caliber, I had no choice but to abandon my plan and join in."

He pantomimed putting a ski mask over his face and, in a Russian accent, said, "Only those who prefer to live their lives unmolested may we rob and beat. For is this not Marxist-Leninism?"

THEY WERE LIT not by the harsh light of a ceiling fixture but by the diffuse warmth of small lamps placed among the bookcases and the soft light of standing lamps in the corners. Saul looked at them now: Leyla in her wheelchair, 3500 years old. Lackman in a white silk overstuffed armchair beside her, 2800. Sitting next to Saul, Carol Denning, nearing two millennia. And, across the room, Howard and Beatrice, hafeems too, although merely children. It felt like a community of his kind.

"Your face was covered by the ski mask, of course," Saul said, "but the way you moved then—your mannerisms, your physical presentation as Alexei—these don't resemble in any way the Howard I worked with today."

"My acting job was pretty good?"

"Remarkable. Allow me to congratulate you."

"Of course. Moreover, let me propose a toast to myself." He held up his cognac glass, but the others ignored him.

"I do have another question," Saul said.

"Please ask," Howard said.

"Well, I have many. But now, I cannot in humanity resist asking the obvious. What is Baehl's project?"

With no hesitation, Howard said, "To turn all his friends into Immortals."

At those words, Saul's exhaustion returned. An entire day of work at Cedar Manor, his catharsis at the beach, his subsequent capture and gagging, and now this.

He looked beseechingly at Denning, at Lackman, at Leyla. "But surely you know it is impossible. Surely, you have encountered numerous fraudulent means of obtaining immortality in your long lives?"

No one responded, and he grew agitated. "The Philosopher's Stone, the competent parchment of Satan requiring a signature in blood, the forest herb of Wen-zhou, the subjunct Delphic spring, the Island of Endless Fog: these were not found because they do not exist. This quest is long since proved a fool's errand."

"I agree," Howard said. "Age is inevitable. We have no choice but to grow old, gain wrinkles like Leyla, and drop dead." He rose from his chair, using his walking stick to bear all his weight. He tottered forward like an ancient, one difficult step after the other. He stopped; he straightened; he tossed the stick high in the air, did a standing back flip and caught the stick effortlessly as it came down.

"Or not," he said.

"LISTEN TO ME, Saul," Lackman said. "While I pretend to be the harried administrator in my drab nursing home office, do you know what I actually do? I read scientific books. Have you done so yourself? Have you kept up?"

"Not past about 1820," Saul said. "I confess to a preference for abstract philosophy, the one subject whose statements are immune to scientific deconstruction."

"Let me loan you a book or two," Lackman said. "I swear to you, these realms of science are dissections of the world, not fantasies of the mind."

"What he means," Howard said, "Is that you can forget the Philosopher's Stone, the competent parchment of Satan, the forest herb of Wen-zhou, the subjunct Delphic spring—whatever the heck that is—and the Island of Endless Fog too. Immortality is a matter of genetics. End of story. Boring, boring, boring."

"No more than several decades until we learn to fix it, Saul," Lackman said.

About the same length of time the Eldest had granted him to consider her question.

Dr. Pierce said, "Though I think it is wrong for them to try, I do believe they shall succeed."

FOR THE FIRST time, Beatrice spoke. She was radiant. "I am a very *young* hafeem," she said. "Only a 150 years old. I don't know much compared to all of you. But I have something you don't have, a disease that plans to kill me. It's ovarian cancer, a disease that enjoys killing young women. If I were a mortal, I'd be dead in a year. As a hafeem, I can probably stick it out for 30 or 40 years, but then, poof. By the way, how did you like *my* acting job at Café Pergolesi? That spontaneous discussion between Howard and me? We deceived you, sorry. It was a written sketch, and we'd rehearsed it for weeks. Weren't we brilliant?"

"Unquestionably," Saul said.

"And I'm brilliant now, too, because I know a particular thing: True Immortals don't get sick, and if they're injured, they heal. So if we find their genes and learn how to use them, and if we can do that fast enough, I don't have to die. And I don't want to die. Do you think I should die, Dr. Pierce?"

"No, of course not." Pierce was clearly pained. "Making everyone immortal is wrong and un-Christian in general, not in particular."

The essence of tragedy, Saul thought.

"And then there's Bonnie Akers." Howard's face was bright with desire, without any trace of his usual irony. "If we learn how to use the genes that make people True Immortals, we can heal her."

If only I could believe, Saul thought. If only I had more of the capacity others possess in abundance—that of believing that which they want to be true. But he realized his doubt had begun to weaken. He knew little of genetics beyond the word, but enough to think maybe these people were onto something.

"You have a certain rapport with her," Howard said. "I can see it. Would you consider sticking around for a bit and persuading her not to starve herself? Like, to eat some food? Just for 10 or 20 more years. I know you don't believe we'll succeed, but would you consider helping her live that long just in case?"

"She means a great deal to you, doesn't she?" Saul said.

"She does," Howard said.

"Then I'll remain here and attempt what you ask. Indeed, with all my heart."

To Saul's astonishment, Carol Denning took him in her arms and kissed him.

SHE DID MORE than kiss him, for she stayed behind when the others left. But the next day, she once more became a charge nurse, a being who moves under great pressure, like those fabled fishes of the deep. She gave Saul his list of patients, informed him that in addition to his ordinary duties, he would feed Bonnie Akers each meal and would he please go feed her now.

Saul paused before passing through the curtain that opened to Bonnie's room. Lacking a door to knock on, he rapped his knuckles on a wooden shelf. She shouted, "Goddamn son of a bitch!" and he entered.

He adopted the deportment of a butler. "Do I have your permission to feed you?" he asked.

She favored him with a glare but didn't answer the question or cease to cyclically throw her legs.

"In the absence of clear directions," he said, "I'm obligated to serve you your meal." He fed her in much the same way that Howard had done. When she declined to eat, though, Saul didn't take advantage of vowels to force the issue. Despite this, she didn't starve herself.

Their ritual remained the same for weeks. And then a breakthrough came.

As usual, Saul asked permission to feed her breakfast. Instead of ignoring the question, she met him eye to eye and, in a profoundly disparaging voice, said, "No."

"Very well then," he said. He gave a deep bow and departed.

When Saul returned at lunchtime, Bonnie presented herself at her most ferocious but with a distinct variation. Instead of merely screaming, "Goddamn Son of A Bitch!" she prefaced some of her repetitions with the words "Feed me," and as a suffix, occasionally added the words, "starving hungry."

"Of course, I'll feed you, my dear," he said. "I didn't intend to starve you, but only to obey your commands." He lifted her from the bed. In that intimate moment of physical closeness, he added, "You have so little free choice in your life, I wouldn't deprive you of any more."

Bonnie ate avidly for 10 bites before she clamped her mouth shut. As Saul began his preparations to leave, she thought better of it and opened her mouth again.

The extent of their interaction and the cordiality of its content increased steadily over subsequent months. She eventually came to a point where she would voluntarily relinquish her death grip on the rails; the quantity and violence of her "Goddamn son of a bitch" recitations subsided greatly. Saul and Bonnie began to develop a form of communication that was peculiar in nature but conversational nonetheless.

On the first warm spring day, he opened the sliding glass door and arranged the Geri chair so she could look out at the green cliff and the ocean beyond.

"Time for your useless nourishment, then?" he asked.

"Useless," she said.

"Useless and disgusting," he agreed.

"Truer words."

"Were never spoken." Saul dipped a spoon in green liquid, examined it, shook his head with distaste, and brought the food to her mouth. She parted her lips and gently closed them on the spoon. He had a washcloth at hand, and when a fraction of the liquid dripped toward her chin, he wiped it off.

After a dozen spoonfuls, she clamped shut her mouth, but in a benign rather than furious manner. Together, they watched the ocean make white circles around a large volcanic rock some distance from the shore.

"The waves never stop," he said.

"Never," she said.

"They come and go for centuries."

"Dessert," she said and opened her mouth. He obediently served her a spoonful of applesauce.

"The ocean is an old son of a bitch, wouldn't you agree, my dear?"

"Old *goddamn* son of a bitch," she said. And she laughed.

Saul had never heard her laugh. He even saw, or thought he did, a glint of happiness in her eyes. But this quickly faded, and as if in reaction, she reverted to her standard phrase and her customary tone of malice and spite.

"God damn son of a bitch! Goddamn son of a bitch! Goddamn son of a bitch!"

Saul chimed in. They chanted together, a kind of infuriated mantra. Her anger drew out his anger; her misery touched his own. He shouted "GODDAMN SON OF A BITCH!" with all his heart, pouring millennia of self-hatred and remorse into the words; he dug up corpses of sorrow and pitched them into his voice. He didn't realize to what a violent height he'd reached until he felt a tap on his shoulder and discovered Howard standing above him.

"You don't have to stop," Howard said. "Just turn it down a trifle? You have a fine baritone, and it's scaring the neighbors."

But Bonnie had stopped screaming when Howard spoke and showed no inclination to start again.

Saul sat with her in silence for a while. Then he said, "It's undoubtedly a great piece of wisdom, your 'goddamn son of a bitch.'"

She glared at him with a mixture of rage and amusement. She opened her mouth, and he fed her the remainder of the food on her tray. When they'd scraped the last bowl dry, she raised one of her arms and looked at it. "Old," she said. It was a report, not a complaint.

"Judging by your physical appearance," he said, "I'd estimate you're anywhere from two to two and a half thousand years old."

"Hafeem goddamn son of a bitch," she confirmed.

"You and I both, my dear."

"You, I, both?" she said, almost sweetly. But then her tone reverted to its norm, and she shouted, "Fornicating goddamn syphilitic whore!"

"Oh, too severe."

"Adulterous Goddamn Slut Of A Bitch! Whore! Cunt!"

"What's the source of this self-slander?" Saul asked.

"GODDAMN POXY SON OF A BITCH!"

"I'm a physician. You may speak freely with me. Did you, perhaps, contract syphilis by having sex with someone to whom you weren't married?"

This invocation of his semi-priestly status succeeded, and she ceased to scream.

"And is that the extent of your crime?"

"Goddamn son of a slut whore bitch bitch bitch," she said.

"You feel morally distressed by this, I see."

"SLUT GODDAMN SON OF A CUNT WHORE BITCH."

"Hold on," he said. "I'll be back in a moment."

He found Carol Denning at the nurse's station furiously filling out forms. "Ms. Denning," Saul said, "I need to borrow your authority for a moment."

"Can't you see I'm up to my eyeballs in paperwork? What do you want?"

He poured out the words without pausing for breath. "It appears Ms. Akers contracted syphilis from an extramarital affair and that her insanity derives not only from mercury- or syphilis-induced brain damage but also from self-judgment regarding what she perceives as a serious moral crime."

Denning stared at him from under her black beret. "Seriously?"

"Afraid so."

She shoved the pile of unfinished paperwork into a corner of her desk. "Get Howard. I'll join you there in 90 seconds."

BONNIE WATCHED WITH interest as they lined up before her, Carol Denning in the middle, Saul and Howard on each side.

Using her most emphatic charge nurse voice, Denning said, "Ms. Akers, I want you to know that over the last 10 years, I've slept with five men to whom I wasn't married, and I don't feel guilty at all. And the public doesn't condemn me either."

Standing in for the general populace, Saul and Howard variously expressed their lack of condemnation.

"Five?" Bonnie said.

"Yes. No, six. I'd forgotten to count my current lover. I've had sex with six different men over the last 10 years. Well, I mean, I've had ongoing sexual relationships with six men. There were a few shorter episodes. I guess if you include those, let's make it ten. Yes, I've had sex with 10 men in the last 10 years, and I've been married to none."

Bonnie's face reddened; she positively blushed. "Ten?"

"Come to think of it, 11. This idea of female chastity is patriarchal crap, Bonnie. But it's finally changing. Wonder of wonders, after endless centuries, the system of female subjugation is finally breaking up."

Denning had much more to say on this subject and expressed her thoughts at length, both then and on numerous subsequent occasions. Saul supplemented these teachings by bringing Bonnie magazines that expressed similar opinions in clear print. He also brought in various members of the staff.

At first, it shocked Bonnie to hear that so many women in her vicinity had engaged in unsanctioned sexual congress; later, her response progressed to amusement. A stage arrived where she would name names. Saul would say, "Yes, her, too," and she'd laugh. Later, she found words to confess her own history, and when Saul summed it up as, "Barely a misdemeanor, my dear," she wept.

He wept too. As a devoted Christian, he'd helped create the truncheon Bonnie had later taken up to beat herself.

The Eldest had commanded him to cease penance, but she hadn't forbidden tears. He wept with Bonnie for days, stretching out into months. And over time, they both grew peaceful. Bonnie ceased to thrash or scream and spent much of the day watching the ocean. For his part, Saul felt a certain inward calm but an unsteadiness too, rather like a sailor stepping ashore after years at sea. After living so long with self-reproach, he found it difficult to achieve balance without it.

IT WAS SAUL who noticed the physical changes. The initial sign was a drop in appetite, followed several days later by a subtle increase in the rate of her breathing. This strengthened to an overt increase, and a frank bluish discoloration suffused Bonnie's lips. In Saul's day, he would have bled her. Instead, he called Dr. Pierce.

Saul watched this 20th-century practitioner of the medical arts examine this now very lethargic and breathless woman.

"Good call," Dr. Pierce said. He applied a device to her back that very much resembled the instrument invented by Saul's old friend Laennec. "I can hear faint rales," Pierce said. "Here, would you like to listen?"

When Saul inserted the rubbery ends into his ears and placed the diaphragm on Bonnie's back, he was astonished by the technical quality of the device. He would certainly not call the sounds faint. In the region of her lower left lung, he could hear very loud rales indeed. Grown peaceful, Bonnie had lost the protection her violence had previously provided, and she'd come down at last with pneumonia.

Saul rode along in the ambulance that took Bonnie to the hospital, and he stood with the other doctors as they looked at the image of her lungs revealed by invisible rays. The disease had spread even to the apex, sparing only a sliver of lung with which she could breathe. She was sufficiently ill that they placed her in a portion of the hospital devoted to particularly intense care, and so-named because of it.

Bloodletting, Saul discovered, had not entirely lost its currency: nurses withdrew vial after vial of Bonnie's blood. In addition, they attached plastic bags to poles and arranged matters so that clear liquid dripped back *into* her veins. He found this a logical innovation, and it raised his spirits. He waited with some hope that she might improve. But she did not. She shifted through varying states of delirium as Saul kept a continuous vigil.

She sank deeper. She spoke on one instance only, when sweat poured from her forehead and the fever briefly broke. "Goddamn son of a bitch."

She said it with a lovely smile.

OUTSIDE BONNIE'S HOSPITAL room, a phalanx of residents, interns and medical students huddled in grave discussion with the attending physician. Dark looks and quiet words passed. The flock of white coats shifted formation, and the chief resident stepped forward to announce their prognosis. Bonnie would not survive another day.

Howard and Carol joined Saul for these final hours. Lackman made an appearance too, but only long enough to conduct a process he called "sweeping the room." This expression indicated a systematic hunt for hidden microphones or other spying devices. He found the room pristine, gave his respects and departed.

The walls in the intensive care unit were almost soundproof. With the outer door closed, they could hear only the sounds inside. They listened to the beeping of various machines and the bellows-like huff of the respirator. Bonnie was the center of all this mechanical attention, but they could barely see her. Most of her body was buried beneath hospital blankets, and her face was half covered by the strips of white tape that held the respirator tube in place.

Howard fretted and muttered and exhibited other signs of distress. Saul suggested he sit beside Bonnie and hold her hand. Howard was uneasy; the intravenous needle inserted at her wrist disturbed him, as did the numerous bruises left behind by needles previously placed. But with Saul's continued encouragement and the final assistance of a single, authoritative "go ahead" from Denning, Howard gingerly touched Bonnie's fingertips. Nothing untoward happened, and he gently stroked the violated skin at the back of her hand.

"She was the one who discovered me," he said. "To myself, I mean. Told me I was a hafeem."

Saul said, "I'd guessed as much. Please, tell me more."

"I met her in Paris in 1748. She presented herself as a matronly noblewoman from an untraceable duchy in Romania. I worked as a professional juggler then and performed at her salon one afternoon. My act went well, and I was called back for two encores. At the end of the second, Bonnie took me to a side room and invited me to undress. Naturally, I assumed she wished to make love with me, because so many women do. Of course, she appeared—and actually was—considerably older than me, she had a lovely grace and carriage. I was more than willing."

Howard bent down and gave Bonnie's hand a lingering kiss. "I was 42 years old. The fact that I showed no signs of aging had become a matter of some conversation, especially among women who'd had the chance to observe me up close. Bonnie observed me too, but clinically, with no evidence of desire. She even examined my teeth. She asked me whether I'd ever had an adult tooth fall out, and I said that, yes, in fact, this had happened twice. 'But you have all your teeth now,' she said. 'They grew back,' I said."

One of the machines beeped at a different pitch, and Carol Denning rose to her feet to study the green electronic tracings.

She found nothing alarming and returned to her seat beside Saul. "Please continue, Howard."

"Should I? All right. Next, she pointed to a very slight scar on my face. I explained that I had gotten it from a sickle. Though I was, and remain, a marvelous juggler, I occasionally slip up. I had already been slightly sickle-slashed on the wrist, hand and knee."

He broke off and engaged in whispery self-reproaches; he wiped his hand along his forehead. "You were right, Saul, when you said that humor has limits. I'm at that limit now."

"But you'll pass over it," Saul said.

"Will I? I'll try. Once, while performing at sea during a gale, I slashed my face. This event had been widely discussed, for the public relishes a gash, and Bonnie had heard of it. She asked me whether the wound had been deep. I admitted that it had allowed the curious to see the deeper tissues of my face. (I was not one of the curious. I could happily have gone through my whole life without sneaking a peek at my own orbicularis oculi muscle.) She said, 'And it resolved to this scar? Why, it is as small as the nail of my little finger. Is it still shrinking?' When I told her that, no, it had stopped shrinking, she said, 'Then I know what you are.'

"She gave me a dissertation on hafeems and True Immortals. She particularly stressed that while True Immortals heal perfectly and never get sick, hafeems only heal amazingly well and seldom get sick. But teeth wear out, and all True Immortals as well as most hafeems grow new ones. When, at last, she'd persuaded me, she helped me carry out my very first frame change.

"She continued to act as my benefactor for frame after frame. More than once, she rescued me from great dangers: hangers-on, husbands, revolutions, that sort of thing. She helped me so much that it was a relief when she finally wanted help from me. And that's when she told me she had syphilis."

He grew tearful; Denning handed him a tissue. He blew his nose. "This is hard." He blew his nose again. "She'd had advanced syphilis for years, but her symptoms had lately gotten much worse. I took her to all the best doctors in London. Please don't be offended when I say I settled on Dr. Lindenbaum rather than you. You were also on my list; perhaps you would have done better."

"I would not," Saul said. "I admired Dr. Lindenbaum, and our methods were of a kind. I would've poisoned her just as effectively."

But Howard wasn't listening. "Why couldn't she have lived just a *tiny* bit longer? A decade or two? We'll have the key by then—unless Alexandros wags his tail at us, God forbid—and she can live forever."

The mention of "Alexandros" opened new realms of consideration, but Saul didn't have time to explore them, for machines had begun to beep wildly. Denning indicated a certain green line as the one to watch. Bonnie's heart made one weak contraction, fell flat, tried once more, and then, almost two thousand years after it first began to beat, subsided forever.

THE FUNERAL WAS held deep in a redwood forest. Dr. Pierce, in his capacity as lay minister, presided.

They sat in chairs arrayed around a grave dug between the trunks of ancient redwoods. Mr. Bates wore a black silk suit and tie, and the vest that constrained him to his chair was made of black silk, too. Leyla sat in her wheelchair on one side of Saul, and he felt honored by the company, for she was venerable. Carol Denning sat on the other and gripped Saul's hand.

Pierce spoke the familiar invocation. "Into your arms, oh Lord, we commend our sister. May we who are left behind take comfort that she is at last at peace, that no effort or need or pain shall ever trouble her, but that she will dwell forever in the peace of God's eternal sabbath."

Why is it, Saul wondered, that I can't believe she's gone? Why does my heart believe I could still carry a tray into her room and hear her lovely, "Goddamn son of a bitch?" Why does her lack of being fill me with such horror?

"From earth we come, to earth we shall return," Pierce said. "The common lot of all mankind. And so let us be at peace with it."

"At peace with it?" Leyla whispered.

Saul leaned toward her to hear better.

"At peace? Ridiculous. It's nothing but a waste. If she could only have held on for another speck of time, we would have saved her. If only she could have held on."

Howard threw in the first clod of earth.

"If only *I* can hold on," Leyla muttered.

SAUL STOOD ABOVE the rock where Blair had dismissed him. His eyes traced the yellow arms of the cliff that isolated the little beach north and south. He remembered the moment when, just down below, Blair had transformed him from mentor and friend to a mere mortal, a transient, forgettable object consigned to the devouring mouth of time.

"You've been a great help to me, Saul," he'd said. "But we're different sorts of creatures, you and I, different orders of being. As different as—I don't know—tuna and dolphins. We'll shake hands, I'll thank you and we'll go our separate ways."

Saul didn't beg or argue. Nor did he point out that tuna are warm-blooded and therefore not as different from dolphins as it might at first appear. Rather, he'd taken Blair's outstretched hand and hid all emotion. And from then on, he'd kept his pride intact. Until now.

The disk of the sun touched water, and its rays traced runes and cuneiform symbols over the flat of the sea. For the first time in 75 years, Saul climbed down to this beach.

He approached the rock. He circumambulated it. He ran his fingers over its entire surface. With the flashlight he'd carried along, he searched its indentations and depressions, hoping against all reasonable expectation that Blair had inscribed a message for him into the rock's soft sandstone.

But there was no message, only the customary names and scrawled schematic hearts, along with phone numbers to be called for satisfactions lewdly described.

Saul removed from his wallet the nail he'd placed there months ago, not admitting to himself why. On a low, flat surface, he scratched out words and numbers. He stretched himself out on the sand and incised the message more deeply. He would soon go on to live out a series of 12-year frames elsewhere, seeking an answer to the Eldest's question. He would study philosophy, religion and psychology and speak with the greatest authorities in those fields; he would spend decades thinking. In the meantime, he would also fully live, as the Eldest had commanded. And he would occasionally return to re-scratch his message in case it had begun to fade.

But for a long time, he lay there outstretched, signifying by his position that universal longing for the infinite, expressed in its endlessly varied ways, of all mortal beings.

CHAPTER 3

THE MORTAL

"Lucky from the cradle
Creation's cherished darling
A blossoming godhead
in crossroads of light
Do the Angels really
Recapture only the radiance that streams out from themselves?
Or sometimes, by mischance,
Is there a bit of our being brought back?
Do we ever figure in their features
even a little?"

RILKE, *DUINO ELEGIES*

Time for a regular mortal;
they're the most fun, anyway.

—THE CHRONICLER

JANICE

BLAIR WORE HIS heavy coat and a black watch cap pulled low to cover his missing ear. Behind him, the sky put on its typical dawn show: streaming ramps of light, cathedrals in the clouds, heavenly mountains of glory. He looked just as beautiful as the sky. You could get stupid and fall in love with someone like that if you didn't watch out. Extreme beauty will do that to you.

"Where's your car?" I asked. "We can't take my piece of junk." I pointed to the sweet, little piece of junk in question, a beat-up, old Dodge Colt station wagon I wouldn't trust to take us much past Walmart, let alone wherever we were going.

"It's still parked at the motel," Blair said.

"I'll show you a shortcut."

We cut through the prairie dog field behind my neighborhood to get to the motel from behind. I wanted to hang onto his arm that stupid way girls do, but I kept both hands in my pockets even though it wasn't cold. The prairie dogs skittered around chatting and posing, and Blair chattered too. He told me how he almost got caught by World War I but got away to Canada just before the Germans started sinking ships. Then people started talking about a draft, and he ran to Argentina, which wasn't easy with world wars going on and so forth. He'd worked as a bartender in Buenos Aires.

I'd worked as a bartender, too, so we had something to talk about besides his cute Argentine wife. But when I saw his car, a snooty green Volvo with a filigreed nose, I felt lost. I couldn't see myself in that kind of world. People who drive expensive Volvos are afraid of life and have too much money.

We found the tracker and tossed it. Blair drove. The seats were made of white leather that got warm when he pushed a switch. It felt good on my butt, but it put my head back in college when I dated this rich guy who tried to share me with his friends. I was a mess then. But in my latest, greatest incarnation, I've been getting healthy.

We turned around a corner and pulled into my crappy neighborhood. I made Blair park behind my house so my neighbors wouldn't see his car for a while. I got my suitcase from my house and asked him to open the trunk so I could toss it in. He opened it, screamed, jumped back and put out his hands to push away someone I couldn't see. I looked in the trunk, and whom should I find there but Richard Menniss?

He'd been duct-taped up and down and looked pretty hangdog, but his eyes could move, so he wasn't dead. "It's OK," I told Blair. I handed him my suitcase and told him to put it in the trunk of my Colt, but he looked ready to run, so I touched his arm and said, "Running is about the stupidest thing you can do right now. Chill." I put my eyes onto his eyes, all definite, and he settled down.

I got my handgun out of my purse and showed it to Menniss. I had a permit for my handgun, and I also knew how to handle it because I was a responsible girl and had taken classes. I put the gun back in my purse and brought out my hunting knife. I always carried my knife with me. Mr. Movable Eyes watched the knife, and his eyes widened as I brought it close. I could have said calming things, but I let him grunt and struggle against his duct tape, then carefully sliced a small hole in the tape over his mouth so he could breathe if his nose got stuffed and also so he could talk. "Did they take Blair's ear?" I asked.

He mumbled in that charming way you mumble when you have duct tape over your mouth, even with a hole in it. One useful thing that came from the year I spent doing BDSM was learning how to understand people with tape over their mouths. Yes, they did take Blair's ear. No, he didn't know who they were except they were big and lots of them. He had no idea why they'd stuck him in Blair's trunk. And, no, he didn't find it comfortable, fuck you too. I said he was probably cold, and he agreed, so I had Blair get a pile of blankets from the house, and I draped a bunch over Menniss.

"I can't see letting you loose just now," I said. "You're too scary. But I'll call a friend once we get away. His name is Maurice. You be nice to Maurice when he comes! He'll be doing a favor for me, and he won't hurt you unless you act stupid, which would be particularly dumb because he's as badass as you are. Well, maybe not quite as badass—I don't know if anyone is—but your joints will be stiff, and that'll give him an advantage. Also, he's younger."

That bit at the end where I ranked him high on the badass scale was me being friendly, and I think Menniss got the message, although, with all that duct tape, you couldn't read his body language. Still, he looked about as agreeable and content as you can expect someone to look who's tied up in a trunk and expects to stay that way long enough to piss himself. I found a piece of plywood and positioned it so the lid couldn't latch closed and suffocate him. Then I closed the lid as far as it would go, setting a cinderblock on top to hold it in place, but also wanting to scratch the paint on that damn perfect Volvo. I locked my house and said goodbye because I knew I wasn't coming back. Say goodbye to that life, dear girl, because you're starting another.

None of this took long. We got in my piece-of-crap car with me in the driver seat, and I made Blair switch over because, control queen or not, I don't want the responsibility of an Immortal's life in my hands, thank you very much.

THE DODGE COLT was no sports car. Blair floored it, and not much happened; the beat-up old girl slugged ahead pretty much the same whether you floored her or not.

"She needs a new fuel pump," I said. "But she'll get us there."

"Get us where?"

"To the Denver airport. We'll buy tickets to London, but we won't get on the plane. Instead, we'll jump in a taxi and hop to the train station where we'll buy tickets to Atlanta and get on a train to Chicago, only we'll sneak out halfway and slip onto a train going a different direction and then buy a ticket from the porter." I had the habit of reading thrillers when I was depressed, and I was depressed a lot. This was straight out of Thomas Perry.

"That makes good sense," he said, and his hands looked pretty on the Colt's cracked wheel. "The only problem I see is with the trains. Amtrak stations aren't busy enough to hop from one train to another. Mostly, the rails in the US carry freight."

"This is something you've looked into?"

"A little. According to Saul, I'm supposed to have half a dozen escape routes figured out at all times. Only I don't do it."

"Why not? You're scared shitless, aren't you?"

I wanted him to get angry, but instead, he got sad. "When I'm not running, I get so lonely I forget to be scared."

Fair enough. I messed through the CDs scattered under my feet, found a live performance by Leonard Cohen, and put it on. The words are pretty good on their own, but with the music, it comes out so passionate and romantic that you can hardly stand it.

Who wouldn't want to make an Immortal fall in love with her? Only, it was crazy. No matter how much he loved me now, I'd turn into an old lady in a snap of his fingers, and he'd leave. He's definitely that shallow. Put up with wrinkles? No way. One snap later, I'm dead, and after a dozen or more wives, he'll have forgotten me.

The music sounded whiny, and I shut it off.

"I met Leonard Cohen when he was starting out," Blair said.

"That's nice. Tell me about it sometime when I'm interested. Do you have any idea who stuffed Menniss in your trunk?"

"I have no idea at all." He looked scared, the way most people would be right after someone hacked off their ear and then the person who did the hacking reappears turkey-trussed in your trunk. But he also looked happy. That confused me before I figured it out: he likes running, and so long as he's running, he feels good even though he's also scared.

Not at all hard to understand. We had things in common. I kept looking over at him. Even with that big honking bandage on his ear and a pitch-black five-o'clock shadow, he was incredibly gorgeous.

"Do you suppose they put a GPS tracker in my car?" I asked. I felt an urge to bust up our little honeymoon. "I mean, maybe the whole idea was to get us to take my car instead of yours, and then they can follow and kill us when they want to. Does your Volvo have bulletproof glass, flame throwers under the doors, self-sealing tires, that kind of thing?"

"No flame throwers, but the other two, yes." He craned his neck to look at the other cars on the freeway. "Do you really think they put a GPS tracker in your car?" He floored my Colt again, and we went maybe one mile per hour faster.

The idea didn't make much sense since they could have grabbed us or killed us in the prairie dog field if that's what they wanted. But now that I'd brought it up, I couldn't help wondering. We'd have to ditch the car at some point.

We took the tollway because it was the fastest way to get to Denver International, but it was also practically deserted, and someone could shoot at us without anyone else seeing. Each time a car came racing past, I shrank away.

A big bug smacked on the dashboard, and I jumped—if you can jump with your shoulder harness on. "Good thing I got bug-proof glass installed," I said.

He didn't laugh. He was Mr. Total Fear right now, hyperalert, like a guy I used to know who spent two years in Iraq, has PTSD and is probably messed up forever thinking some little kid at the store is going to hand him a live grenade.

Denver International sits in the middle of a big empty area that is sometimes planted with sunflowers. It has a weird statue of a blue horse with glowing eyes, supposedly something to do with the New World Order, or maybe space aliens, or both. We drove into long-term parking, but it looked lonely and exposed out there, like someone might drive up in a limousine and kidnap us, so we drove into the five-story garage and found a space close up. We took a bronze elevator up to the ticketing floor, and a teen with curly blonde hair got on with us. I wondered whether she might have a live grenade in her mouth, but nothing happened. I didn't have a passport, damn it. That meant even pretending to leave for London was out. Instead, I had Blair reserve seats on a flight leaving for Miami in an hour. He paid full price like it didn't matter. I suppose that if you live for centuries and have some money you don't need, you can put it in the bank and let it grow.

Instead of going through security, we left the terminal and jumped into a taxi. No one jumped into the taxi right behind us. Not right away, anyhow.

Our taxi driver was a young Ethiopian-looking guy with delicate features. I asked him to make sure no one followed us. He said it wasn't his job to do things like that, and he got on his cell phone.

"Blair, do you know how to make sure no one tails you?" I asked. "You must. Tell him how."

Blair was stuck in some helpless trance, but I elbowed him out of it, and he gave the driver lots of instructions and 500 dollars. Now we were a happening act. I sat back and watched the cloak and dagger: driving in and out of parking garages, making U-turns on empty streets and taking shortcuts through alleys. It was a giggle. The taxi driver did a great job, adding his own curlicues and really getting into it. But not so into it that he stopped looking at us in the mirror, trying to figure us out: movie-star-beautiful Blair and me with my short spiky hair and nose stud.

Blair was working us toward the train station, but I had another idea that was about three ideas stuck together. I got back into the game and gave directions. The driver added his spins and Blair his weaves, and we staggered our winding way to a certain alley paved with frozen mud. Our totally-into-it-but-curious driver drove slowly by a bunch of bushes, and we jumped out into a space between the bushes while he was still moving, and no one could tell. He also promised to keep doing crazy spy stuff for a while, as if he still had us inside. People are decent sometimes, especially when you give them enough money. And when they think you're hot, which we were. Both of us.

UNDER COVER OF the bush, I towed Blair into the back entrance of my favorite piercing parlor, Holes and Poles. My friend Jason, who runs the place, is one of those huge tattooed guys with 100 pounds of metal in his body, the kind of guy who looks like he eats people, but he's sweet. Only, he's not that subtle (hence the parlor's name).

Jason was working on someone else, so Blair and I stood around the waiting room looking at pictures. Blair especially couldn't take his eyes off one that showed a girl's back with a shoelace threaded in and out like the laces on high boots. I have a picture a lot like that one at home; I mean, the home I used to have, the one in that crappy neighborhood where I can pretend I'm still living and going about my business. Only it's not really me; it's a Sim back there, a computer animation, a sexy and shabby Janice carrying wine bottles past the crack houses to her house.

Waiting for Jason to finish up, I got nervous as hell. I wanted to tap my feet and fidget, only I wanted Jason to remember me as cool, so I posed as Goth and grave. My long black coat helped.

Blair couldn't understand why anyone would want to weave shoelaces through their back.

"It's like connecting the dots," I said. "You feel damaged, so you damage yourself. You make the outside match the inside. I used to be more into it than I am now."

"I got shot in the knee with a musket ball once," he said.

It was cute. He wanted to find a way to relate.

"My bones were sticking out, and I touched them with my fingers," he said.

"That's cool. Show me."

"There's nothing to show." He lifted his pant leg and showed a perfect knee.

I felt sweet toward him, but my voice turned hard. "Then it doesn't count, señor: if you know you're going to heal perfectly, big deal. The idea is that you'll end up with physical scars to match the other kind. Do you get it at all? Do you know what I mean about the other kind of scars? The ones inside?"

A barrier went down in Blair then, not to the outside but to the inside, like he was letting himself see *himself*. He looked so husked-out and grief-ridden, my angel did, that I couldn't stand it.

"Good then," I said. "I'm glad. You're a person. Whew. I was wondering." I babbled on like that for a while until he happily closed himself up again. If he wasn't ready, I certainly wouldn't push him.

Jason finished with his client and took us back to the piercing room. I told him Blair needed a big fat stud in his nose because when you've got one of those, no one notices anything else, and, at the moment, I had an urgent need to turn Blair invisible.

"That'll help," Jason said. "But what about that bloody bandage on his ear? It kind of sticks out."

I pulled Blair's black watch cap down over his ear, and Jason studied him judiciously. "That might do, provided you remember to keep it pulled down. Better yet, let me give you one of mine. It's bigger. Also, it changes things up because it's red instead of black. Can I work on that bandage?"

"Be my guest." I knew Jason wouldn't talk, even under torture. Or ask personal questions. Also, he was better than I was at bandaging hard places, like ears.

He expertly re-bandaged the empty spot and didn't ask any questions about how Blair had lost an ear. After that, he got into his methodical piercing mode, like a lay midwife I once knew who stuck to the straight and narrow even more than a doctor would. He slathered purple antiseptic all over Blair's nose and set a timer to the exact number of germ-killing minutes the antiseptic needed to do its thing.

Meanwhile, I took out my nose stud. While his timer ticked away, Jason gowned his metalloid self in a blue elastic hair cap, a matching facemask, and a throwaway paper gown that covered his whole body and made him look even huger. I was still unscrewing piercings; I had a lot.

Jason unfolded a sterile cloth on a tray, careful not to touch the part that ended face up. He took a smaller folded cloth from a cabinet and unfolded it in a special way so that the big metal punch dropped straight down onto the sterile cloth. Clunk. I had gotten to removing my tongue piercing by the time he started the sterile-glove trick. You have to make sure the magically clean surfaces of the gloves never touch anything earthly. The gloves have a cuff a couple of inches above the wrist opening, and that's part of the trick. You grab the outside of the cuff with your left hand to hold the glove still while you shove in your right hand, then you use your covered right hand to help in your left hand, only now you have to slip your fingers *under* the cuff, so the magic clean surfaces only touch other magic clean surfaces. Clean to clean, foul to foul.

The timer beeped. Jason settled the punch on Blair's left nostril. He told Blair what he would do and distracted him with a funny story about a poodle before he squeezed.

Blair winced a lot. I liked that.

THE MOMENT THE stud is installed, the game of holy vs. tainted ends. Jason threw his gown, cap and mask into the trash and launched into his hygiene speech, the one about how you have to clean your piercing with benzalkonium chloride six times a day for the first week and then four times a day for three weeks, and each time you clean it, you have to rotate the stud two full turns and keep rubbing for a full minute because if you skip any steps, your nose will rot out of your head. Blair's nose couldn't rot out of his head, not even if he wanted it to, but we listened patiently until Jason finished talking and then left the back room to pay.

Blair looked good with the stud in his nose: less perfect and more human. A trickle of blood dripped to the tip of his nose, and I wiped it with my sleeve. I smoothed down my hair, got some goop from my purse and spiked Blair's hair. Jason had a box of clothes, his lost-and-found, and I rummaged around until I found a respectable business outfit and changed into it. If anyone asked around for a Greek god traveling with a pierced slutty-looking girl, they'd only get blank stares because we'd turned the picture inside out.

Blair and I waited by the shop door until a bus came by. We ran out at the last second and got on. We changed buses a few times, not to confuse people chasing us but to get where we wanted to go, which was almost as complicated. We got off of our last bus at Coors Field and crossed over a fat street in a complicated part of downtown Denver, where overpasses and underpasses sweep this way and that, leaving secret spaces beneath them. Sneaking was just a game now because if anyone had followed us this far, they could surely guess that we were headed to Union Station, with its huge glowing sign and bright, colorful lights only blocks away.

I was scared to death, but if something bad was about to happen, I wanted to go out playing. So we slipped down a stairway into one of those wonderful abandoned spots you can always find in cities if you have weird taste in places. Our little hideaway was tucked beneath flying swoops of concrete where about four freeways and three train tracks met.

There used to be businesses down here, but they were boarded up because no one could ever find them after the freeway grew overhead. Hand in hand, we hurried through a parking lot covered with crumbled cement and a sad "Morning Light Café" sign peeling its paint away at one end.

It was cold.

I had my gun, and Blair had one too, but we were the only people around. At the end of the lot, an iron chain painted yellow protected nonexistent drivers from cruising down a flight of stairs into a sunken pedestrian walkway that looked like no one had used it for years. We stepped over the chain and walked down the stairs, making our way like good underground pedestrians. The walkway led to a normal intersection, but Blair turned athletic and helped me climb a flat concrete face to another hidden space. We crouched, ran, and slipped between buildings where no one could see us. I love these lost urban landscapes where broken windows bare their jagged glass teeth and bricks crumble out from their centers.

I put my frozen fingers in Blair's back pockets to warm them. Usually, you find needles and condoms on the ground in a place like this, but there weren't any. Maybe Al's Vacuum Repair took responsibility for this stretch of nowhere the way he did for a piece of the interstate near where I lived.

I heard music through one of the walls.

Deep in our clean hidden place, Blair took me in his arms and kissed me. He kissed me for a long time. He got into it so much that I wondered if he liked semi-public sex. (I don't, but I can adjust.) Then he stopped kissing me, held me a bit away from his face, and stared.

He stared at me for a long time with his eyes all amazed.

I'd seen that look on the faces of the drug dealers and other friendly assholes who hang around my neighborhood 7-Eleven. One time I was stuck inside the store for a while behind someone who'd bought a lot of lottery tickets and needed to scratch each one open, then buy some more (depending on how they scratched out). But I didn't mind waiting because it had started to rain outside. The guy scratched and scratched, and the downpour let up, and I paid for my frozen burritos.

When I left the store, I was hit full in the face by a double rainbow stretching across the whole sky. There was even a piece of a third bow close to the ground, and the assholes and drug dealers were staring at it, this gift from the sky, their attitude gone, no fucking with each other, grateful, exposed, open like little kids who've never been hurt.

Blair was staring at me like I was a rainbow. Part of me loved it. Part of me hated it. Because what's so magical about a rainbow is that it doesn't last.

I KNOW I'M going too fast. But that's how it felt: running and blurring, always moving, whether it made sense or not.

At Union Station, we bought a ticket to Atlanta—leaving in four hours—then jumped on a train going to Chicago right then. (Hah! Blair was wrong about how we couldn't do that.) But Amtrak trains aren't like subways; they take forever to get moving, and if there had been a spy in the station, they could've followed.

We paid the conductor, and once we had our seats settled, I went off to the toilet to call Maurice. The cell connection was good in the train toilet, even with the metal walls. I asked Maurice if he'd free a certain guy stuck in the trunk of a Volvo behind my house, and he said no problem. I told him he could have the Volvo too, but he should sell it fast because someone might come looking. No argument. Chop chop (shop).

Talking to Maurice made me miss my old life, but this new one was fun too. Then I imagined Blair jumping off the train while I was gone, rolling down a hill with that athletic body of his, the bandage over his ear falling off, leaping foot after foot into the countryside, and never coming back. I wanted to rush back to my seat, but I walked slowly. When I entered our car and found that Mr. Beautiful hadn't fled, I wanted to hug him. But I was angry at him for running away even though I'd only imagined it. Instead of hugging him, I delivered a thick on-the-spot lecture on gender roles and identity issues to bring him up to speed with the modern world. He listened to every word, wearing that "I'm seeing a rainbow" look, and I wanted to melt but forged ahead, covering everything I'd been taught and adding some of my own ideas for good measure.

It was fun to have an audience, but I must have paused at some point because Blair got a word in about being exhausted since he hadn't slept more than a few hours in the last few days. He said he wanted to hear more, a lot more, but he couldn't stay awake.

I said fine and meant it. I melted some, and I stroked behind his good ear until he nodded off, his head falling on my shoulder while I petted his spiky hair. My eyes closed too, and I felt his perfect immortal life resting against me, trusting me, and in the dark of my eyelids, he was a life bulb, glowing through everything. I stroked his hair and melted some more, and I could feel how I was choosing life because Blair had so much of it. Only, would I lose everything if he left?

Shoulders and heads aren't soft but become soft when you fall asleep. I awoke with Blair whispering in my ear and telling me to pretend I was still asleep. Fine, I said and did such a good job pretending that I fell asleep again. He had to tell me about five times until I woke up enough to hear him say that we were about to reach Omaha and we should pretend we were half-asleep until the last second and then grab our stuff and jump off the train. He stroked my hair, and I didn't want to go to sleep at all—I had something else in mind—but I pretended my lights were going out instead of turning on, and I snuggled like my muscles were relaxing instead of coming alive. Then, at his signal, we seized our stuff without a fumble and dashed out.

We took a taxi to the Greyhound station, and no one followed us. Or, at least, we didn't see anyone follow us. We took the Greyhound to Kansas City and a train from Kansas City to Albuquerque. We took another Greyhound to Salt Lake City, and then Blair said he thought we were probably safe, and he sounded like he knew what he was talking about. Plus, I wanted to stop this damn running.

He wired money from a Swiss bank to someone in Texas, paid off his old landlord, wired more to a local bank and bought a BMW for cash. I bought some clothes and other stuff, and so did he, including an extra-good shaver to smooth away his gorgeous but itchy 500-o'clock shadow.

Now he wanted to leave for Santa Cruz, California, immediately, the place where he'd last seen Saul, but I needed a break from running. And since we were safe, couldn't we hang out for a while? He surrendered, and we checked into the most expensive hotel in Salt Lake City.

It felt weird, I promise you. This was nothing like any life of mine, and the only thing I had to hold onto was some immortal guy growing an ear back.

THE ROOM HAD a huge bed and a tiled hot tub that rose from the center of the floor like an altar. We lived in the bed and the hot tub for a couple of days. We ate boiled shrimp; we had sex; we ate more boiled shrimp. I had a god with me in that ridiculously fancy hotel room, a piece of perfection, an angel dropped from the sky. There's that expression "a delight for the eyes" that I obviously never understood before because now I did: he made my *eyes* happy. Nay, Rosencrantz, my nose and fingers too. Everything was right about him, perfect to look at and touch and rub your nose into. The whole world is broken and partial and dying, and then there's Blair.

I was so high those couple of days that it's hard to remember details. When I think of that time, I mostly think of these lines from Rilke that one of my professors made us memorize. (The only poems I love are those I studied in school.)

> *Lucky from the cradle*
> *Creation's cherished darling*
> *A blossoming godhead*
> *in crossroads of light*

Feelings and fantasies can get so mixed up that when fantasies run out, you can't remember the feelings that went with them. My skin remembers better than I do. There's a violin-shaped space from my crotch through my stomach into my heart that knows what it's like to open up and let immortality enter. To enter and dwell within from heart to crotch. How's that for a beatific vision? But there were giddy and stupid ideas mixed in too, and I can't go there because I've come down since then and can't imagine him as a god, myself as a goddess or any of the other inflated lovey-dovey things I don't want to talk about because (looking back) they're embarrassing.

I crashed on the morning of the third day. I had a headache, and creation's darling was getting on my nerves. We were sitting in the hot tub, and looked a lot like the boiled shrimp I never wanted to eat again. The scabs had peeled off Blair's ear, and the new, pink skin glowed. He was admiring himself in a mirror.

My head hurt, my nerves were scraped raw and I thought, that's what he's been doing all along. When he did his great job of touching me, he was watching me respond so he could admire his great touch. When I admired him, he admired himself through my eyes admiring him. It circled around so that, in a way, he was the only one in the room. Where did I fit in? Would he ever see anything of me?

Blair was admiring his legs now. Yes, his legs were beautiful. Not just nice but perfect. "If you weren't so beautiful," I said, "I wouldn't be able to stand you."

He stopped eyeballing his pretty leg and turned uncomfortable but didn't say anything.

"You're too in love with that perfect body you're wearing," I said. "I wish I could rip it off and see if there's anyone underneath."

But you can't take off someone's body to see them better the way you can make them take off their glasses or silly hat. And, anyway, he looked so forlorn and ashamed I felt sorry for him. Addictions aren't easy to overcome, especially when the drug is draped over you.

"Don't worry," I said. "You happen to be beautiful, and I love you, but I'd like to get to another level. Like maybe one day, you'll see me."

"But I do see you."

We looked at each other and got beyond the "in love" thing, and I let Blair try to look into me as a test. He passed and failed. I affected him, which meant that some part of him saw me. But he couldn't look at me directly. He saw me only in the mirror of his reactions to me. And that meant he only saw me through himself, which I guess is all you could ask for, and, anyway, I was bored.

I climbed out of the hot tub and dried myself with the bedspread because we'd used up all the towels. I looked down between my legs, so recently crammed full of god, and noticed I was getting cellulite in my thighs. Or that I was about to get cellulite. I'd have to start exercising so I didn't turn into a fat chick. I wasn't fat yet, but I could go there. It was obvious.

I got dressed in clothes for going out, but Blair was still in the tub, and I turned on the television and watched an old episode of *Alias*. He came out and watched with me. Mistake. The show mentioned sticking a GPS tracker inside someone's body, and right away, Blair was sure someone had done that to him. He got the idea that while we were on the train, someone had drugged us and operated on him to insert the tracker. Only we didn't remember because of the drugs.

It would have been ridiculous except that Menniss *had* tracked Blair from Texas to Fort Collins with a GPS tracker in his Volvo and then from the Volvo to my house with a GPS tracker in his coat. The leap from a coat to a body isn't so huge. They do stick GPS trackers under the skin of pet cats. Besides, someone had trussed up Menniss and left him where he could have dropped dead if we hadn't found him in time. That someone could successfully do that to a guy like Menniss made you take paranoia seriously.

"If someone had operated on you," I told Blair, "there would be a fresh hole in your skin somewhere."

"True," he said. "So, would you check out the places I can't see?"

I looked over his whole body with my fingers and eyes, not sexually (because I was too worn out), more like a nurse. I didn't find anything.

"What if they put something in my food? A transmitter the size of a grape nut, for example."

"Wouldn't you shit it out again?"

"Maybe it hooks onto your gut."

"You could get a full-body MRI to find out," I said.

He jumped on the idea and wanted to get one right away. I told him he was a crap-in-the-pants chickenshit scared of shadows, but I wanted to get out of the damn hotel room anyway, so I agreed.

I had read somewhere that you can get a full-body MRI on request if you have the money. I rode with him to one of the big Salt Lake City hospitals, but damn if I'd wait around for three hours like a nice Mormon wife while he got scanned, so I walked off in my business suit and enjoyed the game of dressing up like a normal person. It was fun for a while, but then I began to feel like a sketch of Janice drawn by the wind. I could disappear if I didn't watch out.

I'd dressed in not-too-tight black pants, put a bra on under my shirt and had my hair brushed back instead of spiked so I wouldn't freak out the Mormons. But a couple of blocks from the hospital, the damn domesticated neighborhoods got to me, and I put my nose stud back in. I came to a park with big oak trees and a couple of eucalyptus groves. I startled a sprinkling of sparrows, and they flew up from the sidewalk into a nearby bush, looking like one of those reversed videos of a cup unbreaking. I sat on a bench and ignored the moms watching their kids on the playground and the dad playing chase with his two kids. Domestic phlegm. I put a huge bar in my ear piercings, and it was a comfort to see that I made them nervous just sitting there with my metal.

One of the kids playing chase made a break from his dad and ran in my direction on his way toward a stand of trees. As he flew past, he tripped and fell sprawling on the cement. The dad had his hands full with another kid, who'd climbed too high up a tree, and I couldn't ignore a sprawled-out howler five feet away. I went over to help him.

He was six, maybe seven. He'd scraped himself here and there, but it was his hand that scared him most. He held it up in front of his eyes so he could stare at the blood dripping from it. His face twisted up in horror like that soldier in *Saving Private Ryan* who discovers he's had his leg blown off. The soldier thinks: I'm wrecked; I'm not a me anymore; I've become a thing. When you're a kid, and you get a tiny cut on your hand, it's the same discovery. Blair doesn't know a damn thing about it because he can't be damaged.

I kneeled beside the boy and said, "Show me where you're hurt."

He showed me and screamed a lot to let me know his opinion, but he wanted my opinion, too, since I was an adult, and maybe I could tell him he wasn't permanently wrecked.

He had a scrape in the shape of an *X*, and it was bleeding a little.

"It's a treasure map," I said. "X marks the spot. You have your own special treasure map."

He stopped crying and looked interested. I took his other hand. "Let's go find the treasure. Keep looking at your map to make sure we're going the right way."

I took him to his father and handed him over. The father thanked scary me a little too much. I turned around and walked into a eucalyptus grove.

It was a huge eucalyptus grove. I felt alone, like I could be in Australia. I loved it. I did a little dance and then got depressed because I felt isolated, and my usual shame dripped out of the trees. I wanted to go back to the hospital and wait for Blair. I wanted to go back to Fort Collins. Then a guy about my age came walking through the trees.

He wore dirty jeans and a dirty t-shirt and looked unhappy, like a pissed-off loser on his way to his lover's house to pick a fight. Of course, he attracted me. My friends in the sexual abuse group say I need to open up to a different kind of man. But a scared-shitless narcissistic Immortal isn't a big step up, and the closer this new guy came, the more easily I could breathe.

He didn't look up at me as he walked by, keeping two trees away so I wouldn't feel threatened. Thoughtful. But I didn't want him to pass by, so I did the calling out. "Hey, any place good to eat around here?" Random.

He stopped walking and looked at me in that polite way guys do where they force their eyes to stay on your face and not look south. He had his lips pressed tightly together. When they opened, his lips expanded—as big as Angelina Jolie's. "This is Salt Lake City," he said. "There's nowhere good to eat."

"Oh. Then I guess I won't eat till we get to Santa Cruz."

He laughed. "I'm going to the Bay Area too. But I think I'll eat something on the way."

"You have a cigarette?" I asked.

He did, a Camel Red.

I smoked it and enjoyed poisoning myself. There's more life in poisoning yourself than in trying to live forever. It lets you know you're dying little by little, and that helps you live.

I'm so profound.

THE GUY'S NAME was Marcus, and he was staying in a motel on the other side of the park. Instead of leading me to a shitty restaurant, he made me a shitty omelet himself. It had black spots from the frying pan and tasted great.

Marcus wrote screenplays that no one bought and made his living putting together a stupid newsletter for the plumbers union. He lived in New York City with a singer named Rebecca, who had groupies. Reading between the lines, she mostly liked messing with Marcus. She'd get him all worked up romantically, talk dreamy-eyed about their getting married, and then tell him to go away and never return. Not only had they never had sex, they'd never even kissed properly. Sometimes he tried, but she would make her lips wood. Naturally, he loved her desperately, but he ran away sometimes, and that's what he was doing now. He'd stayed in his hotel room for two days writing Rebecca a letter, telling her off and begging her to beg him to come back. He'd been on his way to mail it when he got accosted in a eucalyptus grove by me.

I said I wanted to see the letter. Marcus fumbled in his pants and found the letter in a back pocket. But instead of showing it to me, he tore it up. I grabbed for the pieces while he fended me off, my arms brushing all around his skinny legs, ribs and shoulders. I couldn't make out much from the fragments I managed to grab. After all that wrestling, you'd expect us to have sex, but Marcus had Rebecca on the brain and looked too sad. I didn't feel rejected even though he was the one who said no.

He asked me what I was doing in Salt Lake City.

"Traveling with a guy," I said, "but he's not really my kind of guy; too prim and proper."

"I don't see you with someone prim and proper," Marcus said. "What do you do with him, shine his shoes?"

"It might be sexy to shine his shoes. Also, he's incredibly rich."

"Then you should siphon off his money and support me."

"In exchange for what?"

"In exchange for immortalizing you in my screenplays and books." He leaned over the side of the bed again and came up with a college-ruled notebook in a ragged, red cardboard cover with a pen clipped to it. He took off the pen and opened the notebook to somewhere in the middle. "What was your childhood like?"

"I had a great childhood." Then I told him about how my dad died while I was sitting in his lap, how my mom became an alcoholic and how I got molested. He didn't say anything sympathetic, which made me like him a lot.

"I got myself together somehow," I said, "and I graduated from Bennington College with a BA in English lit."

He looked up from his notebook and said, "That's great."

That annoyed me because saying "that's great" about one part of someone's life is the same as saying "how awful" about the other parts.

I got over being annoyed. "After that, I got into meth. I paid for it by doing Internet porn—you can find me online if you look. It was bad. Though not everything about it was bad. You feel humiliated and used, true, but you also feel like a goddess with all those men around. Is this too raw for you?"

"Not at all." Marcus moved his arm wide with his elbow stuck out as he scrawled cursive in big loopy letters. "It's great material."

"You think? Next, I got lucky and met some cool folks in Denver who got me out of bad weird sex by getting me into good weird sex. B&D is what most people call it. Bondage and domination. People who don't know anything call it S&M, but if you know your kink, it's called "power exchange." Because that's what it is. B&D is all about playing with control and surrender. You learn how to respect other people's boundaries, to let your own boundaries down when you want to let them down, and to keep them up when you want to keep them up. And how to know the difference, like the serenity prayer. That's often the hardest part."

"I agree," he said.

"Then maybe you should try B&D. Those Denver folks used it as psychotherapy. They were also crazy, but I learned a lot, and after a while, I left off weird sex and joined a sexual abuse group. That's helped too. And now I'm working on getting my life together."

"How's that going?" His pen must have dried up because he scratched it all over the page, then threw it across the room. He found another pen under his bed.

"It's going." I tapped his thigh with my pretty foot, then remembered we weren't going to have sex. "I'm thinking of applying to graduate school."

"In what?"

"History, like my dad." It just came out. I hadn't blushed for a long time and forgot that I couldn't stop it once it started. But he had the brilliance not to notice. "I have an idea," I said. "When I get to Santa Cruz, I'll go to the biggest library and write my cell phone number on page 47 of *Northanger Abbey*. Then, if you want and I want, we can get together again."

He looked up from his notebook, though he didn't stop writing, and gave me a sweet smile. Not the sorry-for-yourself, needy kind of sweet smile even though he did feel sorry for himself. Also, not the kind that's part of a plan to sleep with you and throw you away afterward like a gnawed bone. It was that wonderful two-people-can-be-friends smile you don't see a lot.

"What if they have more than one copy?" he asked.

"I'll put it in the oldest and ugliest copy."

"It's a deal," he said.

But as I left, he was fiddling with the shreds of the letter he'd written to Rebecca. People get stuck on other people for no reason. It even happens to me sometimes.

I TURNED A corner and saw Blair leaning against a brick pillar near the hospital entrance. He looked so beautiful that I got short of breath and heard more lines from Rilke.

If an angel
Suddenly held me against his heart
I would fade in the grip
Of that greater existence.

Couldn't everyone see it? Why weren't they all standing around him in adoring circles?

"Nothing inside," he said. He pointed from his head down to his toes and smiled the way you do when a police car comes up from behind with its lights flashing and speeds past you.

So we hadn't been tracked. We were invisible.

I wondered if Blair were *actually* invisible, an angel only I could see. Then a ferocious old lady with oxygen prongs crammed up her nose and a green oxygen tank on her wheelchair said, "Get out of my way" directly to Blair, so I guess the invisibility theory was wrong. She cut between us, and I stopped feeling like an angel's wife and realized I was the same kind of creature as an old lady, just younger. Something I never knew before.

Blair drew me to him in a nice hug, but now it felt messed up; he was an angel, and I was a dying thing. He said he wanted me to get scanned for transmitters too.

"Oh fuck." I twisted around, annoyed, and then said sure, why not? Because I was curious to see how my insides looked. My friend died of ovarian cancer, and sometimes I worry about the state of my inner organs. If your mind affects your body, then I should have weird tumors all over the place, and I didn't want to die just yet, especially not now that I was getting myself together.

I got into the MRI machine and lay still in my paper gown as its weird mechanical eye ogled me. I didn't hide any part of myself from it. During my religious period at age ten, I did the same with God, but this was just a physical confession. Still.

Afterward, I got dressed and waited. I waited a long time, and then a cute, young male nurse wearing those clothes that aren't forest green or lime green but the special green that the hospital world owns came in to get me. I felt like a sick person as he ushered me into a dark room to talk to the radiologist.

The only light came from a computer screen showing pictures of my insides. The radiologist was sitting in front of the screen, and my insides lit him enough for me to see that he wore a fluffy white shirt, like a French gentleman dressed for dueling, only he was an old guy with nose hair long enough to make a mustache. And he sat so collapsed in his padded chair someone should have told him to get up and do exercises because, otherwise, he might grow into it.

He pointed to a messy white thing on the screen. "This is your uterus here, your *womb*. There's a half-millimeter fibroma right *here*. Nothing to worry about. Not now, anyway. Though, it could get bigger. It could get as big as a grapefruit, and then you'd bleed and have pain. You'd have to get it cut out, and you might never have children. But it's small now, don't worry about it."

I'd never seen a person's face lit by the glow of my uterus before.

"And here's your large intestine. No polyps. You have nice intestines. Your breasts look healthy, too. But there's something in your brain. See this in the right temporal lobe?"

He pointed to something that looked like a walnut.

I leaned forward. I was not too fond of the walnut.

"It's odd-looking," he said. "Maybe an artifact? Or could it be cancer?" He turned his head sideways, like a bird checking a seed, and flipped through views of my brain. "You should talk to your private doctor about it. You do have a private doctor, don't you?"

"Of course I do," I said, though, of course, I didn't. "Where is it in my head, exactly?"

He motioned me over, made me lean down, and touched a wormy finger to the right side of my head. As soon as he touched it, I felt the ache there and realized that it had always ached there, never stopping for a second, a big tumor eating out my brain.

"Does it look dangerous?" I asked.

He turned back to the image. He drew a red mark on the film with a grease pencil. "Not really." He tapped a pencil against his teeth and thought about it some more. "Probably a random nothing. I sit here all day looking at bodies, and you know what I see? Ugly cysts, rotten bones, stinking pouches, big fat bulges. We all have that kind of stuff inside. And we get by anyhow." He stuck the grease pencil in his mouth like a cigar. He grunted and took it out. "I lie. Not everyone is ugly inside."

He was a gross old slug, but now he turned beatific, his jowls reaching toward his shoulders and a smile stretching out between them. "I saw a gentleman earlier today who *amazed* me. An MRI to die for. Not a single flaw. The luckiest man in the world." He clicked buttons on his computer and showed me some different black-and-white stuff. "Look at that spine." He pointed with his grease pencil, and the light from the screen gathered around his eyes in a big sheen.

Even if I didn't die of brain cancer, Blair would leave me in 12 years. Even if he didn't leave me in 12 years, I'd get old and shriveled and have to breathe oxygen and bust aside people in my wheelchair, and he'd stay his Greek god self forever.

The luckiest man in the world. Lucky from the cradle. Creation's chosen darling. A damn blossoming godhead in damn crossroads of light.

I didn't tell Blair about the walnut.

That night when we made love, I grabbed his nose stud and twisted it. He breathed in sharply. I scratched his back and made him bleed, and he liked that. I bit his re-growing ear, and he liked that too. The perfect bondage partner. In power exchange, you have to watch what you're doing so you don't leave scars, but with Blair, you could flog away, and it wouldn't matter.

"Don't stop," he said.

I twisted his nose stud hard. He pushed my hand away.

"Make up your mind," I told him. "Do you want me to do it or not?"

"It's only a reflex," Blair said. "I do want it."

I could see it was true because he was hyper-awake, with springy lines of sexual craziness drawing through him. I know a lot about those springy lines.

"Fine," I said, and started up again, maybe a little mean, but after a bit, he pushed me away again.

Making my voice seductive, though mostly I was just annoyed, I said, "I could tie you up so you stop interfering."

When I said it, I didn't think ahead to the special way an

Immortal guy like him would react to the idea. Blair reacted all over the place, getting off and going crazy at the same time. He was already breathing hard from the sexy stuff we'd been doing, but now he panted as fast as a dog on a broiling-hot day. And it would have scared the shit out of me, except I understood. I watched his eyes lurch to the door, pull back to me, then lurch to the door again. His beautiful six-pack abs tightened, and he half sat up and then dropped down. All the usual power exchange stuff even without the bondage yet: aching to let go and scared to death of letting go. That's why people do it.

Blair must have already thought about it, maybe read a Victorian bondage book, because otherwise, he wouldn't know enough about it to react so strongly. But I also knew he'd never let anyone tie him up; his life was about running. Well, everyone is running, but most people don't have to deal with a guy like Menniss, a James Bond type getting old but still vicious and stalking them across the world to cut off an ear. What if another hanger-on came crashing through the door, and Blair was tied up? He'd need me to untie him so he could escape. That was asking a bit much on a first bondage date.

But Blair was unfolding, and I realized I could make it work. I lost my anger and became a power exchange professional, though maybe not entirely since I still wanted to poke a needle in. On the other hand, wanting to stick a needle in isn't necessarily anger because when you're in love, you want to poke too, poke deeply and let some juice out. I calmed enough to realize I had to chill the guy fast before he freaked.

I sat cross-legged on the bed, a little distance from Blair to give him space. "Blair," I said, "Come back. I'm not going to properly tie you up. Not so you can't move."

"But I want you to."

"No, you don't. You're not ready. Anyway, tie up an Immortal? Do you think I'm going to take that responsibility? Fuck you, asshole." Pretend-mad, to shift him.

It worked well, as it usually does. I let the relief and disappointment go on a little, then said, "I'm going to pretend I've tied you up.

Not just pretend in my head. I will tie you up, but with something too weak to hold you. Here, let me find something."

He breathed hard while I dug around in my purse and found a roll of Scotch tape. I bound his wrists to the bedposts with ridiculous little loops that wouldn't hold a baby. With his arms stretched up and out like that, chunky lines of muscle stood out between his nipples and shoulders. I reminded him he couldn't move, not using my real voice but the kind of voice you use when playing a game. I tapped my fingers over his chest and reminded him again. His chest was beautiful, tan with drops of sweat arranged just right, like in a movie about gladiators where it's probably staged. The hairs in his armpits fell into perfect black curls, but I didn't touch him there because it might tickle. He had his usual, thick five-o'clock shadow even though he'd shaved again at about five o'clock, which gave him a nice gaunt prisoner's look.

I used my real voice to step out of the game and ask if he was okay. He said he was. In my pretend voice, I said, "You can't move your hands. You're in my power, and you're stuck unless I let you out. You can't move. You're trapped." I dropped back to my real voice and told him he was supposed to imagine all this.

But he couldn't. That is, he couldn't keep it an imagination. He wasn't playing at being scared; he was damn scared, even by loops of Scotch tape. And he loved it.

We broke the tape pretty quickly, which would have happened even with regular sex, but this was hot, hot sex. I leaned all my weight on one of his arms to make it stay up by the post and told him to pretend he was still tied and not to touch me. Extremely hot.

He was surrendering. He was surrendering to *me*; in his mind, it was more than play. For a guy like him, it was real surrender.

I'm not sure who cried first, my downed angel or me. I've never had tearful sex before. Not that I let it go on long. I sucked up my tears to watch my downed angel let loose with his.

BUBBLED UP SAFE in the new BMW, we left Salt Lake City on a long black highway west. The sky was clear, but high mountains in the distance wore private clouds. Yellow signs every couple of miles said, "Watch for eagles on the road." I'd never traveled west of Colorado before.

I got bored and asked Blair about his childhood. It was hard to get the answers I wanted because he mostly wanted to talk about wars, the way guys usually do. Well, what guys usually do when you ask about their life is talk about their jobs; it's when you try to talk about history that they talk about wars. But Blair's life had a lot of history, so it mixed.

Blair and his perfect eternal body were born into a family of worn-out Hungarian aristocrats in 1671. Hungary specialized in worn-out aristocrats in those days, according to Blair. Also, broken-down peasants and piles of stone that once were castles. According to him, your average worn-out aristocrat, depressed about his smashed castle, would cheer himself up by gouging out eyes. In some villages, all the broken-down peasants were one-eyed and pissed about it.

This is Blair's version of history. I'm not saying it's true.

"Yes, but tell me about your childhood," I said.

"My childhood," he said.

"Growing up," I prompted.

"Well …" He thought about it. "I remember when I was 10 and the Transylvanians and Austrians had a battle near my house. Neither army was on *our* side, exactly, but the Austrians had nicer uniforms."

"What did your mother say about her 10-year-old kid going out to watch a battle? 'Have fun, don't get yourself shot, make sure you're home in time for dinner.'"

"My mother? I don't remember her saying anything about it." It took him a second to put things together. "Oh, I know why. She died when I was nine."

Normally, if you get a guy telling you stories and he forgets that his mother died, it's a red flag, but I decided to give Blair the benefit of the doubt since it happened about 300 years ago, and maybe he'd forgotten. So I only asked him what she looked like.

"She had black eyes and hair, was about your height, and had beautiful rounded features like yours."

"How great. I'm a mother figure for a 300-year-old man." But he had no idea what I was talking about. So old and so little pop psychology. Oh, the ignorance.

We finished discussing his mother in about three more sentences because he hardly remembered anything. I made him count how many of his wives and girlfriends looked like his mother, which took much longer because he'd had so many.

It added up to more than half of them. Theory proved.

Next, I asked him whether he'd been physically abused as a kid. For me, that's basic background information, what you ask a guy on the third date if you're interested and want to get deeper into your new dysfunctional relationship. But no one had ever asked him the question before, and he screwed up his face like a kid doing a difficult arithmetic problem. Calculate, figure. "My father didn't beat me any more than was usual, probably three or four times a week."

Not with his hands either, Blair hastened to explain, meaning it as a positive thing, even though what his esteemed daddy used instead was a leather strap with metal studs that made him bleed.

It took me a minute to take that in. Then I asked him about his own kids. He said he only beat his boys; the girls he usually locked in the root cellar.

"In the cellar? In the dark?"

I'd read an essay once by a girl who'd had this done to her and begged parents *never* to lock their children in a dark cellar because it fucks with your brain a lot worse than, say, getting beaten with a studded leather strap. "That's supposed to be awful," I said.

"They certainly didn't like it. During one of my frames—no, not a frame, because I didn't know I was an immortal yet—"

"What's a frame?" I interrupted.

"That's what Saul calls the 12 years an Immortal can stay in one place. But what I was about to mention happened when I was still with my first family. That is, the family I had before I discovered I was an Immortal. When I was married the normal way."

"I *get* it," I said.

"Back then," he said, "we had a ghost living in the cellar. All my wife had to do was send one of the girls down, and the others would obey for months."

"You believe in ghosts, Blair? Are you that ignorant?" I don't have a problem believing in ghosts, but I was jealous and wanted to poke him.

That hard arithmetic problem again. "No, of course not," he said. "Not anymore. But back then, everyone believed in ghosts. It was a superstitious time."

"I thought the late 1600s was the Enlightenment."

Blair put on a professorial voice and explained that the Enlightenment took its time getting to Hungary. Witch trials were the thing there, not Voltaire. And that's how Blair got in trouble. When he turned 40 and still looked 24, people began to talk. One day, his wife made him stand beside her and look in a mirror, and she asked him whether she looked old enough to be his mother. Blair, a model of sensitivity even in his youth, said, "My God, it's true. You do look like you could be my mother."

"You didn't say that, did you?" I said.

"I did."

"You're an idiot."

Blair's wife settled it in her mind right then and there: her husband was in league with Satan. Which was understandable.

Blair went straight to the family priest and asked for help.

I wondered whether priests were the same then and if this guy had molested Blair, but the story kept moving, and I didn't have a chance to ask.

"Father Stephen was a kindly man," Blair said. "He reminded me that Jesus had already paid for my soul with his life. All I had to do was confess my bargain with Satan and ask God for forgiveness, and everything would come out right. We'd know if it was a true confession because my missing years would return, and I'd die."

The clouds on the distant mountains had snuck up to us and dropped huge rain splats. But that was outside the BMW. Inside, it was just quiet. Blair turned quiet too, and I asked why. He said he hadn't thought about this part of his life for a long time and that thinking about it made him feel awful.

But I was stuck on something, "Why would you die? Wouldn't you turn your real age of 40?"

Father Stephen had a formula. I don't know where he got it. Every year the number of years Blair looked younger than his natural age had to be counted in. When he was 26, that was one year; at 27, another two years, and so on. One plus two plus three, etc., up to 15, a big number stuck on top of 40. Like about 150 with only the Devil's cloven hoof to push the years down. And if he lifts his hoof, you're dead.

Basically, he could save his immortal soul by losing his immortal life.

"That can't have been appealing," I said. "Considering how into staying alive you are."

"I wasn't yet. All I cared about then was my soul's salvation. I was extremely religious and was more terrified by the possibility that my soul would roast in hell for all eternity than anything else."

"More terrified of hell than of dying?"

"Hell seemed real in those days." Mental arithmetic problems again. "I can't remember what it felt like to believe that, but I do remember believing it."

He told the priest he didn't remember making any pact with Satan. The priest explained that it wasn't like borrowing money, where you make a formal contract in the presence of three witnesses; you could make a pact with the Devil so easily you hardly noticed.

"Hold on," I said. "Satan makes you sign your name in blood. Fact."

"That's what I thought, but Father Simon told me those stories were superstitious nonsense. He explained that when people make a pact with Devil, it happens not in the outer world but in the heart. He called it 'an inward turning of the will.' He said that people sometimes sold their soul to Satan in a fit of anger or even in a daydream."

That scared Blair silly, and he dug through his memory, looking for instances when he could have given his soul over. He found several and confessed, and though he built up a big Hail Mary debt, he didn't suddenly turn old and die, so they knew he hadn't gotten to the right confession.

Father Simon offered to hide him in the monastery and sit by patiently while Blair confessed every possible thing, no matter how long it took. (Probably because he'd once molested Blair and felt guilty—my theory.) But the pair didn't make it to the monastery. On the way, they got attacked by a village of pissed peasants.

"Early class warfare," I said.

But Blair had mostly missed Marxism, just as he'd entirely missed pop psychology and didn't get it.

The way he told the story, the crowd had pitchforks, torches and sickles. I imagined scenes from an old black-and-white Frankenstein movie, and I mentioned this, and it turned out Blair had seen the same movie, and he might have mixed the two in his mind.

Blair managed to escape to a barn with thick walls and locked himself inside while the black-and-white peasants cinematically waved their pitchforks and sickles. When that didn't work, they piled stacks of hay to burn him out. Blair could see the hay burning all around the stockade, apparently from the perspective of a camera about 20 feet up and filming in black and white—something was wrong with how his brain had stored the memory, especially because he also remembered getting saved in the nick of time before any fires were started. I think he was mixing real memories with a movie.

He got saved by a group of soldiers who galloped up and commanded the peasants to keep their torches to themselves unless they wanted their remaining eyeballs gouged out for harming the hair on an aristocrat's head.

"They'd get in trouble even though the aristocrat in question was the spawn of Satan?"

"They weren't allowed to hurt aristocrats under any circumstance," Blair said, sounding shocked.

The leader of the soldiers promised the pissed-off peasants that if they dispersed right away, they could come back later and see Blair burned at the stake after he got tried and found guilty, provided they still had eyes, and they scampered home like good little proletariats.

Then the rain hit us. I'm talking about the real world again—sort of. The rain was coming down like firehoses, but through the BMW's windshield, it looked as much like a movie as Blair's memories. Blair pulled off the road because he's not a fan of risk. He turned on the emergency lights so no one would smash into our butt. I pushed my seat back, kicked up my legs on the dash, and told him to keep telling the story.

Big-time arithmetic problems to solve in his head. "I remember the things I was thinking then, but I don't understand them at all." Eyebrow crunches. Crunch, crunch, crunch. "It was as if I *liked* the idea of getting burned at the stake because I thought it would save my soul. I *wanted* to open the door and let the soldiers in."

He sounded real now; this wasn't from a movie. "Go on," I said.

"Except I was too afraid."

"Naturally."

"I hated myself for it. I cursed myself for being a coward, but I couldn't get myself to move. I commanded Satan to get behind me and begged Jesus to save me. It still didn't work. Then ..."

He stopped.

"Don't stop."

"It's agonizing to remember this part. It's humiliating."

"What part?"

"What I did next."

"Tell me."

"I ... I switched sides and begged Satan to save me." He looked at me like a little kid who's been bad. Much worse than drawing on the wall.

"Well, why not?" I asked. "You'd sold your soul to him. Shouldn't he help you when you need it?"

Miscellaneous squirming: forehead mopping, raking hands through hair. Poor Blair. "But it was wrong. It felt wrong."

When the soldiers battered down the door, Blair screamed, "Great Lord Satan! Save me!" That spooked the soldiers, who crossed themselves and wouldn't come closer. But the leader wasn't spooked. He threw a bag over Blair's head, tied his arms behind him, carried him out of the barn, and threw him over a horse.

That last part sounded a little movie-ish to me, but whatever.

The horse galloped for a long time, then someone took Blair off and threw him into a carriage. He lay crumpled and helpless on the carriage seat for hours. After a long time, the carriage stopped, and someone came in and took the bag off his head.

"Let me guess. It was Saul. He told you everything was okay and that he was saving you. And you were incredibly grateful."

"I wasn't grateful."

"Why not?"

"Because now it seemed to me that Saul was an emissary of Satan come in answer to my prayer."

What an ass. As soon as he wasn't in immediate danger of being burned alive, he got his courage back, switched sides again, begged Jesus to forgive him for his abject behavior back in the barn and jumped out of the carriage.

But Saul chased him down easily since he had guys on horseback with him. From then on, Saul kept him in chains and gagged him when they passed through towns so Blair wouldn't scream he was being held in bondage by Satan. Later, when crossing from country to country, Saul not only tied and gagged him but hid Blair in a coffin.

So I was dating the original vampire.

Blair finally decided Saul wasn't an emissary of Satan, and they became friends. Saul protected him from hangers-on and helped him leave his family every 12 years. (I should also add he tried to talk Blair out of having families because of how it made the poor wife and kids feel, but he never succeeded.)

Saul hung out with him on and off for a couple of hundred years. At the turn of the 20th century, they went traveling together. That's when, on some beach in Santa Cruz, which was where we were going, Blair decided he was too good for Saul and ditched him.

"You ditched your only friend, the guy who saved your life?"

"I did."

"You're an ass."

"I know." He felt really bad.

I felt really good. If he'd ditched Saul, he'd ditch me. What a fucking relief.

ON OUR WAY to Santa Cruz, we stopped in Ely, Nevada, under a
20-foot guy with one blue leg straight and the other bent and holding
a lariat in one hand festooned with Christmas lights. The place was a
casino with a hotel curled around it. Besides Big Blue Guy, the place
had sculptures of stirrups, whips, horseshoes, spurs and chainsaws.
I'd never been to a casino.

We checked in, and I put on a jean-jacket shirt I had (luckily)
and some pants that almost matched and left Blair in the room to
shower. I knew he'd be at it for a while. He liked to admire himself
in the mirror, do push-ups, and admire himself in the mirror again.
He was an addict, but like I think I said before, if you had your drug
of choice draped around you, how well could *you* resist?

You had to climb three tiny steps to get from the lobby to the
casino. The point was to separate minors from the evils of gambling
and maybe to remind everyone that a casino is a higher and better
world than this one. A little boy had climbed to the landing at the
top of the steps, where he shouldn't have been, but only to pet a
bear chain sawed out of a dark-brown root. I patted the boy's head
as I walked by.

I walked here and there in the casino and checked out the people putting quarters in the slots. I watched their dried-out faces get
excited when some of the quarters came back (when you smoke for
30 years, your skin turns to cardboard; I really should quit). A girl
wearing orange nylon, but not very much of it, walked around giving
out free sodas. I took a root beer. I sat at a blackjack table and threw
away a little money so I could enjoy the creepy dealer with his green
visor taking it seriously. And I enjoyed the players, too, cowboys in
their string ties, medallions, huge belt buckles and polyester jackets,
solemnly absorbed in the business of betting.

The cowboy sitting next to me won a big pot. He jammed it
in his pockets and wished everyone good luck. They cheered him
even though it was their money he'd stuffed away. Then he left to
get drunk or buy a horse or to get a horse drunk—I didn't quite follow. The seat next to mine didn't stay empty for long: a flamboyant
weirdo appeared from nowhere and took his place. Not a cowboy,
this one. I didn't know what he was.

He wore a handlebar mustache and a goatee and carried a cane with an ivory handle. He looked a little older than me. He wore a black silk suit jacket over a white t-shirt and had long, straight brown hair tied into a ponytail. His fingers moved in a kind of fussy way that could go along with being gay, but he wasn't gay—you could tell—just sexy. No one else paid attention to him because they had their cards to tend to, but Sir Weirdo paid attention to me from the corner of his eye.

We played a few more rounds. In the middle of one, he said, "Are you a lesbian?" He didn't look at me when he said it but said it loud enough for everyone to hear. Since I was the only woman present, he had to mean me.

"What the fuck?" I replied. I flipped my cards up in the middle of the game, a shocking act, but I was pissed. I popped around in my chair and faced him instead of the green table. "You think I'm lesbian because my hair's short?" Not that I cared about the lesbian part. But what a jerk.

"I never said I thought you were a lesbian. I just asked *if* you were." He smiled and adjusted his mustache.

Hell, it was a pickup line. "That's your pickup line?"

"Invented on the spot for you, darling. My name is Zeke." His blue eyes twinkled, and he held out his hand for me to shake.

I didn't shake it. "Zeke, that's a hysterical name. Zeke, Zeke, Zeke. So Mr. Zeke, why do you have such a big mustache and carry a long cane? Because you're tiny down below?"

He pointed both his index fingers at me and, without missing a single beat of the soundtrack that should have been playing, said, "That is a matter of some controversy. I'd greatly value your detailed appraisal."

The dealer smiled. A minor miracle. I smiled too.

"You want some coke?" Zeke asked. "I can get you coke. Or Dr. Pepper."

"I only like classic coke." I rubbed my nose.

He patted his jacket pocket.

"I'm done here," I said.

I cashed in the rest of my chips. He did the same, and we left together.

WAS I DOING it to lose Blair? To defend myself from getting too attached?

I'm not sure.

I knew I was being crazy, but I couldn't stop myself. Mostly, I was a girl on vacation having her fun.

Zeke's room was three floors higher but looked exactly like ours: cowboy pictures on the wall, a couch of no color, a padded chair that matched the couch and a scratched-up coffee table between the couch and chair.

I sat on the chair. He sat on the couch.

I held the purse on my lap and unsnapped it in case I needed my handgun; I'm not stupid, just irresponsible.

I watched Zeke pour two glasses of water from a pitcher on the coffee table. Mostly I watched his hands because they were interesting. Sometimes they made magic flourishes, but mostly they did fastidious things, like closing each action before starting the next. They unzipped one pocket of his jacket, took out a silver spoon, set it on the table, and rezipped the pocket. They unzipped another pocket, took out a zip lock bag and rezipped that pocket. And so on, until there was a line of cocaine and a razor blade to square it up, and the cocaine and the Ziplock bags were back where they came from. Then a magician's flourish and the razor disappeared too.

I hadn't done cocaine for two years and didn't want to start again. "You go first," I said. "And please say something witty. I'll make up my mind once I see if you're witty."

"I thought I already proved I was witty." He made a sad clown's face. He made a dollar bill appear from nowhere, rolled it, and made a happy clown's face. He snorted the whole line of coke. He pulled a red and green handkerchief from yet another pocket, shook it open and delicately applied it to his nose.

"I'm waiting for the witty remark," I said.

One of his fingers told me to wait. He opened the drawer of the coffee table and pulled out a big handgun, a semi-automatic with a silencer like you see in spy movies. He held it in the most non-threatening way possible—balanced on his palm with the barrel pointed away from me. With his other hand, he pinched the tip of the barrel and lifted it like a dead rat by its tail. He handed it to me and said, "Be careful. It's loaded."

It *was* loaded. But the safety was on.

I set it in my lap and took out my own gun, which I could trust. I pointed it straight up as if I wanted to shoot some cowboy couple going at it on the next floor. "You have the hiccups?" I asked. "You want me to scare you?"

"I want you to know that if you ever need help for your boyfriend, you can call me."

"Your gun doubles as a spy telephone?"

"I gave you the gun the way I asked you if you were a lesbian."

Maybe this made sense in some genius way that I didn't get, or maybe it was the punchline of a very long joke. I couldn't tell. "I admit it, you're witty," I said, and then the tension got to me, and I cracked up. I laughed myself silly. When I could talk again, I added, "But I still won't sleep with you."

Three fingers flicked off the idea of sex and applied the handkerchief to his nose again. "Milk sugar. Quite irritating to the nostrils." He put the handkerchief away. "Thank you for laughing. Life is quite unbearable, and I need my hourly dose of hilarity to bear it." He extracted a business card from his sleeve. "There is madness to my method and the opposite too. Please take this."

It was the business card of Holes and Poles, Jason's tattoo parlor in Denver. I had one on my refrigerator at home. (The place that used to be my home, I mean.) It was a very nice card, mauve and full of symbols and patterns laid out carefully, just like Jason's work. But the phone number was wrong. I remembered Jason's number because it has a pattern.

"Call that number whenever you need me. For Blair. Or for yourself, too."

"Why the hell do you care?" I asked politely.

"I care about Blair because he's a gentle, lonely soul. Oh, and also a True Immortal."

Just like that.

"Regarding yourself," he went on, "in the first place, someone important has decided to adopt you, so I'm on the job. Also, I've decided I like you on my own account."

"Who adopted me? And how did you follow me here?"

"Someone else followed you. They are nasty folks, but they have a much bigger organization. We followed them following you." He produced his handkerchief again and wiped the remaining cocaine, or milk sugar, from the coffee table. "I'll grant you, he's beautiful, isn't he? They're not all like that. Healthy, yes, symmetrical, okay-looking. But your Blair, he's on the movie-star scale. To be born that way and to stay the same forever … no wonder he's a bit blank. And, of course, you're in love with him. I'd be, too, if I were a little gayer than I am."

There was a knock on the door. I shoved Zeke's gun under the cushion of my chair and put mine back in my purse.

"Janice, are you in there?" Blair's voice.

I called out that I was coming and hurried to the door so it would be obvious that I didn't need to get my clothes back on. Blair was furious anyway. "We were doing some cocaine. Want to join?" I opened the door wider so he could see Zeke had his clothes on too.

Zeke stood up and bowed. Blair stayed mad and didn't bow back. "I'm leaving in five minutes," he said. "You can come with me or not."

I leaned on the hard line of the open door and watched him disappear into the elevator.

"Asshole," I hissed. I imagined myself running to the stairs at the end of the hall, making a beeline to the BMW, and sitting meekly in the passenger seat until Blair showed up. I said, "Fuck you, I'm not doing it," and closed the door. I sat in the sofa chair again and took the gun out from under the cushion.

"I'm impressed," Zeke said.

"That I pissed him off so much?"

"That you refrained from running after him."

"Don't be impressed. If I really cared, I couldn't hold out. My problem is I don't know how to care."

"Acts of courage are never entirely pure, yet they remain acts of courage."

"Whatever." I gave him back his gun.

He wiggled the fingers of one hand expressively and then pointed at me. "Immortals don't usually reveal themselves to mortals, you know. You have something."

"Nice boobs," I said.

"Those too. So where are you going?"

What the heck. "Santa Cruz."

He didn't fall off the sofa but looked like he would have, except he was too genuinely startled to manage something so theatrical. "Santa Cruz," he said. "Holy donuts. Why Santa Cruz?"

"Because he abandoned his old friend Saul there 100 years ago."

"My oh my," Zeke said. "Oh my my my. Talk about long-term planning. Saul the hafeem?"

"Yes, that one."

"Holy, sacred, consecrated, sterling bat shit. The most revered and blessed of bat shit. Talk about cogs within wheels within gears. So this is what it feels like to be a cog." He'd recovered enough to get theatrical again: he fell on his side and rolled up into a fetal position.

"What's wrong?"

"Nothing's wrong. I'm being a cog. The fact is, I'm sure everything's exactly right, considering who's running the machine. But it scares me. The other problem is that I know the hafeem named Saul who has a thing about Santa Cruz, but I didn't know he was Blair's old friend. He might not be happy about—" He touched his ear.

"You're responsible?" I asked.

"Indirectly," he said.

"Damn," I said and walked out.

It was 15 minutes, not five, but Blair was sitting on the bed in our room instead of gone like he'd threatened, and when I saw him there, I felt giddy and feminine as if he'd gotten down on his knees and asked me for my hand in marriage. But I didn't let him see it. "Let's go," I said.

WE ARRIVED IN Santa Cruz late afternoon the next day. Before finding a hotel, Blair insisted on driving around in search of the exact beach where he'd blown off Saul a century back. But the city had grown just a little bit enormously since then, and Blair couldn't find the right spot.

There's a cliff that runs along the ocean everywhere in Santa Cruz. In some places, it sticks fingers out into the water, dividing the sand into separate beaches. The cliff is 20 or 30 feet high, and to check out each beach, you have to peer down from the cliff's edge, which means parking the car and stopping. We parked at lots of beaches, but none of them was right. Blair remembered a certain rock, and though we saw a wazoo of rocks, he didn't see *that* one. And then it got dark.

I had never been to the ocean. It's a place you can't get cynical about, even though it's smelly. I wanted to hang out at one of those beaches, stare at the waves, and listen to them crash. But Blair was in a hurry.

We checked into a homey motel sprawled along the side of a hill. Down below was a beach-side amusement park with lights on and a roller coaster like a bright bird's nest. In the other direction, across the street and going up the hill, a bunch of giant Victorians made me want to walk over and look at them, but you couldn't see much in the dark. Blair was sweet. In the middle of the night, he woke me to say that he'd remembered something important. I told him to write it down, and I went back to sleep. When it was barely light, he woke me up and said, "Can I tell you what I remembered?"

"Sure," I grumbled.

"I remembered something Saul told me before I abandoned him. He said, 'Shall we go on a short walk to the lighthouse?' So the beach must be near a lighthouse."

I threw the motel-provided phonebook at him and tried to go back to sleep while he looked at the glossy pages to see if Santa Cruz still had an old lighthouse. It did. Only one, and it had been sitting in the same place since Blair's day. Forget about sleeping. We drove to the lighthouse and parked. The sun was getting ready to rise—I could tell because the stars had disappeared.

Piles of seals on an offshore rock barked like musical dogs. They were aggressive, too, knocking one other off the rock and into the water to swim with surfers who, in their slick black wetsuits, looked like seals themselves. A wind blew ocean smell on us, and flowers like colored asterisks hung down the cliff in strands. Fort Collins had been a dry, bare desert. I liked it here.

Santa Cruz is on the north end of a bay, and that messes with your expectations. You're looking south when you look out to sea. We parked as close as we could to the lighthouse and walked on a sidewalk that ran along the top of the cliff. Signs posted everywhere warned that we should stay on the sidewalk and not hop the barrier because the cliff was undercut and could give way. To make sure you got the idea, they showed an icon of the ground crumbling to rocks beneath the feet of a person heading toward a fatal fall. This image scared Blair retroactively because yesterday we'd gone up to the edge of a dozen similar cliffs and missed the signs. But then he forgot to be scared because his whole soul set itself on finding that beach with its rock. He wanted to make amends.

I could respect that.

We hiked at least three miles, first one way then another, and climbed down to maybe 30 beaches using wooden staircases or steps cut into the cliff. People in the 19th century had a very different idea of what a "short walk" was than people in my time, and my feet hurt. But every beach was beautiful in its particular way, the ocean crashing up on flat rocks or over round rocks or into caves, and I wasn't bored, just tired.

Blair wasn't bored either—he was a nervous wreck. He worried the cliff had tumbled down and buried the rock, or maybe the beaches had shifted after a storm, which happens all the time (according to another sign). Or, worst of all, maybe the city had taken away the rock to build a breakwater. He got so irritating and repetitive that I wanted to ditch him, which would have been poetic justice considering how near we were to where he'd ditched Saul. But then we saw it: a small beach with a huge flat-topped stone like a giant Pegasus had flown overhead and dropped a reddish hoof.

We stood at the top of the wooden staircase and stared down at the hoof. This wasn't one of the better staircases we'd seen. Its rotting gray two-by-fours sprouted rusty nails. Blair was afraid to walk down it because it might break, and he'd crash down like the guy in the icon on the signs. But I didn't think the county would leave up a staircase that was ready to break, so I went ahead. Anyway, I only have a regular short life, not a whole immortal one to lose.

I got halfway down when the stairs shifted side to side, and one step broke loose. I changed my mind about how well the county of Santa Cruz took care of its beaches. I grabbed a thick nylon rope hanging down the cliff next to the stairs. The rope turned out to be solid, probably put there by someone else who'd discovered the county's lousy beach-stair-repair program. I walked the rest of the way holding the rope. When I reached the bottom, Blair pulled the rope up the cliff and gave it the full examination of a professional chickenshit. He decided it was safe and went hand over hand down the cliff side, the showoff.

The beach felt tiny once you were there. The arms of the cliff that separated this one from the other beaches curled toward each other out in the water and almost met. Between the cliff arms, the water cut itself apart on two sharp black rocks. It was a private world of sand, a flat red rock and an orangeish-yellow cliff. Just me, a Greek god, and a rock that had my Greek god all freaked out.

He looked at the rock, and I looked at his butt, thinking: when that butt last sat down on that rock, my grandmother was two years old, just starting her little burp of a life.

A big wave split itself on the offshore rocks and moved toward us between the cliff arms. I wondered if we'd get wet, but the wave didn't reach us. I wanted to wade into the water, but Blair needed to talk.

"Saul had been taking me on a world tour. I'd just changed frames. We planned to travel together for a year. It was the fall of 1899, and we planned to celebrate the new century."

"And then, you'd settle down and make a new family to abandon? Never mind. Go on."

He looked sheepish, but he kept talking.

They started their tour in Europe, but Saul smelled a war coming and suggested they leave. Blair agreed; he wanted to see the Wild West anyway. They took a boat from Spain to avoid icebergs—had Saul smelled the Titanic too? On their journey west, they kept a dozen Pinkertons on guard. Saul didn't mess around with Blair's safety.

Blair looked forlorn as he came to the next part, and I had to force myself not to comfort him. To make amends, you need to feel the pain.

"Saul didn't leave me alone often," Blair said, "but one night, he had to go off to deal with someone who might be a hanger-on, and he asked me to stay put in the hotel's bar, which he'd filled with Pinkertons. They're like a private detective service."

"I know what the Pinkertons are," I said. "I read books. Where were you?"

"Laramie, Wyoming."

"Now that's a true cowboy town." It wasn't far from Fort Collins, Colorado, and I'd gone there for the rodeo cowboys a couple of times.

"Cowboys everywhere! But I got bored and looked for someone to talk to."

"For a woman to seduce."

"Not necessarily. Well, yes. A young woman walked into the bar, and I sat beside her. She let me flirt with her a little before she told me she was a Pinkerton, too, only not one of the ones Saul had hired. She was there on other business."

"A lady Pinkerton?"

"Yes. She said they hired girls—women—because they could snoop around in places the men couldn't."

"And that meant it would be unprofessional of her to take the flirting too far. Poor baby. But she was probably pretty butch."

"Butch?"

"Lesbian. The macho kind."

"She wasn't at all macho. She was very feminine and tiny. Asian, I think. Her English was strange, but she had a lot of presence. She was sure of herself. I tried to make conversation with her, and—"

"You tried to seduce her, of course."

"Yes, I tried. I'm usually rather good at it, but—"

"You're incredible at it. You're brilliant. You're amazing." I took his hand. "But it didn't work?"

He looked out toward the ocean, so much water heaving itself up and down. "She brushed me off like I was a five-year-old in love with his kindergarten teacher."

"Hah!" I said. "Hah." Some chick, all Pinkerton-tough and not taking Blair seriously. It was great. "Sorry. Look, she was a Pinkerton. She probably got kidnapped by Indians when she was young and then slit their throats and later fought Jesse James and recovered from the gunshot wounds. There's a bit of a cultural difference between that way of living and how you live. But I bet it made you mad. Did you have a big screaming fight with Saul when he came back and demand your independence?"

"I didn't scream. I kept it to myself. But it festered. Two weeks later, when Saul left me alone in a hotel bar in San Francisco to deal with another possible hanger-on, I boiled over. The same female Pinkerton showed up, and I told her I'd decided to strike out on my own. I said I needed to arrange transportation and didn't want Saul to know about it."

"That was pretty decisive."

"I tried to come off as decisive, but I wasn't, and if she'd discouraged me in the slightest, I'd have folded."

"But she encouraged you."

"What she did was flip a coin. It came up heads, and then she gave me a look of respect and said that for enough money, she'd arrange it."

"Did you eventually sleep with her?"

Blair huffed and puffed just like when I asked a nerdy bank teller friend of mine whether he was sleeping with his boss, a woman 10 years younger than he was, hot as they get and out of his league for every possible reason.

"No. No, no, no. And she wasn't a Pinkerton. I figured that out later. The Pinkertons didn't hire women back then, much less Asians. It was just a story she made up. But she was extremely authoritative. I trusted her and felt better about my plan when she approved it. We made our arrangements: a coach would drive up while I was having a picnic lunch with Saul on the beach." He pointed at the top of the cliff, where half a dozen cedars had grown in the shape of the wind.

"That's where it parked. When I saw it, I jumped down from the rock and said goodbye to Saul. It felt brave at the time."

He looked at me all vulnerable, like my opinion mattered. I was still holding one of his hands, and I took the other and faced him. "It *was* brave," I said.

"You think?"

"Yes. And also shitty and cowardly. But still brave."

"It was truly shitty. Saul had saved my life many times. He'd educated me, always helped me, and never forced me to do or not to do anything, only gave suggestions. But I cut him off like he meant nothing."

"Okay, you've convinced me that you were an ass. But it was still brave." That was about as long as I could play Supportive Girlfriend. "Was your tough girl waiting for you in the coach?"

"I never saw her again."

Now that was strange. Almost like she did it to hurt Saul.

I let go of Blair's hands.

He didn't move.

"Well, go and look," I said.

"He's probably never thought of me again."

"He's probably been back a thousand times looking to see if *you*'ve left a message for *him*."

Blair still didn't move, so I kicked him. That did it, thank God, and he crossed to the rock. I left him to his fun and wandered down toward the wet brown sand my toes had been aching to touch. A wave came in higher than I'd expected, up to my ankles, but I didn't scream, only checked behind to see how far the highest line of seaweed went up the beach. Ten feet short of the cliff, so we didn't have to worry about drowning if the tide came in.

But what about sneaker waves? I'd read about sneaker waves. They could zoom up and eat you.

I didn't see any sneaker waves, just gentle blue throbs, so I walked further out. The water was cold, and I liked the way the sand disappeared under my toes as each wave went back home. I walked out further till the water rolled in up to my knees and splashed my waist. Far out, a bright white sailboat passed from left to right. I'd also seen it from the sidewalk above, going the other way. Sailboat surveillance? That's what Blair would think. Probably just dealing with the wind.

A big wave came at me, and I turned and ran. I saw Blair crawling all over the red rock. The wave didn't catch me. I put my shoes back on and climbed another rock to better see the sailboat. Then a fat crab stuck out its claws, and I jumped down. The waves looked huge as they came, but they always shrank before they reached me.

Blair came over to me and said, "There's nothing here. No message."

He looked happy, which seemed strange at first. Then it made sense: sometimes you *want* to be rejected to get it over with.

"We might as well go," he said.

"Have you looked around the bottom? If whole beaches can move, the sand level can go up and down. Maybe you need to dig."

He wandered back dutifully, and I teased the crab with my foot. I got clipped but it didn't hurt too much.

And then Blair yelled for me to come.

He'd taken his shirt off and looked like an actor in an arty French beach movie. He'd carved away some of the sand at the bottom of the rock and was rubbing the wet, flat surface with his shirt and yelling his head off.

I squatted beside him. He showed me where the words "Eiffel," "Monet," and "Rimbaud" were carved in deep, blocky letters.

In a voice so murmury I had to bend down to hear, Blair said, "It was in December of 1899. We visited the Eiffel Tower. The next day, we saw an exhibition by Monet. On the street outside, a young woman was reading Rimbaud poems aloud."

"And you seduced her, so that's why you remember?"

He didn't answer, the tactful guy that he is.

I kneeled beside him, put my hand on his bare shoulder, and touched his neck with my fingers. He was trembling. He dug away more sand and wiped at the rock again. There were two letters and five numbers carved in the same blocky way.

"It's a phone number. They used to use letters for the first numbers of a phone number."

I didn't know that. It was a habit the phone company got over before I was born. I got out my cell phone to call the number, but Blair said I shouldn't. What if Saul had been captured and tortured, and a hanger-on kidnap party was hiding nearby, waiting for us to call? Saul had trained him to take precautions. He sounded pious.

We climbed up the hill and drove back to town. He didn't feel safe using our own phones to call, so we purchased a burner. Before he could come up with something new to worry about, I dialed and handed the phone over.

"Answering service," the voice said.

"I'm trying to reach someone named Saul," Blair said. I huddled close to hear.

"Do you have his last name, sir?" the voice said.

"I don't know his last name. Just Saul."

"Without his last name, sir, I won't be able to help you. Hold on. Pardon me. We do have a plain 'Saul' listed. Is that the one you want?"

Blair looked at me. I nodded. "Yes," he said.

A long pause. "He's not in now. Can I take a message?"

"Yes. Please let him know that I apologize."

Long fingernails clicked on computer keys. "What name shall I give?"

"Blair."

"And how can he get in touch with you?"

I took the phone from Blair and gave the lady one of my email addresses. Then we got off the phone and ditched.

I KEPT CHECKING my email, but there wasn't any message from Saul. Blair got depressed, but I said, "What do you expect, that he's been waiting by the phone since they used letters for numbers?"

I was starved, so we ate lunch at the restaurant next door, a bizarre place called the Saturn Café that served natural food and had tables whose surfaces were six-inch-deep transparent plastic cases filled with weird tableaux way past anything you'd dare try in Fort Collins. One showed dinosaurs wearing corporate flags, like cars at a racetrack, and competing to see who could slash up the most Bambis.

Fake blood everywhere. Someone was sitting there, though, and I only saw the scene while we waited for the butch hostess on rollerblades to take us to our table.

She placed us—without any prompting—at a Barbie-doll layout with a B&D theme: Barbies in chains, gagged and getting hot wax dripped on them. To get Blair babbling, I asked him how he planned to prove to Saul he was Blair and not a hanger-on.

I wished I hadn't asked. He started pouring out details. He told me about the advances of a maidservant in Port Mahon, a Spanish girl he fell in love with at first sight. I heard about his Russian adventure with Saul and the countess he fell in love with at first sight. Wonderful. He listed the names of his sixth to 15th wives. He filled me in on his 15th wife's birthmarks.

I felt erased. "No more wives, Blair, please."

He apologized. He described the appearance of the coach he'd escaped in and the breeds of the horses pulling it, the furnishings of their cabin in the ship that took them to America and an episode in 1871 when a man of 89 recognized Saul as his father. Over his plate of tofu chicken on barley noodles, he acted out the scene.

We checked my email again twice before we went to bed. No answer. We didn't have sex because Blair was still talking. He had to tell me all the things he'd done with Saul and what he'd done by himself but that Saul knew about. Wives popped up everywhere, and so many little Blair children you'd need a giant crayon box to fit them in. He talked and talked, and when he finally fell asleep, I sleepwalked wide awake to the bathroom.

I looked in the mirror and couldn't see Janice. Blair might be an empty suit, but I didn't exist. That wasn't a good line of thought for me. Too much more, and I'd start cutting on myself to remember I was real.

But I didn't cut on myself anymore. I decided to be brave and go to sleep.

GOING TO SLEEP is hard when you're not exhausted, drunk or on Ambien. You lie there, and nothing is good about it. No happy sigh of contentment. What you're supposed to do is let go and let God, but I don't believe in God. There was no one who loved me and who I could will my life to. Only emptiness.

BLAIR GOT UP early and took a dip in the ocean. I didn't wake till maybe nine. I opened my eyes and found Blair sitting in bed beside me. He smelled like seaweed but in a nice way.

Blair ordered breakfast in bed. He cut up the strawberries thin and fed them to me slice by slice. As if that weren't far enough over the top, he peeled grapes and popped them in my mouth. He told me I was beautiful and brushed my hair. He gave me a massage and was good at it.

It pissed me off. "You're just afraid Saul won't answer." I pushed him away, got out of bed and put on a white, short-sleeved dress shirt and red pants.

"I am?"

"Either that or you're having a manic episode. Yesterday you couldn't wait to check email; today, it's a massage and peeled grapes. Here's my plan: you keep yourself busy today doing something fun, like push-ups. We'll meet up back here again at five, which will make it a little more than 24 hours since we emailed him. If he still hasn't replied, you can freak out, but not before. Deal?"

He was touchingly childlike. Would I really not mind? He would love to go for a long walk by the beach. Not *that* beach. Other beaches. He loves the ocean. It's his role model because it goes on forever and ever.

There didn't seem to be much point in getting jealous of the ocean, so I got out of there.

I climbed the hill behind our hotel and admired all the Victorians up top. They had unbelievable paint jobs. I met a gay guy who owned one, and I told him his house was fantastic. He told me how to get to the library. I had to climb down a long staircase, but this one was in good shape. There was a river flowing through town, and I walked along it. I met a great blue heron standing on a rock, looking for a fish to stab with its beak. Getting beak-stabbed must suck. I threw a rock at the bird and made it fly away. I hate nature. Nature's all about eating things while they're still alive.

I left the river, walked through a Safeway parking lot, and said hello to a lady with four kids who looked frumpy and normal, except she had as many piercings as I did. I decided I liked Santa Cruz. It was another sunny day. I walked another 10 blocks and reached the library. On a bench outside, two lesbians held hands and touched tongues. I remarked to Toto that we weren't in Fort Collins anymore. (Youngsters, back in the old days, lesbians were shy in hick towns like Fort Collins.)

I wandered to the fiction section and found *Northanger Abbey*. I found three paperback copies, each one new and reissued with pretty covers, and also an old dusty hardback. Like I had promised Marcus, the screenwriter I'd met in the park in Salt Lake City and didn't have sex with, I chose that copy. I stuck myself in a hidden carrel, wrote my cell phone number on page 47 of the book, and put the book back on a gray metal cart where the sign said you were supposed to put books instead of re-shelving them yourself.

Still no email. I thought about calling Zeke, but I had a headache. I walked back outside and sat on a bench. I had a lot of email accounts to check, and I started by checking the ones I hadn't given to Saul's answering service. There were messages from some friends in Fort Collins wondering where I was. I wrote back a group email telling everyone I'd taken off with a guy, and though I loved them all, I wasn't ever coming back, and they should go to my house, have a party and take all my stuff. While I was doing that, a new email arrived with the subject line "old acquaintance." I took a big breath and clicked on it.

"If you are, in fact, the person you say you are, your communication is infinitely welcome."

I had no idea how to handle Saul. I knew I should call Zeke and ask for advice. Only, he'd given *me* the gun (even though I'd given it back), so I just handled it myself.

Dear Saul,

Thank you so much for replying. I am so, so sorry about what I did to you. What I did was more than ungrateful; it was criminally wrong. I would understand if you can't find it in your heart to forgive me. But your email suggests that maybe you can. The coach was a brown Brougham with purple trim, drawn by two dapple-gray Percherons and two brown Belgians. Seven days earlier, I flirted with a woman in a green dress, and you told me she was a prostitute. A year before that, approximately, I ordered a set of white leather shoes, and when they arrived, I promptly muddied them.

Saul must have been glued to his computer because the reply came back instantly. "It's really you?"

"Yes, it's me. Saul—or whatever you call yourself these days— I'm so profoundly sorry."

"No, you aren't. You're in trouble and need my help."

"Yes, I am in trouble, but I do feel sorry. And I don't deserve your help."

"Nonsense. Being who you are, you deserve everything."

My eyes teared up. When you and someone else love the same person, it's a kind of relationship.

"Don't get careless," Saul wrote. "Verify my identity. Here are some random facts: the HMS *Resolve*. The Polynesian with a tattoo of a palm tree on her left buttock. Those long brown leather shoes you thought so fashionably modern that it made the butler laugh."

I knew about the HMS *Resolve*, but Blair hadn't mentioned anything about a Polynesian woman or long shoes. Was this a test? Was I supposed to catch him in a mistake and correct him?

Probably not. If Saul said something wrong as a test, Blair might think Saul wasn't Saul. And anyway, memory is fallible. "I thought it was a guest who laughed at my shoes," I wrote, "but maybe it was the butler. I can't remember. I'm calling myself Blair again."

"I've given up calling myself anything other than Saul."

"That's not safe."

"These days, my caution has limits. But please, gather your thoughts and consider that I might not be Saul but rather a hanger-on who's captured Saul and tortured him for information. Ask me questions—the more obscure, the better."

Apparently, I'd been listening during all those hours when I didn't exist. "In our estate in Prussia," I asked, "what wine did I drink to intoxication, and how much of it?"

"It was a 1792 Madeira, the so-called Napoleonic vintage. Over two weeks of debauchery, you downed 100 bottles, and in the following month, proved you could renew your liver as well as your limbs. Where are you? In Santa Cruz?"

"Not far from the rock. How about you?"

"I've been away from Santa Cruz for almost 50 years, but I flew in last night in hopes the message from you was real. I'm not far either."

"I should tell you, Saul, there's a mortal woman with me. I've told her everything."

"That was foolish. Abandon her, and let's meet in a different city."

"I love her, Saul. Besides, she's helped me a great deal."

A long pause. "We'll address this subject later," he wrote at last. "Shall we meet at the rock in 30 minutes?"

I should have called Zeke, but I didn't.

It was idiotic to visit Saul without Blair. I knew that. But if Blair met Saul alone, I'd never see him again. Hence the insanely clever plan of impersonating Blair, which some part of my brain must have figured out on its own since I'd never given it a thought.

I didn't want to use a credit card, so I called a taxi instead of Uber and paid cash. There aren't a lot of taxis in Santa Cruz, and I got there later than I'd promised. The driver let me out a few blocks away. I ruined my nails chewing on them. I took out my cell phone to call Zeke, but I didn't call.

I still had it in my hand when I spotted a man in a professorial jacket standing at the top of the stairway. Mostly he was staring out to sea, but occasionally he looked right or left, and when his glance passed over me, he showed no interest. Obviously, I wasn't Blair. But he seemed the right age to be Saul, and I walked toward him. I came up alongside and said, "You must be Saul."

I'd gotten used to Blair's eyes, so innocent and open. But Saul's eyes weren't innocent. I had my gun, but I didn't dare reach for it. If he decided I would die, I would die.

"LET ME TALK to you before you kill me," I said.

"Hush." He took my purse and removed the cell phone and handgun. He put the gun in his pocket, took the battery out of the cell phone and put the phone in his pocket too. He handed back my purse. He took my arm in his arm as if we were friends, but his arm was hard, and he kept his free hand in his jacket pocket. We walked further along the cliff.

"Where is he?"

"He's out for a walk."

"Where?"

"He didn't say exactly. On the beach somewhere."

"Are you working with someone?"

"I'm not working. I'm dating. I'm in love with Blair. And I'm not a hanger-on. He told me about those. You should take a fresh look at that concept. Isn't it totally obvious by now that immortality is genetic? The only hangers-on you need to worry about are scientist types, and that's not me. I suppose some big government conspiracy might come after you. Or a really rich guy who has a secret laboratory. But then you'd have black helicopters swooping down, not some girl by herself."

Saul didn't say anything and kept walking me.

We crossed the street and came to a black Lexus parked in a grove of cedars. He led me to the passenger side, where the cedars completely hid us from view, and opened the front door. He pulled out a metal detector wand from under the dash and ran it over me. It found my belly button stud but nothing else. He opened the back door and gestured for me to get in.

"You have a gun in your pocket pointed at me, don't you?" I said.

He gave a slight bow.

"How fun," I said. "It's so deterministic. Takes away all my choice, just how I like things."

He smiled. It was quick but beautiful. I felt fantastically less scared.

It was one of those cars with a thick glass divider between the front and back. He closed the door from the outside, and the locks clicked down. He got into the front seat and took an unfamiliar electronic device from a slot in the dash. He studied it and said, "You're not transmitting anything. That's good." His voice came through a speaker.

"Blair's hopeless with technology," I said. "You're not. Is that because you're a hafeem?"

"I regularly hire professionals to teach me so that I can keep up. Where are you holding him?"

"I'm not holding him. Sometimes I do, with Scotch tape, but that's with his permission."

"Scotch tape?"

"A light form of B&D. Bondage and domination. My idea is that if he plays at surrender with me, maybe he'll learn something."

That made a dent. "He lets you do that?"

"He loves it. Also, he hates it."

He started the car and pulled out.

"Life messes us up," I continued. "I have a scar on my knee. You have gray hair. So we've both become used to getting hurt. And we know we're going to die. Probably closer to the surface for you than for me, but I've been through enough bad stuff that I'm precocious, and I feel it too. Mortality, hurting and being screwed up are all the same thing. Only Blair doesn't have the first two to help him face the last. Life can't mess up his body, and he doesn't have to die. So I think he needs some other way to see himself."

"You interest me," he said. "Where did you say he is now?"

"Going for a walk on the beach somewhere. He was afraid to check the email himself, afraid you wouldn't answer."

"Any idea which beach?"

"No. But I know when he's coming back. And I know where." I considered holding onto the hotel's name for leverage but decided I better not. "At the Surfside Hotel, in the Boardwalk area."

He asked me how I met Blair and laughed when I told him how Blair misinterpreted my chance comments and decided I must be an Immortal. When I got to the part about Menniss breaking in and how I'd held a gun on Menniss, but the hanger-on had managed to slice off Blair's ear anyway, he turned serious. He brightened at the part where Menniss left the house, and darkened again when I told him about finding Menniss tied up in the trunk.

"That bothers you," I said. "Why? Do you know who did it?"

"I have an idea. And, yes, it genuinely bothers me. Are you in love with Blair?"

"Most of the time. I don't know why. He's beautiful, of course. But I don't think I'd love him this much just because he's beautiful. Because he's so innocent? And so lonely? Even so, he's an asshole and shallow as hell. Maybe it's the challenge. I hope it's not just the challenge."

"I share some of those hopes and fears. There is, of course, the hypnotizing effect of the perfect. I've wondered whether it's only that. But I believe there's something quite precious in his soul … ineffable, perhaps, but real. Or something that might one day become real if he's taken care of properly."

"You mean you think you can make something of him? And since he lives forever, it's like you do too, in him."

Saul looked startled. Apparently, I'd told him something he didn't know. "Indeed. Yes, I believe you may have identified the crux of the matter."

I hoped I wasn't motivated by the same dynamic. All the pop psychology in the world says you shouldn't go into a relationship wanting to fix the guy. It was OK for Saul because he was like Blair's father, and it's fine when a parent wants to make something of their kid. But not a girlfriend with her boyfriend.

Still, if you put your imprint on an immortal and make him remember you, that imprint and that memory are forever. Pretty damn seductive. Also, to be honest, I enjoyed having so much power over him. Obviously.

Saul pulled over to the side of the road. We were on a suburban street somewhere, but the houses were beautiful—like Munchkin Land in the *Wizard of Oz*—and the street made a circle.

The door locks popped up.

"Why don't you come sit beside me?"

I got in next to him. "Trying to find you was my idea. I don't know enough to protect him, and he can't protect himself. He needs you."

Saul frequently glanced over at me as we drove.

"What are you looking at?" I knew it wasn't my looks; Saul was too chivalrous for that. I'm not into chivalry as a general rule, but he was enough older than me in appearance and so ridiculously old in years that I could deal.

"You bear a certain resemblance to many of Blair's wives," he said. Before I had a chance to get too pissed, he added, "There's a fundamental difference, however. Blair's wives were always pure and childlike. You're not. You're fierce. Now, now, don't bristle. It's entirely a compliment, my dear. I think he's lucky to have discovered you. I'm unsure as to whether you are quite so lucky to have fallen in love with him. I, too, love him—as if he were my child— yet I couldn't swear to my good fortune in the matter." He laughed gently. "Would you like anything to drink?"

I said I would, and he opened a compartment in the dash that turned out to be a cooler. He pulled out a bottle of iced tea cold enough to have condensation all over it. He had a towel handy, wiped the bottle down and unscrewed the top before handing it to me.

I knew I should tell him about Zeke, but I didn't want him to think badly of me, so I kept my mouth shut on that subject. Ditto for Marcus.

"Why did you pretend you were Blair?"

"I was improvising. I guess I had an idea that if he talked to you first, you'd convince him to dump me."

"I might have," he said. "But I would've been wrong."

That was so sweet I wanted to throw my arms around him and kiss him. But he was two thousand years old, or whatever, so it didn't seem right. Instead, I asked him for a tissue to wipe my eyes. He gave me some and pretended not to notice my tears.

"Still," I said, "it's a kind of enabling."

"What is?"

"Helping him leave all his wives."

I had to explain the Alcoholics Anonymous concept of enabling, but he picked up on it fast. "A valid point that I hadn't considered. You've opened my eyes to a veritable realm of potential errors."

"Don't nail yourself too hard. Overprotection is better than no protection."

"Perhaps," Saul said. "In any event, it occurs to me that one of the things excessive protection attempts to guard against is chance, and this may be its fundamental error."

He stopped talking, and we drove toward the center of town. I don't think he was aiming for anything in particular, just driving.

"You're still nailing yourself," I said. "I know it's fun, but you should quit."

That made him chuckle. "May I ask you something?"

"About what?"

"It's a philosophical question," he said.

"I'm brilliant at philosophical questions. What do you want to know?"

"What would you change about your life if you knew you'd live forever?"

My first thought was that I might be able to have Blair if I became immortal. But I kept that quiet and asked whether other people would live forever too.

"For the purpose of our discussion, let's say that everyone becomes immortal."

"What would be different about *my* life? Nothing, really. You should ask someone older. People my age don't believe they'll even get old, never mind die. Oh shit. *Shit!* Up there, up ahead, across the street on the left. The man in the brown coat walking on the sidewalk. It's Richard Menniss. The hanger-on, the one who cut off Blair's ear. The one we found in the trunk."

Calmly and without touching the brake, he said, "Duck."

I put my head down like I'd lost a shoe under the seat, which I had. Saul made a lazy left turn. We parked, and he told me I could sit up again.

A huge bougainvillea spilled down onto the sidewalk. Saul got out of the car and fiddled with the trunk. I watched through a side-view mirror as Menniss came around the bougainvillea, and Saul jumped him.

CHAPTER 4

THE HANGER-ON

Thou slept as I arrayed the first tier of brick and the second
Thou slumbered through the third tier and the fourth.
Only when I set mortar and brick upon the fifth
didst thou awaken to thy woe.
I paused in my labors and listened
to the noise of thy chain as thou shook it.
And then I resumed the trowel.
I laid the sixth tier of brick and then the seventh.
Into its place I compelled the final stone of the eighth.
Against the new mortar I now erect the old ramparts of bone.
And unto thee I say:
at last unliving, thou hast found peace.

EDGAR ALLEN POE
FROM *THE CASK OF AMONTILLADO*
(REWRITTEN KING JAMES STYLE)

He's not such a bad guy once you know him.

THE CHRONICLER

MENNISS

THE TARGET: FRANCINE Selis, Ph.D., professor of molecular biology.

By all appearances, the standard-issue, out-of-touch-with-her-feelings, never-married, 50ish female scientist. However, success in such matters depends on seeing the target as an individual rather than a type. To get to know her better, Menniss invaded her home.

She lived in a new house in an upscale Santa Cruz neighborhood. She kept the exterior light fixtures on her house plumbline vertical and polished to perfection, their brass brilliant and glass housings close to invisible. The lawn was trimmed perfectly from edge to edge and radiated a green so uniformly resplendent Menniss wondered if she dyed it. Only on her front door did the pattern of visual perfection break down: flyers, newspapers and phone books littered the front porch because she always entered the house through the garage.

At 6:30 each weekday morning, she drove her green Toyota Prius up the hill to the university, occupied herself all day in the molecular biology building and returned after dark. She stayed home most weekends to work on grant proposals. The only break in this ritual occurred on the occasional weekday night, when, after nine o'clock, and always after several false starts, she'd dash off to The Catalyst, a local bar.

She would hurry through the outer rooms and their crowds of young people (possibly including her students) and make her way to a classy stand-alone bar on the second floor, designed to attract an older clientele. Francine never sat at the room's half dozen small tables but rather at the gray-granite bar itself, usually at its furthest end. This position made her difficult to approach, and most nights, she talked to nobody but the gay bartender. Occasionally, men would take it upon themselves to sit beside her and attempt a conversation, but they never succeeded. She would respond with a charmingly shy smile and a few hesitant words, but after a few sentences, her vulnerability always evaporated. She began to speak more quickly and in a progressively more professional voice. Though she never became unfriendly, she would cease to be friendly; soon, she would pick up her purse and leave. Watching from a nearby table and drinking expensive scotch, Menniss observed several debacles of this type and recognized the pattern, if not how to break it.

After two weeks of close surveillance, Menniss felt he knew her habits well enough to proceed. When the little Prius disappeared down the street, he didn't follow her to The Catalyst but slid around the back of her house, deactivated the security system, picked the lock on her back door and walked in.

Her kitchen was impeccable, with granite countertops, windowed cherry-wood cabinets and hanging copper-bottom cookware. The refrigerator, gleaming stainless steel, matched the convection oven. But there were no photographs, lists or birthday cards on its door, and the granite counters were bare except for a stray issue of *Cell Biology*. He opened the dishwasher, pausing its cycle, and discovered that it contained a single glass tumbler, two coffee cups, two saucers, a plate, a saucepan and a fork. He closed the dishwasher and let it finish its job.

He studied her living room, with its white couch of raw silk, matching sofa chairs, dark-brown coffee table, white entertainment center, and an area rug patterned in brown and white rectangles on an otherwise bare hardwood floor. The art that hung from her walls was tastefully abstract, mostly linear in design and toned solely in brown and white like everything else. Along one wall, glass bookcases held 100s of Modern Library classics, but he found no evidence that she'd read any of her books, nor for that matter, that a human body had ever pressed itself onto the luxurious couch except maybe to test it at the store before she bought it.

Menniss wondered whether a bloodhound could find a starting point here or whether it would wander aimlessly, unable to sense a human presence. He certainly couldn't sense any.

Until he inspected her computer.

The small room off the main hallway was set up as an office, with filing cabinets, a shredder, a postal scale and a writing table, but it was dominated by a computer desk, a tremendous construction of sweeping glass curves bare except for a MacBook Pro sitting open with its screen alight. It had no password.

Menniss opened her email program. He scrolled past folders devoted to particular classes, publications, research projects and grants until he found one titled "Relationships." Under this heading, the only significant subfolder was named "Mike."

A glance at the five years of correspondence collected under this category showed Menniss his home invasion had succeeded. The folder was a sewer, a primordial stew. Exactly what he wanted.

Even so, it was hard to stomach.

HE COPIED HER hard drive and returned to his hotel room to read through the emails at his leisure.

> From M'Pecker@pugel.com
> Subject: A confession
>
> I love you to death, my dear Francine. I dream of marrying you. But I have a confession. After I left your house, I stopped by The Catalyst and picked up a beautiful young girl who looked a lot like you used to look before you got old. She wore black underwear that reminded me of that photo of you in a black bikini at age 21. You were a real babe, then. <sound of licking lips> I wish I could take that young, ripe Francine and nuzzle her smooth stomach. I want to rub my lips up the fuzz on the back of her neck. I want to take off her bikini top and kiss her nipples. But I can't because you're so old, so I did it all to Barbara instead.
>
> That's the girl I picked up.

You were still pretty OK in your 30s. But now you're last week's leftovers. Women fall apart at 40, don't they? It's sad. A man of 47, if he keeps in shape, he's still attractive. A woman of 47, like you, she's a crone. I love you dearly, Francine, but I'm a normal guy, so it's only natural that your stinking crone body makes me sick. Still, I put up with you because I love you.

Sincerely,

Mike

Disgusting as that was, her reply was worse.

From Fselis@UC.santacruz.edu
Subject: Oh, by the way

Mike, dearest. I can't do anything about being old, but I am so, so sorry if I have an odor. I bathe daily, but maybe I should bathe twice a day. Or use more deodorant.

And I do so much appreciate how much you put up with in me. If I didn't have you, I wouldn't have anyone. So please be patient with me, and keep teaching me.

I love you,

Francine

Menniss wanted to hear sarcasm in her responses, but after reading dozens of similar exchanges, he could tell she meant it. It never ceased to amaze him how you could get under someone's skin and get them to believe whatever you said. Especially given the nude photos they'd traded because, objectively speaking, it was Mike who'd gone to pot, not Francine. She was quite an attractive woman, and he was a disgusting slob—piggish eyes and pale, oily skin hanging down in rolls. Francine was a world-class scientist, while Mike was a handyman, and a small-time one at that. But he treated her terribly, and she took it because he had his finger on her weak spots.

Francine had kept up her horrific relationship with Mike for more than five years. Toward the end, she began to react to his insults, not as forcefully as he deserved, but at least she'd get a little annoyed and occasionally snappish. She wanted to break up but didn't know how. And then he made a big mistake: he finally allowed her to visit his apartment, something he had consistently refused.

Dr. Francine Selis had a nearly limitless appetite for emotional mistreatment, but she drew the line when it came to a messy home.

From Fselis@UC.santacruz.edu
Subject: You're a very sick man.

You're a very sick man, Mike. I had no idea how sick. You live in subhuman conditions. You have a pile of dishes three feet high in your sink, and it stinks. Haven't you ever heard of cleaning a toilet? Or around a toilet? There's urine on the base. Or sticking the toilet paper roll in the dispenser instead of leaving it on the back of the toilet? That's what the dispenser is for. That's why it's a roll of toilet paper.

Your apartment is objective evidence of your psychological problems. With a bipolar aunt and brother, I've had enough of mental illness in my life. I don't need more.

You need help. I'll help you get help if you ask. But I'm breaking up with you.

Sorry to have to say all this, and I hope it doesn't hurt too much.

Francine

Human nature. She needed a reason to hang her breakup on, and she found it in the toilet paper roll rather than in his emotional abuse.

That one home visit did the trick, and they never had sex again. But they continued to exchange emails. Sometimes they even went out to lunch. And Mike still treated her like shit.

Poor lady.

Menniss wanted to beat Mike with a bullwhip and drag Francine to a psychotherapist. But he'd already made too many mistakes. He sternly reminded himself that he'd come to exploit her, not help her.

HE WENT DOWN the list of his fuckups.

He said he'd notify the I-H the moment he found an Immortal, but instead, he'd kept his discovery to himself and written Blair a personal letter. Why? Because the idea of meeting an Immortal had made him idiotically worshipful; he'd thought Blair would *want* to talk to him. Sensibly, Blair took off like a bat out of hell, and if Menniss hadn't managed to tail him the ordinary way and then place GPS trackers on the car and in his coat when Blair stopped at that restaurant, he would have lost him long before he reached Fort Collins.

He'd screwed up again in the restaurant and let Blair escape. Then he went on that ridiculous car chase that could have ended with him in jail or dead. In Fort Collins, he was stupid enough to let that girl draw a gun on him. And he got caught with his pants down when whoever the fuck it was sandbagged him and stuck him in the trunk of a car.

Then, after Blair let him out of the trunk, he'd procrastinated another whole day before calling the I-H. His boss could have sliced him to shit.

Only he hadn't. He'd acted as if he trusted Menniss *more* after that. He'd let him hear his natural human voice rather than the usual electronically altered one. He even cracked jokes.

"That was a trifle foolish of you, Richard," he'd said. "Several trifles. A truffle of trifles. From the moment you found Blair, you needed protection. But, no matter, you did find a True Immortal, and you managed to salvage a piece of his tissue. You're the first. Heaps of Congratulations Upon You. Only—did you have to cut off his ear? Couldn't you have just scraped the inside of his cheek?"

"I was under stress."

"Stress? How could that be? I always find naked girls with big guns relaxing. But from now on, be more careful. Alexandros is not an innocent like Blair. I'm surprised he didn't take the ear away from you."

"He did, but I had previously torn off a small piece and kept it separate. Who's Alexandros?"

"Good thinking. That's why I hired you. He's the guy who put you to bed in a trunk. He doesn't like me."

"Doesn't like *you*? It's me he bushwhacked. What's to stop him from doing it again?"

"Because you have protection now and not from me. A *cordon sanitaire*."

"You're protecting me?"

"Well, yes, but you have a better protector too. Don't ask because I won't answer."

"What's to stop you from taking what's left of the ear from me, kicking me aside and doing all the rest yourself?"

"I like you. Anyway, it's against the rules."

"What rules?"

"There are always rules. All the leading roles in this drama must be played by … by people like you. I'm only the best supporting actor. Well, ready for your instructions? Here they are: go to Santa Cruz, California. At the university, you'll find a molecular biologist named Francine Selis. She believes humans possess a biological clock that sets the rate at which we get older. She calls it the aging clock and has been trying to find it for over a decade. If her theory is correct, and I think it is, then that remaining bit of Blair's ear will give her the information she needs. I've set up a safe laboratory where she can take her time to analyze the tissue and find the answer. Your job is to get her to trust you enough to go there voluntarily. It must be voluntary, though. No kidnapping."

"More rules?"

"Exactly."

"And how am I supposed to get her to go with me voluntarily?"

"In your inimitable way. I'd send someone else if I didn't think you could manage. But I have perfect pitch in such matters. You two are a match made in Heaven—well, in Purgatory. It'll be good for both of you in the end. Just don't overdo it in the beginning, okay?"

His *inimitable way*. What way was that?

The way of Mike. Find her weak spots and take control of her. Mistreat her until she falls in love.

Menniss told himself: you have the right skills.

Yes, but I hate to use them.

One last time and then never again.

RAIN POURED ON a bright green square of lawn illuminated by the light in Francine's kitchen. The green turned gray at 9 p.m. when the light switched off, and soon after, a white square of light appeared where the garage door had been.

An interval passed.

The garage door closed and the kitchen light turned on again. It was Francine's typical indecision.

Ten minutes later, the lights switched places once more, and the little Toyota Prius darted out of the driveway in a backward arc, reversed direction and raced up the street.

Menniss took a different route, drove much too fast and reached The Catalyst before her. He parked close to the entrance and waited. He watched her hurry past in black high heels, rain sluicing off her transparent raincoat. After waiting another minute, he followed.

The Catalyst was decorated greenhouse-style, with plants everywhere on yellow-tile mounts or wrought-iron stands. Wide windows separated the inner rooms, and the tables were made of white-enameled metal in a spiderweb pattern.

The place reminded him of the greenhouse where he'd captured Cowper. The formidable hafeem had been sitting at a table much like these, planting seedlings in small pots and brushing away spilled dirt through the holes in the tabletop. He'd been unprepared when Menniss entered with a small army.

But here, the tables were filled with young men and women, not kidnappers, and their chattering flirtation echoed off the skylights overhead and the surrounding walls. There was a live band, too, and Menniss worried about further damage to his age-damaged ears. He hurried through the crowd toward the stairway at the far end. Besides the decibels, he also wanted to escape all the young women whose artfully displayed sexuality caused him pain.

Menniss squeezed between two girls, accidentally rubbing against breasts in the process. The brief contact set off waves of erotic discomfort. He turned away from the crowd to let his arousal settle, but The Catalyst catered to local artists, and the pieces on display were allegorically sexual oils. Menniss found himself staring at a mountainside in the shape of a vagina. He turned around and bore forced witness to a profuse fountain of sexuality—acres of creamy skin, a torment of young breasts and an eye-compelling length of naked legs. All were beyond his reach.

The Richard Menniss of 40 years ago could have seduced any of these girls and would have spurned all but a few as beneath him.

Perhaps he would have deigned to go after that redhead at the bar, the one with shimmering hair pouring in streams down a bare shoulder. Menniss looked with irritation at her young admirers, especially an ostentatious fellow with a long ponytail, wearing a white tuxedo and bowler hat, the damn peacock. Menniss wanted to punch him.

In the old days, he would have had only to walk up to the bar, and the little boys would drift away. The red-haired girl would defend herself with banter, but after 10 minutes, 15 at the most, his intelligence, charm and aura of danger would bring about the inward melt. In the end, she would drag *him* to bed.

Perhaps he hadn't always been instantly successful, but he'd succeeded often. These days, he could perhaps get into the pants of the occasional half-psychotic chick with a father complex or the young experimenter up for something new, but they never forgot he was a failing old man starved for youth and that they were doing him a favor. It shamed him.

And his desires had turned bizarre. He wanted to consume these women as if they were ice cream, to lick their creamy skin, to devour them. He was becoming a leering old man.

To Menniss' horror, he felt drool descending his chin. He hastily wiped his face and made for the restroom. Alone, he stood before the mirror and carefully combed his surgically augmented and professionally dyed hair. He saw a few stray neck whiskers but nothing too bad. He checked his recently waxed chest, all the white fur pulled off. It would soon be time for another botox injection, but his face looked good at the moment. He took out his makeup kit and gave himself a touchup.

He adjusted his battered brown coat. At the last minute, he'd decided to stick with it instead of wearing a newer one. The old coat gave him a coarse and disreputable look that would play off nicely against his charm and intelligence, that is if the I-H's confidence wasn't misplaced and he actually could seduce Francine.

He'd used Mike's general method more than once, that combination of charm and cruelty many women inexplicably fell for. And he was more subtle and skillful than Mike. But this Mike guy was Francine's age while Menniss was 20 years her senior. What if she found him disgusting?

He checked to make sure his shoes were tied and his fly was zipped. To his horror, his fly was unzipped. He'd caught himself that way twice this month, the first signs of a doddering old man.

But that's why he was doing all this; he was looking for the cure.

MENNISS LEFT THE restroom and climbed the stairs to the small, quiet bar on the second floor. In one corner, a musician played soft jazz on a cello. The walls were made of a blond wood, ash perhaps, refined but not oppressive. Unlike the sophomoric theme pieces below, the original artwork up here reflected an adult's artistic sense, similar to Georgia O'Keefe's style but depicting scenes from Santa Cruz rather than the Southwest.

All but one of the room's small tables were occupied. Menniss glanced with envy at a professional man in his 40s sitting with a woman in her late 20s. She seemed sophisticated, perhaps a concert musician or ballet dancer. You could still get away with that in your 40s. The 40s were okay. The first big change happened when you reached 50. That's when the warranty wore out. And 60, well, forget about it.

As usual, Francine sat alone at the bar, nursing a glass of wine and talking with the bartender. He must have said something funny because she laughed. She lit up when she laughed. Her long, crimped blond hair gave her a wild look, and she looked good in her red silk blouse. Francine was quite sexy, and if she could only stop her unconscious desires from undermining her conscious ones, she could be in a relationship tomorrow. But she didn't have the self-awareness to work out the conflict, poor thing.

Menniss sat at the bar several stools over from Francine. The bartender asked if he wanted his usual, an 18-year-old Glenmorangie scotch, a sophisticated and expensive drink. Instead, Menniss ordered a 25-year-old Glenfarclas, impressing the bartender. Menniss took advantage of the shared moment to ask confidentially what the woman at the other end of the bar was drinking. It was an excellent cabernet. Francine glanced at the two of them talking, and Menniss raised his scotch to her. She responded with her wine glass, and they sipped together, 12 feet apart, his drink just as sophisticated as hers but more violent on the tongue.

Picking a moment when the jazz cellist was sawing away more rhythmically than not, he brought his drink over to Francine and asked if he could join her. "You have great taste in wine," he said. "The 1985 Mayacamas cabernet is remarkable. I'm Richard."

"Francine. I've taken classes in wine. A full summer session in enology at UC Davis."

That would certainly scare off the cruder men. "It doesn't surprise me," he said. "You have the intellectual look. What do you do for work, if you don't mind me asking?"

She eyed him over her glass, her mixed feelings obvious. She knew that the truth drove men away, and she didn't want to drive him away; however, she also wanted to hide and knew that giving an honest answer would accomplish that. "I'm a molecular biologist," she said. In her confusion of feelings, she partly swallowed the words.

"I've worked closely with biologists," he said.

"Really? What do you do?"

"I used to work for the CIA," he said. "What I did is classified, so I can't give any details, but, speaking generally, I can say that my work involved biological terrorism."

"Oh really? That's interesting."

"At times, although the most interesting experiences were the most terrifying. One time we ran into a set of people … I'll just say *terrible* people … who knew much too much about retroviruses."

She moved an inch closer. "What did they know? I have some expertise there."

She was making herself vulnerable and also giving herself an escape: she could always convert the interchange into a lecture. He wanted to let her feel safe but not too safe, a fine line. "Do you really?" he asked.

"I was awarded an NIH grant on the use of retroviruses in warfare."

"Were you?" Menniss had read the grant application and all the papers that had come out of it. "Then you might find this interesting." He looked around, leaned toward her, and in a quiet voice said, "We found a lab trying to make a retrovirus that spreads like measles and produces sterility in humans."

"Oh my goodness!" she said. "That might be the end of the species! But wouldn't it sterilize the terrorists too?"

"They weren't exactly terrorists. More like religious fanatics. They'd vaccinated themselves and their families. The idea was to kill off the infidels and repopulate the world with the pure."

"Oh my." Her eyes were gleaming. "What happened? That is, if you can tell me."

Menniss pretended to consider, then looked around again. He beckoned her to come close so she could hear his whispered reply. "One of my friends penetrated their lab. It was as much a safe house as a lab, and it was full of vaccinated fanatics. However, they'd booby-trapped the place with live virus, and while he was exploring, a needle popped out and stabbed him. So by the time he knew what was going on, he couldn't leave or he'd spread it." Menniss paused to let that sink in.

She was horrified and enthralled. "What did he do?"

"What he did was—because he couldn't think of any other option—was to call in an air strike on the lab with him hidden inside."

"Oh wow," she said. "How awful."

"I'd known him for years. And I was the one who had to send in the planes."

You see, Francine, I'm on intimate terms with violence. But it's virtuous violence in the service of a good cause. How will you resist? Of course, the story was made up.

She couldn't resist. Her hand darted out and touched his briefly. "That's terrible. So terrible." Her fingers were ice cold. "And what a noble act on your friend's part. But why didn't he just stay there and wait until he stopped being contagious?"

Good point. He thought quickly. "He knew they would find him soon if he didn't leave and was afraid they would let him go in the middle of some large city."

"Oooh," she said. "He really did have no choice." Then her voice made a right-angle turn and became cool and analytic. "But how did you avoid vectoring the virus when you dropped the bomb? That would have been a challenge. You must have given it quite a bit of thought."

This sudden arousal of her professional mind unnerved him. Menniss had to be careful. She probably had a 50 IQ-point advantage over him, and his imagination hadn't gone this far. "We did give it quite a bit of thought. As to how we solved it, unfortunately, that part's classified."

After he said this, his imagination caught up, showing him a fighter jet with incendiaries. Or a tactical nuke. He saw bombs drop from the wings and bloom below in a sterilizing nuclear fire. As a child, he'd lusted for nuclear war because he thought he'd make out well in the aftermath. He and his friend Lemon would hide in their treehouse and make plans to thrive in a post-nuclear world.

He'd allowed his mind to wander, an operational mistake. He brought himself back and discovered that Francine was lost in thought and hadn't noticed. She had one hand up in the air, and her fingers moved slightly as if she were working an invisible 10-key. Her eyes were unfocused.

She suddenly re-emerged. "What you used was a gamma ray bomb. Nothing so effectively breaks up viral structures as high-intensity gamma radiation. And the government has gamma weapons, even if they deny it."

Francine was right about that last part, as he just happened to know. She was too damn smart.

"I'm right," she said. "I can see it in your eyes."

It scared him. What else could she see?

Her tone shifted suddenly. "The government has lots of things it doesn't talk about. The Republican right-wing Christians have been planning a coup for years. And with gamma-ray weapons, they could do it."

He suppressed a smile. It was a strange fact of life that otherwise intelligent people fell for the stupidest conspiracy theories.

As he soon discovered, Francine had fallen in a really big way. He listened politely as she ran through a brainiac version of the paranoid canon, weaving Area 51, the Trilateral Commission and the Twin Towers into a right-wing Christian plot to abrogate the Constitution and establish a theocracy. She grew animated and brushed her fingers through her crimped blonde hair, making it even wilder. "As a biologist, you see, I'm on the frontlines of the battle. Christians don't pick on experts in quantum mechanics, just biologists—because of evolution. I get calls all the time to debate some idiotic creationist."

He found this slightly out-of-control Francine charming, and he egged her on. "Why do you think they make evolution the point of attack?"

She answered enthusiastically. "Because they hate the idea that we're descended from animals. They want a bright line between human and animal, just like they want to find an exact moment when the 'soul' enters the embryo. It's simplistic, black-and-white thinking. My family is full of virulent evangelicals who hate everything we biologists believe and do. But they're hypocritical. The moment we find a cure for a disease one of them has, like bipolar disease or diabetes, just you wait, they'll find a rationalization to make *that* particular kind of playing God okay."

Time to reel her back in. "Your mind cuts right through things," he said. "It's amazing."

Her posture softened; she let go of the conspiracy world and became personal again. "I don't exactly cut through." She was glow-ing. "It's more like I let go. I let the world come to me and let myself see it. I get my best ideas with my mind wide open."

Exactly the right moment to stick a pin in her heart. "What I didn't mention," Menniss said, "is that a dozen families were living in the safe house too." He let his voice falter and start again. "Sixty kids. No fault of theirs. The air strike killed them all. The air strike *I* called in."

He knew how to stab people in the heart. Like when he'd shown Blair that photo of his aging wife, on instinct, for no particular rea-son, sensing he should.

"How *terrible*," she said. "But you had to do it. I think that's noble."

Noble. It was the second time she'd used the word. Only, she's wrong: I'm an unmanly, vile creature. My father wanted a lion for a son. And what did I become? A snake.

"Don't idealize me too much," he said. "When you're in the CIA, you get so single-minded it turns you inhuman."

"You don't seem inhuman." Her voice was full of sweetness.

"I'm close to the edge."

"But you've stayed on this side. And, anyway, you got out." She drew out the words, filling them with warmth. "Scientists can go over the edge, too, you know. They become inhuman because they only care about their work. But I haven't gone over that edge, and you haven't either."

"There's a difference," Menniss said. "Scientists do what they do because they love it. In the CIA, we do what we hate because we love something else; hopefully, it's our country and not our personal triumphs. Either way, it's dangerous."

"What an interesting insight," she said. "You're an interesting man." She gave him a smile that reached down to her heart.

"You're pretty amazing yourself," he said, mimicking the smile.

But he wasn't entirely mimicking.

Reaching for safety, he came up with a non sequitur. "By the way, were you ever married?"

She stared down into her glass. She moved it in small circles, watching the wine swirl. "No, it never worked out. I never found a man I wanted to marry. How about you?"

"No one could ever find me. A spy's life is invisible. We're like secret pilgrims." Pretty romantic. Menniss hoped she hadn't read any John LeCarre since he was practically plagiarizing the guy. "Even when you're married, you're still invisible. The wife of the head of MI-5 lived her whole married life thinking her husband worked at a bank." More LeCarre. "To be seen and not to be seen makes loneliness worse."

"So you're lonely?" she asked.

"Beyond loneliness. I'm invisible even to myself. But lately, I've been on a mission to become visible."

"*I* can see you," she said. Her voice was melodic, harmonized, and so full of energy that he lost his balance again.

THEY TOOK SEPARATE cars to her house, and she drove into her garage while he parked on the street. When Francine opened the front door to let him inside, she noticed the flyers and phone books scattered over her porch and knelt to gather them up. He followed her to the trashcan and took her hand. She looked at the hand and then at his eyes. She smiled again, but this time, she was too nervous to show him even a sliver of her heart.

"The funny thing is," he said, "I was looking for a biologist just now. And I ran into you."

"That's hysterical," she said. "I've been looking for a good carpet repairman. Who goes around looking for a biologist?"

"Seriously. I came to Santa Cruz to find someone with a certain expertise. I was getting ready to go to the department and ask around when fate dropped you in my lap. It must have been meant to be."

"Meant by whom? God? There's no such thing as God."

"Serendipity, then."

But she wasn't listening; she was touching him. "I'm a scientist." She put her lips to his neck. "I don't believe in God. And I don't have any moral restraint about certain things."

They were inside and kissing passionately. "Oh, sweetheart," she said, unbuttoning his shirt. "Oh, baby." She spoke as if they'd known each other for years.

Did Francine even know she was going too fast? That she wasn't herself?

She felt breakable in his arms, and he began gently. But she didn't want gentle sex. She urged him to extreme intensity as if otherwise she couldn't feel at all. She was inexpert; she wiped wildly at his shoulder blades, like someone brushing away dust. She let go of him entirely and threw her arms above her head, letting go for dear life.

MENNISS AWOKE AT seven to the sound of the garage door opening and the little Prius driving out. She'd left him a cold omelet, toast, and a note inviting him to visit her lab that afternoon—a huge term of endearment coming from her. Things were going well.

After eating everything she'd set out, he drove home and ate a second breakfast. It had rained much of the night, but now the sun had come out. He took a shower, changed and went for a walk.

Tendrils of steam rose from flower gardens and the bark of redwood trees. On the Pacific Garden Mall, half-naked girls breathed out sex in much the same way, and Menniss averted his eyes. He fended off sales talk from a Rasta hawking marijuana pipes and admired the hand-eye coordination of three young men juggling sickles. His eyes wandered past an older couple shopping and came to a stop on a solitary male strolling ahead of them.

Vigilance has a smell. The man was dressed like a tourist but was no tourist.

Menniss slumped his shoulders and turned himself into an innocuous old man. Now that he was looking, he saw several others: a man with binoculars on a store's second floor, a woman on a side street, a loose group of young men too well-muscled for average college students.

The same people who'd thrown him in the trunk?

But they weren't interested in him. They were focused on someone ahead.

A small woman of indeterminate age strolled down the mall half a block on. She held herself as if she owned the earth. Probably, she was a visiting dignitary and these were Secret Service. But if Menniss could smell their vigilance, they could smell his. He didn't want any part of Secret Service drama. He turned himself into an old man inside as well as outside and forced his mind to turn sluggish. He turned down one side street, then another.

As far as he could tell, he'd escaped them.

But it was a bad omen. To stumble through someone else's surveillance field right at the start of your mission was the spy's equivalent of a black cat crossing your path. Call it superstition if you like.

Menniss lifted his head at the sound of helicopters and watched three rumble across the sky. Another bad omen.

He came to a spot where untrimmed bougainvillea grew over the edge of a rock wall and partially blocked the sidewalk. His automatically scanning eye looked up at the huge Victorian above the wall and noticed three security cameras facing the street.

He felt depressed and didn't know why.

Detouring into the street to get around the bougainvillea, he passed a middle-aged man bent over the trunk of a parked Lexus with its back door open. He recognized the woman in the passenger seat, but too late because a weight struck him in the back of the head, and he was falling. Someone turned him as he fell, and he landed face-first onto the back seat of a car instead of concrete. The lip of the car door bludgeoned his knees.

Strong hands shoved him inside. Conscious but dazed, he listened to the sound of handcuffs clicking, doors locking and the Lexus roaring to life.

MENNISS STRUGGLED AGAINST the throbbing dullness of his brain and forced himself to inventory his position.

He was slumped forward in the middle of the backseat of the Lexus. One pair of handcuffs closed his hands together; a second pair attached to a seatbelt key held his hands down and to the right. His feet were shackled to a metal bar that ran the length of the backseat. The bar anchored a thick sheet of Plexiglas that divided the back of the car from the front. The windows were tinted, and to anyone outside, he was no more than a passenger. He was entirely trapped.

First, the Volvo's trunk, now this. Menniss fought against a wild urge to yank against his cuffs and scream. He thought: what the hell are *those two* doing together? He couldn't hear them through the Plexiglas divider, but they seemed to be chatting comfortably, like old friends.

A speaker turned on, and the voice that came through seemed familiar, like when you're watching a movie, and you recognize an actor, but you can't figure out what movie you saw him in.

"You're sending a signal, sir," the voice said. "For whom do you work?"

He was speaking English instead of Russian; that was the difference. But the voice was distinctive, and suddenly he remembered. "Nikolai Semyvich," Menniss said. "How the hell do you know Miss Janice? There's too much stinking coincidence going on. And what do you mean that I'm transmitting?"

If being called by his former name startled the hafeem, he didn't let it show. "What do you know of Semyvich?"

"I followed him for years. That is, I followed you for years." Then he remembered he was talking to a hafeem and added, "sir." He took a breath before going on. "Back when you lived in Moscow. You almost got grabbed, too, not by me, but by the I-H himself. But at the last minute, he let you go. Or so he told me."

"Whom, may I ask, is this client of which you speak?"

Instinct and professional habit told him to give away as little as possible, but a deeper intuition advised him to speak without reservation. This man was not only a hafeem but one of the truly great hafeems. "I've never met my client in person, sir. He's only a voice on the phone. I call him the Immortal Hunter. The I-H, for short. He pays me to search for hafeems and True Immortals. My last *object of search* (he'd almost said "target") was a certain True Immortal whom I assume you know, seeing as you're with Miss Janice."

"Someone paid you to cut off Blair's ear?" This was Janice talking.

"What I was supposed to do was capture him and tell the I-H

I had him," Menniss said. "The ear thing is partly your fault. You figured out on the spot that immortality is genetic, and that gave me the idea. And with your shotgun there, I couldn't exactly kidnap him. So I settled for an ear. Anyway, it'll grow back."

"It already has. But that was gross."

"More to the point," the hafeem said, "it's uncivil to handle a True Immortal, or indeed, anyone else, in such a manner. Nonetheless, Janice tells me that Blair harbored no resentment after the fact, so I'll follow suit. May I add that I appreciate your candor? Now, with similar candor, please explain how you came to Santa Cruz. I share your impression that the number of coincidences strains credulity."

"Past straining credulity, sir. Someone's pulling strings." Menniss hesitated. He never gave away information about his missions, but he continued to sense that his only hope was to tell the whole truth. "I'm in Santa Cruz because the I-H sent me here. There's a biologist at the university who specializes in something called the 'aging clock.' I'm supposed to give her Blair's tissue so she can analyze it and figure out how to stop the clock. The idea is to make us all True Immortals. How that fits in with you being here, I have no idea."

Janice twisted around to face Menniss through the Plexiglas. It reminded him of a prison visitation. She wore a conventional blue top, had straight hair and wore no piercings. The last time he'd seen her, she was all skin, tattoos, metal and spiked hair, handling a shotgun like she'd used one before. Quite a girl.

At the moment, she was angry. "I treated you right, Menniss. Remember? I put those blankets on you. And I had Maurice let you out easy."

"I owe you."

"You do. So don't fuck with me. When I found you in the trunk, you told me someone took Blair's ear from you. So how will you get this chick to analyze Blair's tissue if you don't have it? Did you track us here to cut off Blair's other ear?"

"After I left your house, I tore off a sliver of the ear and stuck it in my pocket as an insurance policy. And the guys who put me in the trunk didn't find it."

He couldn't believe he was saying all this, giving away every-thing he had.

"Where's this sliver now?"

"In the freezer in my hotel room."

"Yuck."

"It's in an insulated lunchbox filled with ice."

"That's better. But where'd you get it?"

"Get what?"

"The lunchbox? You didn't know you were coming to snatch tis-sue, so you probably had to get it afterward."

"I bought it at the army surplus store in Fort Collins before I left town. They have red ones and blue ones. I got a blue one."

"I got a red one." She wasn't angry anymore. "Must be a girl-boy thing. So have you fucked her yet?"

"You're going too fast for me."

"Your female scientist buddy. You did, didn't you? Well, I'm glad you're *someone's* type."

The hafeem was working a handheld device with one hand while driving with the other. "It appears that you're transmitting on satel-lite phone frequency."

"Satellite frequency? Fucking shit. Excuse my French, sir. It's just that if it's satellite frequency, they can track me just about everywhere. Someone's been playing me. Someone's been playing all of us."

"We do indeed appear to have been tied together by some unknown power or powers. But I've been impolite. My current name is Saul Velis."

"Pleased to meet you, sir. I'm called Richard Menniss. Formerly of the CIA, now freelance."

"When we have a bit of leisure time," Saul said, "I'd very much like to hear more about your work. But first, we must deal with the problem of this transmitter."

"What problem?" Janice said. "Why can't we just dump him back on the sidewalk and leave him to play with his invisible friend?"

"Unfortunately, the moment we took him into this car, we forged a link with him, and we're therefore duty-bound to quarantine our-selves from Blair until we know more about his secret sharer."

"I knew I should have shot him." Janice turned away from Menniss and leaned her head against the passenger window.

"Don't be too hard on yourself, child. It's safer to know the nature of the threat we're dealing with than not to know, and the transmitter is the key."

"Shit," she said.

Saul looked at her with concern, then addressed Menniss: "I can make you invisible within the confines of the car—this vehicle can block radio transmissions—but the instant I invoke the blockade, you will, in an inverse way, become highly visible, as I'm sure you understand. So please take a moment to consider our best course of action. I'll do the same."

The hafeem was right; he was in a tricky situation. On the plus side, his pursuers' interest in him would have waned once they took his ear. At the very least, they'd stop monitoring him minute by minute.

But he couldn't take Francine to the I-H's safehouse with that signal pouring out. He had to get clean. How?

Lemon, obviously.

He'd have to stay in the car with transmission blocked the whole time Lemon did his thing. But the moment the hafeem blocked transmission, alarms would go off. They'd find Francine, see what she did for a living, and kidnap her themselves.

"Let's go to a parking garage," Menniss said. "A parking garage under a hotel. Because that'll block the signal itself but in an innocent way. Whatever backbencher they have on the job will check the location and go back to eating his donuts."

"I have arrived at the same conclusion," Saul said. "And I've already chosen the hotel. We're here, in fact."

"A Hilton?" Janice said. "My, you're getting the posh treatment, Menniss. I hear they have high-class garages."

Saul glided down several turns to the bottom, parked in a remote corner and worked with his device while Janice bitched quietly to herself. Menniss looked glumly at the concrete walls all around and felt the acres of concrete above. He was safe and hidden down here. That dark mood washed over him again, the one that had troubled him before. He didn't know where it came from and didn't want to know.

"There, it's done," Saul said. "Provided you stay inside the Lexus, you won't transmit any signal whatsoever. Or so my security consultants have assured me. No doubt you understand current science better than I do. Does this seem plausible?"

"Definitely," Menniss said. His concerns were several steps down the road. "So far as electricity's concerned, your car's a sphere. Radio signals can't get out of charged spheres if they're charged correctly. I'm stuck in this car, that's for damn sure."

"I'm not," Janice said. "I promised Blair I'd see him at five. I'm going now." She had her shoulder pressed against the door, her hand on the handle.

"Hold on," Menniss said. "See that security camera up there? Do you want to be their last link to me after I disappear?"

"Hell," Janice said. "Well, let's go somewhere that doesn't have a camera."

"That we shall," Saul said.

He opened the glove compartment and took out white leather gloves, which he carefully pulled on, adjusting each finger. He started the car and drove out of the garage.

They traveled in a meandering way through the city, generally drifting northward. When they came to redwood forest, Saul drove for some time along its fringes, flirting with the canopy. With no warning, he made a sudden sharp turn and dove in.

THEY DROVE DEEP into the forest along fire roads that grew narrower as they went. The canopy grew so dense it could have been twilight rather than late morning.

Looking out on the dim world of living columns, Menniss felt claustrophobic from both the car and the trees. And his neck was getting sore from having his hands pulled across his lap onto his right thigh.

"As an aside," Saul began, "and to pass the time, may I ask you both a question?"

"What's that?" Janice said.

"I wonder whether you believe it's truly possible to attain immortality using Blair's ear."

"Sure, why not?" she said. "You can analyze genes these days. And you can stick new genes in people too."

"So I've been told," Saul said. "And yet I find the proposition exceedingly far-fetched."

"Well, maybe you're wrong." Janice stared out the window, the smooth white skin on the back of her neck flushing red.

"I'm wrong often enough," Saul admitted. "May I ask another question? If it's possible to artificially acquire the traits of a True Immortal, would you consider that to be a good thing or a bad thing?"

"Ask *him*."

Saul gave her a lingering look of concern. "Mr. Menniss? Your opinion?"

"My opinion? Whether it's good or bad? The question doesn't make sense. If someone's thirsty, is it good or bad for them to drink? Right and wrong don't enter into it. If they're thirsty enough and they find water, they'll drink. And immortality is all thirsts rolled into one."

"A marvelous answer," Saul said. "And here's a marvelous spot to stop. Notice how the trees up ahead lean in together? They'll hide us from the prying eyes of satellites while leaving a large clear space underneath. We can park in the center and avoid injuring their roots. For all their height and girth, redwoods possess exceedingly vulnerable roots, or so I'm told."

He peeled off his gloves, placed them in the glove compartment and opened a notebook. "Allow me to write down what you just said. 'All thirsts rolled into one.' Very, very nice. Give me a moment … there." He put the notebook away. "And now I'll take the detector I have here and come around back to sit beside you." To Janice, he said, "This will only take a few minutes."

The detector was a flat white device with buttons and two screens. "May I examine your clothes?" Saul asked Menniss.

"If you want, but it's not in my clothes. Too unreliable. Someone sank a chip in me, I promise you that."

Saul came around back and opened the door, letting in the tangy odor of redwoods. He removed the leg cuffs so Menniss could adjust his position.

"If you would be so kind to bend to the right?" Saul said. "And now to the left? Yes, exactly so. Thank you."

Saul persisted in what Menniss regarded as a remarkably respectful examination while Janice fidgeted and muttered to herself.

After several minutes, Saul said, "I'm amazed. I believe the device is located some distance beneath the skin of your abdomen."

"Like I said. A subcutaneous chip. I've stuck them in people myself."

"Without their knowledge?"

"You bump their shoulder as you walk by, and at the same time, you pop them with an air gun that shoots in the chip. They think it's only an insect bite."

Janice turned around in her seat and faced them. She was smiling. "You know, it's all a little ironic. Because a few days ago, Blair got the idea someone had stuck a tracker in his body or mine, and he made us get whole-body scans. I thought he was being paranoid, but obviously he was not. Hey, I have an idea. Maybe guys like you should get yourself scanned after each mission, the way the rest of us get HIV tests between relationships?" Having said this, she burst into nervous giggles.

Menniss couldn't help chuckling a little himself.

Saul looked on blankly.

Menniss sobered and said, "If you have a knife, we can try digging around for it. Only, they're hard to find. I suppose you could kill me, scoop out enough flesh, so you know you got it, and then dump the rest of me here. But if for some reason, you want to put yourself through an incredible amount of trouble and unpleasantness, I know a doctor up in Oakland who can take the damn thing out, and he won't ask questions."

Saul sat placidly with his hands on his lap. "Neither your first suggestion, that of digging, nor your second, that of killing you and, as you say, 'scooping,' merit consideration."

"Why not?" Janice said. "Except that they're messy."

"I must live with myself, my dear, and for a very long time. I've made a habit of avoiding actions that would weigh on my conscience."

"Oh, come off it, I was just kidding." She turned away.

Saul looked at her with concern before speaking to Menniss again. "Could you tell me more about this doctor in Oakland?"

"Hell, I'm not going to Oakland." Janice opened her door and jumped out. She came around by the open rear door, though not too close. "Byes-bye. You guys have fun. I'm going to meet Blair like I promised."

"Janice, calm yourself," Saul said. "We're a very, *very* long way from town. Far too great a distance to walk."

"So? I'll hitchhike." She bounced up and down in place, a bundle of nervous energy. She stuck a knuckle in her mouth and chewed on it. "So how do I get to the road?"

"This isn't the wisest of decisions," Saul said. "You should stay."

She backed away from the car. "Indeed, kind sir," she said, "I doubt not that were I to travel with you, some other misadventure would befall me. You'd make sure of that. Because you're jealous, and you don't want me to see Blair again before you do, and that's why you didn't let me out anywhere in town though there are lots of places you could. If you're half the gentleman you pretend to be, let me go."

Menniss was shocked that Janice dared talk to him like that. He was a hafeem, a truly great hafeem.

But Saul only looked unhappy. "Surely you don't believe I'm intentionally keeping you from Blair? Mr. Menniss, do you think she puts Blair at risk?"

"No, probably not," Menniss said. "There were video cameras where you folks were so kind as to pick me up, and I'm sure they caught a picture of you. But, given the angle, they wouldn't have caught a clear image of her inside the car. Not in the parking garage either. I think she's clear."

"Well?" Janice said.

With obvious reluctance, Saul repeated what Menniss had said.

"So it's fine, then," Janice said. "Look, if you're worried about losing your link to Blair, you shouldn't. I told you where he's staying.

I'll give you my cell number, and you can always email me. I *want* you
to connect with him, remember? Finding you was *my* idea."

"I'm worried about you as well," Saul said.

Menniss longed to escape. But even minus the leg cuffs, he
couldn't. He was tied from within by this tracker.

She stepped away as Saul moved to the front seat. He pulled yet
another object out of a slot in the dashboard and pushed buttons on
it. "The highway is 2.7 miles north-northeast. You can follow that
dirt road ahead, which veers off to the left; it'll take you directly there.
We're going to the right to avoid the main highway."

"Good plan," she said. Then her face fell. "You took my gun.
And my cell phone. I need them back." She came closer. She looked
more childlike now, dependent.

"I'd forgotten," Saul said." He took the cell phone out of a
pocket, noticed it was missing its battery, and reassembled it. The
pistol appeared as well.

Janice took them and put the gun and the phone in her purse.
"When you've solved your asshole-in-the-backseat problem, phone
me. Bye-bye."

She began walking but turned around and called out a phone
number. "You got that?"

Saul took out his notebook and repeated it back to her.

"Good."

"But will you be safe on the road?"

"I have my gun."

"Have you noticed it's starting to rain?"

She looked up. "Don't be such a mother hen."

Janice returned, gave him a quick kiss on the cheek and cut
through the swept-clean spaces beneath the trees and onto the road.
She dwindled to an intermittent flash of color, then disappeared.

Menniss said, "I'm surprised you let her go."

Saul had returned to sit beside him in the back seat. "I didn't want
her to go—indeed, I very much did not. But I feel I must not attempt
to contact Blair until I know who's tracking you without your knowledge. And, in any case, I had no right to compel her to do anything. I
do not, except in moments of extreme need, grant myself that right."

Menniss shook his shackled wrists. "Quite the setup you have back here."

"You shame me." Saul searched through his pockets for the keys to the handcuffs, not systematically but in a hurry, checking the same pocket more than once. "One may justify any decision by claiming extreme need." He found the keys, came around back again and unlocked Menniss' hands. "I don't intend to abuse the justification, but no doubt I will at times delude myself. Don't we all? I apologize for confining you to the back seat of my car."

Menniss wondered whether he could physically take the hafeem. Perhaps he could. And how much better it would be to approach Dr. Lemon alone and unencumbered. But the thought of attacking so great a man as Saul filled Menniss with superstitious dread. The gods, if there were gods, would punish him for it. Not only that, he probably *couldn't* take Saul.

Menniss sighed, stretched out his legs and rubbed his wrists. "I don't understand why either of you gives a damn about that narcissistic bastard."

"Narcissistic, yes, but there's a spiritual analog to his physical perfection. He's the loneliest and most innocent soul I've ever met, and I would happily die for him. Or perhaps, as young Janice privately suggested to me, it is only the lure of the infinite. Something to eat or drink before we discuss your physician?"

"What I need most right now is a urinal."

"I don't have one. Couldn't you relieve yourself while remaining within the car? Or would that provide a means of escape for the electrical forces involved?"

"It might. Do you have a different set of license plates to put on?"

"I do, indeed."

"Why don't you switch them over? Then we drive to the nearest pharmacy for a urinal. I'll be able to focus better once I've taken a piss."

IT WAS RAINING harder now. Even under the canopy, water had begun to drip along the trunks of the trees and fall from the overhanging needles. They drove out of the trees into a dense downpour.

Saul parked in a remote corner of a Walmart, put on a plastic pon-
cho, set off at a trot and returned almost at once, not with a single
urinal but with half a dozen. He handed them through the back
window to Menniss, then walked off to a discreet distance. Menniss
found this touch of courtesy strangely moving, as he did of Saul's
effort to smooth over the next embarrassing moment.

"It has been said," Saul said, as he took firm hold of the full
urinal, "that all pleasures are constructed in the same way: they
are preceded by distress and followed by relief. Let us postulate
for the moment that you achieve immortality by means of Blair's
tissue. I wonder if this accomplishment would follow the same pattern, although more subtly. The antecedent would be a long-built-up
loathing toward death and aging. Pardon me a moment."

Saul disposed of the urinal's contents beside a tree and then
dropped the urinal in a trashcan. He came back and continued.
"And, if this analogy holds, once immortality is achieved, it will provide great satisfaction for a time, but that state will prove no more
enduring than the pleasure you experienced some minutes ago. One
that by now has almost entirely subsided."

Menniss felt a rush of gratitude. By making it a philosophical
subject, Saul had removed any humiliation. Saul's thoughtfulness
filled a need Menniss didn't even know he had. Or had forgotten.
He thought of his Sensei.

"Immortality might work like you say," Menniss said. "I don't
know. But we still eat even if we wind up being full. So do you want
to hear about Doctor Lemon now?"

"Please. And in the interest of time, I'll drive toward Oakland
while I listen."

"Maybe you should hear the story first and see if you still want
to go ahead with the idea."

"No need," Saul said. "None whatsoever." He put on his driving
gloves and started the car.

"Well then," Menniss said, and as Saul drove, he gave a brief
account of his history with Lemon.

They'd grown up together in Los Angeles, each of them an
only child. Lemon's father was doctor to the stars and probably gay,

while Menniss' father was third generation buzzcut—Marine, Army, Marine. But their mothers met somewhere and liked each other, and despite the huge difference in their fathers, the boys became inseparable friends.

They attended the same schools from second grade through college. On graduation, Menniss signed up for Army Special Forces, and Lemon attended medical school, but they kept in touch. When, finally disillusioned, Menniss quit Special Forces and transferred to the CIA, Lemon decided to join too, signing up to supervise interrogations.

"We made a good team. Back then, there were strict rules about what you could and couldn't do, and they'd have a doctor on the job to ensure you didn't push the envelope. I would push, and he'd pretend not to notice. But in the 70s, the rules changed, and now you were *supposed* to torture subjects because they tortured our guys. After a year of that, we both discovered we had morals. We quit."

"An honorable decision," Saul said. "And a long association. I understand why you trust this man."

"I trust him some. He's his own guy. After the CIA, I went freelance, and Lemon made another stab at regular medicine. It didn't work out. He got bored and found his way into what he calls 'occupational medicine for those in interesting occupations.' Mostly he pulls bullets out of people who can't show up at a regular hospital, sets their bones or gives them transfusions. Bread-and-butter criminal stuff. Oh, also making new faces and scraping off fingerprints, and, lately, doing things to fool retinal scans. But what he likes most are his sidelines. He can implant a device that automatically releases antitoxins if you're stabbed with a ricin-tipped umbrella or someone throws an asp in your bed. But here's his real tour de force: he installs internal Kevlar shields to protect vital organs."

"How marvelous! Can it really be done? Is it effective?"

"It works, but it's uncomfortable," Menniss said. "I wore one over my spleen for a while, but I'm a stomach sleeper, so I had to take it out."

"Clearly, he's our man," Saul said. "But you spoke of a certain unpleasantnesses involved if we sought his services?"

The rain had stopped, and they were making good time up the freeway. "It's the particulars of the situation I'm worried about. Lemon has lots of enemies. Hezbollah, for example. They think he implanted a poisoned Kevlar shield over the chest of their chief bomb-maker. Lemon would never do anything like that—he takes the Hippocratic Oath seriously—but the Mossad keeps spreading the rumor so it doesn't come out that *they're* the ones who poisoned the guy. So, naturally, Lemon has to be a cautious man. Now think about it from his point of view. I show up stuck in the backseat of a car belonging to someone he doesn't know, and I tell him I can't leave the car until the bug in my stomach is removed. Which means he has to get inside the car. To him, it'll sound like a perfect setup. What if you're a Hezbollah agent, and you've threatened to torture me to death if I don't help you kill Lemon?"

"Surely, having been childhood friends, you wouldn't agree to such a deception?"

"We've had our fallings-out. The fact is, I can think of several ways he could safely handle the situation, but none of them are going to be pleasurable for you."

"Food for thought, certainly," Saul said. "Allow me a moment or two, if you would."

Menniss, too, considered; he speculated on what it would be like to live in the backseat of a Lexus forever. It wasn't the worst prison cell in the world. The seats were luxurious. He could use the ledge under the back window as a kitchen table and a writing desk. Pretty comfortable.

Only, what would he do with himself? Get drunk every day?

Maybe Saul would agree to throw in the occasional badger or ocelot and watch them wrestle to the death. A picture of life: at the end, you realize you've been a captive lion hunting the game God throws in your cage.

Menniss wanted to jump out of the car and take his chances with whoever was tracking him. Only, they were still on the freeway. Maybe he could handle a badger, but semis were out of his league. SUVs, too. (And also badgers.)

"I would survive the experience?" Saul asked.

It took Menniss a moment to remember what they'd been talking about. "So long as you don't make any fast moves. But you'll hate it."

Saul nodded but said nothing. He pulled off the freeway and drove through Oakland. They reached the central BART terminal, and Saul found a place to park.

"I'm going for a stroll," Saul said. "You may hop a train if you're so inclined. Trains leave in four directions, and I could never find you. Alternatively, you could steal my car. I have no way to monitor it remotely."

"What the hell are you doing this for?" Menniss said. "Do you *want* me to run off?"

"Not at all. As I said earlier, I'm deeply concerned that persons unknown have been monitoring you. We must remove this chip from your body, which, perhaps, will allow us to identify them. To do this, I must submit to the jurisdiction of your childhood friend. I'm an ordinary creature in that I greatly prefer not to be kidnapped or killed. But if you choose to remain with me, I'll assume our separate motivations converge for the time being. That, to me, is sufficient security."

With that, Saul unlocked the car doors and started up the street. Menniss noted with admiration that the hafeem moved as if he were going for a pleasant afternoon stroll. His arms moved freely, he almost sauntered, and when he paused momentarily (to contemplate a street performer imitating a statue), he seemed the image of happiness.

Menniss gazed longingly toward the sidewalk. He hated this rectangular prison of a back seat. But if he left the car's radio blockade, he'd appear on someone's map, and he hated that idea more.

The transmitter in his body would need at least a few seconds—probably more—to link up with a satellite. If he jumped out the back and quickly got in the front, he probably wouldn't appear. This was what he'd wanted before: to get rid of Saul and go on his own. And the keys were left on the front seat.

What if the hafeem was lying, and he actually could track the car from a distance? Or shut it off.

But he knew Saul wasn't lying. He knew he could trust Saul. And he was glad of it. He felt more than a bit outclassed and appreciated having a powerful hafeem on his side.

As he'd already observed, the backseat of a Lexus wasn't the worst prison cell in the world. He massaged his knees and worked out their stiffness by stretching. He stretched his back, as well. He did push-ups of a sort and crunches. He watched the street performer.

A quarter of an hour later, Saul returned with a large vegetarian pizza.

They sat facing each other, each leaning against a door, and shared the pizza. "Do you have a guess as to who's tracking me?" Menniss asked.

"I have more than one."

"Which one are you most worried about?"

"Most?" Saul said. "I'm not sure how to rank them. Perhaps the most likely possibility is that you're being followed by the associates of an utterly good man."

"A good man?" Menniss was confused. The words had been reassuring, but not the tone. "Well, that would be all right, wouldn't it?"

"Not at all. He's terribly dangerous."

"Why?"

"Because he believes he knows what it is to do good. I fear him greatly."

"My contact, the I-H, said someone named Alexandros took the ear and put me in the trunk."

Saul sat up straighter. "That's the same man. Our suspicions align. But I would like to know for sure."

They finished eating in silence. Saul cleaned up and said, "Let's go forward, then."

SAUL HANDED MENNISS back his phone, and Menniss sent Lemon an encrypted email. As he'd expected, Lemon didn't jump at the opportunity.

"You owe me for that last thing," Menniss wrote.

"I owe you some," Lemon replied. "But not enough for this. What if they're holding you at gunpoint?"

"Oh, get over yourself," Menniss wrote. "Send in guys you wouldn't mind losing, and don't show up in person until you're satisfied. Come on. Are you a pro or not?"

He'd used this method on Lemon since childhood, and it nearly always worked.

"I suppose it might do," Lemon wrote.

Menniss could hear Lemon's tone of voice in the reply—nonchalant, the way he became when he wanted to prove he was as tough as Menniss.

"Get yourself to Marin County. I'll text you then."

Saul held the wheel lightly in his gloved hands. They drove to San Rafael and waited there until the sun went down. Saul brought Menniss coffee and then another meal. They chatted in a comradely fashion for many hours. Saul admitted that, just as older mortals have trouble keeping up with new tech and current slang, aging hafeems tend to live a century or two in the past. Saul had numerous gaps in his knowledge of the current day that he was happy to fill. In turn, he spoke to Menniss about the typical lives of hafeems and True Immortals and the character differences between them; he postponed speaking of Alexandros. Menniss appreciated all the information, but he continued to struggle with the inexplicable dark mood that had been bothering him for days.

Lemon's text came at seven in the evening. It was a summons to a specific address in Fairfax, a small town on the rugged edge of Marin County. Following Lemon's directions, they drove up the heavily wooded north slope of Mt. Tamalpais, along streets lined with garages dug into the hillside like hobbit holes. Saul commented that the ground must have shifted over time because, in places, the brick walls of the garages tilted from vertical. Menniss said the area was prone to mudslides and earthquakes. Saul noted that some True Immortals regarded earthquakes as a type of god, as they did other powers too great for them to counter.

The address Lemon had given them was written in fading letters over a garage built into the hillside. Saul nudged his car up to it, and the door opened of its own accord. "This is not going to be pleasant," Menniss repeated.

"So you've said, my friend," Saul said. "I must say, I'm convinced."

He drove on. The air was dead and musty inside, stifled by the pressure of the hillside above. Though narrow, the garage was deep enough to allow two cars to park one after the other. Saul drove up to an orange traffic cone set on the floor halfway in and turned off the ignition.

The door closed behind them. Brilliant overhead lights switched on. Video cameras on the walls swiveled to examine them. The lights and the cameras, Menniss noticed, were newly installed, showing the fresh circular scrape marks of electric screwdrivers.

A door at the far end opened, and 10 young men marched in, each carrying a gun. Despite having been chosen for what was potentially a suicide mission, they seemed greatly pleased with themselves. Menniss reflected that he had been like that too when he was young: most alive when throwing his life away. How strange.

Lemon was a doctor first and only incidentally a master of criminal operations. The gunmen positioned themselves inexpertly around the garage and held their guns in a manner that only resembled proper readiness.

The door at the far wall opened again, and a young man entered who looked like he'd been squeezed ear to ear in a vice. Everything pointed forward—nose, thick lips, even the space between his eyebrows. His face was deep red; getting squeezed by a vice would do that too, Menniss supposed. Many people had pointy faces, but this was extreme, verging on the horrible. He looked like an axe blade.

Listing slightly to the left, axe-face shuffled toward the driver's side and motioned for Saul to open the window. He spoke in a voice like someone talking in his sleep, and though Menniss had opened his own window and could also hear the sound transmitted through the speaker in the back, he couldn't understand the words. Saul, however, evidently did. He said, "I'll be happy to."

Saul stepped out agreeably and raised his arms above his head. He succeeded in maintaining his dignity as two gunmen stripped him naked and handcuffed him to bright steel hooks on the garage wall. They yanked forcefully on Saul's limbs to show that they were in control, but he made the unavoidable movements appear voluntary by cooperating. They blindfolded him and shoved orange foam earplugs into his ears. Using a bright red ball gag, they held his mouth open. Perhaps they were afraid Saul had a switch in his mouth that would blow up the car if he bit down.

The guards ran a metal detector over Saul, shoving it so brutally between his legs that Menniss winced. At the same time, axe-face ran some other kind of detector over the car itself, presumably looking for transmissions. When he finished, he left the detector hanging on a cable over the car and connected it to additional equipment. Checking for intermittent transmission? Good thinking.

Axe-face gave the guards additional instruments with which to check Saul. He used one of them himself, his movements awkward and jerky. Apparently satisfied, he motioned the guards away and shuffled over to Menniss' open window. He seemed to feel shy about facing Menniss directly, which was a mistake because he looked best straight on. In profile, he resembled a fish.

"You can't possibly be under any duress now," he said, pointing toward Saul. "He can't hear you or signal anyone. So tell me, is what you told Doctor Lemon the real story?"

All of this came out in an annoying, stumbling way, and Menniss found it hard to be polite; he wanted to either give the man a wad of money or beat him to death. "What's your name?" Menniss said.

The response, after Menniss deciphered it, was "Gary."

"Who are you?"

He rotated his head to show his other profile. "Dr. Lemon's son."

A son? Lemon had never told him he'd had a son.

And he'd included his son in the group of people he might throw away in case this was a trap? "I'm not under duress, Gary. The story I told your father is true. And that fellow you have trussed up naked against the wall is a great man and a friend of mine. Please release him immediately. Okay?"

Gary mumbled, "I can't. I want to, but I can't."

"Why not?"

"I can't do anything until my father comes. I'm not allowed."

"Well, if it's that way, it's that way," Menniss said. "Don't beat yourself up about it. Relax."

Gary, however, did not relax. He walked around uncomfortably. He looked at Saul, tied to the wall with his mouth spread open and his ears plugged closed. He stopped walking and stood at an angle to the car window, his hands on his thighs. "I'm sorry," he said.

"Let go of it," Menniss said. "That's an order."

Half an hour passed, and then Lemon walked in. The gunmen came to attention, and he told them to go fuck themselves. He didn't look at his son, and Gary didn't look at him. Menniss wondered whether Blair's genes would help Gary. If you could grow back body parts, couldn't you unsqueeze a face?

Lemon himself looked awful. While it had been only a year since Menniss had last seen him, his friend seemed to have aged 10 or 20 years. His cheeks had collapsed, and you could see the double line of his lower jaw through the tight skin. His skin was mottled brown and white. The last time they'd met, Lemon had worn his hair long in a thick gray ponytail, but now only a few sickly strands hung from a wrinkled scalp.

"You look like shit," Menniss said.

"Thank you. I need some new organs." He pointed at Saul. "Can I cut him up for spare parts?"

"No, you can't. He's a friend."

"His organs would fetch a good price," Lemon said regretfully. He gently removed Saul's earplugs and said, "I'm sorry for putting you through this." He removed the gag and shackles, and rubbed Saul's face with a tissue, presumably wiping away drool.

Lemon ran a dry hand along Saul's back. "You look like you're in good shape," he said. "No melanomas on your back. Have you had your cholesterol checked? Your PSA?"

"No, I haven't," Saul said. "Are these measurements truly valuable?"

Menniss would not have thought a naked man could look dignified while he pulled on his underwear, but Saul managed.

"You look like you're what, about 55?" Lemon said.

"Exactly so," Saul said.

"Then you need to get your PSA and cholesterol checked, and your colon too. That is if you want to live long enough to become a senile idiot."

"On a recommendation as strong as that, I'll certainly give the proposal serious consideration. May I sit on that pile of decaying tires to tie my shoes? If you haven't availed yourself of it already and don't have your own, you can find the detector, a 'multi-band scanner,' as it's properly called, on the passenger seat. If you wish, once I've finished buttoning my shirt, I'll show you how to use it."

Saul and Lemon joined Menniss in the back, one on either side of him. Surrounded, he felt a wave of claustrophobia but choked it down. Saul gently placed the scanner on various parts of Menniss' anatomy and demonstrated its functions. When his turn came, Lemon was aggressive, jabbing it into Menniss' groin and pressing it far into his lower stomach above the pelvis.

"Hey, cool it." Menniss grabbed Lemon's arm. It felt frail enough to break in his grip.

"Would you like me to go in blind and just scoop out all your guts?" Lemon asked. "Or would you like to find out where it is first?"

This was payback for something, Menniss realized, but he couldn't remember exactly what. In his long history with Lemon, many favors and paybacks were owed in both directions, and it was hard to keep track. He tossed the doctor's wrist free, and Lemon started jabbing again.

"So we'll have to do everything *inside* this car?" Lemon asked.

"Unless this garage is set up to block transmissions," Menniss said.

"What if you stick your feet out? Gary, can he stick his feet out?"

Gary shuffled up to the window. "You can't let any part of his body out," he said. "It'll act like an antenna."

"What about all the dirt above the garage?" Menniss asked.

Gary shook his head. "Not enough to shield it. You'd need a lot more."

"How much more?" Lemon asked.

"Twenty feet. Would you consider …"

"Consider what?"

"An underground … an underground parking garage?"

"I don't have one of those handy, thank you," Lemon said. "Could you build something to shield this garage in an hour?" he asked his son. "No? Very well. Back off now so I don't have to look at you." To Saul, he said, "Now, sir, would you be so kind as to step out of the car so we can arrange the patient?"

Lemon had Menniss stretch out on all fours on the seat, his butt in the air. Lemon jammed the scanner into Menniss' kidneys, his butt cheeks, and up between his butt cheeks. "Hold on," Menniss said. "You're not sticking that thing up my ass."

"I would if it fit," Lemon said. "But it won't. Now roll over. On your back with your feet away from me."

Lemon used his weight, slight as it was, to force the detector far into Menniss' belly. From up close, he looked ghoulish, as if his skin were ready to fall off; Menniss felt like he was trapped in a coffin with a corpse.

"Interesting," Lemon said. "You can sit up now. Quite interesting. It's not subcutaneous. It seems to be down beneath your spinal musculature. This wasn't a jab on the street. Someone knocked you out and took their time. Have you had surgery for anything else recently? Appendix? Maybe someone paid the surgeon to stick it in."

"I haven't had any surgery for years."

"That you know of, you mean. Give someone enough Valium, and he won't remember a thing. Someone could have operated on you in the middle of the night, and you wouldn't know. I've done it myself. You go in through the small of the back with microscopic tools that barely leave a mark and cause no more discomfort than a minor bruise."

"You astonish me," Saul said.

"Sticking in a transmitter isn't the wildest use of memory suppression. I know someone who captured a guy he hated and tortured him every night for a week. Electric shocks, I think. Anyway, something that doesn't leave a mark. The poor guy would scream with pain for hours and then forget in the morning because of the high-dose Valium. The point is the guy didn't remember getting tortured, so he wouldn't come back for revenge. In my opinion, that's rather cowardly because what's the point of torturing someone if they don't remember?" He gave a wet cough and spat on the concrete floor. "Gary, have someone get my surgical equipment. You help me rig up a few things." To Menniss, he said, "Surgery in a box. That's new. Do you want to remember it or not?"

But he had to remember because if Lemon gave him enough drugs to forget, he'd sleep for too long afterward.

MENNISS LAY ON his back on a sheet, his belly smeared with brownish disinfectant. Heat poured onto his face from the spotlights Gary had attached to the roof of the Lexus. Lemon straddled him, one shoulder pushed up against the Plexiglas divider. He wore a surgical mask and head coverings, but sweat dripped onto Menniss anyway. The sweat smelled like cigarettes.

Saul sat on a low stool just outside the Lexus and behind Menniss' head. On Lemon's command, he put his hands under Menniss' shoulders and lifted, raising the right shoulder more than the left. "Hold it there," Lemon said. He stabbed a needle deep into Menniss' belly. "Now raise the other shoulder."

After several more injections, Lemon lifted a scalpel. Menniss could see a reflection of his stomach in the metal housing of one of the spotlights, and he watched the knife slice down. That was about enough, and he closed his eyes.

Lemon, unfortunately, tended to become talkative while slicing. "I grew up with our friend here," he said to Saul. "You knew that, didn't you? Well, let me tell you a story. His dad was nuts. He thought his son was a reincarnation of General Patton. And he thought that Patton was a reincarnation of Alexander the Great. Seriously. Have you lived up to your dad's dream, Menniss? Would your career make your father proud?"

No, it wouldn't, Menniss thought. Dad believed in all-out open battle. He hadn't even approved of Army Special Forces, let alone what came after. Tank battles were his idea of good fighting.

"Stop breathing with your diaphragm, damn you," Lemon said. "I can't get anything done with your belly moving like that. And my back hurts. Chest breathing only. You know how to do that, don't you?"

Menniss knew how, but it felt suffocating, and he ached to take a full breath. Saul lifted Menniss' shoulders toward his ears, and he felt marginally better. He opened his eyes and looked at the reflective metal again. Lemon appeared to be slicing into him randomly, making an abstract canvas of lines on his stomach like one of the paintings in Francine's house.

"Well, well, well," Lemon said. "Well, well. Come back, you slippery bugger. You're a decorative little thing, aren't you? Whoops. Trying to get away? Gotcha."

Lemon triumphantly held up a bloody chunk of plastic about a quarter of an inch square. "How do you like that?" he asked. He held it so Menniss could look at it. The chip was black with a blue fleur-de-lis pattern on one side and a raised letter "S," also blue, on the other.

"May I take a look at that?" Saul asked, and Lemon handed it over. "So gaudy," Saul whispered. "Almost a mental aberration. But the blue and the black? I didn't expect …"

"What are you saying?" Menniss asked. "I can't understand you."

"That's because I'm not speaking," Saul said. "I'm muttering. Be that as it may, we'll return to this topic at a more opportune moment. I'll set this object safely on the car's floor. May he breathe normally now, doctor?"

"I don't give a damn how he breathes." Lemon climbed out of the car, stripping off his gloves and mask. "Bring him out and set him on that table so I can stitch him up."

Blood dripped down Menniss' sides and soaked his leg, but to breathe deeply again and to escape the car, what a wonderful release into freedom.

MENNISS PAINSTAKINGLY CLIMBED the stairs to the house above. It wasn't Lemon's own house, but it was intense, with pipes and ducts visible above a metal-mesh ceiling, hanging airport-runway lights, tables of blue steel and red copper and walls like the metal plates of a battleship deck. The shower he'd come looking for resembled a small bank vault, opening with a lever that had to be turned circularly. Before stepping in, Menniss made sure he could open the vault door from the *inside*.

Lemon met him afterward in the living room. He was sitting on a cylindrical steel stand. There were other such stands in the room, made of various heights and metals.

"Weird room," Menniss said.

"The owner fancies a post-post-industrial aesthetic," Lemon said. "But the whole place blocks radio transmission to a certain extent. I felt safer working here."

Menniss pointed up at the metallic ceiling. "It looks like it could slowly descend and crush you, doesn't it?"

"Like in that Bond movie?" Lemon said. "The villain puts him in the room, explains all his bad deeds, and makes sure the ceiling descends slowly enough that Bond has time to escape. Which movie was it?"

"I can't remember. Not sure it was Bond. But I remember watching that scene at your house when we were in high school. Your father had gotten us some bimbos, and mine looked like a girl in the movie. Which is why I remember."

"Those bimbos were actresses," Lemon said. "Yours was sort of famous, I think."

"Come to think of it, she might have *been* the girl from the movie."

"I think you're right," Lemon said. "We were screening the movie, and you had the real girl with you."

"Your dad was quite the host," Menniss said. "Most dads, maybe they spring for a pizza. Your dad comes up with starlets. No HIV to worry about back then, either."

"It's true, though," Lemon said.

"What's true?"

"The collapsing room."

Menniss looked up nervously at the ceiling. "It really does?"

"I wasn't speaking literally," Lemon said. "I meant life. You're born in a collapsing room, and the ceiling starts coming down from the moment of your first breath. It never stops, and one day it gets low enough to squeeze the juice out of you. So what do you do while you watch it come down? Play cards? Sing a song? Live your life?"

"You look around for a metal pole to stop it," Menniss said. "Or an escape hatch. The enemy always leaves an escape hatch."

"Not in real life. I only have an inch of space left. Lung cancer. And all I'll have left is Gary."

"He's okay."

"He's not okay."

"I'm sorry to hear about the lung cancer. How much do I owe you?"

"Your friend already paid. Now go. I have to give the house back."

He broke into a fit of wet coughs that echoed and reechoed in Menniss' mind as he left.

IT WAS NOW two in the morning. Gary had placed the chip in a metal box to block the signal, a Faraday cage, and Menniss held it safely between his feet. Though his stomach ached, he didn't feel terrible, just tired. Driving south, they were approaching the Golden Gate Bridge. Saul had called Janice three times, and the call went straight to voicemail each time. But on the fourth try, she picked up.

"Janice? This is Saul." Menniss heard Janice say a few words, and then Saul disconnected.

"What did she say?" Menniss asked.

He hadn't seen the hafeem annoyed until now. "To quote her precise words: 'Everything's okay, we're busy, call me in the morning.'"

Menniss chuckled. His wound hurt, and he pressed his forearm against the bandage. "What do you expect? They're lovers. You're going to have to share Blair with her. Get used to it."

Saul reached up with one hand to hold his neck and did something that produced a series of cracking sounds.

"What was it you muttered back there?" Menniss asked. "When you saw the chip. You said we'd talk about it later."

They'd entered the first span of the bridge. "This is indeed a wonder of the world," Saul said. "I never cease to be moved by its beauty."

At first, Menniss thought Saul was evading his question but sensed the hafeem needed to preamble his way to an answer.

"As great in its way as the Great Pyramid. But the Great Pyramid faces backward, to when men were helpless creatures like all the others. The pyramid is like the stamp of man's fist on the earth, as if to say, 'We have established dominion.' This bridge is far more fragile than the Great Pyramid but more forward-looking. It faces the future and says, 'We have no limits.'"

They'd reached San Francisco. "There's no mark of Cain on the faces of True Immortals or hafeems," he said. "They're as hard for us to find as for you."

"True Immortals especially," Menniss said. "I've tracked down several hafeems. You're not quite as careful."

"Agreed," Saul said. "I'm in contact with a number of hafeems whom I discovered or who discovered me and through them, still others, but in this *network*, as you might currently call it, there are no True Immortals. What I know of their general behavior I learned largely from one of them when he attempted to recruit me."

"Who's he?"

Saul didn't reply, and Menniss realized he shouldn't have interrupted. They made their way through the city in silence. When they reached the Pacific Coast Highway, and it was only an hour or so to Santa Cruz, Saul spoke again. "I know only one organized group of True Immortals, although there may be more. I've already mentioned its leader, the man of whose absolute goodness I am terrified, Alexandros by name. In legends told by mortals, a group of seven men rule the world as the *Illuminati*. Alexandros' group contains more than seven, women as well as men, but when he encountered the legend, he was amused and adopted the name.

"The Illuminati arrange themselves by age. Being the oldest known True Immortal save one, Alexandros is their leader. There's an Illuminata almost as old as him, Soraya, and she, too, is good and terrible. Others are no older than I am and less terrible.

"The Illuminati wrap themselves in gaudy colors and symbols so exaggerated as to appear, by contemporary standards—standards that I flatter myself I have, to a certain extent, mastered—ludicrously overdone. For example, Alexandros paints a triangle on his face to represent some aspect of his excessive self-regard. Perhaps that tendency is a mental quirk composed of power and self-regard. Or perhaps these are merely archaic creatures, wonders of the world in their own right, and their thinking was formed during another epoch.

In any case, they have considerable gravitas, and in their presence, one finds oneself taking them as seriously as they take themselves.

"When your friend Lemon pulled the chip from your belly, I expected to find it decorated with a white cross or perhaps a yellow snake. Those are the symbols of the two Illuminati who handle minor tasks. They are lesser beings, reasonably decent and not yet appalling. Even saffron symbols I would have taken with equanimity. But the blue fleur-de-lis on black is the gaudy sign of Soraya, a most warlike creature. While the red&white may imprison and the saffron may spy, Soraya possesses armies. They are the blue&blacks, spelled with an ampersand.

"Upon seeing her signature, I felt an impulse to break the thing then and there. I'm daunted at the thought of summoning Soraya. I'm especially uncertain that you should be in the vicinity when I flash the chip. I would go so far as to suggest you get safely away with your tissue sample and your scientist and allow me to take this step alone."

The local anesthetic was wearing off, and the wound in Menniss' stomach throbbed. "You've said that Santa Cruz, especially the area around a particular beach, is under some protection."

"That beach, certainly, but for me alone. And even for me, nothing is guaranteed. You find yourself perhaps on the verge of infinite life. Why take such a risk?"

Menniss thought: he's right. Why should I involve myself with this? At the very least, I should call the I-H first. But he was on the threshold of immortality, and whatever he did now would define his eternal future. He must step toward it with courage, not cowardice.

"I want to be there," Menniss said. "Though I can't explain why. Perhaps it's only an intuition." A superstition is more like it, he thought.

Saul glanced at him. "That is a perfectly good reason for acting," he said.

They drove along a dark road that hugged the surface of a cliff. To their right and far below, ocean waves crashed against black rocks.

"Besides," Menniss said, "You let yourself be pilloried for me. Now I want to stand beside you. At least once."

"You do me a great honor," Saul said. "but at the same time, I'd be less than honest if I failed to say that I fear for you—in no small measure."

THEY STOPPED AT Menniss' hotel to pick up the tissue. Menniss approached with trepidation, but the three hairs he'd strategically placed to signal an entrance were still where he'd left them. He took the blue insulated lunchbox out of the freezer and added extra ice. They drove near Francine's house, and Menniss set the lunchbox in deep bushes where it was impossible to see but could be retrieved quickly. Then they returned to the parking garage.

Once more, they glided to the bottom. Saul removed the chip from its Faraday cage and handed it to Menniss. It would transmit once they left the parking garage, informing whoever monitored it that Menniss had left the hotel.

They drove to a beach south of Santa Cruz proper and parked at the top of a cliff. It was almost midnight. There was no moon, and the beach was dark except where fires lit up circles of young people.

They walked down decaying concrete steps onto the sand. They weren't the only older people down by the water; as they circumambulated the beach, they encountered a few aging hippies among the young ones, men in their 60s or 70s wearing long ponytails and gray-haired women in flowery dresses.

They reached a fire circle where half a dozen young people beat on drums. A topless girl offered them drums of their own, and Saul accepted on their behalf. While Menniss did no more than tap on his drum, Saul knew how to play. Another girl sat on the sand before Saul, raised her arms above her head and moved sinuously in time with his skillful drumming.

Mennis took the insulated box and the chip to a dark area between fires. He put the chip in the box and closed the lid, screening transmission, then removed it. He repeated the process several times at random, then repeated it several more times in the mocking pattern of "shave and a haircut, two bits." When an intuition told him he'd gone far enough, he pushed the chip into the sand, where it would continue to send its signal and set the box beside it.

He rejoined Saul at the drum circle. The fire had died down to embers. A young man set a tubular seaweed on the glowing center of the fire. The air in its various bladders expanded, and the end of the seaweed rose into the air, weaving and bowing like a living snake. The girl who had danced to Saul's playing and who now seemed unbearably beautiful stood beside the seaweed and mimed its movements. A boy joined her, and the two danced together.

When I was their age, Menniss thought, I went off and learned to kill. But they're full of life. I want another chance at that.

"They're coming," Saul said.

Menniss saw nothing unusual on the beach ahead. He turned around, looked back, and still saw nothing. And then he caught the movement. Figures in black were pouring over the side of the cliff and pooling, almost invisibly, at its base.

A young man added logs to the dying fire, and it blazed up. He piled on more logs in a four-square pattern, stacking them high, a burning log cabin. Saul's drumming grew inspired. More young people rose to dance beside the roaring flames. More figures had gathered on the top of the cliff, and others approached along the water's edge from both directions. The light of a passing car caught some, and Menniss glimpsed the blue fleur-de-lis.

At last other people on the beach saw them. "Police!" people shouted. A general panic ensued, young hippies and their elders alike running in all directions.

Saul's admirer didn't want to leave. He spoke to her, and she reluctantly obeyed. She held her sandals and shirt in one hand and gave Saul several soulful looks over her shoulder as she walked slowly away. She disappeared through a gap in the lines of blue&blacks. The circle tightened and tightened further. But before it reached them, its movement slowed. The closest blue&blacks slowed and then halted.

A new presence had appeared on the beach.

They were dressed not in uniforms but in ordinary clothes. They moved in a surge that carried them to the chip in the sand, and the blue&blacks fled before them. The surge passed over the chip and moved on, heading toward them.

Saul stood motionless by the fire, Menniss close beside him. The breaker of people crested, and at its peak came the same vaguely Indonesian woman Menniss had glimpsed at the Pacific Garden Mall.

She was tiny, not even five feet tall. When he'd seen her from afar, he'd noticed her bearing and thought she might be a visiting dignitary. In her actual presence, he felt crushed out of existence.

He ceased to live. He wanted to run, but he couldn't move. There was no air. He fell to his knees.

"Greetings, Eldest." Saul bowed to her.

She didn't return the bow. Menniss watched as she raised one hand and slapped Saul's face.

"YOU HAVE BROUGHT the blue&blacks near my home," she said. "My *home*."

"I am sorry, Eldest. I did not know."

"Sorry? Yes, you are sorry. Very well, for I did not tell you, only that you are protected here. Do you have an answer to my question?"

"I am almost ready to answer," Saul said.

"Bring almost to now. For there is an instant's time between the two." She raised her hand again as if to slap him, but she only held it in the air, her fingers straight out and slightly separated. "Once, I held up all five fingers with my will. Now I hold up only one, and that one wavers." She adjusted her fingers and made a fist with the little finger raised. "This much protection only I give. And when that finger falls, I shall protect only the balance between them, not one or the other of two sides. I need your answer soon."

"I shall answer soon, Eldest," Saul said. "In an instant's time."

"Yes, you shall," she said. "But what of him?"

Menniss, still on his knees, hunched further down.

"Must *I* choose?" she said. "Must *I* decide yes or no? To let him go or not to let him go? To protect or not to protect? I do not wish this. But he is here, and I am here too. How do I leave untouched that which only a god should touch?"

"I am deeply sorry, Eldest," Saul said.

Menniss' stomach cramped, and he wanted to vomit.

"Stand," she said.

He tried to stand but couldn't. His knees shook.

Saul whispered, "Menniss, you must stand. She has commanded it."

He wavered to his feet. And then there was a sudden crack, a flash, a searing pain in his back.

A gunshot? No, only the logs in the fire collapsing and an ember that had landed on his back. He slapped at it. His thoughts and movements were out of sync, and he lost his balance, tripped over his feet, and fell. It was comical even to him, but he knew it was the end; he'd shown disrespect to the tiny woman who now towered above him.

She stared down at him, and her face was grim. Then she burst out laughing. More logs collapsed, and floating embers fell around them. Saul flicked one off his arm. A particularly large ember flew toward the Eldest, and she caught it in one hand; she did not flinch as it burned her.

"Yavànna sees the signs," she said, "and she is like to split her sides that the changing gods have chosen such a one as you. Now stand, child."

Menniss stood.

She said, "Fool thou," and there was affection in her voice. "Deceitful thou but reverent. I shall keep my hand raised, and I shall protect thee even as laughter splits my sides. A bit shall I protect thee—one wavering finger of protection. I will close the sky one hour to your enemies, and on the ground, I shall for one hour impair. Go now. Go and fly from trap to trap. In haste go, before laughter fells my hand. Go in haste."

Someone had gripped his shoulder and was shaking him. It was Saul. "She told you to go," Saul said. "*In haste.*" Saul gave him a push. "You must obey. Run. Find Francine and run with her too. Waste no time. She has *commanded* you. Do it now."

He was running. He ran up the beach. The blue&blacks were gone. He ran toward the tissue and Francine.

IT WAS EARLY dawn. Menniss removed the lunchbox from the bushes where he'd hidden it and walked toward Francine's house as quickly as his aching stomach would allow. On the way, he called the I-H and told him everything.

"Well, well," the I-H said. "Quite a story. A GPS tracker in your ample gut? Amazing. But affairs always work out swimmingly when she's around. I took upon myself the liberty of destroying Francine's lab."

"You did *what?*"

"I did it gently. No bombs. They called her about the damage half an hour ago. Go in, talk to her, and then I'll stage a scene and force you out the back. And all of it super-speedy, just like the Eldest commanded."

A light was on in Francine's kitchen, and a shape moved around behind the drapes. Menniss rang the bell, and Francine opened the door at once. She wore a formal business suit and had on makeup, but her face was streaked with tears. He stepped inside and closed the door. She allowed him to hold her, but she didn't respond.

"Someone—right-wing Christians, I imagine—wrecked my lab," she said. "They stole the experiments, the records, the computers, the equipment. And we had three experiments almost done."

He held her against his shoulder and stroked her hair; it felt amazingly soft, as if she'd spent hours brushing it. Perhaps she had. She didn't bend to his arms when he held her but remained stiff and straight. He remembered a time when he'd tried to comfort a grief-stricken mother whose child he'd just killed with a bomb. Francine felt the same in his arms.

"They left notes saying it was against God's will. That everything I do is against God's will. I wanted to ask one of them, 'If your child comes down with pneumonia, would you say it's God's will and let her die?' Aging is a sickness like any other. What's wrong with try-ing to cure it?"

He must move with haste. That was the command.

He opened the lunchbox and pulled out the plastic bag with the tissue sample packed in ice. "Francine, forget your lab—the secret to the aging clock is right here."

"At least the data from the finished experiments was all backed up on the server," she said. She put a thin hand on her cheek, her polished red fingernails gnawed to the skin. "I can finish the three articles I've already promised. The one proving that the telomere hypothesis is wrong. Another demonstrating the existence of an aging clock in flatworms. And the third, suggesting that the same gene complex that causes aging also suppresses tissue regeneration. But I don't know what I'll do after that."

"Look at me," Menniss said. He had to physically place himself in her line of sight to get her to focus. He showed her the ice in the box and waved the tissue sample again. "Did I do this right? I wanted to preserve its DNA. Was packing it in ice good enough?"

She partly focused on him. "Dry ice would have been better, but water ice should do. DNA is pretty stable."

"Well then," he said, "the way is clear."

"What way?"

"Francine, listen … this happened because of me. Because of this tissue." He didn't want to lie because Sensei said that when you begin a project with deceit, you end with a false success.

"What tissue?"

Menniss opened the lunchbox and showed her the tissue wrapped in clear plastic. "This comes from a man who doesn't age, a man whose aging clock doesn't tick at all. He's a mutation. There are others like him. I have proof. Here, look at this." He ripped open a seam of his jacket and showed her photos of Blair in Australia and Brazil with their date stamps on the back and copies of his driver's licenses from both places.

She gave them a vague glance and stepped a few inches away.

"I know this is all easy to fake," he said. "But it's not fake. I have a dossier to prove it. And think about it. Why would someone wreck your lab right after you meet me? *Your* lab. One of the top experts in the world on aging. Because they don't want you to learn how to do this."

"Who doesn't want me to?"

He tried to think of a truthful way to move her, but only lies came to mind. He struggled against them and came up with a way to use the truth. "A secret cabal that thinks they run the world. They want to be the only ones who live forever. Think about it, Francine.

If a few powerful people live forever and the rest do not, imagine how much power they will have."

His cell phone buzzed with a text message. He tapped the screen and read, "Diversion in 30 seconds. Directions to follow separately." He hit delete.

"Francine, this tissue is the answer to your prayers."

"I don't pray."

"I mean to your hopes. This tissue will give you the breakthrough you've been looking for."

She was pacing around now. "It's not like you think. What am I supposed to do, work from my kitchen? You need a setting to do science: graduate students, equipment, and time. I must put my lab back together and do my work there."

"You won't be able to, Francine. They won't let you. We have to get away."

There was a powerful knock on the door. "Open up, Section Fifty-Nine, Federal."

"Francine," Menniss said, "we've got to get out of here." But he almost laughed out loud.

Section 59 was a standing joke at the agency. "So an agent from Section 59 was walking down the street, and …" His client was having altogether too much fun.

"I'm not going to run from the government. It'll make me look guilty. Besides, they pay for my grants."

"It's not a matter of guilt. They want to put you in a secret prison and make you work only for them. Don't you see? They want to be the immortal masters and control the rest of the world."

He held the cooler out toward her, but she still hesitated.

The knock on the door repeated, angry, forceful. "Open up."

"Make up your mind," he said.

"I can do that." But she still didn't move. She was thinking.

Suddenly, Francine took the cooler, cradled it against her chest and ran with him out the back door. They ran down a sloping back-yard and into the neighbor's yard behind her. On the other side of the street, a Jeep waited, its door slightly open, the key in the ignition, far too much like a James Bond movie.

She came to a stop beside it. "What's going on?"

"I don't entirely know what's going on," Menniss said.

"Well, that's obvious."

"But I think the best thing to do is to take this car."

Francine hurried stiffly around to the passenger seat. She rested the cooler in her lap, sitting fully upright. "I'm not a crank," she said. "I must rebuild my lab, and then I'll work on it."

"You can't rebuild your lab. You can't go back there. But there's another lab ready."

Her upper lip curled. Then she looked down at the lunch box. "We have to get this to a proper freezer *soon*," she said.

CHAPTER 5

JANICE AMONG THE IMMORTALS

"Compared with me, a tree is immortal and
a flower-head not tall, but more startling
I want the one's longevity and the other's daring."
SYLVIA PLATH

In which you meet the bad guys and discover
that they think they're the good guys.
THE CHRONICLER

JANICE

I WALKED ALONG the fire road as fast as I could. It wasn't kept up well, and the forest was trying to take it back. The trees leaned over, stuck out roots and dripped redwood mulch.

People say redwood forests are beautiful, but I don't like them. True, the trees stand there perfectly straight, reaching into the sky cathedral-grand, and you can walk between them like you're in a park, with no shrubs to trip over. But there are no shrubs to trip over because redwood forests block the light with their canopy and poison the ground with their acid bark; they kill off everything besides themselves. They kill each other, too. Quite often. Bigger trees choke out smaller trees, so fallen trunks are lying here and there. Here I was, a tiny thing, scurrying around, tickling their feet. "Sorry for living," I said.

They were choking me along with the small trees. I wanted to turn around and go back to Saul, put up with Menniss and go to Oakland, but chickening out isn't my thing—I'm too depressed for that—and anyway, I wanted to see Blair. So I kept walking.

Temperature-wise, the air was probably warmer than back in Fort Collins, but the air there was dry, and here it was sopping wet and felt colder. The cold, wet air got into the skin of my neck and my back, too, and I had to stop twice to pee. One time, my left hand trembled in a weird way, like it had its own agenda. I could hear myself huffing and puffing. It's not like I've never hiked before, but I've done all my hiking in the desert around Fort Collins, and in the bare desert, you're a big deal, especially when you wear bright colors. Here, the big trees run things, and you don't matter.

I got used to walking on mulch and detouring around roots. Every so often, I passed one of those spots where sun rays break slantwise through a hole in the canopy, and dust motes spiral down on the shimmery light stage. The big tree trunks, in every way the opposite of dust motes, stand still and look solemn, and you hear a heavenly choir whether you want to or not. I tried to act suitably impressed because I knew the trees put a lot of effort into their show, but the mandatory transcendent experience didn't happen for me. I felt sick.

I was never very good at holding myself together. I always needed a lot of things, like my house, some TV shows full of imaginary old friends, my books, my bath, my support groups, my stupid job, my asshole neighbors, etc. And what did I have now? A bunch of arrogant redwoods and an Immortal boyfriend I could only hold onto by tying up. I was falling apart.

I sat on a big redwood log that was moldering itself to pieces. A tiny log considering the neighborhood, but big compared to anything you'd ever find in Fort Collins. The damp cold crawled down my neck and wiggled its way into my armpits. I decided to give up. Go ahead, huge trees, squish the life out of my life. I'll molder away here like you want me to.

Molder, molder.

Then I realized the crawling sensation on my neck wasn't damp but a spider, and I jumped around until I was sure I'd shaken it off. I ran out of there, not because I thought the spider would chase me, but after jumping around, I felt better and wanted to keep feeling better. Running did that. After about 15 minutes of running, I felt the grip of the trees falter. Soon after that, they shrank from giants to normal-sized trees, then to dwarves, then they let go completely. I reached a place in the middle of the redwood forest that the redwoods didn't control. They couldn't poison and shadow out all the shrubs, wildflowers and grass the way they liked. Something about the soil, probably. I hoped it frustrated the piss out of them, but I knew trees were too patient for that. They knew they'd conquer the hidden meadow in a thousand years or so.

The sun suddenly came out. I stretched out flat on the grass in the center of the circle and let the light pour down on me. The sun doesn't care about you any more than a redwood does, but at least it makes you feel nice. I petted a wildflower. Something smelled like mint. Something else felt poky. I sat up, checked for ants, and lay back down again.

I loved the sun. I let it pour and pour. Unlike an MRI, it doesn't know or care what's inside you; it only looks at your skin. Very polite. And the sun only has one agenda: that you should grow, live and die. A doctor I visited one time who was also a kind of amateur biologist once told me that life is what happens when the right kind of star shines on the right kind of planet. As gods go, the sun isn't bad.

Sweat gathered between my breasts and dripped down my arms. I realized I was thirsty. I sat up. I heard a hissing noise and wondered whether it was a serial killer or a mountain lion sneaking into the clearing to murder me. I opened my purse and got out my handgun. But the hissing turned out to be cars; I'd almost reached the road. I fluffed my hair, straightened my clothes and put myself in the frame of mind to hitchhike. Then my cell phone rang.

IT WAS MARCUS. He wasn't happy at all. Rebecca—the rock-star chick who'd strung him along forever, treating him like crap and never sleeping with him, getting him going and then saying goodbye, the one he was over-the-top in love with and whom he wanted to marry, only they'd never done more than kiss—she'd driven him off at last. For real. An official no-contact order from the court, which was rather decent of her because it ended the torture. (Marcus didn't see it that way.) He flew as far west as he could to get away from her, which meant Santa Cruz, and though he hadn't expected to find my phone number on page 47 of *Northanger Abbey*, he'd looked anyway.

"And there it was," he said. "Your number. I felt like an angel touched me. Where are you?"

Too sweet. Guys who say stuff like that you can love forever but only in the fan club way. I would Rebecca him too if he didn't watch out. Shallow me.

"I'm about to hitchhike on Highway 17."

"I don't think you can hitchhike there. I drove over it three times in the last two days, and it looks like you can hardly even walk on it."

"Well, then get here soon." I was already doing a Rebecca on him, even if I didn't mean to. People aren't like redwoods; you can affect them.

I had one more bunch of trees to get through before I reached the highway, so I straightened up and started marching. I marched right out of my sun pool back into the redwoods. This time I was ready to fight, only I didn't have to fight for very long because, after about 20 feet, the redwoods gave up. A bunch of normal-sized trees marched in to replace them. Pine trees at first, then weird olive-brownish trees with bark so smooth they looked like they wore human skin. Unlike redwoods, they didn't mind letting the sun hit the forest floor. I walked around an old rusted car with one of those human skin trees growing through its windshield and a tumbleweed of poison oak in its trunk. Pretty cool. And here was the highway.

Marcus was right; if you tried to hitchhike here, you'd get run over. I used to go to a firing range in Fort Collins where they let you shoot semi-automatics two-handed and fill the air with bullets. Highway 17 was the same, only with cars.

I stuck out my thumb anyway. It twitched again. What was that about? I watched several interesting guys drive by, one with as many piercings as Jason. Another was a cool loser type like Marcus, but none were a tenth as beautiful as Blair, and they didn't stop for me anyway. Three fraternity fucks came by in a convertible BMW, and because I didn't want them to stop, they did. I looked away, but they pulled up close and said all kinds of disgusting things. I couldn't think of the right way to blow them off because they were too stupid to understand anything clever. At least we were in public. Men don't have to worry about getting raped, and it pisses me off. That's one reason I carry a gun.

The college kids suddenly sped up the road. I stared at the backs of their necks and wished I had the kind of psychic power I saw in a movie once, where you can make someone's head explode. Then I felt something tingly on the back of my own pretty neck—probably the way a butterfly felt just before it got pinned to a board. Ahead of me, the leaves of the trees flittered red and blue. I turned around and faced the police car.

The guy who stepped out was young and cute, in a highway patrolman sort of way.

"Excuse me, ma'am," he said. "This is a no-pedestrian road."

"I'd be happy to turn myself into a non-pedestrian," I said, "but it's also a no-hitchhiking road. What would you recommend?"

He had one of those green state-trooper hats on. He pulled it down low and cocked one hip like he was a cowboy. I wanted to laugh, but you don't laugh at police types because that makes them act out.

"How did you get here?" he asked. "Hitchhike part way?"

"No," I said. "I got lost hiking."

He shifted weight to the other foot and changed type. Now he was the generous, know-everything, boy-scout kind of highway patrolman.

"It can happen. The redwoods confuse people's sense of direction. Do you have any ID?"

"Why do I need ID? I'm not driving." He looked ready to escalate if I stonewalled him, and I remembered I had a gun. I set my purse on the ground, disowning it, fluttery, girl-like. "Just so you know, I have a concealed weapons permit in there. And also a concealed weapon. Tell me how you want to deal with it."

He readjusted his hat and said, "May I lift your purse from the ground and open it?"

"Yes, you may, officer, so long as you don't use any of my makeup."

"I'll try to control myself, ma'am."

Total deadpan and very cute.

He found the Beretta and said, "nice gun." I did the kind of demure awe-shucks you can do when you're a girl, getting your breasts involved along with your shoulders and head. I wish it didn't come so naturally. He took the magazine out of the gun, then returned both to my purse that he was still holding. "Any other weapons in here?" he asked.

"A nasty metal comb."

"I think I'll take my chances with that," he said.

He asked where I kept the carrying permit. I told him to look in the red wallet in the purse. He found it and said, "This is a Colorado permit."

"That's because I'm visiting from Colorado," I said.

"Maybe you didn't know this, but you need a California permit to carry a gun here, ma'am."

Kowtowing time. I was only a hot chick, and he was an Agent Of the State. "Whoops," I said.

He shifted hips again, adjusted his hat, and said, "How about I give you a receipt for the gun, and when you get yourself a permit in California, you can go to the Santa Cruz County Sheriff's office and retrieve it."

"That's more than fair." I didn't ask him what he would've done if I weren't white.

He put the gun in the trunk of his police car, gave me back my purse and wrote out a receipt. The purse felt light as a feather without its gun. Only there was still the problem that you couldn't hitchhike on this highway, which was pretty obvious looking at the car-bullets shooting by, and so I couldn't let loose as my movable self but had to say yes when he offered me a lift. He wanted to drive me into town, but I said I didn't need that and asked him if there was a restaurant nearby. He said yes and wanted me to sit up front with him, but I opened the back door and sat behind; my thumb was twitching again, and it embarrassed me.

He let me off at a tacky restaurant right at the summit of the local mountains, above most of the trees. Far away, you could see the ocean spread out like a second sky. I washed my face in the restaurant's bathroom and drank straight out of the faucet. I felt dizzy—sick dizzy—then I drank more water and felt better. The restaurant was some kind of expensive Denny's with disgusting all-American food. I returned to the parking lot and found a giant wooden spool that I upended and sat on. Way out in the water, you could see an island. Maybe Japan. (I'm not that stupid. I know you can't see Japan from the US, no matter how high you are.)

My cell phone rang again. I hoped it was Zeke or Saul, but it was Marcus. I told him where I was, and he said he could see me. He pulled into the parking area, jumped out of his car and hugged me—my first normal mortal hug in a while.

I CLIMBED INTO the car and kissed his cheek. Marcus looked even better than I remembered him: clothes disheveled, face tortured and sensitive (exactly like a guy's face should look). And he hadn't slept with me even when I asked him to because he was too much in love with someone; that's the only legal cause for rejection according to Janice's Rules of Relationships.

I knew that he'd hit on me instead of me on him this time. How guys get over heartache, Step One.

"Tell me more about what happened," I said, suddenly interested. "I want all the details."

We were sitting in the parked car. The things wrong with a guy can be sexy. I mean physical things, too, not just emotional problems. He had pale skin with bumps on it and too-big ears and too-short fingers, not at all like perfecto Blair. It was growing on me.

"Well ..." he said.

"Go on, go on."

"The same day I saw you, she called and begged me to come home. Out of the blue, her apartment was *my* home, too! She said she knew no one would ever love her as much as I loved her. She'd had a dream we got married and wanted me to come out right away and marry her."

The bitch. "Let's drive now," I said. Not that I knew exactly how I would pull off ditching Marcus to see Blair.

Marcus obediently started the car, and we headed downhill toward Santa Cruz. The road dropped back into the redwood forest, but the trees can't get to you through a car. "Okay," I said, "she asked you to come out. What next?"

"I bought a ticket and flew back that same day, so she wouldn't have time to change her mind. Do you know how much it costs to get a ticket on the same day? Thousands of dollars. Anyway, I got the ticket and called to tell her the time, and she didn't answer her phone. I called her again on the way to the airport and right up to when the plane started moving. I didn't reach her till I landed in New York, and then she said she'd met someone else and couldn't meet me but invited me to her concert."

"What about the getting married bit?"

"She said I made that part up, that she'd never said it. She admitted telling me she missed me but explained that she'd only said that because she felt lonely."

"What a bitch." I stroked his neck, not sexually, and he leaned against my hand.

"I'm used to it, so it doesn't bother me as much as it should. I showed up at her gig that night to get closure. But she was so beautiful I climbed up on stage and hugged her knees."

"You climbed on stage. In front of people? What did the bouncers do?"

"They bounced me. And that's when she put out the court order. It's like I'm dead to her, the way the mafia say."

I played with the hair on the back of his head, curling some around one finger. Not sexually.

"I *feel* dead, too," he said. "A soul in Hades. Not hell, Hades."

"Hades specifically?" I asked.

"Where you're a shadow of yourself. A shade. It's dark in there, and you can't see much, and you're not exactly dead but definitely not alive either."

I was still fiddling with his hair. He took my hand and kissed it, and just when I was about to get alarmed in a fun way, he pushed my hand away and stuck it firmly on my lap. Brief interlude for a pout.

Bouncing back, I said, "So that's why you liked getting my message in the Jane Austen book. Like a light in Hades?"

"Exactly. I know you're involved, but it was good hearing from you."

Ooh, I know how that line works. It means, "Please tell me you're not involved, or not so much, or that you might consider deciding you're not involved because otherwise I'm gone, and so's your chance with me." Hard to fight off. But I didn't say anything.

"I'll get over her someday," he added. "Won't I?"

"No, you won't. You'll pine away until you're 75, like the guy in *Love in the Time of Cholera*, and when you finally get together, you're about to die, and then you die, and it sucks."

"That's a little more romantic than I want to be," he said.

He almost sounded like a sane person who was not still hopelessly in love with a woman who'd sicced a court order on him.

I smelled something that made me hungry, and then we drove around a corner and the smell got stronger. When we passed a lumberyard, it faded. How could the smell of redwood chips make you hungry?

"By the way," he said, "if I come onto you, please say no. I know it's a bad idea."

I turned away from him and looked out the window. I was scared that I'd take him up on it. In the Janice Dictionary, that kind of spell is called "backward magic," and it works even when you understand it. But I'd already tried to sleep with him, and he said no, and that gives you some protection because you want to get even.

"And I know perfectly well that what I just said *is* a kind of coming onto you," he added. "I'm sorry."

Backward magic at the next level. I felt myself slipping.

"Of course, I want to sleep with you," he said. "But I don't want to because I know it's a bad idea since I'm not actually over Rebecca, not to mention you're in a relationship. So you don't have to tell me it's a bad idea. I'll remember not to all on my own. If you're free when I'm over her, though, I want to try. Raincheck?"

Kind of assuming but assuming correctly.

The thing is, according to Janice's Rules of Relationships, Marcus was the kind of guy I *should* get into a relationship with. He's screwed up but conscious of it and trying to do better. That's about where I'm at and a step up from my usual guy. Here's the relevant rule: never get into a relationship with someone who's either a whole lot healthier or a whole lot unhealthier than you.

Or a whole lot more immortal.

"Raincheck," I said. "Should I write it out?"

He was looking up through the windshield "What the hell? What are those helicopters doing?"

I'd been hearing the sound of helicopters for a while now, but I hadn't noticed myself hearing them. I stuck my head out the window and saw no less than four helicopters, police, I guess, black with blue highlights and flying low.

They had to be after someone else. Except we were the only people on the road here other than a limousine in front of us that was also painted black and dark blue. And two behind us. No, shit: three behind and three in front.

"Maybe the President's coming to town," I said. "And we're in the way of their motorcade. Better pull off. Right here." Marcus did what I told him and headed down a little road that peeled away from the highway.

Instead of leaving us behind the way they would have if they were escorting the President, the limousines followed us. The helicopters followed too, but the forest grew thick, and you couldn't see them. We were on a road to nowhere with dark limousines closing in. I knew it was bad.

I opened my purse and then remembered I didn't have a gun anymore. I took out my cell phone instead. I fumbled in my purse for the card with Zeke's number, the longest fumbling around of my life, like when you're in the middle of sex and trying to find your vibrator under the bed.

Zeke answered right away. "Whoa," he said. "Slow down. What do they look like?"

"Like limousines and helicopters. I don't know."

"What colors are they painted?"

"Blue and black."

There was so long a silence I thought I'd lost him, and I looked at the phone; there was only one bar, but we were still connected.

"Are you alone?" he asked.

"No, with a friend."

"Blair?"

"Not Blair. A regular person."

"Not good for him," he said. "Really not good."

"Who are you talking to?" Marcus said. Or, rather, shrieked, because the limousines were pushing us off the road into a small ditch.

"What's bad?" I asked.

"The blue&blacks are the worst," Zeke said. "With an ampersand, by the way."

"What are you talking about? Who are they? They're making us stop now. What are they going to do to us?"

"They won't do anything to *you*. You're protected. Your friend, though, I don't know. Listen to me—where's Blair?"

"In Santa Cruz. I'm supposed to meet him in an hour."

Marcus was pretty much just saying "fuck" in lots of different ways.

"You can't get away from them," Zeke said. "But you don't have to. They'll take you to Blair if you let them, and you should let them. Trust me: they won't hurt you or Blair. You're going to have a fun time. You can call it 'Janice among the Illuminati.' Yes, they call themselves Illuminati. Later, you can let me know how it goes. And sorry about your friend."

"Sorry about him? Why sorry?" But the call dropped, and the car came to a jerky stop because we'd been pushed to a halt, limousines all around us. And those damn redwoods closing in and watching everything.

People dressed in blue and black uniforms—too gaudy for police—got out of the limousines. Their leader was a she, and she talked into the air like you do when you have a Bluetooth headset on you, although I didn't see one. Marcus had locked the car doors, but the blue&blacks did something to the locks. The doors opened, and they pulled us out.

I guess I have a normal girl inside me somewhere because, right on cue, I shouted, "Where are you taking him?"

No one bothered to answer. They shoved Marcus into the back of a car the way cops do, pushing his head down first so he didn't bump it. He caught my eye one last time before he disappeared, and I knew that was the last time I'd ever see him. He was dead to me. Whether he was dead to himself was another thing. I hoped not, but I'd never know.

A guy named Marcus pops into Janice World, they connect, and then the parachute strings yank him away, and he's gone. Next movie.

I'M TIRED OF cars.

I was in the back with two middle-aged women, one on each side. Up front, there was a young guy in the passenger seat and an old guy driving. They were dressed in blue and black, and they all wore headsets. I grabbed one of the headsets from the bitch on the right and put it on. I heard a male voice in my ear, and the asshole in the passenger seat turned to face me. (Janice-speak lesson: when you're in a bad mood, the female pronoun is "bitch," and the male is "asshole.")

I snatched the headset off asshole-up-front next. He put on a new headset and the bitches held me back so I couldn't get to him. I yelled, "What's going on?" I yelled other things too, but mostly that. Then I heard his voice in my ear again.

"Please calm down," he said. "You're completely safe. You have never been so safe. We're not the enemy. Once you hear what we plan to do, you'll realize that. Please listen."

I laid off yelling.

"We are servants bound and loyal to the hidden world of True Immortals. Once we've removed all your lice, we'll take you to the True Immortal Blair and invite him to meet others of his kind. But there is no compulsion. If he wants to meet them, we will take him there. If he declines the offer, we shall not further trouble him. Our masters extend the same invitation to you. We shall take you to the hidden world, too, if you choose. If you do not so choose, we won't trouble you either."

"I don't have lice," I said.

"Pardon me. It's a metaphorical expression. To avoid leading a hanger-on to a True Immortal, you must take effective steps to shake off all possible hangers-on before meeting one. The practice is known colloquially as 'delousing.' It is a matter of courtesy and prudence."

Not quite so courteous to the hangers-on, though. I don't particularly like Richard Menniss, but he's a person, not an insect.

I asked the bitch on my right why *I* should have a hanger-on since I'm not an Immortal. She said that hangers-on don't only look for True Immortals but also for mortals who know True Immortals and, perhaps, even mortals who know those mortals. One can't be too careful.

"But what stops you folks—servants—from becoming hangers-on? Or telling the whole wide world?"

The bitch on my left took that one. "Because we're *bound* servants. If any of us committed such sacrilege, the consequences would be terrible."

"What exactly? Spontaneous combustion?"

"No one knows exactly, but it is said to be painful and fatal. We choose to join, and the life is good, but there is no leaving."

Sucks to be you, I thought.

I'll skip the boring details of what happened next—the usual spy stuff but carried out by professionals for once, as if we had the Secret Service in charge instead of Harry Potter. Mostly we changed cars in parking garages. Our last car was a blue Honda Civic. By then, the folks with me weren't wearing blue and black livery, only street clothes with a bit of blue and black flair.

They dropped me off under a tree near the Surfside Hotel, and I walked half a block under cover like they told me to. The idea was to make sure no orbiting satellite camera could pick me out, which I didn't think made too much sense since the fog had rolled in and the sun was going down. Besides, I'd been to this hotel several times before. But it dawned on me that True Immortals and their stans *like* to do this sort of thing, and I played along.

I walked through a vacant lot filled with trees. The weeds that rubbed against my legs were soft and kind to my naked skin. In Santa Cruz, even the weeds are friendly. The hotel looked magical, with flowers growing everywhere and luxurious ivy hugging the sides. It was easy to forget that I'd recently been kidnapped by scary people. I walked under an arch of climbing wisteria to the hotel door, remembering to look down like they told me to whenever I was out in the open. The whole upper half of the entrance was stained glass. I looked through a stained glass wisteria and saw Blair sitting on a couch in the lobby, waiting for me.

The moment I saw him, I came out to my skin and into the moment. It was a long way to travel because I'd fallen about 10 miles inside myself. He brought me back. He always did. I didn't know why he made me soften, and I knew for damn sure I shouldn't love him, but I did. Besides, even if Marcus would be a better choice, he was dead to me and maybe to himself, too. Shit.

I pushed the door open, and then all I could think of was Blair; the other options were grayed out, like a computer menu you can't click on.

Ten miles out to get to my skin and a hundred years of events since I'd last seen him. They flashed before me in a compressed present: Those assholes and bitches in blue and black and their limousines. Marcus squirreling his car across the highway to pick me up. The highway patrolman. The forest choking everything to death. Giving Saul a kiss on the cheek when I realize he's not going to stop me from running. Driving into the forest with Menniss in the back seat. Saul cracking Menniss on the head and shoving him into the car. Meeting Saul on the clifftop, terrified. Checking email because Blair was too chicken to check, then pretending to be Blair when Saul emailed back. Blair in bed in the morning, feeding me peeled grapes. Blair right now, rising from the couch to meet me.

Oh my goodness, was he beautiful. Three hundred years of wide-eyed, open being rose from a leather couch so shiny it reflected him. I saw another Blair reflection on the big glass coffee table between us. I picked the real one and hugged him.

I knew he must be dying to hear what happened all day, so I stopped hugging him. I took his hands and tried to figure out where to start. Only he wasn't with the program. We were out of sync, and it messed up the magic.

I think he said, "I love the ocean," or something like that, but I didn't listen because I was too busy wondering whether I should start with this morning, when I got the email, or with yesterday, when I somehow absorbed enough details to fool Saul. Blair said, "It's amazingly beautiful." I was about to blow that off as Hallmark card crap when he said stuff that took me off track even before it turned awful.

"I spent almost the whole day sitting on a rock watching the waves," he said. "Each one is incredibly beautiful and different from any other."

"Well, yeah," I said because I'd noticed that too. Unique as snowflakes, except better because waves move and do things instead of just lying there.

"You know what I think?" he said.

On cue, I said, "What?"

Then he got all rapturous and said his awful thing: "Waves are like mortals. Each is a beautiful and perfect creation born in the swell, riding through rocks and dying on the sand."

Oh, so poetic. He must have worked on it for a while. "So I'm just a wave? How can you fall in love with a wave?"

"How can you not?" he said.

After all my sweating out there on the road, I needed a shower. He talked to me through the shower door. Between moments when I had shampoo in my ears, I learned that he'd spent the entire day sitting on a rock, watching the ocean. He'd seen a whale. He liked whales because they don't die as fast as most mortal beings. He talked about how waves break around a rock and come together on the other side. He talked about a bird that skimmed so low above the water that it flew through the curl of a breaking wave, which I think he probably made up. Then I realized the obvious, that he assumed Saul hadn't answered his email, and he didn't want to talk about it.

As I dried off, Blair went on to explain how the retreating tide made stairs in the sand, long curling stairs, like the steps to a Buddhist temple he'd seen in Cambodia.

My cell phone rang, and I shut it off. I pushed Blair down on the bed. I unbuttoned his shirt. My left breast is slightly larger than the other, and the one on the right isn't shaped the way it should be, but *his* chest is as perfect as the rest of him. I could either feel envious or lose myself in his perfection. I decided to do both.

I ran my hand over that perfect chest and pinched a nipple. I told him to wait there while I looked for something. When I didn't find what I wanted in the closet or under the sink, I left the room to explore the parking lot. I found a long hempy rope holding down the tarp on someone's boat trailer, and since there wasn't any wind and no one was watching, I set some rocks on the tarp and borrowed the rope. My beautiful Immortal was still lying half-naked in bed when I came back. I took off the rest of his clothes, tied the rope over his chest and watched the hemp bristles make red spots on his skin. I tied his hands and feet to the old-fashioned bedposts, and instead of resisting, he held out his hands and feet.

Was it the magic of Santa Cruz seeping through the walls, the softness and safety of a city where even the weeds are nice? It couldn't be that he trusted me. I'm just one of those dying-in-the-sand waves.

I took off my robe and stretched myself over Blair's tied-up body. I gagged his lips with my tongue. If someone sliced up *his* legs, the scars would disappear. If someone burned *him* with a candle, the burns would go away. I let myself fall into him and thought that if I fell far enough, the slices I'd made in my legs long ago during my bad years might disappear. What about the slices I'd made in my life? Not them. They're for keeps.

Tied up, helpless, loving, my perfect immortal one. Trusting me.

When I untied him, Blair burst out wildly. He was strong when he got going and threw me around some, but that was okay because I had given him permission. I deserve to let things get totally out of control sometimes.

AT TWO IN the morning, I turned the phone back on. Saul had left five messages, and now he was calling for the sixth time.

"Everything's okay," I said. "But we're busy. Call after nine."

"Who was that?" Blair asked.

"Nobody," I said. "I'm going to sleep."

"I love you," he said.

"You too," I said, but I was curled up and falling asleep.

He tried to uncurl me, but I didn't let him. He pushed my arms apart to find my face and, again, said he loved me.

"Fine," I said, "but I'm tired." I turned the other way.

"I really love you," he said.

Which should have been cool since he's an Immortal. But I only felt it in the thin shell of skin around my body. My stomach didn't feel loved. My heart didn't either, and I didn't want him to touch me. Then I stretched out against him and went so far as to stroke his head until he fell asleep. I've never met a better way to fall asleep than that, forgetting everything against an Immortal's perfect skin.

IN THE MORNING, I told Blair that Saul actually *had* emailed, that I'd impersonated him and met Saul at the rock myself.

Blair didn't believe me.

I pushed hard on the stud in his nose, and then he did.

"You kept that secret all night?" He danced naked around the room; he lifted me off the bed and spun me in circles while I tried to keep my dignity—no mean feat in that position—then I let go and let myself almost love him. He sat me down on the floor, and I said the floors in hotels are disgusting, something I knew a little about.

We put on robes and made coffee. He loved how much I admired Saul because it mirrored his own feelings.

But when I got to the part where Menniss showed up crossing the street, I noticed he'd stopped listening.

"What now?" I asked.

He didn't want to tell me, but I made him.

"I was wondering whether you and Saul talked about me," he said. "That's narcissistic, isn't it?"

"Just a little. By pure coincidence, that was the one subject we talked about—how narcissistic you are. And we tried to figure out why we bothered with you, considering that you're a total nobody."

The funny thing was, Blair liked hearing that. He said that it was just what he wanted, to be seen and criticized. That's why he needed Saul—and me, too, although that wasn't the *only* reason he needed me. (He was lucky he added that part.)

He'd worked his way to planning the fifth month of our world travels as a triple when my cell phone rang. It was Saul again. The two hadn't talked for over a century, and I felt bad for putting off Saul all night, so I handed the phone straight to Blair and took another shower.

I love showers.

But I had a headache, too, in my right temple, and when I put my hand on it, I remembered the radiologist's wormy finger touching me in the same place when I asked him where the walnut in my brain lived. I stopped enjoying the shower because my headache got worse, and I began seeing things the way you do with a bad migraine but weirder.

First, the light above the shower acted out. It was normal when I looked directly at it, but I saw purple when I let my eyes fall. I scrubbed my hair with shampoo, and when I opened my eyes, purple had dyed its way further down from above, so the whole top half of whatever I looked at was purple. Violet, really. A nice shade. Little by little, the violet crept further, and the light above the shower turned into a Halloween black light and stayed that way even if I looked directly at it. I could hardly see anything. I felt for the shower knobs, made the water nice and hot, and squatted on the floor.

I'm not stupid. I knew I was in trouble. But I wanted to grow my hair long, and I'd go bald if they treated me for cancer. Besides, I felt wonderful just then: squatting purple-blind under a hot, hot rain. I've been at birthings, and I wondered whether that's how it is for babies before they come out (only for them, it's red).

Gradually, the violet haze backed itself up, unfurling from the bottom until the shower was normal again. I got out and pretended nothing had happened. I looked at myself in the mirror and tried to imagine what it would be like to be Blair and look at your body and see perfection. I saw how my breasts didn't match and where I had fat that I didn't want, and I imagined the walnut under my skull bulging itself a good time. Oh well. Death strikes the innocent, too. Not that I'm innocent.

I THOUGHT I'D done Blair a favor by leaving him alone to talk with Saul, and when I came out of the bathroom, I intended to be annoyed with him for staying on the phone for so long when all three of us could just meet. But he wasn't talking on the phone. He was sitting petulantly on the bed, and my phone was lying on the floor across the room, case popped open and the battery out.

"You didn't have to throw it," I said.

"He can't come see me right now," Blair said.

Premonitions popped over my forehead like beads of sweat. "Why can't he see you now? What's happening?"

"He was busy doing something else. Mostly he just called to tell me he'd call again later. He didn't even sound friendly. I don't think he wants to see me."

Naturally, Blair thought it was all about him. "I promise you, he loves you," I said. "Something big must be going on for him if he had to get off like that. I hope he's okay."

"I doubt he loves me. Why should he?"

I rubbed my hair with a towel. "He shouldn't, considering you're a self-centered fucking two-year-old, but he does. I spent half a day with him, remember?" Which sounded funny, considering that Blair had spent a couple of centuries with him.

He didn't stop pouting. I got annoyed, and I wanted to find something sharp and slash the beauty out of him. Only, it wasn't possible. You could give Blair the death of a thousand cuts, and he'd come back as beautiful as before. He had too much life, way more than he deserved.

I got dressed because I knew he'd want to leave the moment I told him the next thing. I spiked my hair for old times' sake and inserted a few bars and studs. "Do you want to go talk to an organization of other True Immortals?" I asked. "I met a crew yesterday, and we're invited to their HQ. Interested?"

The pout disappeared. He stared at me. "You met some True Immortals?"

I drank some water and put on some sunscreen. "Their servants, anyway. Remember Zeke at the casino hotel in Ely, Nevada, the guy who made you so jealous? It turns out he's a hafeem and knows things. And he told me we'd be safe with these Immortals even though he hates them."

"But how did you find them? What happened?"

"I was with an old boyfriend of mine, and they picked me up, a whole army of people dressed in blue and black who work for these Immortals. They brought me here." Cell phone reassembled, stuff gathered, all ready.

"How are we supposed to get in touch with them?" Blair asked.

"They're swarming around outside, and if we do so much as snap our fingers, they'll take us to their masters. Could you act a little less jealous about the old boyfriend I just mentioned?"

"An organization of Immortals?" He caught himself almost in time and said, "But yes, I'm jealous. Of course I'm jealous. What old boyfriend? What do you mean you were with him?"

At least he was trying. But I knew that the idea of meeting other Immortals had made him forget about me.

I opened the window and waved goodbye to all those beautiful Santa Cruz flowers and plants. About two minutes later, a couple of big guys and a woman showed up at the door wearing street clothes and blue and black Bluetooth earpieces. We got in a blue and black car and drove into the Land of Faerie.

YOU KNOW HOW in books like *Jonathan Strange* you can leave this world by landing on a particular step with your left foot as you traipse down the Spanish stairs and find your way to the land of fairies, goblins and other magical creatures? But I'm not talking about the magical endpoint, only the funny rituals you do to get there. This was about the sixth time for me, so I minted it as an expression in Janice's private language. "We drove into the Land of Faerie" doesn't mean we saw fairies but that a horde of super-professional Bluetoothified blue&black folks rang out the changes that erase all trails.

After about three days of cars, trains, subways and parking garages, we got on an airplane that didn't have windows. It would've been more romantic if we'd been blindfolded or forced to sit in a bare compartment with raw metal walls, but Blair and I had a nice room with a fold-out bed, like Air Force One on *West Wing*.

We flew for a long time. There was no turbulence because, with Blair aboard, they took the safest route. The plane had six engines, although it could fly with only one working and many other safety features. For all I know, we went in a circle and ended up back in Santa Cruz because when we landed, a ladder rose up into our flying bedroom from a hatch on the floor, and Blair and I climbed down into another comfy room with no windows.

A chick joined us and said we had to wear seatbelts because we were in a truck. She was done up in a black cloth uniform with dark blue embroidery that made a fleur-de-lis pattern on the back and the letter "S" on the front. She made it work for her, too.

We drove for half a day and got out in a parking garage (surprise, surprise). On the way to the elevator, I looked back at the truck and misread the words written on its side. The words actually said

"Serapis Van Lines," but I misread them as "Sisyphus Van Lines," which would have been pretty funny if you think of the myth of Sisyphus and put it together with furniture movers. I guess you end up with Laurel and Hardy moving that piano upstairs.

Another done up blue&black stuck a key into the elevator's control panel, and we went down at least four floors lower than the lowest one marked. We got out into a concrete passageway under a loud river or sewer. There were swiveling video cameras everywhere and lots of heavy doors. If the FBI or the X-Men discovered the place and broke in, the Immortals would have plenty of time to escape or to fill the tunnels with poison gas. Okay, I admit this was fun.

We usually had about six blue&blacks with us. Some were men, others were women, and none of them talked much. One of the women opened a hidden door in the wall, and we stepped through into a passage with a thin gray carpet and ugly wallpaper. A little further along, we climbed up through a hatch into a corridor full of fancy doors. Far away, someone walked out of one door, crossed the hall, and disappeared into another.

Things got fancier as we went along. We reached a hallway covered in paintings, copies of works by Rafael and Rubens and DaVinci. Or maybe originals. The fat women in the Rubens paintings had lots of cellulite. There were also fancy statues, some of them a little weird, and, here and there, string quartets and other live music.

We turned a corner, reached a set of double doors guarded by guys all decked out in livery, gold over green, so fancy I wanted to laugh but couldn't because the place stifled me. They let us through and the space opened out to a huge cavern, something like what Tolkien's dwarves might have built when they carved out the inside of a mountain. We walked on polished stone sidewalks swooping in great, grand curves above an abyss, watched over by statues of a scary guy with a triangle on his face. Fake stalactites in weird shapes hung from the ceiling, people wearing silly uniforms of various colors walked busily this way and that, and in one place, I saw what looked like a spiral staircase reaching upward to the ceiling.

I wondered how they kept this place secret. Did they hire mortal builders and then murder them? Or were they kept locked in fancy suites with lifelong room service? I saw old people in the distance and figured my second theory must be right. I remembered the part about how you die painfully if you transgress, and I wondered whether the Immortals—the Illuminati—installed remote control poison capsules in their mortals. Or maybe the threat was imaginary, something the Illuminati made up to keep their servants under control.

I swear I saw Marcus for a second, far away on some other level. I wanted to run up to him, but then I'd have to explain to Blair who he was, and anyway, some friendly folks in yellow had already shepherded Marcus offstage.

After a while, we entered a normal enclosed corridor again, and the style turned classical, with Greek or Roman statues in niches. I was starting to miss the real world. I thought about tying up perfect Blair, hanging out with Marcus, who's sweet, and talking to Saul, who's wonderful. I even missed sitting in the Lexus with Menniss, who's not so wonderful, but he's real. Down there in Illuminati Land, nothing was real. I lost track of Janice all over again.

We arrived at a door carved in fancy images and guarded by stacks of butler types in gold over green. The butlers pulled the doors open, and we stepped into the secret chambers of the Illuminati. (Zeke was right—they actually called themselves that.)

I THINK I was hoping for the Palace at Versailles or maybe the counterterrorism bunker from the show *24*, but what I got was a corporation boardroom with dark wooden walls, a long table and pitchers of ice water every couple of chairs. I'd imagined grave, ancient sages, but that was all wrong since we're talking about True Immortals; the folks who rule the world looked about my age or younger. A few did seem a little old in the eyes, but I have a picture of myself at age 13, and my eyes looked old too. Not only didn't they appear ancient, they mostly didn't seem grave either, except for one scary lady up by the head of the table wearing a black silk gown with blue trim and a blue fleur-de-lis on the chest. Duh, she was the Immortal who runs the blue&blacks.

Another guy wore a forest green suit with gold buttons, and he looked cheery, with his fat, red cheeks, more like what you'd expect of the cook below stairs in a British class comedy than a head butler.

Here's another funny part: the chairs matched the people. Madam blue&black's chair had fleur-de-lis designs carved into its wood, and the fabric backing of King Butler's was a tapestry of gold leaves over a green forest. Pretty silly and like stepping into a comic book. Why didn't they look ridiculous? Then I thought of the Aztecs with their green quetzal-feather headdresses and gold embroidered shoes studded with jade, and the Pope with his silly hat and funny shoes, not to mention British judges with their red and black silk gowns, gold braided vests and horsehair wigs. Suppose you get arrested in England (as did one of my friends for smuggling speed in Marmite jars), and the judge walks in and bangs his gavel. You're not going to even think about laughing because he takes himself seriously and so does everyone else in the courtroom; besides, he has the power to do awful things to you. After a couple of seconds, these guys stopped looking silly.

A servant in gold-and-green livery graciously pulled out a chair at the foot of the table for me. I checked to see whether the chair had piercings or anything to match yours truly, but it didn't; probably, you have to place an order, and that takes time.

The Immortal sitting on my right reminded me of a type you often see in sexual abuse support groups: a little overweight and dressed in loose clothes that made her look more overweight than she was, with sad, friendly eyes and a lower lip that got chewed on a lot. I was glad to see that Immortals came in different shapes. She looked less mature than the others, and I got the idea they arranged seating by age, which would explain why they put me down at the end. They stuck Blair next to me on my other side, which fits my theory because he's young for an Immortal.

A woman with short red hair sitting halfway down the table winked at me. She looked nice but shallow, like a professor's wife I once knew who took in stray cats but wouldn't give money to the Humane Society because she didn't care about stray cats in general, only the ones that came to her door. According to my theory about the seating, she would be middling ancient.

The guy sitting opposite Professor's Wife gave me a seductive look that was *really* well done. Like, incredible. I felt the way a piece of iron feels when a magnet walks by, but it's attached to something and can't follow. The guy was nowhere as beautiful as Blair, but he had seduction down pat, and that made me curious.

Most of them weren't particularly beautiful. They were all *perfect*, in the sense that none of them were cross-eyed or had big warts hanging off their noses or even a blemish, but being perfect didn't make them gorgeous. I don't think it was only my feelings about Blair because one Immortal in a saffron shirt looked pretty good too. But he was too old for someone like me to get under his skin.

I felt someone reaching around under the table. It was Blair, and I let him take my hand. He seemed scared, so I gave his hand a squeeze.

All the chairs around the table held people except for the two at the far end. One was made of white stone and looked uncomfortable. The other, composed of thick, dark wood, tapestry fabric and a big gold halo over where the sitting person's head would go, was more like a throne. The tapestry and the wood were full of symbols: a talking mouth, a clay pot, a woman menstruating onto a field, a chicken and a woman giving birth to a horde of little people. The image of the woman giving birth was carved into the wood, but the little people seemed to be crawling off the wood onto the tapestry and up into the gold halo—quite a chair.

Black velvet curtains rippled, and a man walked out and sat in the stone chair. His face was relaxed, and yet made strange by a triangular symbol painted on it with the point up; I realized this was the guy who had images of himself all around that big cavern. "The Illuminati are now convened," he said. His voice with a radio voice— serene, melodic and warm. "I am the oldest present and, therefore, by custom, the voice of the Illuminati. But consensus rather than custom rules. Do we all agree that I should speak?"

Apparently, they'd already agreed to agree because no one said anything. He went on. "To the True Immortal Blair, I, the voice of the Illuminati, say, welcome to the realm of our love. As myself, as Alexandros, I say this too. To the mortal Janice, I say, feel thou equally welcome, for, having of your own free will befriended and aided a True Immortal, you take, by right and gratitude, a place of high honor among us. As myself, as Alexandros, I say this too."

Other people around the table told us their names, and they all murmured welcoming things. I couldn't help smiling because the feeling in the room was rather wonderful. I took a quick look at Blair to see if he was smiling. He was. I looked down at my hands because otherwise I might have done something silly, like kiss him.

Speech time next. I wouldn't be surprised if Alexandros had been the one who'd written Shakespeare's plays—he was *that* good. When words are beautiful, you shouldn't even try to quote them unless you have a perfect memory. I don't, so this next part is just an impression.

Alexandros started off by telling us the history of the Illuminati. He and his close buddy Soraya were the ones who founded it. (Soraya was the scary woman sitting beside him with the blue fleur-de-lis on her gown.) They did this about eight thousand years ago, but it wasn't their idea; someone else had told them to do it. Her name was Yavànna, and she was much older than Alexandros and Soraya put together. Whenever she showed up, she sat on the fancy throne, only she hadn't shown up for quite a while, which bothered Alexandros.

He talked about how everyone used to live in the old days, stuff historians and archaeologists would die for because this was thousands of years before people invented writing. I liked it for a while but stopped listening when he started on kings and their battles. My mind rambled off to the important question of who these folks had sex with.

I tried to put them in couples, but I couldn't. I wondered if they often had sex with mortals. The guys would. Thousands of years of practice, and you still look like you're 24? Like living in a bowl of cherries. But I worried about the female Immortals. I'm sure they could give themselves great orgasms, all the practice they had. But what about sex? Fucked up as I am, even I don't like one-night stands, and if you're thousands of years old and trying to hang with mortals, pretty much anything would feel short. I tried to do the math in my head and couldn't get it exactly, but I think one of those 12-year frames Blair talked about converts into something like a week. Depressing.

Maybe they took hafeem lovers. If you met a hafeem when he was young, you'd have him for a few thousand years. That would be a chunk, even for Soraya. I tried to put Saul together with Soraya but couldn't.

I returned to listening. I'd gotten in my head that the Illuminati led the world forward, bringing down fire from heaven and putting up black monoliths like in *2001*. Only, that's not how it worked. Sometimes they did help out after a dark age or a bad plague, but only by reminding the living of what their ancestors had already discovered. All the new inventions and big advances came from mortals.

"And then the mortals invented the alphabet," Alexandros was saying. It made me feel proud of us.

I learned that the Illuminati are big-time do-gooders, or at least mean to be. They mess around with history to make things better. For example, they helped some ancient king named Sargon beat up a bunch of other kings whose names are harder to pronounce, but when Sargon and the Ammonites tried to wipe out Lugbutt of the Goddamnites, the Immortals stopped him because they didn't think the Goddamnites should get wiped out. Things worked out according to plan, and for the next five centuries, good stuff happened to the people there.

But the Illuminati didn't always get it right. In the land of Canaan, they picked some off-brand tribe instead of the Hebrews, and the only reason we have the Bible is that the Illuminati got distracted by things happening elsewhere; by the time they looked back, Solomon had built his temple. Or something like that. I might have the details wrong. The main idea is that the Illuminati mean well and can admit mistakes. That's cool.

They worked hard. They put leaders in power and took others out; they protected crucial ships and kept caravans safe; they stopped a lot of wars and started others. They turned back the Mongols at

Vienna and helped Abraham Lincoln get elected, and it wasn't so Eurocentric as I just made it sound because they did a lot in China, Korea, Japan and India, too. Only, I know even less about Asian history than I do about our history, so I couldn't follow much. I imagined a blue&black cavalry galloping to the rescue. In some ways, it was easier for them back in the old days because they didn't have to worry one of their mortals would tell all to the tabloids.

A ton more of spoken iambic pentameter, and we reached the 20th century. Alexandros paused to drink from a glass someone behind the curtain handed him. He started up again in a quiet voice, and what he said was boring (mostly about cotton, manganese and interest rates), but my mind didn't wander because I could tell he was building up to something.

He stopped talking about cotton and manganese and turned poetic. It was really beautiful. When you dazzle someone with beauty, they let their defenses down. He was King Lear and the King James Bible rolled into one, with Ian Mckellan doing the voice. I said I shouldn't paraphrase, but here goes.

> *I was young when the ice sheets melted, and the ocean rose to flood the world. I was young when the first great fields were tilled, and the foundations of Jericho laid. These I remember and much more besides. So do others among us. We look back and see the human world becoming, and with memories so full, we can also foresee. So it was in 1919, when as one world war ceased, we saw a second one coming. As did many others, mortal as well as Immortal. But we saw what others did not: a flood of fire, a catastrophe so fearful only a god could have created it yet made by the hands of mortals. Yavànna, too, envisioned the great fire, and she was amazed. And she gave us leave to stop it.*

That meant nuclear bombs. Nuclear bombs scared them shitless, which makes sense if you remember that these folks grew up when bronze javelins were the baddest thing around. The name they used was "nuclear gods."

We could not stop the Second World War from coming, but we could shape it. And so we did. We found two terrible men and brought them to power. Why? Because in blurred future sight, we saw that the great horrors of Stalin and Hitler would prevent a greater horror.

And so it came about. The nuclear gods were born, but the two powers that wielded these gods were chastened by the horror we had caused them to know and found the wisdom not to destroy the world.

Though narrowly. During those first few decades after the nuclear gods came into being, even the Eldest cowered, and that is how we came to live underground.

And here is the question, rendered in contemporary terms, which we have faced before and shall now face again: were we right to have touched history in this terrible way? Did we do good or evil? Was it an act of compassion to cause in plain sight the death of millions because we saw, in blurred future vision, that the alternative was the death of tens of millions?

Was this egoism or wisdom? Did we have a right to act? Or did we have the right not to act, foreseeing as we did?

Wow. Talk about over the top. You create a Hitler knowing he'll kill millions because you think that, otherwise, nuclear bombs will kill 10 times more. That's what you call stepping up. Or really awful. I'm not sure.

And I didn't have time to get sure because he went straight from there to Blair's missing ear. If the last part was intense, this part went to a whole new level. I'm not going to try to quote it because I don't remember the words at all. I was too freaked out.

Some hafeem named Baehl intended to use Blair's ear to figure out the secret of immortality, and if he succeeded, terrible things would happen, even worse than nuclear war. A population explosion; war; chaos; a dark, grim world that banned children to prevent the world from drowning in them and drowned instead in the cynicism and fatigue of unrelieved age. The Illuminati wanted to protect the world from this horror, and the most important first step was to stop

Baehl. Only there was a problem: Yavànna, the oldest Immortal in the world, the one who was supposed to be sitting on that throne, wouldn't let them do it. Back when they wanted to put Hitler in power and all, she said sure, fine, whatever. But she wouldn't allow them anywhere *near* this guy Baehl.

At this point, I was a little confused because I thought it was Menniss who wanted to figure out immortality using Blair's ear. Was Menniss Baehl? Or did Menniss work for Baehl? Was Baehl the Immortal Hunter Menniss always talked about? Or was it Baehl who stole the ear and stuck Menniss in the trunk?

Then Alexandros looked directly at me. He talked straight at me, too, and in the grandest voice I've ever heard. I think I remember the words verbatim.

> *The hand of Fate declares itself and guides*
> *Us to the youthful mortal sitting here.*

He raised a finger. He gave me a lofty stare. I don't think anyone in the world can do lofty stares as well as he can.

> *Immortal-friend, Immortal-lover,*
> *Thou art chosen, three times chosen.*
> *Fate has chosen thee as servant,*
> *Setting brief and mortal life*
> *on the path of great designs.*
> *Baehl, whom by Eldest order none can touch,*
> *Has chosen thee, in speech and deed.*
> *Yavànna the Eldest chooseth thee,*
> *The choice of fate by Immortal will.*
> *She says that thou art sacrosanct,*
> *And gives to thee the rights and roles*
> *that she withholds from us.*
> *She is the Eldest, and we must obey,*
> *But while we wait, the enemy proceeds*
> *Toward nightmare.*

I wanted to say, and this affects me, *how*? But these folks had the seniority thing going big-time, and since I was the most un-senior person in the room by far, I knew I wasn't supposed to say a word.

But what the fuck? I'm Ms. Sacrosanct. *His* words. "This affects me *how*?"

The Immortals acted suitably shocked. Blair, that asshole, even let go of my hand. But being chosen by fate and all, I didn't care. Besides, I had to pee, and the room was so stuffy I could hardly breathe. I wanted this damn thing to finish up. "Is this a Frodo thing? You gave that long speech to fill me in, and now you want me to carry off a ring somewhere?"

> *Truly, we do have need of thee,*
> *and truly, that is why we reveal*
> *our purpose and our history.*
> *For we seek your help.*
> *Today the Eldest ties our hands,*
> *but tomorrow she may release us from her bonds*
> *and let us save the world from danger.*
> *She is changeable by choice.*
> *And she has decreed that we cannot to her directly speak,*
> *But only through the medium of mortals.*
> *Therefore, Janice, Immortal-friend,*
> *We ask of thee:*
> *Wilt thou a message carry?*
> *Wilt thou seek Yavànna the Eldest and speak to her on our* *behalf?*

Oh, what the hell? Anything to get out of this room where the Immortals had breathed up all the air. "Sure," I said. "No problem."

I wanted to bargain for Marcus' freedom, but I realized they couldn't let him go now that he knew about the underground world.

They stood and bowed. Did it feel solemn? Yeah, it did. Remember before when I said I felt like I'd stepped into a comic book? I take it back. Funny chairs and all, this was real.

"YOU SHOULDN'T GO alone," Blair said. "I want to come with you."

We were tucked away in bed in a fancy room down there in the underground Hilton. The mattress was some luxurious inflatable kind with his-and-hers tension adjustment. I'd always wanted one of those. His-and-hers closets, too; mine would be stuffed full of silk nightgowns and outfits Jennifer Garner would feel proud to wear when she went on one of her missions. An incredible hot tub, unlimited room service, video on demand, Internet and a library card that could get you any book you wanted. What more could anyone ask for?

In the days after Alexandros gave me that speech, other Immortals stopped by to put in their own two thousand cents, and they had me convinced that they were wise (a word that sticks to the top of my mouth like a mushy graham cracker) and that they thought they were good. The bottom line was that I should get going with the message as soon as possible.

"I don't think they're going to let you go with me," I said. "You're a precious Immortal, and they don't think Immortals have any business running around in the outside world. But I like it that you asked."

"You're saying I'm a prisoner? I can't leave if I want to?"

If. So he didn't, not really. Well, at least he'd pretended to consider it.

"All I have to do is hand this Eldest person a piece of paper," I said. "I'll be back soon."

"Will you really come back?"

I'll be damned. The guy did have insight sometimes.

Going on missions and then returning home to some wimped-out house-husband watching TV in an underground palace where you can't breathe? "Of course I'll come back," I said, and he believed me, though I couldn't see it.

THE ARTSY IMMORTAL with short red hair was the one who came to take me out. She said her name was Maggie and called me "dear." She was holding a silk-covered tube about a foot long with the message rolled up inside, and we had to figure out the best way for me to carry it. First, she offered me a big fat purse, but I said no. Then she tried to get me to wear it around my neck, but that was ridiculous. Finally, she scrounged up a black backpack, and I went with that. Ms. Maggie said it was time to go and asked whether I wanted to say goodbye to Blair. I said I already had, and let's get going.

She led me the whole way. We had escorts dressed in tie-dye uniforms, but they stayed at a discrete distance. I got the feeling I was Maggie's pet project, which should have pissed me off, except she didn't scare me the way Soraya or Alexandros did. Also, I liked her. We talked about relationships some, and she knew a lot—you would think so, after six thousand years—and she told me I was right about female Immortals taking hafeems for lovers.

I wondered if Saul had ever been her lover but didn't ask.

She led me to a hallway with a one-way mirror running along one side, and we could see into a cafeteria where lots of mortals and maybe hafeems milled around and couldn't see us. She pointed out Marcus. He was sitting at a table eating lunch with some chick who looked exactly like Rebecca and making lovey eyes at her.

"He's nice-looking," Maggie said. "But from what I heard during your last conversation with him—we managed to snoop—the two of you never made love. I approve."

"Christ, you Illuminati are nosy! But why do you approve?"

"Because, dear, you've gotten a True Immortal to fall in love with you, and that's remarkable. You're very talented."

When someone who looks your age patronizes you, it's annoying—even when you know they're five thousand years old. "I didn't *work* at it," I said. "It just happened."

"Then you were very lucky," she said.

The snot.

We walked for another half-hour and got into an elevator. The elevator doors opened, and we looked out into a parking garage that might have been the same parking garage we came in by. Hard to tell. Maybe there's only one parking garage in the world, and all parking garages are parts of that same one, with walls put up discreetly so you can't tell. The Platonic parking garage theory: aren't I a giggle?

Maggie kissed me, said she'd always look after me, and got

teary-eyed. The elevator doors closed, and she pushed the button to open them again. She kissed me again, said a lingering goodbye to her rescued alley cat (me). Then the doors closed, and she went away for good.

A voice said, "Hello, Janice," and Maggie came out from behind a pillar in *front* of me.

Well, not really. She wore Maggie-type clothes, had Maggie-type mannerisms and did Maggie's voice perfectly, but she looked a little different. She was also mortal. The real Maggie wouldn't risk the outside world, so she sent a fake Maggie to take care of me.

Mortal Maggie took me through a bunch of Faerie-world stuff I won't get into because you know all about it. She dropped me off at the Pacific Garden Mall in Santa Cruz with money and a special cell-phone. Another Maggie would contact me in an hour or so and give me directions to the Eldest, but in the meantime, I could go shopping.

I went to a convenience store and bought some gum, cigarettes and a throwaway cell phone of my own. I called Zeke on that one and asked him to meet with me. He said he'd find me at the mall.

The Pacific Garden Mall isn't the kind of mall you're probably thinking of, just a street with shops, planters full of flowers and piles of post-modern hippies. The air smelled of roasting coffee, lilacs, ocean and marijuana. I declined a bong hit from a Rastaman on the sidewalk and waved at a baby who smiled at me over her father's shoulder as he lurched her along. I sat on a stone ledge beside a concrete planter and watched a girl with heavy garden gloves and a sleeveless t-shirt dig in a flower bed. Santa Cruz is lush in a way Fort Collins could never be.

It's strange how you can treat flowers as decoration even though they're alive. The flower girl yanked out plants whose flowers had withered and stuck in new ones. I wanted to take home the used plants so they didn't have to die. Only, I didn't have a home, and Flower Girl had pulled out 100s of plants.

At a used clothing store, I bought a green t-shirt, red half-calfs, white Converse and a backpack, and changed, shoving my old stuff in the backpack. I went into a juice bar with huge wooden menus on the wall that listed juices on one side and the supplements you could mix in with them on the other: ginkgo, echinacea, zinc, etc., and also "Doctor Harry Boullard's Longevity Cocktail." That last one made me smile because I knew something about longevity that Doctor Quackster Baxter didn't. I knew about Immortals.

But my left hand did its shaking thing again, and I got a drink with his cocktail, just in case. He had a brochure about how alternative medicine treats the *cause* of diseases, not just the symptoms, and I read it while the juice barista mixed my drink in a large chrome blender. But it was all wrong. Mortality is what causes disease, and food supplements can't treat that.

My dosed-up carrot and broccoli juice tasted weird and healthy, and I could feel it cleaning me out. I thought about that Immortal who didn't look happy, and I wished she were with me so we could talk about things that suck. I missed my support group. I missed my crappy neighborhood, my house, and Maurice but I didn't miss Blair.

"Excuse me."

I looked up. "Hey, Zeke."

"Hey, Janice. Would you like to go for a walk?" He put out his arm, like Darcy in *Pride and Prejudice*, and I took it.

We made quite a pair, him with his goatee and handlebar mustache and me in my Converse. We crossed the street at a six-way intersection, and because the other side wasn't part of the mall, the shops were old and needed paint; I liked them better than the fancy ones on the side. Behind the shops, a chalky cliff waved flags of pampas grass. The shops petered out, and we climbed a stairway cut into the side of the cliff. We stopped to rest on a carved-out landing halfway up, and I asked him why he wasn't afraid of going out in public like all the other Immortals were.

"Because I'm a coward," he said.

"How does that work, Zeke?" I knew he'd say something cute.

"I'm scared to death of safety."

"Cute."

"Anyway, I'm not an Immortal. I'm a mortal like you."

"You're not at all like me. You're a hafeem. You live three or four thousand years."

"I'm more like you than not. I know I will get old, and my life will end. Immortals don't have that, and most of them become worn out and empty, sad like the elves that stayed too long in Tolkien's Middle-earth. If I ever became immortal, I'd play Russian roulette every New Year's, so that wouldn't happen to me."

He'd seemed pretty sexy under fluorescent lights in that hotel casino in Ely, Nevada. In bright daylight, he was the sexiest guy I'd ever seen. I had no idea why. "Why are you so sexy?"

In a detached voice, as if he were an anthropologist and I'd asked him about the habits of the ruling class in Medieval Korea, he said, "The question of my ineffable sexiness has stumped the world's brightest minds for centuries."

"Tell me more."

He twirled his goatee. He looked down at his feet, leaned on my shoulder and brushed chalk off one of his burgundy wingtips. "An example," he said. "When I turned 16, my nursemaid confessed that for many years she'd felt tempted to relieve me of my virginity—long before it was physiologically possible."

"I assume you didn't call child protective services."

"Wow." He sounded sincerely impressed. "I never thought of that. That's true."

"What's true?"

"That maybe it wasn't good for me that my nursemaid offered to sleep with me. But they didn't have child protective services in 1683."

"What did you do instead? Blush? How old was she?"

"Twenty-four. I may have blushed. What I most clearly recall, however, is my state of mind as I requited her frustrated desires."

"Let me guess: you felt like a true do-gooder."

He gave me an astonished look. "How'd you know?"

I didn't answer. We started up the cliff again. When he'd recovered from the brilliance of my insight, he said, "But getting back to your question, after we finished our third round, she said I was the sexiest young man she'd ever met. I asked her what was sexy about me, and she said she didn't know. No one has ever answered the question to my satisfaction. It appears to be a matter of fate."

"A heavy burden."

"Indeed."

When we reached the top of the stairs, he led me past white-washed buildings that were part of Mission Santa Cruz. He'd been there when they were new and had stories to tell.

We reached a modern neighborhood full of houses painted in bright colors and surrounded by pretty gardens. A small sign by one house read, "Santa Cruz Zen Center."

Zeke said, "A mission and a Zen Center. I'd call this clifftop holy ground."

"Are you religious?"

He gave the question some thought. "Religious enough to be afraid of Yahweh. He's not very amusing and doesn't like my chief hobby."

"Which is? Oh."

"Exactly. Yahweh doesn't like people to like sex as much as I do. I hope Satan is funny because I'll be spending eternity with the fellow."

"No, you won't."

"I won't?"

"Not a chance."

"Will you put that in writing?" He took out a notebook.

I wrote it down for him and signed my name. He looked relieved, and I kissed him on the cheek.

We sat on a green cast-iron bench by a park, the ocean stretching far away and the sky even further. I felt ridiculously peaceful, like I was on holiday. I'd just left a bunch of scary Illuminati, and I was about to see this Eldest person, who I was pretty sure would be even scarier than the Illuminati. But I was with Zeke right now. And even though I had no say in what he did next, I felt fine.

A city truck drove up to the park, and a woman dressed in a brownish uniform climbed out to work on the flowers in a planter.

"She could be a spy," I said.

"She could. And a damn beautiful spy at that." He reclined on the bench and sighed. Then he took a piece of paper out of his pocket and gave it to me. "Please, my love, would you give this to the Eldest?"

"It doesn't say 'kill the bearer?'"

"My dear Janice Guildenstern, of course not."

"But why me? Why can't you bring it to her yourself?"

"Because I'm not allowed to. She insists that mortals do all the work just now. Did I mention how lovely you are?"

Though I recognized magnetic charm, I was no better at resisting it than anyone else, especially when I didn't want to resist it. But there was nowhere nearby to go and no time.

Anyway, this was holy ground. Yahweh would be watching right along with his frenemy, the Buddha. Zeke only kissed my hand.

A CAR DROVE up and Zeke got in, leaving me alone on the clifftop. I took the scroll out of my backpack, unrolled it, and stared at a page of incomprehensible writing divided into formal sections and subsections, like the United States Constitution in Minoan. When I watch a foreign movie with subtitles and go to the kitchen to get something to drink, I feel like I'm still following the words even though I'm not. Same here. I can't read Minoan as well as I used to, but who could argue with an argument so well organized?

Zeke's letter was written in plain English, and I could hear him saying it.

Oh, Beautiful One,

Your obedient worshipper wishes you to know that Step Three, The Bringing, well that's all done now. Up next: Step Four, The Knowing. Should I proceed? Give me a jingle.

PS. Janice is a real find. I like her lots.

Could you get away with talking like that to the oldest human being alive, someone who'd already been old when agriculture got invented? You had to hand it to Zeke's cheek. Then my left arm started twitching, and the violet came down. Straight lines inside my head chopped up the "me" in there until there was no me. But only for a few seconds, then it passed.

I thought about going to the doctor. But I didn't know any doctors in Santa Cruz other than Dr. Quackster Baxter, and by the time

I'd finished putting the scroll away, one of the Maggies called and gave me directions. She texted them, too, so I wouldn't forget.

Three buses and a happy of hippies later, I got out in front of an ice cream stand. I bought a double-scoop of double chocolate. I licked the first scoop slowly and chowed down the second because it was starting to melt. I felt crappy. The ocean was two blocks away, and the text message told me to go to it.

I sat on the sand at a beach with dozens of fire pits and watched the beautiful college students tan themselves. No one looked unhappy. Santa Cruz is weird that way.

I took off my shoes and wet my feet in the waves. How had I managed to live my whole life so far from the ocean? Maybe cold ocean water would wash me clean, and I wouldn't need psychotherapy. But I knew it wouldn't work. Janice was a sick, sick girl, not only because of the cancer in her brain but every other way too. I needed a coven of doctors.

I walked in the direction I was supposed to walk. The usual Santa Cruz cliff ran along the beach with beautiful Victorians on top and rickety wooden steps descending down from them. Here and there, the cliff stuck an arm deep into the water, and you had to work your way around. In one place, the cliff stuck out so far I couldn't get around at all. Luckily, there was a hole in the rock. I pushed my backpack through, then crawled, a happy little kid on her hands and knees getting wet sand on her pants.

The hole led to a small closed-off beach, like the one with Blair's rock. This beach had a rock, too, though not as big, and my highway patrolman friend was sitting on it.

Oh, he worked for the Eldest. No wonder he didn't arrest me for the gun.

He wore a bathing suit instead of a uniform, and hair covered his head instead of a trooper's hat. He looked like a model.

"Nice uniform," I said. "What's up? Aren't pedestrians allowed here either?"

"They're not unless you have friends in high places, miss." He hopped down from the rock. "Luckily, you do. May I show you the way?"

"If you insist," I said, though I couldn't see there was much showing to do. *Two more beaches,* the message said.

But to get to the last beach, we had to get around another spot where the cliff reached far into the water, and this time there wasn't a hole to crawl through. He took my backpack and said I should go around anyway. It looked crazy, but I'm brave. I waited until the waves pulled as far back as they would go and ran for it, but even so, the water reached my knees, and before I made it around, a new wave came and soaked me to the hips. I might have washed away if he hadn't grabbed me and carried me through.

Somehow he'd kept the backpack dry. I put it back on. "Was it really chance?" I asked.

"Not sure what you mean." He wasn't so fast in the head as Zeke.

"Obviously, you work for … my friend in high places." I almost said, "the Eldest," but realized he might not know whom he worked for. "But how did you find me on that road? Were you just driving by?"

"I got a call to look for you."

"Did they tell you why?"

"No." He sounded like he didn't want to know, so I dropped it. Anyway, we were there.

This beach had a sea cave, and when waves shot up into it, the cave boomed. There was an elevated ledge on one side, and we walked on it to stay dry. We were above the water, but the floor was slick with rainbow-colored seaweed, and my policeman friend gave me his arm so I wouldn't slip. He was nice but empty. Marcus had a lot more soul. What about Blair? He was lonely, and there's soul in that.

And me? It depended on when and where. Back there in the Illuminati hole, I didn't exist, but this was Janice's renaissance.

We crawled through a slimy hole at the back of the cave into another, larger cave, a really big one. The cave had electric lights and at least 20 bodyguard types who looked on-the-clock, plus a German Shepherd doing her best not to look cute. A female body-guard climbed off her rock and came up to us. She was about my size and shape, wore her hair like mine, and was dressed in my out-fit down to the sockless feet in red Converse.

My policeman said goodbye, and the two wormed their way back out. If anyone was watching, they wouldn't see anything odd, such as two people going into a cave and never coming out. It would look like we went in, looked around and popped back out. Pretty amazing. This Eldest lady knew how to get things done.

My left arm shook, and I got nauseous and threw up on the sand.

A lady bodyguard said, "Everyone's nervous before they meet her. Don't feel bad."

I said, "Thank you," but I wasn't nervous, just dying. I threw up again, felt better and kicked sand over the vomit.

She ran a wand over me, the way they do at airports, then searched my backpack. Another woman brought the German Shepherd over. The dog sniffed me, got bored and went off to dig up my buried vomit.

This cave also had a hole in the back. It was as big as a door, and I walked through alone. I was in a long tunnel. After I'd walked 15 minutes, the tunnel ended at a set of stairs. I climbed I don't know how many stairs, felt sick and sat down, then climbed more. I reached a landing that had a closed door. No one answered when I knocked, so I opened the door.

I stepped into shaded sunlight under a kind of arbor, with flow-ering vines on trellises far above blocking any view from the sky but in the prettiest way. The floor was made of dirt, and so were the walls. At the far end of the arbor, a woman sat in a big wicker chair. The moment I saw her, I stopped feeling sick. I was in a secret gar-den, alone with the Eldest.

ALTHOUGH BY THEN I should have known better, my mind expected her to *look* old. Of course, she didn't. She could have been my age. She had shining, long, wavy, black hair and perfect skin without wrin-kles. Her skin had some color, and I thought she looked Indonesian. She wore a lime green sari. She sat quietly, and my first thought was that I'd met the Buddha: still, detached, cool. But that was wrong. The Eldest had about as much passion as a human being could; she just kept it in check.

She kept her body in check, but her face kept changing. Or at least I think it did. Faces change on me sometimes when I fall in love with a guy, and we're close in a half-darkened room: he starts looking like everyone who ever was. But I've never seen it happen in daylight or to a woman. Feral. Refined. Asian. African. Angry. Kind. Gray eyes. Violet-gray.

I was wrong when I said she could be my age. No way. By the time a normal person gets this deep and complicated, she has lines stamped all over her face. The Eldest had nothing permanent written on her skin, not even as much as I do. But there are non-permanent things you can see in a face too, and hers had a million more words to say than anyone my age could think of.

The arbor was dead silent, except for a breeze that stirred the plants highest up. The closer I came to her, the more I wanted to kneel. When I got close enough to touch her, I decided *what the hell* and knelt. Kneeling felt great, so I put my head on the floor, and that felt even better. Like checking your whole fucked up self at the door.

I'd waited my whole life for this.

"I AM YAVÀNNA," she said. All kinds of crazy accents juiced up her voice. "I am Yavànna, and you are Janice, and you shall rise."

I managed to get my head off the floor but not my eyes. As for standing, my knees didn't believe a word of it. Her chair creaked. She got up. I watched her feet as she walked toward me. With each step, those feet gave the ground a whole-body hug.

She touched my upper arms. Her touch moved down toward my hands. She clasped my hands in hers, and then I was standing.

We were face to face. She didn't say anything, but she didn't have to, not with a face like that. Like many women who've been abused, I tended to spend more time with men than with women. Backward, I know. This made up for it.

She touched me with her hands. She touched my face, my neck, my stomach. None of this was sexual. My legs. My cheeks. My hair.

She touched my forehead with her lips. She lifted one foot, balanced on the other, and rubbed her toes on my calves and ankles.

I'm not sure which things she said in words and which parts I got directly. And I'm not sure how to write them. I'll try a poetic form, but don't take the words literally.

Have you been raped and beaten and raped and beaten? Yavànna has.
Have you given birth to baby torn from you and
taken? Torn from you and killed? Yavànna has.
Have you been caged and starved? Have
you been enslaved? Yavànna has.
Have you known the shame there was before words were made
and mind could not protect itself with words? Yavànna has.
Were you there when words first came, and you could
hear your shame told to you by others? Yavànna was.
Long ago,
Words became thought, became power.
Words enslaved her.
Then she became free.
She became Yavànna.
Yavànna the Eldest.
Yavànna who is not a god,
and yet a god to men and to women.
And to Janice?
What shall be Yavànna to Janice?
She shall be your friend.

That's the general idea, though it wasn't as verbal or corny as what I wrote.

Anyway, after that came the rainstorm. I mean tears. I let her see them more than I let myself see them.

She licked the tears from my cheeks. No one had ever done that to me before, and I don't think anyone else will unless it's her again, and she can do it all she wants.

She cupped her hands and filled them with Janice tears. She ran her hands through her hair. She pushed me down and made me sit cross-legged, and she sat cross-legged too. I realized that one reason her face kept changing is that my face was changing. Each face of mine called out a different face in her and vice versa. A way of holding a conversation I never knew about.

She laughed, and I laughed. Or I groaned and she did the same. We did this until I couldn't stand it anymore. And then we kept on doing it.

WHEN WE STARTED talking again, she'd lost her accent and spoke in standard English; apparently, she performed her unusual speech style for effect.

She asked me for the letters, and I got them out of the backpack and gave them to her.

"I love writing," Yavànna said. "I think of it as words captured from the moving air. It's still magic to me. I remember when words couldn't yet be captured, and when they first were. Now, I will look at these, and we shall see what I do."

She set Zeke's folded paper in her lap, patted it, and smiled at me like we were sisters. She unrolled the scroll from Alexandros. Moving her lips silently, she ran a finger down the page. Her hands were beautiful.

After reading half the scroll, she looked up at me again, holding her place with one finger, and said, "This is a language from long ago. A beautiful lost language. Its spoken form has no descendants, and its writings disappeared in fire and water. Alexandros knows that I know this language and that I love it. He wishes to charm me. But he is so heavy handed."

She returned to reading. Her finger reached the bottom of the page. "So heavy handed," she repeated. "He demonstrates like Euclid what I should fear and lays out like a code of law the actions I should take and that he would take on my behalf, would I allow. Very well. But he lies. He does not truly want to stop it, but to place it under his control." Her accents were coming back. "He plans and thinks I do not see? That I do not know. He thinks he can fool *me*? Deceive *me*? Add together all the lives of all the Illuminati and so many years and more have I Yavànna lived.

"And yet, he speaks truly of the danger. So many people on this earth already, and if all become immortal, all are doomed. He speaks of this in his scroll, and he speaks truly. But he does not speak of what is behind the words, the rule of the small by the great. Alexandros and Soraya on Olympus. This he means but dares not say. And so he lies. He lies to *me*. And so I shall set down his letter and fail to decide. I shall hold the powers equal and let chance decide."

She put Alexandros' scroll back in its tube. Her voice returned to standard English, and she said, "I am fond of not deciding. Why? Because I trust fate. I trust Her. Although she is not kind, she is wise."

She set the tube on the sand beside her and unfolded Zeke's note. This time she read without moving her lips. Her eyes glittered, and she laughed. "This is a man who is not wise at all. This man is not grave. He cares but does not take care. He cares with careless-ness. He is full of care but not careful. English has these words, and I play with them. Because he plays. You have read this note?"

"Yes, I read it." I felt an urgent need to add that I'd never slept with or even touched him but kept silent.

She laughed, and I may have heard a giggle in it. "He is a lovely man. A man to touch. Do you agree with the Eldest? Do you agree with Yavànna? That he is a man one wants to make love to?"

"Yes, he's very sexy, Eldest."

She adjusted her sari so the fabric draped beautifully between her knees, then turned cool and rational. "A lovely man he is. But shall a man so ungrave make so grave a change on this earth? Is not the gravity of a man like Alexandros or a woman like Soraya more fit to carry so much weight? More fit, yes. But whom would we more enjoy trusting? The other." She sighed. "And so, I remain indecisive. Because I do not decide, I do decide, and the amusing man, he carries on. You need not tell him so, for no answer is all the answer he needs. Would you like to be immortal, little sister?"

Talk about a slight change in direction. It took me a while to catch up.

Of *course* I wanted to be immortal. I wanted to match up with Blair better than I did. But now that I'd seen something of immor-tality, it scared me. "I don't know," I said.

She definitely giggled now. It sounded natural in her, and that surprised the heck out of me. "One older than all the Illuminati placed head to foot, the other just born, and we are the same. I have a question. Please, will you advise me?

"Advise you? Eldest, what could *I* possibly advise you on?"

"Oh, hush." She pushed on my knees, like girls at a slumber party. "Our friend Saul, he protested the same."

"Saul's wise," I said.

Her voice turned soft. "Yes, Saul is very wise. But you stand in one place, he stands in another, and I stand in yet another, and so you may see what I cannot and he cannot. My question now, and sister Janice, please do answer me, for I need to know: is it a gift or a curse?"

"Is what a gift or curse?"

She giggled again. "You do not think about this day and night as I do? I am glad. I mean immortality. As you've known it in your lover Blair and seen it in those weighty people underground, and in me. This power that stops the body's time: if our amusing friend brings it from the few and gives it to the many, will they thank him for it? Will it be good for them?"

I wanted to tell her I was just a fucked up girl who couldn't possibly advise her. But her ancient eyes looked at me with such respect and need that I hushed myself, as she wanted, and thought about it.

Would people feel thankful for immortality? That wasn't the right question. People aren't usually all that thankful, except for the wrong things. Would it be good for them? What does "good for you" mean? Maybe it means "healing." Would more time untwist my twists and turns and help me heal? Or would my twists and turns congeal to rock? It could go either way.

But before I could say anything in words, bad things happened. Very bad things.

I was dizzy and hot in the head. I heard myself think, *this is a shitty time to get sick again.*

I saw two Yavànnas. My left hand shook. My whole left arm shook.

Time broke into different lines.

I was lying on the ground in wet clothes, and my tongue hurt. Saul was standing over me.

I said, "You're the one who should answer her question, not me."

He didn't hear me. The redwoods were too tall.

Zeke was there too. Saul called him Baehl.

A woman in a black beret touched my hand. She squatted beside me and put her hands on my chest like she was going to do CPR.

Many people have died before, but it was a new experience for *me*.

CHAPTER 6

THE SCIENTIST

"We hung our harps on the willow trees.
We wept, and we remembered Zion."

PSALM 137

Real scientists are the real saints: they are truly pure.
Or, at least, Francine is.

THE CHRONICLER

FRANCINE

HOWLS ROSE IN her mind, like when high winds poured around her house and made sounds like wailing ghosts. She'd wake in terror, clutching her big down pillow. Only when she'd become fully awake would she grip reality and remember that the human-sounding groans came from nothing more supernatural than flow turbulence around the edges of her new solar panels.

But what could she hold on to now? Her lab was wrecked, and she'd fled her beautiful solar-powered house. No graduate students. No research. Nothing to clutch as protection against the howling except this blue lunchbox and the tall tale inside.

Tires shrieked as the Jeep lurched around a corner. Richard was driving like a madman. She thought of her bipolar brother, Sammie, and his endless car crashes. Her hands ached and her fingertips had turned purple from gripping the lunchbox so hard. She relaxed her hold to let the blood flow back. She should take better care of her hands.

Once upon a time, she'd had beautiful hands. That's what everyone told her. She'd taken the compliments for granted—until they stopped coming. Cooking, chemical reagents, and obsessive cleaning had taken their toll. No elastin left. These days she had the hands of a fishwife. She owned closets full of moisturizing lotions, but none helped. What was a fishwife anyway? Probably, someone who wrecked her hands scaling fish because she'd married a fisherman.

She set the lunchbox on the floor between her feet and leafed through the dossier Richard had given her: birth certificates,

281

fingerprints and passports, police reports of missing persons and a single faded photo from a newspaper. Taken together, they told the story of a man who didn't age.

"It's so easy to fake photos," she said.

They were driving on a two-lane highway now, steadily and evenly, but above the speed limit. Richard twisted around in the seat, struggled with a pocket, and pulled out a cell phone. "Use the web browser," he said. "Find the *Sydney Tribune* archive page, and look at August 11th, 1958, page six." He slammed on the brakes and made a sudden U-turn.

She wasn't good at typing with her thumbs, especially in a constantly braking and swerving car, but she found the story from the dossier, and the photo, too: a man in his mid-30s who'd gone missing in Australia.

He looked younger than mid-30s, looked as young as the graduate students who used to come to talk to her during office hours, bashful and shy because they'd fallen hopelessly in love with her. One or two a semester. When was the last time that happened?

"Found the article?" Menniss said. "So you see, I didn't fake the photo. Now go to the Homeland Security website, www.dhs.gov. Under sitemap, you'll find a login option. Use this name and password."

He gave them to her, and she laboriously thumbed them in.

"Now search for Alan Davidsen. No, first, enter your own name. Just to see how much they know."

It took a while to type her whole name, but when she did, the things that came up filled her with outrage. "Oh my God! They have every place I've lived. All my driver's licenses and passport photos. Even my high school yearbook. And what's this part? Phone log? They have every single number I've called? Going back 20 years? And my emails. Is this because—because you brought me the tissue?"

"No, not at all. They have that kind of information on everyone."

"But that's unconstitutional! The Republicans are turning the United States into a dictatorship."

He twisted the steering wheel, and they left the highway at such a sharp angle the force slammed her into the passenger door.

"Stop it!" she cried. "You're going to get us killed."

"I'm trying to save us from getting killed. Now type in Alan Davidsen."

She did. And there he was, the same man 50 years later, but he hadn't aged a year. Maybe a man could stay young-looking all the way up to 40, or even 50, if he used enough makeup. But given the time interval, this man calling himself Alan Davidsen had to be at least 70 years old. It wasn't possible to look like a beautiful young man at 70.

Unless he didn't have an aging clock.

"You'll want to close your eyes now," Richard said.

She closed her eyes and put her palms over them as inertia tossed her. She heard horns and tire screeches and plugged her ears with her index fingers to make the outside world disappear.

A human who didn't age. A science-fiction story.

Not at all. She should have been looking for such cases herself. If all higher organisms possess a genetic clock that initiates and controls the rate of aging, mutations that disable the clock could certainly occur. Perhaps, as she suspected, the clock was linked to the citric acid cycle or some other essential physiologic function. In that case, non-fatal mutations would be extremely rare. But rare isn't zero.

You meet someone at a bar, seduce him, and he gives you the key to winning the Nobel Prize. It sounded like the punch line of a joke.

Only, it wasn't a joke. Someone had wrecked her lab, and a few hours later, Federal agents were pounding on the door of her house.

Her eyes popped open. "Are they still following us?"

They were on the freeway, past Capitola.

"Hold on tight." He jerked the wheel, swerved across three lanes of traffic and raced down an exit ramp. "I don't think so. I think I've lost them."

"If you've lost them, why are you still driving like this?"

"Just to make sure."

He made another of his violent U-turns and threw the car up an on-ramp, putting them on the opposite side of the freeway.

You meet a man in a bar, and he gives you the tissue of an Immortal. You sequence the tissue's DNA, which doesn't take more than six months. You use a computer to compare the tissue genome against the normal human genome—that doesn't take any appreciable time at all, given the speed of computers—then you do some digging. With any luck, a few weeks later, you find the genetic clock, the goal of your whole professional life. What a funny joke. Especially when you can't sequence the tissue because you don't have a lab anymore and you're running away from someone who isn't chasing you anymore. Hysterically funny.

But she didn't let herself laugh because she was afraid she wouldn't be able to stop. She was on the edge. She didn't have full-blown bipolar disease like Sammie and her aunt Evelyn, but she'd known for a long time that she had the tendency. If she went too far down that road, she might not come back.

She looked at Richard, his big body hunched around the wheel, his eyes flashing in every direction. Although he was driving like a madman, she found his presence calming.

She wondered what he thought of her. She wasn't beautiful anymore, not like she once was. And she wasn't a normal woman. She was a science robot. Mike had told her that a thousand times. Men want women who can feel, but she lived in her mind, not her feelings. Did Richard like her anyway? Last night, while they were making love, he certainly seemed to. What about now?

As she tried to concentrate on the question, she ran into the familiar obstacle that impaired her ability to understand other people. When she was a child, she'd named it Blocking Monster—a mental block she imagined as a giant creature made of stone that plopped down out of nowhere and blocked her perception of other people.

She had so many mental blocks. The worst was Gray Fog, the dense mental mist that sometimes impaired her concentration when she wanted to think.

Other people didn't have the same blocks. Mike said her problem came from focusing on facts too much, and he was probably right. Mike said she was afraid of emotions, and that's why she was a scientist—because she wanted to think instead of feel.

But he had that last part backward. She pursued science because it *made* her feel. She loved science. What was more worth getting passionate about than the truth?

Consider, for example, this piece of truth: Japanese quail and common pigeons each weigh about the same as the other, but pigeons live 10 times longer. A Japanese quail begins to show signs of aging at a year and a half, something that won't happen to a pigeon for another *15* years. Isn't that enough in itself to prove that aging is under genetic control?

An entire factor of ten. Apply that to a human, and what do you get? The lifespan of Methuselah. Not that there ever really was a Methuselah.

Richard lifted a hand off the steering wheel and stroked her once-beautiful hair. "I think we're safe now."

"You do?" On impulse she leaned over and kissed him. He was such a good, kind man. She knew that from the stories he'd told. She trusted him. How wonderful to have someone you could trust.

FRANCINE UNZIPPED THE lunch box and checked on the sample. A dozen ice cubes were floating in the water, and the sample was wrapped tightly in a thick wad of Saran wrap. "How far do we have to go? We may need to get more ice."

"I'm not sure. But the directions are in the most recent text message on my phone."

She found the message and read through it. "Based on the mileage, it looks like an hour or two. The ice should last that far. But what's this place we're going to? It's deep in the redwoods."

"A hidden laboratory for you, Dr. Selis." He pronounced "laboratory" the Boris Karloff way. Her non-scientist friends in college used to say it that way too. "Francine has to go to her la-BOR-a-TOR-y." Back when she had non-scientist friends. Most of them were English majors. Then molecular biology took over her life, and she didn't have time for friends.

She had a frightening thought. "Who sent you these directions? Are you sure they're not in on the conspiracy?"

"They came from my client. He's the one who convinced me that Immortals exist in the world and paid me to search for them."

Francine imagined Richard dressed like Sherlock Holmes in a deerstalker hat and holding a magnifying glass. She smiled. "Who's your client?"

"I don't know. I've worked for him for 25 years doing this and that, but I've never seen his face. I call him the I-H, the Immortal Hunter. I've lately realized he's a character."

"How so?"

"He has a weird sense of humor. He thinks life is a big joke."

"I hate that attitude," she said. "Life's not a joke. There's so much greed and selfishness in the world that you must take it seriously. Watch out!" A truck carrying redwood logs appeared out of nowhere, filling the road. She cried out and closed her eyes. She didn't want to die. Not now. There was too much left to discover.

But Richard made a smooth turn, and the huge crash she expected didn't happen. She opened her eyes, and the road was clear. "You're a good driver," she said.

"It's the car. It has stability control. It also has a really good radio. How about we listen to some music and relax?"

They were driving in a suburban neighborhood in the foothills of the Santa Cruz Mountains. He tuned the radio to a classical station, and she would have liked it except he turned the volume up too high. She reached toward the knob to turn it down, but Richard grabbed her forearm before she made it there.

He put his mouth to her ear. "I have something important to tell you, and I have to assume this car is bugged."

The car was bugged? Howls of terror rose again. But she was also curious. Putting her mouth to his ear now, she asked, "Bugged by whom?"

"My client. I only trust him so far. Right now, he needs you, but the moment you discover how to make people immortal, he won't need you anymore. That worries me. Don't the directions say I'm supposed to hop the curb somewhere around here? We're on Bridgelane Drive."

The sudden change of subject confused her, but only for an instant and then she was on top of it. She scanned the text message. "There's supposed to be a green two-story house across from a house under construction. Oh, here we are. Hop the curb at that empty lot past the yurt. But are you sure we should follow these directions? What if it's a trap?"

"We don't have much of a choice."

He drove the Jeep over the curb. They passed through a large clearing between two houses and came to the dirt road leading into the redwoods.

"If we stay out in the open, the guys chasing us will find us, and even though I don't entirely trust my client, I trust *him* more than I trust *them*. We have to go to ground somewhere, and I don't see any other option. But once we're at the I-H's place, we'll need to handle things carefully. The point is to manipulate things so you stay essential. As long as the I-H needs you, you're safe."

She was in the middle of a real-life thriller. "But if I have to worry about manipulating someone, I'll be too anxious to work. When I'm anxious, my mind goes sideways."

He put his arm around her. "How about this for a deal ... you do the science, and I'll do the manipulating? It's a way of life in my line of work, and I'm good at it. When am I supposed to turn next?"

"Not for another mile."

They were deep in the forest now. She loved redwoods. Beautiful trees towered up around them, trees so high that when you looked up you felt like you were falling. They made all your personal problems seem so small.

MENNISS

I KNOW HOW to protect her, Menniss thought. But how do I protect myself? The moment I deliver her to the I-H, I'm disposable.

Or worse than disposable—I'm an active problem. Francine may be brilliant, but she's an innocent. With me gone, the I-H would have complete control. If I were him, I'd get rid of me. And I'm going straight into the I-H's lair.

That terrifying woman on the beach, the one Saul called the Eldest, what was it she'd said? "Fly from trap to trap"? She sure had that right. Menniss held his hand to his stomach and pressed into the soreness.

"What's wrong?" Francine asked.

"I had surgery last night to remove a transmitter implanted in my stomach."

"Oh my goodness. Really?"

"Yes. It's a long story."

"You had an operation just last night? You must be in a lot of pain."

"Not so much, really. But I'm exhausted."

"I'm sure you are." She rubbed his shoulder at the collarbone. She did it in a repetitive way he found annoying, but he put up with it and tried to think. He was getting too old for this business of staying up all night.

That other thing the Eldest said: "I will for one hour close the sky to your enemies, and on the ground, I shall for one hour impair them." He'd woven his way through innumerable cars filled with

289

blue&blacks and never would have escaped if she hadn't protected him. Now it was long past an hour. For now, he was safe under the canopy, but they'd find him the moment he left the forest.

He could take Francine somewhere else, but she'd need a lab and expensive, cutting-edge equipment. He was well off, but not *that* well off. And there would be only so many places to buy the stuff. He'd get traced.

What about Lemon? The immortality genes should cure his lung cancer and might make his son look more normal. If he and Lemon pooled their resources, perhaps they could finance an adequate lab themselves. But Menniss still faced the problem of leaving the forest without getting caught. Fleeing from trap to trap.

"What're you thinking about?" Francine asked.

"I'm just tired, sweetheart," he said.

She inexpertly massaged his neck.

"That feels great," he said, though it didn't.

What I have to do, he thought wearily, is carry forward what I've already begun and make Francine fall desperately in love with me—so desperately in love that if anything happened to me, she'd fall to pieces. More precisely, I have to convince the I-H that this would happen. But they both go together.

As he knew from her emails with that terrible boyfriend, the key to Francine's heart was to treat her like crap (but keep your house neat and tidy, he added with an inward smile.) And the key to convincing the I-H that Menniss possessed the key to her heart was the same: he had to show the I-H he could treat her like crap and get away with it.

That's my insurance policy. At least I have one.

"Take a sharp right after the green propane tank," Francine said.

But as he yanked the steering wheel and craned his neck to see ahead, he caught sight of her sincere and innocent face and softened. Mistreating a damaged, brilliant woman—for all he wanted to be young again, he wasn't sure he could do it. And what more terrible way to start on a journey into immortality could there be? As Sensei said, howsoever you start, that's where you end up.

But did he have a choice?

FRANCINE

THE REDWOODS WERE so tall that when she looked up, she felt like she was falling. But it was more than the trees. Was she falling in love? So soon? Was that a good idea?

And now Richard was looking at her strangely. Was he falling in love too?

She'd read a historical fiction novel about a man and woman fleeing the Nazis. They were fleeing separately and didn't know each other beforehand, but chance pushed them into a tiny cellar together. Even though they had nothing in common, they fell in love. Come to think of it, she'd read more than one novel where people fell in love while escaping an enemy. Shared danger supposedly does that to you.

And he was such a noble, kind man. "Get ready for another turn," she said. "Just after a blue water tower. There it is, that logging road."

They drove into a dark forest where the trees were as thick as grass. It must be early second growth. After a clear-cut, redwoods re-grew with trunks packed tightly, racing toward the sun. The ones that grew the fastest shaded out the others as the forest matured. Not that this forest would be left to mature—the corporations would log it all first.

The logging road climbed up a hill. At its peak, the trees gave way to a splendid view. She looked down onto a green ocean brightly lit by the sun, woods that spread for 20, 30 miles in every direction, cleared here and there for houses but mostly untouched. She'd never

imagined such vast expanses of redwood forest in the Santa Cruz
Mountains. You could hide 100 laboratories beneath these trees.

"It's beautiful, isn't it?" he said.

"It is," she said. She leaned her head on his shoulder.

The road dropped back under the canopy and followed the
course of a river. Enormous rocks lay jumbled about in its bed, creating steep waterfalls and deep pools. They came to a broken-down
bridge exactly as described in the directions, and she told Richard
to slow down. A small house, a meadow and a grove of flowering
hawthorn on the far side of the bridge made an enchanting scene.
But the house was ruined.

"We're supposed to cross the bridge, yes?" he asked.

"Yes, and turn right soon after that house." When they'd gone over,
she cried out, "But where are we supposed to turn? There's no road."

"We turn up there," he said, pointing. "See the cairn?"

He left the pavement at a pile of rocks, changed gears, and drove
directly into the trees.

Though they were in the middle of the woods, they didn't need
a road. This was fairly old growth, and the forest floor was empty
except for the rising redwood trunks.

The cairns guided them up over a small rise and down into a val-
ley. They came to a steep incline, almost a cliff, the hillside dropping
at an angle of more than 45-degrees toward a small stream. A cairn
led them straight ahead, but it didn't seem possible.

"Wait," she protested, but he ignored her and drove directly over
the edge. She pressed back in her seat as if her shifted weight could
stop the Jeep from flipping over.

They drove down the middle of the creek, their tires throwing
great splashes on each side.

The floor of a stream is a fragile ecosystem, she thought, *and the Jeep's
tires are tearing it up.*

But it wouldn't be a great idea to drive through open redwood
forest either. Redwood trees have shallow roots, and the pressure of
a vehicle can kill even the grandest.

They came to a waterfall, and again Richard took a path she
would have thought impossible, balancing the Jeep's tires from one

rock to the next as they lurched along. She closed her eyes at one particularly frightening lurch. When she opened them again, the trees were very large, their trunks eight feet or more in diameter. She looked around, first with interest, then awe.

"Is this original forest?" she said. "Oh my God, I think it is. We're in a hidden stand of untouched forest."

She'd read about patches of great trees hidden along stream-beds and canyon bottoms, but up in Humboldt County and further north, not down here.

She had a student who spent his vacations searching out undiscovered groves of ancient, giant trees. He had to search for them on foot because they don't stand out in a flyover; trees growing on higher ground may look taller than the great ones. Her student had told her stories about the-earth-above-the-earth, magical places where enough mulch had accumulated on the canopy to create a false forest floor 100 feet up, a fully three-dimensional world of trees, bushes, birds and animals growing in the sky. She'd love to see something like that.

But they'd reached the last part of the text message. The directions were a bit peculiar, and she read them aloud. "Look for a barn on your right, painted a moldy, decrepit, peeling green sort of color. Beside it there's a rectangular, white rock, a 20-foot tall standing sentry. Don't worry, the sentry's unarmed. Leave the horse outside and unlock the barn door." She stopped.

"And then what?"

"That's all. The message ends."

"Damn him." He pounded the steering wheel. "Damn him."

RICHARD PARKED AT the barn and pulled aside a huge sliding door. Francine wasn't sure exactly what she'd expected, perhaps a sign reading, "Entrance to Laboratory," but there were only bales of hay.

She handed him the phone so he could look at the message himself.

"Damn him," he said again.

"Why don't you text back and ask for more directions?"

"No signal."

"So what now?"

"I don't know what now. How about you leave me alone so I can figure it out? Go look at some trees." He sprang forward to the hay bales and set about violently tossing them aside.

She'd hoped for at least some acknowledgment they were in this together. Bringing the blue lunchbox with her, she walked out of earshot so she couldn't hear him cursing.

Second-growth redwoods had worked their way into the clearing around the barn, but behind them, she found old-growth forest again. The furry bark of young redwoods felt fine enough to comb or brush, but these trees were stringy and coarse with age. She rubbed her hand on one enormous tree whose trunk disappeared into the canopy 100s of feet above her. She walked in still deeper. Another massive tree stood at an alarming angle, 20 degrees or more from vertical. What havoc that one would wreak when it fell! She'd read that sometimes trees knocked each other down in sequence, like dominoes.

She passed the tree on its safe side and kept going. She listened for Richard but couldn't hear him. She couldn't hear anything: the forest was still and silent. In places like this, one could feel religious without having to believe in anything. She thought of the underground churches she'd visited in Cappadocia and the New Camaldoli Hermitage, a Benedictine monastery in Big Sur, where she'd gone on retreat during her brief Christian phase.

By the waters of Babylon,
we hung our harps on the willow trees;
we wept and remembered Zion.

That was Father Bruno chanting at two in the morning when they got up for prayers. And chanting the same words again during Sunday morning Mass, his eyes bloodshot from a night spent in meditation. How long had she been Christian? Two months? But she still thought fondly of Father Bruno and remembered that sermon verbatim.

"Zion represents eternal being, our original life with God," he'd said. "We are exiled for a time into this world of imperfection—I have seen this—and whenever we weep, it is eternal life our tears flow for. The Greek philosopher Epicurus said, 'Death does not concern us because as long as we exist, death is not here, and when it does come, we no longer exist.' He meant this as comfort. But do these words comfort you? They don't comfort me. I recoil with horror from non-Being. And last night, in prayer, I discovered why.

"Because in our souls, we remember Zion. Zion is not just a place. Zion is eternal life. To remember Zion is to know that Being cannot die; that, though the body dies, the soul returns to its eternal home. For—I have seen this—at the end, we shall take our harps off the willow trees and go home."

How nice to believe all that. How comforting. It was all wishful thinking but very pretty.

Christians were right to fear Darwin because science frees the mind from faith. She now knew perfectly well there is no God, soul or eternal life, only digital information compiled into the genome and other, extra-genetic mechanisms through the iterative power of natural selection. And isn't it obvious why people recoil from death? Survival of the fittest has programmed living creatures to fight to stay alive.

Obviously, this was a much less comforting tale. But people should look truth in the eye rather than console themselves with fairy tales.

She retraced her steps, but not precisely, and emerged from the woods behind the barn. An interesting structure caught her eye, a crumbling concrete wall that climbed up the hillside and trailed vines of flowering, wild sweet pea. She loved flowering pea. There were old stairs beside the wall, and she walked up them carefully, testing each one to make sure it was solid before putting her full weight on it. When she reached the platform on top, she knelt to study a peculiar, decaying wooden object. She saw bits of rope. Oh, I see, she thought. This was once a system of pulleys to haul objects up the hill.

A rabbit hopped across the concrete and drew her gaze. And then she saw them: five aluminum pipes, each a meter across and opening a few inches above the ground. They were the outflow pipes of a fume hood.

The lab was somewhere below.

MENNISS

HE'D CLEARED ALL the bales from the back wall and found nothing. He'd moved them all to the left and again found nothing. Just bare wall. That damn I-H. Menniss was hot and thirsty and irritated by the bits of hay that clung to his sweaty neck. Would it have been so hard to add a single sentence explaining what to do once he got to the barn? The I-H was entertaining himself, and it pissed Menniss off.

"Any luck?"

He saw Francine standing just outside the barn. Against the backdrop of his mood, she seemed absurdly delicate. He shook his head, not trusting himself to speak.

"I was walking around the back of the barn," she said. She moved her index finger in a broad circle. "And I saw ventilation pipes. I think the lab's underneath them."

The back of the barn? Fuck if he was going to move all these damn hay bales a second time.

But he followed her out, and together they climbed the staircase beside the concrete wall. She pointed at a set of wide metal pipes. "Those are fume hood vents," she said.

"What's a fume hood?"

"Like the fan above a stove, only more powerful. When you have to work with volatile chemicals, you take them under the hood."

"Volatile? What good would a fan do if your chemicals explode?"

"Volatile means 'evaporates easily,' not 'explosive.' It's a common misunderstanding."

Now he felt doubly stupid. He climbed down the ladder and studied the base of the concrete wall. He saw signs that a truck had driven close by, but the wall didn't have a door in it—not that he could see. He was too irritated to speak. He hurried back to the barn and, once again, tore away the bales that covered its back wall. Once he'd cleared it, he tapped along the wood, listening for resonance. A long splinter stabbed his pointer finger. He suppressed all expression of pain, pulled out the splinter and let the blood drip freely. He tapped again and heard a hollow sound. He tugged on a long diagonal two-by-four, and a piece of the wall came away.

Between the false wall and the real, there was a space wide enough to stand. He put his head inside and saw a stairway leading down. Without turning to look at her, he said, "Follow me," and stepped inside.

"What about brown recluse spiders?" she asked.

"Of all the fucking ridiculous things," he said.

She touched his shoulder from behind. "I'm sorry. It's just that I've studied brown recluse immunotoxin, and I know what it can do."

"I wasn't talking about your fear of spiders. I was talking about this whole setup. Why's he being so theatrical? I don't get it." He shrugged her hand off his shoulder and walked down the stairs.

The door at the bottom was normal in size, but it opened onto a corridor no more than five feet high, and he banged his head on the strip of concrete that formed the top two feet of the doorway.

"Jesus Christ." He stooped uncomfortably and walked into the corridor. "Come on."

She followed and he finally turned around to face her. She had the lunchbox in her hand. He kissed her and wondered.

The tunnel was dark ahead, but he had a small flashlight, and they moved carefully forward in its small circle of light. The tunnel curved, and around the corner, parallel lines of bright lights appeared on the ground: white bulbs set every six inches along the intersections of wall and floor, like the lights along the aisle of a passenger plane that show you the way to the emergency exits.

They came to a T-intersection, a crossing corridor of bare concrete whose ceiling, though still oppressively low, was high enough for

Menniss to stand up. Lights outlined the floor here, too, flashing in a flowing manner that directed them to the left. Menniss overcame a perverse urge to go the other way.

The corridor began straight and then curved gently to the right. Here and there, fake red bricks were painted on the bare wall. Real bricks gradually replaced the painted ones until they took over entirely. The concrete corridor became a brick corridor with an arched brick ceiling and incandescent lights designed to look like flickering torches stuck in holes in the wall. Entirely ridiculous, Menniss thought.

When they came to a lifelike bust set in a niche in the wall, he said, "Ridiculous" out loud and added other words besides. The face wore a smirk along with a goatee and a handlebar mustache, and its eyes, though mechanical, moved to follow them.

The passage turned again and ended at a metal door whose surface was decorated with raised symbols. "Like a fucking computer game," Menniss said. "I suppose we have to solve a puzzle to get in."

Francine merely turned the knob, and the door opened. She stepped into the brightly lit room and gasped. "It's my laboratory."

THE PLACE STANK like perfume made from turpentine and rancid wine, but Francine didn't seem to notice. She looked positively radiant. She walked in the cramped space between two lab benches, trailing her hands on the surfaces of both, holding the lunchbox in the crook of her left elbow. The lab was exactly the opposite of Francine's house—cluttered, more than cluttered, crammed full of objects. The benches on both sides were covered with items he could identify, such as centrifuges, warming plates and autoclaves, and other scientific appliances with buttons and sliders that he couldn't. At the back of each bench, shelves stuffed to bursting held labeled brown jars full of chemicals, spiral distilling tubes and other glassware.

"It's a replica of my lab," Francine said. "Everything is in just the right place. But the supplies, the equipment, they're all completely new." Her eyes were opened wide, dazzled, the eyes of a child opening presents. She pulled a brown bottle from a shelf and touched its clean white label. "Ethylaldehyde," she said. "It's never been opened."

At the end of the aisle, they came to a long rectangular niche in the wall that held various pieces of equipment. An arrangement of sliding windows covered the top half of the opening.

Francine flipped a switch, and a sound roared like a small jet turbine. "I have my fume hood on this same wall, and it's the same size. But this one is so much better. It's the kind you buy when you have all the money in the world."

And it's loud enough, Menniss thought, *to shave off more of my fading hearing*.

She shut off the jet turbine with a flick of her fingers, turned around, and broke into giggles. "And there's Christina, our mascot." She pointed to the ceiling, where an inflated vinyl orca hung on a rope from a hook. "Someone either brought it or bought another. How funny."

Hilarious, Menniss thought. And so was the video camera unabashedly installed next to the orca. He scanned the ceiling and found five other cameras, all in plain sight.

Why cameras? And why no attempt to hide them? He could think of several explanations, but none made sense.

Whatever the reason, he could use them to demonstrate his power over Francine.

He leaned his head toward Francine and whispered, "I have something to tell you."

She paid no attention and walked rapidly away from him along the lab's far wall. Menniss followed her, passing row after row of narrowly spaced lab benches. They passed a utility closet, a small restroom and a walk-in cooler whose oversize metal door was secured by a rotating metal lever. She stopped at another metal door, this one of normal proportions and opened by a normal knob. A label on the door tilt read, "Clean Room." She turned the knob and gasped again. "Incredible." She set the blue lunchbox on a lab bench behind her and stepped inside. Not wanting to leave the tissue unprotected, he took it and followed her inside.

The outer lab was full of apparatus and jumbled machines, but this room was mostly empty. It had long lab benches like the other lab, but they were separated by gaps broad enough for several people to stroll abreast. The air was so clean it tasted like metal or electricity. Only the ceiling was busy, packed tight with intricately bent and brightly colored ductwork.

The lab benches were almost entirely bare except for a single large stainless steel machine on each, accompanied by a computer. Menniss walked up to the closest and looked through a translucent plastic window at a factory in miniature: 100s of tiny tubes, metal arms, glass circles, laser eyes and plastic trays in various colors.

Francine came up from behind, found a clasp at one end of the plastic window and pulled it open. Blue, green and red LED lights inside began to flash.

"What are the lights for?" Menniss asked.

"Nothing important," she said. "The more expensive the equipment, the fancier the lights. And this equipment is *really* expensive." Her face was glowing. "I've read about the prototypes," she said, "but I didn't think you could buy them yet."

"What does it do?"

"It's a fully robotic rapid genome sequencer. It does everything from beginning to end: extension, substitution, blasting and analysis, with almost no human intervention."

"And how long will it take to decode Blair's DNA?"

"The first time we decoded the human genome, it took years. Basic analysis only takes a few weeks now, and it's down to an easy six months for a complete analysis, including single-nucleotide polymorphisms, non-coding DNA and analysis of methylation patterns. With this machine? Maybe two or three months? I'm not sure."

Only a few months. And what then? What use was he to the I-H after that?

Francine slid into a chair and turned on the computer attached to one of the machines. He got bored watching her explore the software and left to explore the room. The walls were made of drywall panels six feet by three feet, held in place by metal bars. He pushed against one wall and felt the panel give way a quarter of an inch. He spread out his fingers against the drywall and exerted vertical pressure, using the friction of his fingerprints as a grip. The panel slid upwards, and blue light came in through the crack at the bottom. He bent down to look and saw a large hexagonal room lit with blue light. There was a door at its far end that opened to another hexagon. This lab was inside a much larger underground space.

He let the panel slide back down into place. He studied the ceiling for cameras and found two.

Time to get started. But Francine was already on her way out of the Clean Room and back into the lab. He gave the nearest video camera a vicious glare and hurried to follow.

FRANCINE

FRANCINE IMAGINED CELLULAR DNases destroying all the information coded in the tissue, and she felt an enormous urge to hurry. But she knew from experience that when doing science, one must never get into a rush, and forced herself down to a fast walk.

She leaned with all her weight on the rotating metal lever protruding from the walk-in freezer's door. The handle turned, and the thick, insulated door swung open, billows of condensation swirling from its edges. Stiffening herself against the cold, she entered. She found the large Dewar flask of liquid nitrogen right where she expected to—the same place where it lived in her own lab. She lifted the insulated cap that fitted over the opening like a cork-lined metal helmet and used a ladle with a cork-insulated handle to transfer steaming liquid nitrogen from the Dewar to a small wide-mouthed thermos.

"You look like a goddess in there," Richard said. He was standing at the door to the freezer, the blue lunchbox in hand. "A goddess striding through clouds and mixing the elements of ambrosia."

"You're too imaginative," she said, but she smiled.

Using a hammer to break up a slab of dry ice, she slid the chunks into a plastic bucket and brought the bucket and thermos out to a lab bench. She took the lunchbox from Richard, unzipped the Thinsulate and was relieved to find that there were still a few ice cubes floating in the water. She pulled out the Saran-wrapped bundle and dried it with a towel. At least 40 layers of Saran wrap. "What exactly was your system?" she asked.

"What do you mean?"

"How you wrapped it?"

"I put it in a baggie. A sandwich bag. And then I rolled Saran wrap around it. Wasn't that okay?"

"Oh, it's fine. I just wanted to know what I'm facing."

At least 40 layers of Saran wrap *and* a baggie. The overkill was cute.

Unwrapping it presented a challenge. When she finally reached the sandwich bag, she carefully turned it inside out so that the sliver of tissue fell into a strainer without touching her fingers.

Richard hovered beside her as she poured a liter of sterile saline over the tissue, and she felt compelled to explain. "You held this piece of tissue in your bare hands. The idea is to wash away any of your DNA that might have rubbed off on the sample."

Using sterile tweezers, she dropped the tissue into the thermos. The liquid nitrogen boiled briefly and then settled. "There," she said. "Now it's safe from decomposition."

He looked worried. "Should I have frozen it in liquid nitrogen right from the beginning?"

"Ideally. But I'm sure it'll be fine."

She found a mortar and pestle, washed it with soap and water, and put it and a few other tools into a desktop autoclave. She opened a liter bottle of 100% ethanol, emptied it into the bucket of dry ice and stirred it with the bottom of a second, unopened bottle. She inserted the second bottle into the dry ice bath too. "We'll need the cold ethanol later," she explained. "It's about minus 100 degrees centigrade in there."

He was in her way, and she gently pushed past him, fetching some proteinase K from the freezer and spooning a dollop onto an eppi tube. She set the eppi tube in the rubber cup of a warmer to defrost it, but the warmer was an unfamiliar model, and she couldn't find the on-off switch. She was really out of touch. You get pushed up the ladder until all you do is write grants. Her graduate students and post-docs did all the grunt work these days.

"Francine," Richard said, "We have to talk."

She sensed the urgency in his voice but couldn't tear her mind away from what she was doing. "Sarah, one of my post-docs, orders all the equipment," she said. "And so I don't know how things work anymore." She rotated the warmer and finally found the switch recessed beside the cord.

When was the last time she'd done her own experimental work? You could get more done by relying on others, but nothing felt as good as doing the lab work yourself.

For the moment, though, there was nothing to do. "This little plastic tube is called an eppi tube," she explained. "The pointed bottom gives it several useful properties. For example, it increases surface area for heat exchange. I'm using the eppi tube to thaw out some proteinase K, a chemical we need for the next step."

"What's a proteinase?"

Like freshman-in-the-lab day. "The suffix 'ase' means an enzyme that breaks something down. Proteinase K breaks down proteins but not nucleic acids. That's why it's so useful. The idea is to destroy all the DNases in the tissue without damaging the DNA itself." Painfully, she added, "DNases are enzymes that break down DNA."

"I thought you said that proteinase K breaks down proteins. It breaks down enzymes too?"

"Enzymes *are* proteins," she said. Worse than freshman-in-the-lab day. More like take-a-clingy-child-to-work day.

"Anyway," Richard said, "the tissue's safe now that it's in liquid nitrogen."

"Absolutely safe." She began to arrange the equipment for the next stage.

"That means you can stop for a moment now, doesn't it?"

"In principle, yes, but I'm too excited to stop." She reached for a bottle of SDS on the shelf, but her arm wouldn't move. She looked down and saw a big hand gripping her wrist, gripping so hard that it hurt.

"Stop that," she said. She tried to jerk free, but he was too strong. "You're hurting me. Let me go."

But he forced her arm out straight and pushed her forward. The stool she'd been sitting on crashed to the floor as he made her walk away from the bench and toward the door. She felt like she was in a dream or a movie. She wanted to scream, but Blocking Monster sat on her tongue.

They walked back through the brick-lined corridor, past the bust of the goateed and smirking man and back to the T-intersection. This time, they took the other side of the T. The corridor gradually transformed into an ordinary household hallway with doors in it. On one door, a loop of string over a pushpin held a label that read "Kitchen" in fancy calligraphy. Francine realized she was hungry and wanted to stop. She said so, her first words in a while, and struggled when he paid no attention and pushed her further on.

She gave up struggling. They passed doors labeled "Library," "Cleaning Supplies," and "Theater." When they reached one labeled "Master Bedroom," Richard opened the door with his free hand and forced her inside.

The bedroom was set up as a suite, and they were in its small living room. On one side, there was an antique overstuffed loveseat with flowery fabric and, on the other, an entertainment center that looked a lot like an antique dresser she'd once coveted: dark hardwood inlaid with lighter, cross-grained wood in the shape of roses.

It was romantic. But if he meant to have sex with her, he should have waited until she'd finished purifying the DNA. She was far too distracted just now.

She tried to tell him that, but he hushed her.

The living room was divided from the bedroom by a slanting wall of fired gray pottery pockmarked with niches that held wineglasses, CDs and candles. It reminded her of Gaudi's architecture in Barcelona. Richard picked a CD at random and stuck it in the stereo. The music came on very loud, Dvorak's seventh symphony, one of her favorites. He lifted her bodily, carried her around the dividing wall and set her on the bed.

The power of the music strengthened her. "If you're trying to seduce me, you're going about it fine, but the timing is off."

He put his mouth to her ear. She tried to wriggle away, but he held her with his weight and whispered, "I'm not trying to seduce you. I have to talk to you."

"Well, talk to me," she said or tried to say. She'd only gotten out the word "well" before he flipped her onto her stomach and the rest of the sentence disappeared into a plush microfiber quilt. He held her down with the weight of his body and kissed her neck. "Hush," he whispered. "There are microphones and cameras everywhere. And there's a second underground city surrounding this one. We're only separated from it by the thickness of a wall, and some wall panels slide upward. This is the only way I could figure out to talk to you so they wouldn't notice."

Microphones everywhere? Cameras? Panels? The beautifully equipped laboratory, her return to bench science and the project's grandeur had made her forget everything. Now the sick anxiety flooded back.

She remembered the early morning phone call from the university to tell her that her lab was wrecked. Her first thought had been concern for her ongoing grants. She'd spent an hour brushing her hair and worrying about them. Then the doorbell rang, and time sped up: Richard, the federal agents, the car, the hair-raising drive.

"Tell me what I should do," she whispered.

"You're with me?"

"I'm with you."

"Good. In a moment, I'll roll off. Then I'll get a little wild and undress you. We'll make love, and while we're making love, I'll whisper what you need to know. Got it?"

"I got it." It was a sensible plan. No one would suspect that two people making passionate love were secretly conversing.

But as they undressed each other, a part of her mind rebelled. It was a part she couldn't see because Blocking Monster got in the way, but she heard it complain. Then she went blank. When she came back, they were having sex.

She couldn't tell whether her body was responding or moving passively as he pushed her.

"That's good," he whispered. "Act excited like that."

Was she acting excited? The Dvorak symphony turned coarse with bassoons, and Richard squeezed her buttocks. "Listen to me carefully," he said. "We're in more danger than I thought."

She heard herself gasp and moan. She might even have begun

to enjoy herself if Richard hadn't talked on and ruined it. "People could rush in on us any second. Don't be surprised if tomorrow or the day after you find me shot dead, my brains splattered against the wall."

She froze.

"It could even happen now," he said.

He was still making love to her, but she was disassociated.

"It could happen right now," he said. "You hear a gunshot, and my blood starts running in rivers over you, dying the bed red. But even if I become a corpse before your eyes, *you* can survive this. Listen closely, and I'll tell you how."

Listen? All she heard was the howling. The bed rocked as his body thrust against her. She heard screams or sobs and someone gulping and gasping in fear.

MENNISS

SEE HOW BADLY *I can treat her? See how she takes it?*

Menniss damned well *hoped* someone was watching. He was behaving abominably, but he couldn't think of a better demonstration.

Do you see how unstable your scientist is? Do you dare mess with me?

Poor girl. She was sobbing like a child. Only he didn't see any cameras in this room. Was the bedroom supposed to be a private space? He didn't believe it.

Even if no one's watching, it's still worthwhile doing this because that's how I make her fall in love with me. It's like psychotherapy, only in reverse. You find the buried illness, and you grab hold of it. You take the twisted primal needs and twist them further.

He was too good at this. Someone should stop him.

Her crying changed its tone and became animal-like, not entirely human. Now Menniss worried he'd pushed her too far. What if she broke?

A voice appeared in his head, cruel and cutting: *What kind of person makes love to a woman while telling her bloody stories, intending to control her? What kind of person would do that to someone as innocent as Francine? A person like that doesn't deserve to become immortal.*

It's not like I enjoy torturing her, Menniss thought. *I'm just doing this to survive. And to help her survive too.*

Are you sure you don't get off on this?

She sounded like an infant crying.

He remembered the time he'd pulled an infant out of the wreckage of a safe house he'd bombed. Glorious pleasure as the walls exploded outwards, billowing orange pleasure turning dark when the search teams found the infant, and he'd held the baby against his shoulder until she died.

He couldn't do this anymore.

He pulled out of Francine. He held her as she shuddered against him. He stroked her back. He held her close until her manic sobbing subsided. He ran his fingers gently through her wild blonde hair. Her face relaxed, and her breathing slowed. She fell into her look of abstraction, her right hand up in the air, fingers moving.

They were stretched out on the bed side by side. She pushed herself up on one elbow so her face was above his. She put one hand on his face and gazed at him quietly. Menniss didn't realize until he opened his mouth that he was about to tell her the plain truth. "The only way I'll be safe is if we can make them think that you need me. We have to make them think that if anything happens to me, you won't be able to work. Can we convince them of that? They won't dare touch me if we can make them think it's true."

"But it *is* true," she said.

FRANCINE

IN LOVERS' WHISPERS, they worked out how best to manage the situation. They showered and dressed in fresh clothes from the bedroom's huge walk-in closet. One side was a replica of Francine's closet and held clothes very much like her own, while the other consisted entirely of brown suits in Richard's size. Twelve identical suits; Richard said it was yet another joke. She told him she liked him in brown because the color brought out his natural resemblance to a bear. She wanted to return to the lab, but he reminded her that she was hungry, and they stopped in the kitchen. She heated a can of Amy's Black Bean Vegetable soup, her favorite. In the time it took her to finish, Richard had microwaved and wolfed down the contents of three frozen packages of lasagna. He seemed inclined toward a fourth, but she said she needed to get back.

"You go ahead," he said. "I'll catch up in a while."

The idea terrified her. "Wander this place without you? Not a chance."

"I'm sorry. I'll come with." He held her.

She smiled, realizing that he'd set her up just like they'd planned and had done so using her natural reactions rather than asking her to pretend anything.

Back to the refuge of work. She removed the frozen tissue from the liquid nitrogen and ground it to powder. She spooned a gram of the powder into the eppi tube filled with proteinase K and touched the tube's pointed tip to the vibrating surface of a vortexer. Richard, hovering as always, asked what she'd just done.

This time she didn't mind explaining. "We call these vibrating devices 'vortexers' because they move in circles, not just up and down. This model is called 'belly dancer.' It can mix the contents of an eppi tube in under a second of contact." She added some sodium dodecyl sulfate, vortexed the tube again, and set it back in the warmer. "Now we wait for an hour."

"And then?"

"Then we do a little more biochemistry, and after that, we go to the Clean Room."

"That's where you'll decode the DNA?"

"That's right." Francine spooned the remainder of the sample back into the liquid nitrogen in case they needed more later.

"And once the DNA is decoded," Richard asked, "can almost anyone figure out what makes Blair immortal?"

"Not just anyone. You couldn't."

"I mean, any molecular biologist."

"Not to brag, but it's a little tricky."

She found some ordinary liquid soap and wiped the bench clean. She liked her surfaces spotless, at work and home. But in a lab, you couldn't get rid of clutter. "This mutation is unlikely to have occurred in a typical gene region because—well, for various reasons. Identifying it won't be a piece of cake. To avoid going down blind allies, you probably need specific knowledge of the aging clock."

"But there are a few people besides yourself who could do it quickly, aren't there?"

"A few. Most are in my study section. A study section is what you call the group that helps the NIH decide how to apportion its grants. Frank Semmons isn't quite as good as I am, but he could do it. Lisa Proudon, on the other hand, she's better than me. She'd win the race if we started together. And then there's Martin Stockman." Thinking of Martin, so impressive professionally—his publications a yard long—and yet a total idiot in so many ways, she grinned.

"What about him?"

"He's the senior member of our section. If an outsider tried to pick the best expert on the subject, they'd probably pick him." Her grin turned into a chuckle. "But that's only because Stockman's good at self-promotion. He's more a bureaucrat than a scientist. Still, I suppose he'd eventually claw his way through to a solution."

"Then there's something else we have to do," Richard said. "Come on." He grabbed her forcefully by the wrist, and she went along without resistance even before she remembered the plan required her to act submissively.

He didn't let go until he'd tugged her to the Clean Room. "Which of these machines do you plan to use?"

So much wealth: three robotic sequencers to pick from.

She randomly chose one of the sequencers and watched with startled concern as he grabbed the computer attached to it and roughly turned it around. He traced the computer's cables, followed one to where it connected to a networking plug in the wall and yanked it out. More gently, he disconnected the cable's other end, where it was attached to the computer. He asked her to help find him a small screwdriver, and she searched obediently, but his violent attack on the drawers succeeded first. He loosened the screws that held the computer's metal case closed and tossed the cover to the ground with a clattering bang. He was a tornado. Ransacking drawers again, he found a smaller screwdriver, unscrewed the computer's hard drive, and set the hard drive on the desk, still attached to the computer through a long ribbon cable. "I can shoot the damn drive if I have to," he said. "I think a few bullets would damage the data." He reached inside his coat and showed her his gun.

She didn't know anything about guns. She was pro-gun-control and hated the NRA. But at this moment, she liked it that Richard went around armed. So many alien concepts to grapple with, such a confusing new world.

But by then, she'd figured out what he was about: he was afraid someone would copy the data as fast as she got it.

"What about a wireless card?" she suggested.

He gave her a look of respect. "Good thinking," he said. He checked each of the boards rising at right angles from the motherboard. "None of these. But what if there's a wireless adapter on the motherboard itself? I have no idea how to tell. Do you?"

"Not a clue," she said.

Richard, she noticed, never paused; he thought while acting. He was already opening cabinets when he said, "Mesh. I need wire mesh."

This time she was the one who found what they needed, a heavy wire mesh that held a set of cables in neat order under a sink. He yanked on the mesh, but it didn't give. He used a screwdriver to pry off the restraining brads and got it free. He found more mesh under other sinks and wrapped yards of the mesh around the computer. "I need a moving magnetic field," he said. "What do you have out there that has an electric motor?"

Memories from second-year physics. "Magnetic stirrers," she said. They went back to the outer lab, and she found him one. "Suppose you want to heat the contents of a beaker but want to make sure it doesn't burn?" She half-filled a beaker with water, set it on the flat metal surface of a stirrer and dropped in the plastic bar. "Now turn the stirrer on," she said. "That knob. It also adjusts the speed."

Together they watched the white plastic bar rotate, stirring the water from the bottom. "How does it work?" he asked.

"The mixer creates a rotating magnetic field, and there's a bar magnet in that plastic thing. They should sell these in kitchen stores. Perfect for heating sauces."

But he'd already unplugged the stirrer and was gathering others. They found eight and carried them all to the Clean Room. They set up the stirrers around the mesh, each rotating at a different speed.

"That should work," he said. "At least, I think it will. It should induce a current and create a Faraday cage."

He stepped back to admire his handiwork, but only for a second. "Metal coat hangers. You have any?"

She took him to a closet in the outer lab. In her own lab, this closet was full of white coats on metal coat hangers, and sure enough, there were white coats on hangers here too.

He took the largest coat off its hanger and handed it to her. Throwing the other lab coats on the ground, he brought a handful of hangers back to the computer. He twisted several together to make a frame and attached the frame to the computer monitor with duct tape. Cutting off a piece of the lab coat, he draped it over the frame to make a hood, like on an ancient camera. "There," he said. "Now you can watch the screen without any video camera looking over your shoulder and taking pictures of the data."

He stepped back to admire his handiwork again. Before he could jump into yet another project, she said, "Now's the time to purify the DNA."

He didn't move. His eyes were roved, hyperalert, looking for more things to do. It couldn't be good for him.

"Come," she said. She held out her hand. He didn't take it, but he followed her out.

RICHARD SEEMED TO relax a bit as he helped her work, but when she turned on the fume hood, he got nervous again. He looked over his shoulder every few seconds, and when the large autoclave went off with a thunk, he spun around and had his gun out before Francine could tell him what it was.

"Can't we turn it off?" he asked.

"Turn off what?"

"That jet engine. The fume hood."

"But phenol is toxic. That's why we're working under the hood."

He didn't argue but stood with his back to her and kept his gun out. That made *her* anxious, and she fumbled with the eppi tube, nearly spilling the contents. She closed it properly and said, "What's bothering you so much?"

"That fan's so loud we'd never hear if anyone came in behind us."

She shut the fume hood off instantly. After wiping down the tube, she returned it to the bench and placed it in the centrifuge. But she was spooked, and after turning on the centrifuge, she turned it off again. "Is that too loud also?"

"Not at all," he said. "That's fine." He turned it back on and massaged her upper back.

"That feels great," she said. "You know exactly where to touch. How did you get to be so good?"

"My Sensei—my martial arts teacher in Laos—taught healing

arts along with fighting. This is acupressure massage. We learned acupuncture too."

Acupuncture? What incredible nonsense. But she knew better than to say anything. If you wanted to get along with non-scientists, you had to tolerate a high ridiculousness quotient. "I don't want you to stop," she said, "but now it's time."

"Time for what?"

"Time for the magic part." She turned around and kissed him. She put on a set of thick gloves, took the bottle of chilled ethanol out of the dry ice bath, opened it, and dripped a couple of milliliters into the eppi tube. She added an equal quantity of finely ground sodium chloride and re-closed it. White, fluffy flecks of DNA were already precipitating when she touched the tube's tip to a vortexer.

She waited a full minute, then put the tube in the microcentrifuge and spun it down. When she took it out, she said, "Voilà. The DNA of an Immortal."

He took the tube from her and held it up to the light. "The liquid or the white stuff?"

"The precipitant," she said. Painfully, she added, "The white stuff. Don't shake it. We want it to stay on the bottom."

"How amazing."

He looked dreamy. She'd never seen him look dreamy before. She didn't know he could.

"You know," he said, "when I first found evidence of a man who doesn't age, I had all kinds of crazy ideas. I thought maybe he performed some special breath practice. Or that he ate a rare forest mushroom. Or even that he did a magical ritual. And it's only this fluffy white powder?"

Shocked, she asked, "You believe in magical rituals?"

"Not really. But I guess DNA is sort of magical."

"No, it's not. It's just a biochemical form of digital data storage."

"So if I ate some of this or stuck it under my pillow, I wouldn't turn immortal?" he asked.

"Don't be absurd."

"I was kidding."

"We're not done, anyway." She took the tube back. "There's still

RNA copurified with the DNA. To get rid of that, we'll use some RNase."

"I see," he said.

Magic. How ridiculous.

But when she finished the last extraction and had the eppi tube of pure genomic DNA in her hand, she felt shivers up and down her spine. Not because she thought DNA was magic—quite the opposite: DNA is *real*. And truth is better than fantasy.

But she kept her voice flat and scientific so he wouldn't get any wrong ideas. "Now the hard work starts," she said. "Now we go to the Clean Room and sequence the sample."

A CLEAN ROOM should be a sanctuary. But now that she looked, she saw two video cameras on the ceiling. An outrageous invasion.

Who was watching her and why? She could guess that easily enough: billionaires who wanted to steal the secret of immortality for themselves. And right-wing Christians. If you asked them about it, they'd call it a sin against God's law, but the moment a way to live forever came into existence, they'd come clamoring. The hypocrites.

Anger cleared away Gray Fog, and she saw to the endgame. She saw the unseen watchers breaking in to kill her and Richard and to take the secret for themselves. And she saw the simple twist that would change everything, the small variation in method that would save Richard, save herself, and frustrate their unseen enemy in every way.

From a scientific perspective, it was a small step. But ethically, it was an immense violation. Did she dare?

The potential consequences frightened her, and she let Gray Fog roll over the idea. She stuck her head under the hood Richard had set up to hide the computer monitor from the cameras, opened the program that controlled the sequencer, checked the defaults, altered a few and started the process. She blanked the screen and pulled her head back out. "Come watch this part with me," she said

Richard stood beside her at the sequencer's clear plastic cover. A purple light turned on, ultraviolet actually, sterilizing the outside of the eppi tube. A metal arm closed on the tube's lid and pulled it off. The sound of small gears started up. Another lid replaced the one taken off, this one with an autopipette like a moth's proboscis. A flurry of movement, and bits of isolated DNA dropped onto 100s of glass slides.

"What's it doing now?" he asked.

She held his arm and leaned against him. "Replicating the DNA. Making 100 grams of it. You need to have plenty for the next step."

"How long will this stage go on?"

"About 12 hours. We don't need to stay here. Let's go to sleep. I'm exhausted."

"Soon," he said. "But first, we have some work to do."

She had no idea what he had in mind, but she knew it fit somehow into the general plan. She let him forcefully drag her out of the Clean Room, through the outer lab and into the tunnel. They came to the bust set in the wall, and there Richard stopped. He pointed to the snout of a video camera embedded in the brick. He stood directly in its field of view and said, "Don't think you can kidnap her and threaten to hurt her if I don't go along. You don't dare hurt her. You need her too much."

Richard seized her tightly again and pulled her down the corridor so rapidly she had to run. The forced march cleared her head, and by the time they'd reached the bedroom, she could think again. "What are we doing?" she asked.

"We're going to live in the Clean Room," he said.

"But why?"

"So no one can break in and steal the data."

"But what about food? Showers?"

"You can go eat and shower whenever you want. I'll stay in the lab with my gun pointed at the hard drive."

The mattress was terribly heavy, and when they finally set it down on the floor of the Clean Room, Francine's arms trembled. But Richard was a slave driver. He didn't let her take a break as they brought back the box springs, the bedside table and piles of clothes. She said she was exhausted. "Damn you," he said. "Get your head out of your ass. We're in danger of our lives." But when they'd finished, he kissed her and whispered in her ear that she was wonderful.

The Clean Room was now about as violated as it could be. Still, it didn't matter now that the tissue was safely inside the sequencer. "Time for sleep," he said. He undressed down to boxer shorts. He stretched out on the bed and said, "Will you join me?"

It was cold in the Clean Room, and she pulled covers over him. "I'll just straighten up a little," she said. He was already snoring.

She put away the scattered drawers from the dresser they'd brought over and hung up the clothes Richard had thrown in a pile. He'd tossed the contents of his pockets on the counter, everything but his gun, and she straightened those up too. After changing into her nightgown, she found more things to put away and kept working until she could scarcely stand. She finally fell into bed but jumped up again to turn the lights off. She could never sleep with lights on, especially not with all those video cameras watching.

Richard had thrown off his covers, and when she climbed in beside him, his body radiated a comforting heat. She snuggled up close and listened to the sounds in the room: the air hissing through ducts in the ceiling, the magnetic stirrers giving off a faint hum, the sequencer clicking. Though she couldn't see the cameras in the darkness, she remembered where they were, and her eyes darted first toward one and then the other. She imagined people lurking behind the walls. And her mind came around to the idea that had come to her back in the bedroom with Richard.

Only how could she take so much power into her own hands?

Who else should have the power? Better a secular humanist than a religious fanatic, a scientist than a politician. Robert Oppenheimer hadn't wanted the responsibility either. "Now I am become Death, the destroyer of worlds." But he knew he had to make the atomic bomb for America because if the Nazis got it first, imagine the horror.

Einstein, Darwin, Nelson Mandela—they'd taken on huge responsibilities. And Richard too. Having to bomb his friend. She admired greatness of spirit in others; could she find it in herself?

She must be falling asleep because she saw hypnogogic images. A dog with a pink hat. A bright steel cylinder. A gun lying on the ground in a circle of light.

A corridor and bright light pouring in through a doorway at the far end of the corridor. A cross. A Buddha. All those crazy stories people told themselves to deal with death: no one will need religion anymore. Not once they have *this*.

MENNISS

A CONTROLLED COUGH from the foot of the bed woke him, but he pretended he was still asleep. He grunted and rolled on his side. He parted his eyelids far enough to make thin slits and looked through them. The room was entirely dark except for one bright circle of light. The light illuminated a familiar face, the face from the bust in the corridor. A real man now, but with the same handlebar mustache and goatee, the same smirk. He was fairly young, late 20s, probably. In his left hand, he held a bright flashlight. His right hand rested on a fancy walking stick. A single finger lifted from the head of the stick and wiggled in an admonishing fashion.

Menniss abandoned the pretense and sat up in bed. The man tossed his cane pole high in the air, switched on the room light, and caught the cane as it fell, all with the same hand. "Howdy," he said.

Images clashed. Menniss had formed various mental pictures of the I-H, but none resembled this peacock. But there was no mistaking the voice. He gently nudged Francine. "We have a visitor."

Her eyes popped open with the instant clarity of a person used to waking early.

Their visitor said "Madam," and made a sweeping bow. Francine gasped, sat up in bed and held the covers close around her.

"By the way," the young man added, "would you please deactivate that cannon under your pillow?"

Menniss drew the gun out by its barrel and set it on the floor.

The visitor tapped his stick on the wire mesh around the computer and touched the tops of several of the whirling magnetic

321

stirrers. "A picturesque composition. Did you get paranoid and forget what I mentioned earlier, that there are rules? Even if I wanted to, I couldn't steal the discovery from you. A certain elder person would kill me. More to the point, such behavior is foreign to my nature. I'm a good egg, one of the best—if a bit runny and undercooked. Still, I respect your flair for the dramatic. I flair that way too, but my tastes run toward burlesque more than melodrama. And what a temper you have. Cutting off ears. Berating famous scientists. My, my."

"When you sent me hunting for people," Menniss asked, "did you think I'd simply say hello and introduce myself?"

The I-H twirled his mustache. "A palpable hit. Perhaps I am a hypocrite. Or a hippogriff. One of those guys who keeps his fingernails polished and delegates the messier details to others."

Francine, bewildered, leaned in close to Menniss. "Who's he?"

Menniss put his arm around her. "He's my client. The one I told you about. I don't even know his real name."

The I-H made a grand bow. "My names are legion: Zeke, Howard, Ivan, and Maxifestifustuchian, to list a few. As a token of esteem, I shall tell you my most secret appellation: it is as Baehl that I am known in the priviest of privy counsels. Therefore, by this gesture, I confer upon you the coveted status of privet. Now, I know what you're thinking. You want to point out that the word 'privet' indicates not the member of an inner circle but a type of hedge. Well, be that as it may. I do tend to hedge."

"When did you become a stand-up comedian?"

"I've always been considered rather a gas. Or at least gassy. I just pretend to be a cold, hard spymaster because it gets the good stuff. Remember when we pulled you off the job in Moscow? Your friend Grigor must have told you the story. 'Are we not good Marxist-Leninists?' One of my favorite improvs ever."

"That was *you*?"

"In person. When someone works for me long enough, and I like them, I let them in on the secret. Those hafeems you captured? They're all my buds now."

Francine interjected with a vehemence that startled Menniss. "Hafeems? The people Richard told me about who live a few thousand years? If you have access to hafeems, why didn't you start this project long ago?"

"Madam scientist," Baehl said, "I myself am a hafeem. If, therefore, it were the essence of hafeemity I wanted, I could have gone van Gogh on myself and lopped off the handiest of ears. However, what I want, and what my friends most need, is not life extension. Rejuvenation is the rub since we hafeems don't have much of that. We can sometimes grow back fingers and other cosmetic necessities, but we still age. As hard as this may be for you to believe, there is no essential difference between getting old and dying in 80 years or three thousand years. We are as one, you and I, when compared to True Immortals."

Francine threw her covers aside and jumped out of bed. She opened the top drawer of the dresser and started grabbing clothes.

"Have no fear," Baehl said. "I shall avert my eyes." He put his hand on one cheek and pushed, turning his face away from her.

She undressed and stood naked in a pose of concentration for a few seconds, one hand in the air typing on its imaginary 10 keys. Recalling herself, she started to put on clothes, but promptly lost herself in thought again.

"By the way," Baehl said, "we turned the cameras off when you moved your stuff in here. What kind of person do you think I am?"

"I wasn't sure," Menniss said. "That was the problem."

"Why? Did I not sufficiently display my essential nature in the style of this place?" Baehl asked. "Could you not determine by direct observation that I'm fundamentally silly? Or, rather, the class-clown type. My way of dealing."

"I saw," Menniss said. "Just didn't believe it."

"Well, that's something. I do enjoy being found unbelievable."

Francine finished dressing in stages, breaking off several times to think. She turned on the water at a sink and splashed her face. She found a brush and dragged it violently through her hair. She made a final pass with the brush, threw it down and approached Baehl. He smiled at her.

In a preemptory tone, she said, "I shall need a piece of your body."

Baehl staggered backward several steps. He wobbled in place

as if stunned. He rubbed the side of his chin that had been facing Francine and moved his jaw experimentally. "Ouch," he said.

Menniss found it rather amusing, but Francine only frowned. "Come," she said. "Into the lab. Let's go."

"My dear," Baehl said, "Would it be too much out of place to inquire why you so suddenly covet a souvenir of my person?"

"Isn't it obvious?" she said. She held the Clean Room door open and motioned for Baehl to step out.

"Of course. Why didn't I think of that? Thank you for the explanation. There is only one problem: I have no idea what you're talking about. What do you mean, precisely?"

It was obvious even to Menniss. "The change in your DNA must act on the aging clock, although incompletely. But it must affect the same part of the genome. Looking at your genes could help Dr. Selis confirm her work."

"Very good," Francine said.

"How interesting," Baehl said. "Having grown up in an essentialist age, I find it difficult to think in a non-essentialist manner. That is to say, I tend to think of a True Immortal as fundamentally better than me. Much to my delight, I see that I am wrong. Hurray. Alas, I cannot spare an ear, for, unlike True Immortals, we hafeems only occasionally grow back entire body parts."

"I don't need an ear," Francine said. "A scraping from inside your mouth will do."

"Oh, very well then." He knelt on one knee, spread his arms wide and opened his mouth, looking much like a statue spitting water in a fountain.

"Not in here," Francine said. "Out there."

Baehl rose and followed her into the outer lab. He reassumed the position but with less flair.

Menniss helped Francine set up her equipment.

She found a metal instrument, dipped it in a chemical, waved it dry and pulled up a lab stool beside Baehl. She scraped the inside of his mouth rather roughly.

When she'd finished, Baehl licked his lips and said, "That was a unique form of a kiss, my dear."

"You're disgusting." Francine stirred the scraper in the eppi tube Menniss held out to her. She frowned. "No, this isn't enough for full sequencing. I need something more substantial."

"Would blood do?" Baehl asked. He tipped his head to one side and pulled down his shirt to bare his jugular vein.

"No, blood would *not* do," Francine said. "Red blood cells have no nuclei, so obviously, they have no DNA. I need several grams of flesh." She flashed Menniss a brief, private smile, and he remembered what she'd said before, that when it came to DNA, even the tiniest sample would do. She disliked Baehl and was taking it out on him; Menniss found this endearing.

"Flesh," Baehl said. "Yes. Hmm. Let me consider. Well, as it happens, I have not been circumcised. Would you care to obtain your flesh in that manner?"

"You're truly disgusting," she said.

"Not usually." He sounded quite dispirited. "My act seldom falls this flat. You are a tough audience. But let me begin again." He climbed laboriously to his feet. "Though I cannot spare a pound of flesh, perhaps I could manage a gram or two. But I am a trifle vain and should like professional help." He gestured toward the back wall of the Clean Room and, with a stage magician's wave, said, "Open sesame."

A panel on the wall moved upwards and fell back. A balding, gray-haired head ducked to pass through. It was Dr. Lemon.

IN THE BRIGHT fluorescent lights of the laboratory, Lemon looked terrible. The skin on his forehead seemed stretched and ready to break. The muscles between his thumb and index finger were collapsed to a hollow, and his shirt billowed as if it were empty.

He carried a briefcase, and the act of setting it on a bench seemed to exhaust him. "I'd suggest the back of your scalp," he said. "A scar beneath your hairline won't show."

"I do like to look my best," Baehl said.

"May I?" Lemon asked Francine.

"Of course, certainly," she said. "You're a doctor? I'm pleased. I can use your help. Not only with this minor procedure but for the project too. I'm Francine Selis." She held out her hand, and, after a pause, Lemon smiled. When he reached out to take her hand, he looked almost happy.

"Lemon," Menniss said, "when I came yesterday, did you already know?"

"I didn't know a thing." Lemon took instruments out of the brief-case and arranged them on a cloth. "But our friend Baehl here called me not an hour after you left and invited me into the job. I'd been working with him for years on other business. Apparently, you were too. But it's not the kind of thing one talks about in our profession, is it?"

"I would have told you about it if I could," Menniss said.

"Told me about immortality? Maybe after you'd already taken the treatment yourself," Lemon said. "But keeping secrets is what we do. Baehl, lay your head sideways on the bench there."

"I want you to know something," Menniss said. "Remember when you told me that life is like getting trapped in a room with a collapsing ceiling? Right then and there, I decided I would let you in on the secret as soon as possible. I meant for you and your son to be among the first to get the genes."

"I know that. Our mutual client already told me you had it in mind. Very considerate of you."

How did Baehl know? Menniss had never told him. Baehl had come up with it on his own. What covert motives made him do that? What layers beneath layers?

None. No layers beneath layers. Looking at his formerly unseen client, head stretched out on a lab bench as if on the chopping block, Menniss understood that Baehl had no covert motives. What he'd said to Lemon, he'd invented out of pure goodwill.

How wonderful. One fewer enemy and one additional friend. They might succeed.

Again, Menniss wondered why he felt depressed rather than pleased.

FRANCINE

BAEHL WAS GONE. He'd left right after Lemon snipped him, much to her relief. The kitchen was stocked with excellent wine and supplies, and with Richard's help, she put together a civilized meal.

Poor Dr. Lemon, he looked terribly ill. But he was a cultured man and a great conversationalist. Richard, too, proved to have depths of knowledge she wouldn't have guessed. They discussed the evolution of world languages, the history of Russian literature and the ecological effects of the Columbian contact. Later, the two of them began telling her about their CIA experiences. She was treated to stories of assassinations and abductions so Machiavellian and cold-hearted that it made her jaw drop.

Francine loved it. "What about the CIA and 9/11?" she asked. "I watched a lecture where they proved that the towers couldn't have collapsed from the impact of the planes alone. There are videos that show explosions going off simultaneously on lower floors."

The two men exchanged looks, but Blocking Monster stopped her from deciphering them. Probably they wanted to tell her they agreed, but the information was classified and they couldn't. Still, to be sitting near two people who *knew:* that alone was exciting.

"Here's my theory," she said. "I know you won't confirm or deny, but I have to tell you anyway. You know the story about how all the Jews escaped because the Mossad warned them? I know for a fact that isn't true: two of my Jewish colleagues died there. The story is obvious propaganda. But whose propaganda? My idea is that the CIA itself spread the theory. You see, it's diabolically clever. They're covering a real conspiracy story by connecting it to another that's patently ridiculous. Any thinking person will reject the second and, by association, the first."

Again that mysterious look between Richard and Dr. Lemon; undoubtedly, they were astounded that she had figured it out.

She sat back in her chair in triumph. These two are master plotters, but I'm not so bad myself. Dissecting plots isn't so different from doing science once you get the hang of it. She refilled their wine glasses and sat back, feeling like a true fellow traveler.

"Not to change the subject," Richard said, "but Lemon here has a question."

The doctor looked annoyed. "No, I don't. There's no point in asking her now. She doesn't have enough data."

"Try me," she said. "I might be able to make a guess. Some people are great kissers. I'm a great guesser." She giggled. She was a bit drunk, and she knew she could be funny when she was drunk. "Ask away."

"Well … to begin with, it seems clear that Immortals can't get cancer."

"Why? Oh, I see your reasoning. Cancer-causing mutations build up over time. So if they *could* ever get cancer, they'd all have died of cancer. They must have some defense. Interesting. Better cell surveillance? That's adding a new hypothesis. Better to use Occam's razor and limit the hypotheses. Tissue regeneration arises out of the initial theory naturally."

"How so?" Lemon asked.

"One of the actions of the aging clock would be to limit regeneration and thereby allow aging. Therefore, disabling the aging clock could plausibly restore regeneration. But cancer? Why? Perhaps we need to invoke the template hypothesis after all …" Francine broke off, her mind moving faster than she could speak.

"What he wants to know," Richard said, "is whether the immortality genes would cure a cancer that's already there?"

"There's no way she could know the answer to that yet," Lemon said. "Anyway, I need to take a nap. I'm exhausted."

"What's the template hypothesis?" Richard asked.

"It's one theory about how an organism would function if the aging clock were stopped. According to the template hypothesis, the DNA in each cell can be reread from scratch, so to speak, thereby restoring that cell to its initial state. Like when you run a restore program on your computer. All the new software you've put on it, along with any viruses or spyware that snuck in, gets erased, and the computer returns to how it was when you bought it. Returns to the template. A somewhat more complicated method could restore a whole set of linked cells, say, a tissue or an organ."

"Is that possible?" Lemon asked.

There was something peculiar about his tone and the expression on his face. Francine tried to understand what he was feeling, but there was Blocking Monster again. "Theoretically possible," she said. "Tissue template restoration has possibly been observed in certain species, but the idea remains controversial. For example, we know that starfish regenerate. But do they restore to a template? Maybe."

"Lemon's asking for himself," Richard said. "He has lung cancer. He wants to know if the immortality genes will heal him."

So that's why they'd been looking at me like that. Why do I always miss the things everyone else sees?

What do you say to someone who's dying? How do you talk to someone who's about to disappear forever?

"We'll see," Lemon said. "I'd rather not die if it can be helped, but we'll see." He got up from his seat and carried his dishes to the sink. "Excellent meal. And excellent conversation."

Francine tried to respond, but tears stopped her, tears rising from an aquifer she didn't know she had. She'd always recognized that her work might help real people. That's why the NIH gave out grants. But it had always been other people who took her discoveries and used them to create treatments. She'd never done that herself. To have someone waiting on her to save his life? It was a lot of pressure. But she also liked the feeling.

Richard said, "Well, I'm going to move everything back out of the Clean Room."

"Why would you do that?" Francine protested.

Lemon leaned against the kitchen counter. "I want to know why he put all that crap there in the first place."

Richard threw his hands up in the air. "I was just being cautious. I decided Baehl meant to steal the secret of immortality from us as soon as Francine figured it out. That's what I would do. To protect us, I had to—well, I don't want to get into all I thought I had to do, but moving to the Clean Room was part of it. And then I met the guy."

"The picture changes when you meet him, doesn't it?" Lemon said wryly.

"It does. Quite a lot." Richard chuckled.

"Are you sure?" Francine asked. "I agree the man is asinine, but does that mean he's not a threat?"

"I've known him in his true character for years," Lemon said. "He's not going to steal the secret and kill you."

"Are you positive?"

"You can never be positive in our line of work," Richard said. "But none of the things I was trying could have made us safe anyway. Not down here, right in the middle of his world."

She was incredulous. "So it was all useless drama?"

"I suppose you could sum up my whole life from beginning to end as nothing but useless drama," Richard said. "At the very least, let *me* haul everything back."

Which meant she'd have to clean the kitchen even though she was the one who'd done most of the cooking. Typical.

But after the two men left, her usual background level of Gray Fog vanished, and she saw what she would do.

Richard wasn't worried about Baehl anymore. She didn't necessarily agree, but even if he was right, the hafeem wasn't the only possible source of danger. And the step she had in mind would change the game-theory calculus against many potential threats. Hopefully, she wouldn't have to do anything so radical. But if the need arose, she'd have to move fast. And that meant building the second carrier in advance.

While cleaning plates and silverware, she worked out the details. The trick would be to do her work so cleverly that not even someone watching every keystroke would guess. Should she let Richard in on the secret? Better not; he might accidentally give it away.

She felt happier than she had in a long time. This must be why people enter helping professions, she thought: it's intoxicating.

She heard Father Bruno's voice in her head. *Take down your harps from the willow tree, oh my people, and return thee to Zion.*

CHAPTER 7

THE HOSPICE

"Setting: An infant has just been killed. She finds it unfair,
and when Death comes to claim her, she complains.
Infant: 'That's it? That's all I get?'
Death: 'You get what anyone gets. You get a lifetime.'"

NEIL GAIMAN
PRELUDES AND NOCTURNES,

In case you're wondering how I know some of this stuff: I interviewed
folks. (Plus, like Saul's old friend Thucydides, I invented some
plausible details because there's no other way to tell the story.)

THE CHRONICLER

JANICE

FUCK EVERYTHING. FUCK them all. It's ended. It's over.

How wonderful.

No more sexual abuse groups and how much they hurt. No more psychotherapy, and how much that hurts. End of cravings for crystal meth, ever-weirder piercings and sex with men I know will hurt me. No more longings at all—because I'm about to be dead.

Let it go. Let everything go.

But what about the assholes who screwed me? Should I let *them* go? Yes, because they're all going to die, too. Even the primary asshole, the cause at the core, the piece of crap who abused me: he's going to die, too, if he's not dead already.

Ashes to ashes and dust to dust. Let it all blow away.

It goes. It blows. Freedom. Peace.

At least for a second.

Is that all the peace I get, a second? I guess you have to be the Dalai Lama for peace to last longer than that. Because there's all the shit I did to myself. Can I forgive that? Can I forgive *me*?

Forgive who? Forgive Janice for what she did to Janice? Who that girl you talking about? Ms. Janice—she dead. She dead and gone. She is one bitch *all* gone. Not one grain coming back.

What you just now mistook for trash talk was an artistically controlled riff on the "Mistah Kurtz—he dead" quote from Conrad's *Heart of Darkness*. Through a weave of contemporized source-document elements, as well as ironic references to T. S. Eliot's repurposing of the original Conrad quote in his epigraph to *The Hollow Men*, Ms. Janice had found fresh words to express her process of letting go.

So there. I graduated from Bennington College.

"So there" to who? To whom. To whom am I defending my speaking ability? To some afterlife English teacher who's taken a job grading souls? I seriously hope there's no standardized testing in the afterlife.

I hope there's no afterlife, period. Because if death isn't the end, then I still have to deal, and I don't want to deal. I want to go free.

But if I do go on living, can't I dump my baggage and start over? Start from scratch as Janice, pure and simple, not as Janice, messed up and twisted?

Janice, pure and simple: who's that? There's no such thing as Janice unfucked-up. Because Janice without her bullshit isn't Janice. The real, true Janice is fucked up five stories deep. Do you know how twisted she is? She misses Blair, that narcissistic nobody.

I shouldn't give a damn for him. But I do. I miss him incredibly. I miss him so much I don't want to die. That shows you.

"Janice?" A voice has been saying this for a while. "Janice, are you awake?"

I guess so.

I bring myself awake.

I wake up.

THE FIRST THING I saw when I woke up was Saul leaning over the rails at the side of my hospital bed.

"Hi," I said.

"How do you feel?"

"I don't know, haven't checked lately." I closed my eyes to check and felt myself drifting away. I opened my eyes. "I feel crappy. I have a headache, and my back hurts from lying on this mushy mattress too long."

"I'm sorry." Saul put his hand on my arm with a firm touch that reassured me; it didn't signal sex, but it didn't signal distance either because it wasn't *too* firm.

"I feel like I'm on a bad high. Spaced-out and sick, like there's poison in my veins."

"I believe these are expected side effects of the medications they've administered to forestall further seizures."

I tried to scooch up in bed, but I didn't have the strength. He put his hands under my armpits and pulled me up to a sitting position without once touching my breasts or acting like he had to try hard not to touch them.

I looked around at my beautiful hospital room. A nice gray plastic TV hung from the ceiling. Handsome metal poles were everywhere, decorated with blue boxes and plastic IV bags. A friendly fake wood bedside stand was covered with squished juice boxes, their sucked-on straws sticking out. Decorative puke-green wallpaper and puke-green furniture completed the picture.

On the far side of the room, Zeke lounged on a puke-green faux-leather recliner. He wore a white tux.

I didn't mind Saul seeing me like this, but Zeke? Even the Eldest called him sexy. I could normally hold my own against him, but not with a tube up my nose.

Zeke looked amused, as he always did.

"What's so funny?" I asked.

"Life is," he said, "for presenting itself in sonata-allegro form." He posed every inch the armchair philosopher there in the armchair, one hand in his jacket pocket, the other stroking his goatee and mustache, his voice sincerely enthused about talking nonsense.

He threw both legs over the chair's right arm and pulled himself onto what you could call the edge of his seat although people don't usually pick that particular edge to sit on. "The classic sonata-allegro form: exposition, development, recapitulation. In the first few moments of our initial acquaintance, Saul and I raised from the floor a man with Parkinson's disease—the exposition. We went on to all manner and kinds of raising as well as of patients there on the cliff where we were nurse assistants—the development section."

He took a break from talking and hummed instead, waving his finger like a conductor's baton in rhythm with his humming. "Saul and I lose touch for a bit. A modulating bridge." His waving finger flopped about drunkenly before collapsing. "Then the Eldest snaps her fingers, and we're in the recapitulation, the same theme in exalted form. Previously, a large hospital for the old and infirm; now, a single hospital room for the young and beautiful. And sexily begowned to boot." He hummed again, focused on his finger, got cross-eyed, and stopped humming.

"I'm missing something," I said.

"About 50 years," Zeke said.

"Shall I make good on the elision?" Saul asked.

"Please," Zeke said. "I say so on behalf of Janice as well, for she is too busy clearing a disgusting liquid from the back of her throat."

"Are you, dear?" Saul asked.

I waved at him to go on.

"Nearly five decades ago," Saul said, "your friend and I became acquainted as fellow employees in a convalescent hospital. In that era, he lived as a young and egocentric but rather philosophical college student. He'd worn the white uniform of a nurse's aide some months before my arrival, and therefore to him fell the task of tutoring me in the vows and duties of the profession."

"Saul was a novitiate of nurse assistance," Zeke said. "A supplicant of the soporified, an acolyte of Alzheimer's, a postulant of pustulance. I taught him all he knows."

I couldn't laugh because a new glob of the aforementioned disgusting liquid had collected at the back of my throat. I concentrated with all my might to swallow it, and once I pulled that off, I didn't feel like laughing anymore. "You're Baehl, aren't you?" I said. "Alexandros hates you."

Zeke slipped from the chair onto his feet and bowed. "I have both privileges."

"He hates you a lot. But the Eldest likes you, and that counts more, doesn't it? She says she's good with you going ahead. Though supposedly I am supposed to tell you that by not telling you."

"The Eldest likes you, too," Zeke said. "And so do I. Personally. I mean, even if she hadn't threatened to hang me from a tree by the foreskin and make batter-fried calamari out of my nostrils and run me through with a sharpened boa constrictor if I didn't take care of you, I'd take care of you anyway."

I laughed a little at that. "And how did she threaten Saul to make him care for me?" Mostly, I wanted to hear more of his funny riffs.

"She didn't threaten him," Zeke said. "He loves you for yourself."

"Because I helped Blair?"

"That was, perhaps, a door," Saul said, "but my affections stepped through on their own."

He said it so sweetly I forgot to feel cruddy for a second. "So I'm not going to die right now?"

Saul took my hand. "In all honesty, my dear, you're seriously ill. However, as we are informed by the best, if not the politest, of physicians, you remain a respectable distance from death's proverbial door. Your symptoms, it seems, derive from a tumor pressing upon your brain. You'll undergo surgery, during which the bulk of this malignant growth will be removed. Though this extraction won't entirely cure you, it will relieve your symptoms and, to use an idiom typical of this unabashedly capitalist culture, *buy* you time."

With one hand, Zeke (I mean Baehl) threw a bagged set of hospital slippers high in the air. He caught it in his other hand and returned it to the first. He tossed up the set of slippers again, and while it was midair, he added a pair of balled-up socks. Every little while, he added something else to the growing Ferris wheel between his hands: a fork, a boxed juice, an apple. He managed it all without a sound, and because of where he was standing, Saul didn't know he was doing it. While Zeke juggled and made funny faces, Saul kept talking to me, his voice earnest and concerned.

"Fortunately, my dear, this surgery will leave you with very little pain. Indeed, perhaps none at all. That fact is said to follow from the anatomical terrain; there are no pain nerves in the brain."

An empty IV bag joined Baehl's circle and, after that, a bedpan—hopefully, empty.

I still felt too sick to smile, but my frown must have lightened; Saul (such a sensitive man) noticed and misinterpreted the change in my expression as a reaction to what he'd said. He added hastily, "Much as it pleases me to encourage you, I don't for a moment wish to be misleading. The incisions in your skull will ache—although, apparently, not as much as one might expect. And after the surgery, you'll endure a course of chemotherapy, which has been advertised as profoundly unpleasant. Still more disheartening, even these medicinal assaults on your body won't entirely eradicate the cancer. They'll only induce what your surgeon is pleased to call a 'remission.' Unfortunately, like remission of sins, your state of grace won't endure."

"Quit talking so fancy," I said. "And why do you care, anyway?"

Saul stopped talking and looked hurt.

The Ferris wheel thinned and disappeared as Baehl pocketed the juggled objects (except the bedpan, which ended up on a table). He came up to me and said, "Saul cares for you greatly, m'lady. Because you both love Blair? In part. But that's not the whole story. Saul is the sort of man who can care, and for some reason, you particularly appeal to him." He leaned forward and whispered, "I think he's adopted you." In a normal voice, he added, "Perhaps Saul speaks with more elegance than necessary, but the topic is painful and it's his way of coping. Here's the most important point: after all this unpleasantness, we'll spirit you away to my secret underground lair, Baehl's Underground, so much more whimsical than the other underground (or so I've been told). There, we'll cure you completely."

"To be honest," Saul said. "We only *hope* to cure you. We aren't certain we'll succeed."

"Thank you for being honest," I said. "I mean it."

"Still, we do have high hopes," Saul said. "There's a project underway, and, if luck favors us, it may …" He broke off and held a finger to his lips. The door opened, and an incredibly cute doctor walked in.

I KNEW HE was a doctor because he wore a dress-length white coat and a stethoscope necklace. He stood about 10 feet away and sprayed me with fancy words that can be summarized as, "I plan to carve into your brain." So arrogant and sexy. Even his wavy black hair bragged about how smart he was.

I would have messed with him in the old days, back before I had a tube up my nose and a big honking tumor in my brain. I might have hinted that if he worked hard enough, he could get me to worship him. I'd make him struggle for my devotion, feed him bits, withhold and feed some more. Once I'd persuaded him that he had *me* persuaded of his godhood and that I was ready to fall on my knees, I'd blow him off. You're a shallow egotistical nobody, I'd say, and you can go fuck yourself. No charge for the lesson.

But I was tired of all that.

"Do you know what day it is?" That was him in real life asking me a question.

You don't go through drug rehab without getting asked these questions a million times: oriented to time, place and person, serial sevens. "If you tell me how long I've been unconscious, I'll tell you the day," I said.

"About 72 hours."

"Then it's Friday."

"Very good. And your name and why you're here?"

"My name is George Sand. I'm here for gender reassignment surgery. If I'm going to call myself George, why not go all the way?"

Doc doesn't get the joke. He comes to my bedside, shoving Baehl aside, and takes my arm ungently. Reading the band, he said, "Your name is Janice, not George."

Baehl explained the joke. "George Sand was a female author who wrote under a man's name."

From close up, dockety-doc looked cuter than ever. But he didn't have a bit of bedside manner, towering over me like a coroner studying a corpse. He glanced sideways at Baehl and didn't (I'd guess) think much of him. He glanced at Saul and recoiled; I would have, too, if someone had glared at me so ferociously. Good old Saul.

Doctor Neurosurgeon-the-God introduced himself all over again. "I'm Dr. Ogsbury. I'm going to perform an operation on your brain, and …"

"Big news," I said.

"Don't interrupt me."

"Don't treat me like I'm not a person."

Saul contributed a lizardly glower; doc backed up. "I apologize if my manner is brusque."

"Surgeons like their patients unconscious," I said. "I know

because I, uh, *dated* a surgeon once. So naturally, you want to get this part over quickly and come back when I'm unconscious."

"I will *not* be using general anesthesia," he said. "You will remain awake during the entire procedure."

Score one for you, Doc Neuro.

"You intend to operate on her *awake*? Please explain."

Dear Doctor climbed high up on his own nose—he couldn't help himself—and asked, "Who are you?"

"A friend," Saul said.

They stared at each other; Saul won. Doc Neuro climbed down off his nose. In a nearly human voice, he said, "Conscious sedation reduces morbidity and mortality during this procedure."

"In what manner, may I ask?" Saul said.

Docket-doc wanted to say something arrogant, but he didn't dare. Not to Saul.

"The primary challenge that faces us during a debulking procedure for glioblastoma is that there is no clear boundary between normal brain tissue and cancerous tissue. To the naked eye, glioblastoma and healthy tissue superficially look much alike. Conscious sedation allows us to establish tissue identity by patient report. We insert a probe into borderline tissue and apply an electric current. If we've contacted brain, she'll have an interior experience, and she can tell us that. But if it's cancerous tissue, she won't notice a thing. She can tell us that, too."

"These interior experiences of which you speak," Saul says. "They do not involve pain? I was informed that this procedure would not cause pain."

"There will be no—" He amended himself. "There will be little pain. The brain itself lacks pain nerves. A few of the early steps may cause a moderate level of pain, but she won't remember them afterward. So far as she's concerned, they won't ever have happened."

"Why won't I remember?"

It's hard for the guy, but he lowered himself and addressed me instead of Saul. "Because we'll give you Versed. It's a strong tranquilizer that also blocks the process of permanent memory lay-down. Once the Versed reaches the central nervous system, your brain won't be able to permanently record any of its experiences. Everything you think and feel will drift away about 10 minutes later. You won't even remember the conversation we're having now because the amnesia is retrograde—it reaches back. It will be the same for you as if it never happened."

"Oh really?" I ask. "You think so?" Setup.

"Absolutely."

"Then, after you die, it will be like your whole life never happened, right?"

Neurosurgeon's eyes darted around. He realized he was caught. "Unless one believes in an afterlife."

"But you don't, do you?"

More eye darting. "I need to get started."

"Sure. And afterward, I'll have one of my gangster friends kidnap you and go all medieval on you like in *Pulp Fiction*, and once they've finished torturing you to death, it won't matter because you won't remember because you're dead. And so you're cool with all that?"

Points for me. Even if I wouldn't remember scoring.

I told him I was just kidding. I told him I thought this was the kind of issue all neurosurgeons get analytic about, but maybe I'm thinking of Oliver Sacks.

He clucked and stumbled and left. He wasn't a philosophical neurosurgeon.

I felt ice in my arm as the nurse, who'd been puttering around the whole time without my noticing, pushed in the drug.

I COULD GET used to mainlining tranquilizers.

I'm not ashamed of anything. The life of Janice happened to someone else.

Her father dies when she's a preteen, so she has a male-shaped ache. Some guy she can't remember molests her. Her mother gets killed in a drunken car crash, so Janice also has a female-shaped ache. That is the recipe for a Janice, a girl who cuts and slices and pierces herself and grows brain cancer.

Who was it who molested me?

Even on IV drugs, I could feel it, my original sin. But I had no idea who was responsible; no face, no name.

If I knew who did it, I could hate him instead of hating myself. After another 10 years, maybe I'd forgive the asshole. After that, I'd go to therapy for another 10 years and get into the underlying abandonment. But Jeez, molested *and* two missing parents? A piece of work.

Let me announce to all the fucked up assholes and bitches who act out their fuckedupedness on themselves and everyone they know: I bless you and forgive your shit. Even if you're so fucked up that you run for President, I bless and forgive you.

Aren't I a regular Dalai Lama? Only, I don't think it officially counts if you need IV drugs to get there.

THEY'RE SHAVING MY head. Buzz, buzz. Thick spiked hair falling on the floor, the bald-headed badge of a cancer patient. They say the grumpiest cancer patients live the longest. Lucky me! Only I don't feel grumpy now, not with this tranquilizer.

They wheel me into the operating room. It's pretty inside. Everyone wears heavy blue gowns like it's a hospital soap opera. Is that a warm Chihuahua under my feet? No, a heated blanket. A big oval light like the light at the end of the tunnel you see after death blinds me, and I shut my eyes. I keep my eyes shut and feel that good-ol' narcotic warm and happy. Now, this is the life.

"Janice? Are you awake? Open your eyes."

I open my eyes. A doctor's face swaddled in a blue surgical Burkha partly blocks the bright light, but rays leak around like a halo. He's one sexy angel. "Have I met you before?" I ask.

"We first met about an hour ago, and since then, we've talked twice. But you're on a drug that blocks the laying down of permanent memory. You're completely conscious in the moment—quite intelligent, too, and rather funny—but you only have a 12-minute window of linked awareness. Because that's about how long you can keep things in short-term memory. I've been testing you. Twelve minutes is a bit higher than average."

I know what he's talking about because I've taken Ambien and had long conversations with people that they tell me about later, but I don't remember.

"It's time to get started on your surgery," the doctor says. "Versed at this dose is a *very* strong tranquilizer, so what I'm about to say shouldn't bother you a bit."

"Go ahead, good doctor, sir. Spill."

"I'm about to saw open your skull. Are you okay with that?"

"No problem. I love it when my soul gets sawed. I mean my skull. Same idea."

He chuckles. "I've used a local anesthetic, and I've also given you IV fentanyl. So you won't feel too much discomfort."

Fentanyl? That's dangerous stuff. But powerful; I thought I felt a narcotic glow.

Wouldn't it be funny if this got me started back on drugs? I knew a girl who started drinking after 16 years of sobriety because she sipped wine at Christmas midnight Mass. "Not feel much?" I shout. "You're a liar. It hurts like hell! You're shaking my brain to pieces!"

"Sorry," he says. "It's almost over. More fentanyl, please."

Almost over! Grinding, sawing, ripping. More ripping. Some serious grinding. Now the two-handled lumberjack blade. I get into it. Bring it on! Cut me. Rip me. Pierce me.

Then it's over.

"That took longer than I expected," the doctor says. "Sorry. But it's done now. Are you doing all right?"

"No, I'm not! I'm permanently traumatized."

"You won't remember any of it."

"Like hell, I won't. Getting your head sawed open isn't something you forget. Is there a huge gaping hole in my head? It feels drafty up there."

"More than a hole. We've removed almost a third of your skull. But we'll put it back afterward."

"If it's not too much trouble."

He chuckles. I've impressed him: I'm pretty bright and don't scare easily. "Skull bone heals quickly," he says. "So you don't have to worry about it falling off again."

"That's a relief. But tell me, why didn't you put me out before you did this, like any normal doctor?"

"This type of surgery is best performed with conscious anesthesia.

I need your help distinguishing between brain tumor and real brain, because glioblastoma is a kind of brain tissue. Just for the record, I've already explained this to you several times, but the drugs make you forget."

To show him I'm not just a lowlife chick with tattoos, I ask, "If the tumor is made of brain tissue, how do you know there isn't any of *me* in it?"

"An interesting question," he says. Squishy sounds. "I suppose it's because cancer cells don't talk to other cells. They're not part of the whole system. They've become immortalized, and they live on just for themselves."

Immortalized cells in my brain. How funny. Like pieces of Blair.

I miss Blair. I've never missed anyone like I miss Blair.

Ooh, those are disgusting squish-squish sounds.

"I've opened the dura mater," doctor man says. "That's the tissue around your brain. You won't feel any pain at all during this next stage of the procedure because there are no pain nerves in your brain."

"Did I feel pain during the last stage?"

"When I opened your skull, you certainly said you did."

"I must have been asleep," I say, "because I don't remember."

He mucks around in my head some more.

"I'm going to use the electric stimulator now," he says. "When I stimulate cells that belong to your brain, you'll have subjective experiences. Could you report them to me? That's how I'll know whether I'm in healthy or cancerous tissue. For example, when I touch here, what do you feel?"

Everything is such a waste. You try so hard, and it goes nowhere. Even this horrible surgery; it's not going to cure me. I can tell. Tears well up. I've been sad like this forever, and I'll always feel sad. A whole lifetime sad.

Then I feel fine again.

"What was that like?" he asks.

"Horrible," I said. "Like a major depression. You can do that just by touching my brain?"

"That's why neurosurgeons don't believe in souls," he says.

"Everything's in the brain. *Everything*." He doesn't sound happy about it. "Do you feel anything when I do this? No? How about here?"

"You fucking asshole," I say. I want to bite him. My jaws click.

"What about here?"

I don't want to bite him anymore. "Nothing that I can tell."

"You sure? Here? Here?"

"Nothing."

I hear wet, mucky, slurping sounds, and I like how they sound. I smell something burning, and what a gift to smell things. My stomach feels good, and so do my toes. This is what life should be like. I've always felt like this, and I always will. This is my whole life forever and ever.

"Janice, wake up. Open your eyes."

I open my eyes and see a beautiful doctor all Burkha'd up. He tells me I know him. He tells me I'm on a drug that blocks memory, and also on fentanyl, which is why everything feels so good and so new. Next, he's going to put a probe into my brain and zap me with it. Which, he says, he's already done a few times.

A brilliant, lucid memory floods and flashes. I'm right there. I can see it and feel it too. On the goddamn couch in his office. Oh shit. In my worst fantasies, I never suspected *him*. I thought for sure it was one of my mom's boyfriends. But my therapist, Dr. Stott? He was one of the good guys.

I thought he was one of the good guys.

The room fades.

"Go back there a second," I say.

"Does it feel pleasurable?" he asks. I imagine I catch a hint of a leer. "There are several pleasure centers in this part of your brain."

He's talking sexual pleasure centers; screw yourself, dockety-doc. And why the hell does my abuse memory have to camp out near a pleasure center? I don't need this.

I'm back in my therapist's room, and I see everything. Janice is 11, and she's way past scared. But Dr. Stott is one of her only adult friends, and she can't say anything.

My whole life will change now that I know this. This will turn everything around. "That's enough," I say.

"There are certain centers in the brain that stimulate pleasure."

That's my doctor. The creepy jerk thinks his brain probe is giving me orgasms. "Just so you know, what you had your finger on there was a memory of childhood sexual abuse."

He's taken aback. "I'm sorry."

"Don't be. I spent years in therapy trying to remember who the guy was, and now I know. He's dead, unfortunately, so I can't sue the hell out of him. But that's fine. I'm just glad to know."

Now he becomes unsure of himself, weird for a doctor. "Do you want to tell me anything about it so I can remind you after surgery?"

It doesn't get any slimier. "No, I fucking don't want to tell you the details."

"Listen, Janice, seriously, I know you think you'll remember, but you won't. You're on a drug that blocks memory. In 12 minutes, you'll forget this entirely."

"Hah. Not. I'm not going to forget *this*. Not a chance."

"But you will. Your brain stores 12 minutes of current experience in a temporary buffer, and the drug you're taking stops you from writing the buffer to the hard drive. Everything you're thinking and feeling right now won't leave a trace."

Is it possible? They'll all disappear, this moment, this incredible discovery, these awful images? I can't believe it. This is too powerful. He's wrong.

But even if it does disappear, even if this 12 minutes of existence goes down the drain forever like one of Blair's 12-year frames, it's real now. This moment means something.

A woman is talking to me, and I like that better than a man talking to me. "Janice, he's right when he says you'll forget. I think you should at least give us a name. When you wake up, one of us will tell you what you said, and you can go from there."

"Who's that?"

"Carol Denning. I'm a friend of Saul's."

A friend of Saul's? Saul snuck a friend into the operating room to watch over me? How cool. "Okay, then. When I wake up, tell me, 'Dr. Stott did it.'"

"No more than that?" That's the surgeon.

"Don't be a pervert. Go back to work."

"We're almost done," he says.

"Done with what?"

"Operating on your brain."

"That was fast."

"We've been at this five hours. You did very well."

I WAS LYING in a bed. Saul sat beside me, squeezing my hand.

I loved Saul. I trusted him like I'd never trusted anyone before. I felt like a little girl, and I didn't mind feeling like a little girl with him. "What exactly did they do to me?"

"To use your surgeon's inelegant term," Saul said, "he success-fully 'debulked' the tumor."

"Did I just wake up from anesthetic?"

"Interestingly, they chose not to utilize that magnificent inven-tion. Instead, they employed a drug that in some peculiar manner interferes with memory."

"You've told me this already, haven't you?"

"Several times in the last hour. However, this marks the first time that you guessed the repetition, and therefore we may conclude the drug's effects are waning. But compose yourself, my dear. The heroic neurosurgeon arrives."

I composed myself as much as possible with a tube up my nose. Dockety-doc said a lot of boring stuff, mostly about what a great job he did, and I promised to nominate him for America's Best Doctor if he'd just shut up. I had a headache, and my arm hurt because one IV pulled. And I had to pee. Or maybe not. There was a catheter between my legs.

Superdoc's voice changed, and I paid attention. He leaned closer. Saul leaned closer too.

Superdoc said, "During surgery, you told me to tell you something."

"I did?"

Doc looked at Saul.

"It's okay. Whatever you're going to tell me, Saul can hear, too."

"This is rather confidential."

"I issue him security clearance to hear Janice's secrets. Spill."

He swallowed. "I want you to know that not everything you remember under electrical stimulation actually happened."

"Yeah? For example?"

"For example, when I was a child, I spent a lot of time pretending to fly a fighter jet. Under electrical stimulation, I might remember those fantasies as if they happened."

"That's great. Now get to the point."

There was no one else in the room, but he dropped his voice anyway. "You told me to say the following words to you: 'Dr. Stott did it.'"

I didn't get it.

Then I did. It was a bombshell.

"You're kidding. I said that?"

"We were stimulating parts of your brain to identify healthy tissue, and you experienced a vivid memory."

Dr. Stott? The therapist who helped me so much after my dad died?

Not him. He couldn't have abused me. He was one of the good guys.

Row, row, row your boat, life is just a dream.

I did feel good, though.

Probably leftover narcotics. Good drug. Good dog.

THERE ARE GOOD drugs, and there are bad drugs, and then there's chemo.

After two weeks of chemotherapy, I was the incarnation of nausea. Nausea made flesh, and she shall dwell always and forever among us. She is the Alpha and the Omega, the one who was and who is to come. The almighty urge to vomit.

Nausea started at the soul and went out to the throat; no holding back or faking; always full disclosure. I'd never felt so honest. Letting everyone and myself see the deepest, sickest me right there in the bucket.

Six weeks later, it was over. I was empty and clean. Maybe even purified.

That Janice chick, she was so polluted, so sinful it took chemo to detox her.

Oh, don't be so hard on the girl. She's been through things.

SAUL WAS TALKING to me. I worked hard to push my eyelids open.

I had the blankets up to my chin. I was cold and didn't want to look at myself. I was a shrunken nothing, which was what happened when you spent more time vomiting than eating.

"It's time to go," Saul said.

"Go where?"

He looked around to see whether anyone could hear. In a quiet voice, he said, "Ostensibly, to a hospice." He leaned over and whispered in my ear. "To Baehl's underground establishment beneath the redwoods."

I weakly tugged on his collar and pulled his ear next to my mouth. "What's with this underground fetish? Baehl and Alexandros both."

"Secrecy and safety, and, for Alexandros, fear of nuclear bombs."

"So you think I might live?"

"The hope, I believe, is not vain, not far-fetched." He kissed me on the forehead.

I still didn't get why he cared about me. I turned my head to cry. Only, I didn't have time to cry because a flock of EMT types swarmed in, moved me onto a gurney, swaddled me with blankets, and strapped me so tight I felt like a corpse with movable eyes.

They carried me to the hospital's roof, where I watched a helicopter land. The pilot was another hafeem, Saul told me, and she helped the EMTs set me gently in the back. She lifted the helicopter off the roof pretty smoothly, but then the wind hit us and my internal organs jounced around. Stomach, say hello to spleen. Guts say hello to liver. You're supposed to have fat pads around your stomach, but three weeks of chemo gets rid of that. Internal anorexia.

We did the usual Faerie-world routine and changed helicopters a lot, with me getting more airsick each time. Screw that. Nausea likes to pretend it's the whole you and the whole world, too, but it's just one little thing, like a stuffy nose or a stubbed toe. Once you've had chemo, you know how to put nausea in its place.

After a pile of parking garages, car switches and helicopter changes, we landed soft as grass in a meadow surrounded by giant redwoods. They carried me out on a stretcher. I wanted to stay out there and soak in some moonlight, but Saul, Baehl and some other folks hurried me into the woods. Baehl had one of those huge flashlights. You know the kind: the guy who has one when you go camping thinks he's cool. He used it to show me four cars parked neatly under the trees. No, hearses. Each was a different color: white, red, black and beige.

"The Four Hearses of the Apocalypse," Baehl said. "Antichrist, War, Famine and Plague."

I gave him the laugh he expected, and he held up a wineglass. "A toast to your health, milady." He handed me the glass.

I sat up and drank it. It was a protein drink, not wine—cold, luscious, strawberry-flavored Ensure. I gulped it down and broke into a shiver. Saul made me lie down and piled more blankets on me.

Baehl asked me to choose a hearse, and after profound consideration, I picked Antichrist. They bundled me onto a soft mattress with silky sheets where the coffin usually goes. Baehl climbed inside and expertly tucked me in. He moved in that industrious, right-angled way men use when they want you to know they have no intention of getting sexual with you, but they're tempted. Not that he truly felt tempted, considering how I looked. But it was nice of him to pretend.

He shut the back, got in the driver's seat—Saul was sitting shotgun—and opened the window partition behind which there was usually a corpse. "Indigo Girls?"

Though I don't like to admit it, I love them and told him yes.

We drove into the woods, and Saul and Baehl got into a heavy conversation, which I ignored. I let the music make a soundtrack to my life. That's what music does if you trust it, and I trust Indigo.

The best thing you've ever done for me
Is help me take my life less seriously
It's only life after all

With that, I became Claire from *Six Feet Under*, bopping around in her hearse, doing her sincere best and making mistakes. Bopping around in a redwood forest. The trees didn't oppress me like they usually do because I had nothing inside to *be* oppressed, only protein drinks. You can't oppress liquids because they slither away when you press on them.

The less I seek my source for some definitive
The less I seek my source.
The closer I am to fine

"Closer to Fine." Half-dead and swaddled, brain-tumored to the gills, but in a hearse named Antichrist with two half-immortal friends and bopping around a redwood forest that can't squish you because you've turned to slither. Pretty damn fine.

"She showed up one night and stared at me," Baehl was saying. "That's all—just stared. That's when I promised to ask her permission before taking the final step."

"And you did ask?" Saul said.

"Janice asked for me. I sent her to the Eldest with a message. Remember before her surgery when she said, 'the Eldest is good with your going ahead'? That was the answer. But I already knew that must be her answer because if the answer had been 'no,' I would have heard about it. When Janice had her big seizure, the Eldest sent me word to drop everything and come help, which I did, of course. On the way, she appeared briefly and handed me a message. It says … well, here, read it for yourself."

"What does it say?" I asked. I could hardly talk, and I didn't think they could hear me, but one of them turned down the music, and Saul said, "May I read it aloud?"

"Please do," Baehl said.

"Very well," Saul said. "This is in her hand, without a doubt. She writes in Portuguese. Please excuse my poor translation. The Eldest often intentionally transgresses conventional grammar, and I lack the poetic skill to carry through the spirit of her speech. However, since both of you have met her in person, perhaps you can fill in where I fail.

I now begin the message. 'You have met Janice and you care for her. This pleases me, for I have chosen to have love for her, and I do have love for her. And this I command: treat her as if she were my child. I command. Hear? A command. To all, and especially to you. And after this command, another. The hafeem Saul, who is dear to me …'

"To pause and interpolate: perhaps she means 'useful to me.' The language is archaic and unclear. But to continue, 'I trust Saul greatly, and I trust you little.' That is a rhetorical flourish, for I know I'm not worthy of so much trust. 'In all matters relating to the care of my adopted child, you shall obey Saul. That, too, I command. And now I cease commanding. Now I answer. To that which you have asked of me, I say I will allow, and I will protect. For a little while.'

"That's the end of the message though I should add that the style of her handwriting has a certain irony to it, a certain humor."

"You noticed?" That was Baehl.

"It's present in the curl of the vowels. You observed the vowels, did you not?"

"Maybe, I don't know. But, you see, she assures me again that I have permission. So why am I so nervous?"

"You are right to be nervous," Saul said, "For as easily as she gives, she takes away. The Eldest is both a very patient and a very *sudden* being."

Bouncing away in a hearse while two half-immortal guys, my best friends in all the world, talk away about crazy things—including the fact that the oldest person who's ever lived loves me—I'd never felt so happy.

"Hark," Baehl announced. "Forsooth also. We are here. Where, you ask? Why, at the hidden hafeem hobbit hole." He braked more suddenly than my internal organs liked, switched into reverse, drove backward in a circle and stopped again.

Baehl got out, opened the back of the hearse and gave me another protein drink to sip. I looked past my stretched-out feet as I sipped and saw a concrete wall lit by a piece of bright moon. Baehl handed Saul a flashlight and asked Saul to shine the flashlight on him. He asked me to watch. With that protein drink to fortify me, I pushed myself up on my elbows like there was nothing to it.

Baehl arranged himself in a precise position beside the wall as if there were special markings on the ground that matched his feet, and he had to place them properly, but you could tell he was faking it. He lifted one leg and wobbled like Charlie Chaplin trying to keep his balance on roller skates at a cliff's edge. Finding his balance, he pushed the toes of his raised foot behind the knee of the leg still in touch with the ground. He crammed his thumbs in his nostrils and said, "Fizzleswit."

Nothing happened.

He intoned "Fizzleswit" again and again nothing happened.

He mimed deep disappointment.

Then Baehl stood up normally and pulled a long black thing, like a TV remote control, out of his shirt. He pointed it at the wall. Still nothing. As if he had no idea what he was doing, Baehl ostentatiously pushed buttons. Again nothing. "Oh, what the hell." He mashed the buttons of the remote all over his face. It was hilarious. And a section of the concrete slid away.

Baehl put his head in the back of the hearse. "Even if the ritual is not in itself efficacious, it does put one in the right state of mind. Do you think she can walk?"

"I think so," Saul said. "She was walking a little in the hospital."

"Hey, I'm here," I said. "You can talk to me. Yes, I can walk."

Saul found my shriveled feet among the covers and slipped a pair of silly hospital slippers over them. He gave me his arm, and I wormed my way up to sitting. I rested then stood. Hurray. I had on one of those hospital gowns that keeps untying and shows your butt out the back, but Saul wrapped me in a blanket.

I leaned on Saul's arm and walked slowly. I looked at the redwoods with trepidation, but they kept their distance. We followed Baehl through the opening in the concrete wall into what turned out to be an elevator. The door closed, the elevator dropped with a lurch, and my internal organs said "pleased to meet you" to each other again.

"I'm sorry," Baehl said. "The elevator was built for freight, not beautiful convalescents."

I felt a lot more like freight than a beautiful convalescent. Anorexic freight—cheap at the weigh station.

THE ELEVATOR CAME to a jerky stop. The door opened, and we walked out into a large, bare, hexagonal room lit by rows of pale red floor lights that turned the white walls pink.

"You live in a pink beehive?" I said.

Baehl laughed, and the rims of his eyes turned red as if the me-corpse had said something hilarious. Pure generosity.

"It is indeed a beehive," he said. "A beehive of industry, conspiracy, plotting and planning, of devious scheming. The outer beehive of Baehl's Underground is vast and contains, or shall contain, multitudes. The inner beehive is a laboratory for a few. Shall we sally forth?"

It was only 30 feet or so across the room, but it looked like miles. "And do what?" I asked.

"Attain the aperture at the far end." With a big, graceful wave of his right arm, he pointed across the hexagon to a door labeled "Aperture."

"And go through it too, I bet." It being an aperture and all.

"Not much further than that."

The floor was made of rubber like they use in playgrounds, only it was white and turned pink by the lights. It squished, and I felt unsteady.

Walk across that? No.

I put one hand against the wall and sallied forth along the edge like a bug.

I managed one whole edge, but halfway down the next, I had to rest. Like most of the other hexagon edges, this one had a door in it. I opened the door a crack and saw a long corridor stretching away and a few people walking along it. The walls were covered in bawdy murals. I closed the door because my stomach was sore and I didn't want to laugh.

I made it to the door set in the next edge and again stopped to rest. This one had a sign that read, "Master Control Room." Instead of opening it, I asked what was in there.

Baehl imitated a medieval footman, or one of the Illuminati green&golds, and flourished it open. The room was crazily decked out in tasteless gangster style: royal-red carpet, purple velvet chairs, a green silk sofa, brass standing lamps with red, tasseled hats, stands with curving gilt legs and black-marble tops, tons of Asian vases and a white Venus de Milo wearing a peacock feather hat.

"Your love bower?" I asked.

"My Master Control Room. As the sign says. A place of wonders. As, for example, yonder device." He pointed to a black rotary phone sitting on a gilt stand. "You no doubt will disbelieve me, and yet I speak the truth when I say that via this wonder of science, I can put myself in contact with virtually any person on this latitudinous and longiglobius earth. Are you not amazed? Do you not wish to prostrate yourself before such mighty might?"

Saul chuckled. It sounded amazing, like he was brimful with sorrows, and each chuckle was a sorrow falling out. I'd never heard Saul chuckle. He frequently smiled, but he wasn't the chuckling kind of guy.

"You, sir, are a master," Saul said. "I am awestruck. I salute you from my heart. You have raised the art of foolery to the sublime. This is luminescent whimsy, humor transcendent, superabundant, and perhaps capable, as you once said, of turning back all the tragedies in the world, if only for an instant."

"Wow, sir, and wowza," Baehl said. "I am deeply complimented. More deeply than I can say."

He bowed, and so did Saul. Bow, bow, bow, and, I'm sorry, after a while, they looked like those fake birds dipping their beaks into a cup of water, so I stuck my thumb in. "Nowadays, what Baehl does is called 'over the top.' This place is completely over the top."

Saul stopped bowing to Baehl and finally gave me the attention I deserved. I'd never seen him so happy. "Thank you for the explanation, my dear," he said. "I've heard the expression but misunderstood, knowing too well its original military application. And yet, on reflection, perhaps it's appropriate. This world he's created—in merely one of its multitudinous aspects—isn't it a parody aimed at a certain other underground world?"

"You're right," I said. "It's all a campy take-off on Alexandros." I heard someone tittering and realized it was me. "Only, since he's not the world's funniest guy, Alexandros won't get the joke, and he'll take it as a big fuck-you, won't he?" After I said that, I wished I hadn't because I was talking to Saul and didn't want to act gutter around him.

Luckily, Saul still had his high chuckle on. "Yes. And, as such, might it not be regarded as a gesture of brave recklessness that, coincidentally enough, resembles the action from which 'over the top' derives? That is to say, leaving deep entrenchments and dashing through No Man's Land? But you're exhausting yourself, standing without support. Here..." He offered me his arm again, and I took it.

Baehl said, "Shall we make a final push? We don't have much further to go, and when we reach it, we'll find cans of delectable protein supplement in abundance."

"A wheelchair might be useful," Saul suggested.

Spurred on by visions of Ensure, I said, "No, I'm fine," and let go of Saul's arm. I walked the last 10 feet like it was nothing and got through the "Aperture" door and into another hexagon, this one blue.

The floor was covered with white sand blued by the lights, and five of the six walls wore white silk stained blue the same way. One of the edges had a giant TV showing rippling bluish colors. But the carpenters who built this place had gone on vacation early and left one edge unfinished. You could look through to the back of a wall facing the other way, but the side facing us wasn't covered, and you could see those metal strips full of holes that walls get attached to.

The carpenters, I realized, hadn't forgotten anything. Baehl sauntered over, reached between the metal strips, took hold of a handle and lifted. Part of the wall came away, and he set it to one side. He ducked his head under a metal crossbar and called out, "We're *here*. Anyone home?"

A voice, so tired and exhausted I felt like Supergirl by comparison, replied, "Do you have to enter like that? Would it break some sacred rule to install a door? Well, bring her in and let me take a look at her."

I STOOPED UNDER the metal crossbar and considered myself quite the athlete. Afterward, I felt dizzy and had to lean against a cabinet. The room was a medical clinic filled to overflowing with an addict's dream of needles and drugs in glass-covered cabinets, piles of black machines on rollers ready to beep and flash, red trash bags with that biohazard symbol on them, a big microscope, an examining table and, above it, a huge swiveling surgery light with removable plastic covers on its handles like the gloves deli cashiers wear.

The room was normal-shaped, not a hexagon. It had a little office attached at one end, and an old man stood at its doorway, leaning most of his weight on a desk just inside. He looked sicker than me. If he'd started out as an eight-legged spider, he was down to maybe two legs. He wobbled a few feet from the office door and dropped onto a stool, and I remembered how that felt, except now I was closer to fine. Or I would be after another can of Ensure. Better yet, a pizza.

"Good evening, Dr. Lemon," Baehl said.

Dr. Lemon said, "Is it evening? You can't tell in this dungeon." He started a wheezy coughing fit that went on forever and ended with a huge hock into a handy cup.

Saul walked over and said, "I am most pleased to meet you again, Dr. Lemon, but I confess I've yet to take advantage of your counsel: the level of my cholesterol remains unmeasured."

The old man wiped his lips on a tissue and dropped the tissue into a red biohazard bag. "Levels,'" he said. "Cholesterol 'levels.' It's a panel. But I hardly think it matters, considering *what* you are, as I now know. Please allow me to apologize for mistreating you during our last encounter."

"Not at all, doctor," Saul said, "you were quite kind."

They shook hands, or at least Saul shook Lemon's hand; when he let go, the hand dropped into Lemon's lap. Some people wave their arms around when they talk, and even regular people emphasize words with their bodies, but Lemon spoke without gestures, not even with his face, as if he didn't have the energy.

No *physical* energy, anyway. He still had a lot of mental energy. "How old are you exactly?" he asked Saul.

"Two thousand, five hundred sixty-eight years."

"Therefore, based on your appearance," Lemon said, "I would calculate you have another … say one thousand years or so before decrepitude sets in. Does this give you a sense of urgency?"

"More than you might guess," Saul said. "Nonetheless, I respect-fully acknowledge that your urgency exceeds mine."

"You guys keep talking," Baehl said. "I'll be back." He hurried out of the clinic through another door.

"Mr. Baehl tells me you're a doctor yourself," Lemon said. "I hope we can work together."

"Alas, I last practiced in the 18th century, and what I learned then is best forgotten."

"But I'm sure you have the instincts," Lemon said. "You certainly have more physical strength than I do. I'll appreciate any help I can get. Do you have her medical records?"

"I do." Saul handed Lemon a thick chart that he must have been carrying all along, only I hadn't noticed. I thought, If I die now, that chart is the closest I have to a biography. What a sorry biography.

Lemon flipped through my records and grunted in that comfort-ing, professional way doctors do when they feel like it. He waved me over. Because I was the healthy one compared to him, I unleaned from the cabinet and forced a hint of bounce into my step as I joined him and Saul.

"I'm Dr. Lemon, and I'll be managing your care from now on."

"I'm Janice. My brain just got carved up, and I'm hungry."

"Do you know your diagnosis?"

"Grade four glioblastoma."

Lemon repeated the words slowly and with reverence. "Grade four glioblastoma." He put his lips together and blew through them just short of whistling. "Young woman, you and I are in the same boat. I have stage four lung cancer. If what they're doing out there doesn't work, we're both dead and probably at about the same time. So we might as well be friends." He held out his limp hand.

I shook it, but I wished I hadn't because his nails were orange around the edges and his fingers felt like greasy popsicle sticks.

"What did it do to you initially?" he asked. "Headaches? Sei-zures? Personality changes?"

"Headaches and seizures. I don't know about personality changes. I fell in love with a total narcissist the other day, which is pretty much what I always do, but I'm still in love with him, and that's not normal. So yes, you can write down personality changes."

You know that annoying habit doctors have of ignoring everything they can't use? Lemon skipped over that moment of stunning self-revelation and asked, "Weakness? Stumbling?"

"One of my arms used to twitch, and they called that a 'partial seizure.' But I feel good now." We might both have fatal cancer, but I was in remission and young and healthy; cancer or not, he was almost dead with old age. "Do you have any Ensure around?" I asked. "Or a taco? A Snickers bar?"

"You'll stick to Ensure for now," Lemon said, "but you have your choice of flavors. We're well-stocked."

Saul got two cans and a straw for me from a cabinet. He and Lemon put their heads together over my chart and talked *about* me instead of *to* me, except for the three or five times Lemon looked up and told me to sip more slowly.

I was halfway through the second can when Baehl returned. He had two people with him: my dear friend Richard Menniss, he of the knife in the night, and a straight-backed woman of maybe 45 who looked so prim and civilized that right off I didn't like her.

I GAVE MENNISS a cheerful hello. I expected him to give me some shit back, but he looked weirdly helpless, like when I'd found him tied up in the trunk. Saul gave him a great big two-hands-around-one handshake, and that perked him up a little. The ladylike lady wanted to get back to doing something much more important than meeting us; you could tell.

Saul bowed to Francine, and she smiled, even giggled. He knew how to say a lot with a bow. "You must be Professor Francine Selis," Saul said, "the distinguished scientist directing this project. Deeply honored to meet you."

"What a nice thing to say," the professor lady said. "Thank you."

"Now, don't spoil my fun," Baehl said. "It's my job to introduce you. Dr. Selis, please meet Saul, a hafeem of some two and half thousand orbits 'round the sun and a right good guy on top of it."

"Two and a half thousand years old?" Lady Professor said in a gleeful tone worthy of a child. I liked her better after that.

"Indeed, ma'am," Saul said. "And my fond hope is that at some point in the near future, you'll manage to find time to sketch for me the current understanding of biology—an excellent Greek-derived neologism, by the way. The original term was, I believe, 'naturalism.' I was once a naturalist myself, to a modest extent. I like to believe that my slight investigations contributed in some minute part to Darwin's great work."

"You were a naturalist in the early 19th century?" Her rising voice signaled how thrilled she was.

Saul bowed again. "I had that honor."

She clapped her hands and gave a little jump. Her frizzy blonde hair bounced with the jump. "Amateur naturalists in the 19th century were the key to everything!" she said. "Did you go on sea voyages? Discover new species?"

Saul lifted his chin ever so slightly. "I had the privilege of naming one species of moss and another of beetle."

"Oh what a time to have lived!" Her eyes glittered.

She'd have come off super-nerdy if she'd been a guy, but it felt different coming from a woman. I thought of Theresa (the Little Flower, not the orgasmic of Avila). Imagine a lady sparked up with God, except it's science, not God, and her hair is hilarious.

"Oh, what a time to be alive!" she said again.

"It was indeed," Saul said, and they jumped into talk about beetles and moss.

Which was fine, except the woolly hospital blanket that covered my bare butt made me itch, and Lemon hadn't finished discussing my case with Saul: Menniss looked sad and I felt left out.

"Excuse me, Professor Francine," I said. "I wonder, could you help me find some clothes? Is there anything down here I could wear? A little less casual than a blanket and somewhere near my fit?"

While I was talking, I worried that she'd write me off as trashy because of my spiky hair, piercings and tattoos. Then I remembered that they'd shaved my head for surgery, and six weeks of chemo had made sure none of it grew back; plus, dockety-doc had made me remove all my piercings. This meant I probably came off as a typical cancer patient instead of a trash girl, and almost anyone will give the benefit of the doubt to a bald cancer patient, even if they can see a few tattoos on her calves.

Her face turned properly sympathetic, though in a distracted kind of way, and she promised to answer all Saul's questions as soon as she had the chance. Then she tried to sneak in a few answers, something about organic molecules. Dearest Saul didn't let her get going.

"Much as I ache to be instructed by you," he said, "I would take it as the greatest kindness if you would help my dear friend Janice just now."

"Oh, certainly." The professor fumbled about in her brain until she found the right gears, and with a clank and a grind, changed direction and invited me to come with her and look over the clothes in her closet.

Dr. Lemon made me gag down about a dozen pills, which I did like an expert. I took Francine's arm for support without her offering, and her eyes moved amusingly back and forth between my face and the hand clutching her forearm. But when a bald cancer lady grabs your arm, you can't just shake her off.

I steered her toward the door, and she came along without argument. Behind us, I could hear Saul asking Menniss and Lemon the question that bugged him a lot, about whether there's anything good to say about mortality.

As we walked down a corridor, I tried to work out how to talk to a science professor. Over the last several years, I'd acquired a bad case of potty mouth, in case you hadn't noticed, and didn't want to come off that way with her. So I put on the New England version of the Queen's English—by which I meant that, if our conversation were to be transcribed verbatim, I'd have received top marks in grammar—and fished around for common ground. It didn't take more than five steps down the corridor to hit on Jane Austen. Francine loved *Pride and Prejudice*, and, as you already know, I do too. Maybe not in precisely the same way; while she'd fallen in love with Darcy, I'd once written a paper titled "The Trope of Failed

Bourgeois Masculinity in the *Pride and Prejudice* Narrative." But at least we appreciated the same book.

I let her do most of the talking. She believed books should tell the stories of admirable people behaving admirably, didn't I agree? I pandered and said that she had a point there. That's the importance of learning the Western Canon, I pandered further; it teaches us humanistic values and how to apply them in life. Francine couldn't agree more. It's so important to read about people behaving nobly, she said, because real life is filled with ignoble people, Republicans for example, and without the example of characters in books, we might all act like Republicans. She was kind of simple outside of science, but I liked her.

After a while, we used up *Pride and Prejudice*. To keep the conversation going, I brought up that dean of Harvard who'd called women biologically inferior in science and asked whether she'd had to face similar prejudice in her career. Score. She gave me fervent lectures about women in science all the way to her bedroom, where she apologized for its messiness.

"Richard is incorrigible."

How interesting: Menniss and the professor were an item. Well, good for him.

"But we've only been talking about me," she said. "How about you? What do you do?"

"I've had a difficult life for a few years," I said. "I'm not proud of all the things I've done." I came to a full stop at the end of the sentence, the way you do when you want to signal an end to questions.

"What kinds of things?" she asked.

Clearly, she was a tad weak on the matter of boundaries.

"Embarrassing things." I drew up my shoulders—signal, signal, signal. "I don't much like to talk about them."

"Could you give me just a hint?"

She couldn't read signals, could she? Or was it something else? Maybe she had a personal interest. Maybe she had a few secrets of her own and wanted to hear mine so she'd feel less guilty. Fine with me, only not just now.

"I graduated with honors from Bennington College. English

literature," I said. "But that didn't lead to a job. I work in the hospitality industry."

She looked disappointed "Have you thought about returning to school for a graduate degree?"

"Definitely. But what most appeals to my interest doesn't lead to a job either. If I could do whatever I wanted, I'd get a Ph.D. in history."

"You could become a professor of history," she said. "That's a perfectly respectable job."

I tried to bite my tongue, but it came out anyway. "My father was a history professor, and I've always wanted to follow in his footsteps."

"I think history is fascinating," she said. "Where does your father teach?"

"He died when I was 11." And the rest came out, too, though I told it not to. "He had a heart attack and died while I was in his lap."

"Oh my goodness," she said. "Oh, I'm so sorry."

And also interested. She wanted more.

Not now, lady professor. You'll get your voyeuristic suffering another time. "Did you say you had some clothes I could borrow? This blanket is itchy."

"Yes, of course, I'm sorry. Right here. Take anything you want."

She had a huge walk-in closet full of boring clothes for the flat-chested, but at this point I was a walking skeleton. I picked out a frumpy, floral long-sleeved shirt and some jeans and dressed in the bathroom so Francine wouldn't see my zillion tattoos. I put on a boring, white lacy sweater over the shirt because I was cold with my bald head and no fat. As for shoes, with the help of double socks, I fit into her bigfoot shoes just fine.

The closet also had a row of wild, wild hats way up high. I pulled down a bright red one with a feather that Jane Austen might have worn to the races and felt quite the fashionable cancer girl. When I modeled the hat for Francine, she laughed, said I looked nice, and added that she'd never worn any of those hats herself; Baehl must have put them there as one of his jokes. She gave me an impish smile, reached up, snagged a cobalt-blue hat, and modeled it for me.

I told her she looked nice, too. We were getting along.

Maybe having your skull lifted off, your brain chopped up, and your blood filled with drugs slows you down because it took me until then to figure it out. Saul had never explained what he meant. Neither had Baehl. Maybe because they worried about microphones. But they'd hinted around plenty.

If Blair could grow back an ear, I could grow back a normal brain. They meant to cure my cancer with immortality. And they were counting on Professor Francine to do it.

She was my savior, and so I *had* to like her. Damn—just when I was getting to appreciate the lonely and noble lady just for herself.

SHE ASKED WHETHER I wanted to see her laboratory, and I lied and said yes.

Francine's lab stank like cleaning products from a far-off galaxy; I held the steaming latte to my nose. Francine didn't seem to notice the odor. I'm sure because she was used to it. She hauled me through her territory like a house-proud lab rat. I especially liked the fetishy parts: the black rubber hoses, beige surgical tubing and glass rods. I put certain thoughts aside and asked about the six-foot, inflated plastic orca that dangled from the ceiling. She said one of her graduate students had gone on a whale-watching trip and brought the model back as a souvenir. When Baehl copied her whole lab, he'd copied that too.

"Of all this stuff," I asked, pointing to everything, "what's your favorite?"

Her eyes glowed the way a girl's eyes do when her first true boyfriend catches her alone by her locker and says he loves her. "My favorite?" she said. "Come look at this."

She brought me to a door marked "Clean Room." The sign wasn't kidding. This room was *really* clean. Zen Center clean, except with machines instead of people doing the meditating. The air smelled thin and electric, like at the top of the one high mountain I'd climbed, Torres Peak in Colorado.

Francine jumped onto a chair in front of a computer, pulled out a keyboard from under the counter and clicked up a storm, leaving me forlorn and chairless. I found a hard stool that hurt my shrunken butt, dragged it over, and sat on it.

"Look at this," Francine said. She moved aside so I could see her computer screen. "It's 40 percent done."

The screen was a zoo of graphs. I hate graphs, but since these graphs talked about Blair's ear and my cancer cure, I tried to look and listen as she explained everything. She called Blair's ear "the tissue sample" and didn't have a clue that I'd fondled and kissed that tissue sample before it got cut off. She described the whole process from start to finish, and I remember some of what she said, such as the story of blasting Blair's DNA into tiny pieces.

I remember the explanation because it involved books. Begin like this: take a copy of *Pride and Prejudice*, cut out each line of print and tape all the lines together, lengthwise, in order. What you'll get is the whole book in a strip about five miles long. That's Blair's DNA.

Now suppose Kinko's can handle five-mile-long strips, and you make a thousand copies of your longways *Pride and Prejudice*. That's what the sequencer machine takes as its starting point because a piece of ear contains billions of cells, each of which holds the same DNA as all the others. The next part is weird. You take all those five-mile-long strands and randomly cut them up into tiny strips about five or six words in a row long. Sometimes you cut out words from the middle of a single sentence, and sometimes you get the end of one sentence, a period and the beginning of another sentence, etc. It has to be random to work. You have to do it to each of the five-mile-long strands differently.

So now you have about 10 million strips of five or six words each. You mix them all into a big pile, and you call over all your friends for a jigsaw party, and using all those strips, you recreate the original book. According to Francine, it's always possible to do that, provided you start with enough copies of the book (the DNA) and you're random about how you do the cutting. You can reassemble the message because certain words and punctuation overlap. It sounds like a ridiculous amount of extra work, tearing it apart and then putting it together, but apparently, it's easier to read short pieces of DNA than the whole thing at once.

I thought of the movie *Argo*, with 100s of students reassembling strips of shredded paper, but scientists use computers. That's what the sequencer was doing right now, Francine said, sorting through the pile of blasted-apart copies of Blair's DNA and reconstructing what it said originally.

Francine had a clock-like widget on her screen that counted up the percentage completed. While I watched, the number changed from 40% to 41%. When it reached 100%, we'd have the story of immortality written out for everyone to see. Well, almost. Francine would still have to figure out what Blair's DNA had that a normal human's didn't have, and that wasn't so easy because single-nuclear polyamories (or something like that) trick things up.

The air in the Clean Room was way too thin, and I felt mountain sickness coming on as Francine talked and talked. She had a lot to say about retroviruses, which aren't viruses dressed up in '60s clothes but what you use to insert new DNA in people. She babbled about histones, codons and reintroducing mammoths to the world by using elephants as surrogate moms. I quit paying attention to the details and listened to it as a love song.

It wasn't the normal kind of love song. When you sing to a person, you open up wide and human. This was different. I know a guy who rhapsodizes about his collection of vinyl recordings, and a girl who sings the praises of her Smartwool socks. They're nerds. Here's the definition of nerdy: you get love-crazy over things that shrink you instead of grow you.

But that didn't fit Francine. Yes, her love song reached toward little things, but they were powerful little things, genes and retroviruses and nuclear tides, things that can give you blonde or black hair, turn you female or male, make you smart or stupid. Grant eternal life. So maybe it's like loving Mount Everest, the Grand Canyon or the stars. Way better than socks. Her little things make you grand. But still, when you pour your love into something that isn't human, you turn less human yourself. Was that what she wanted? To get away from being human?

If so, I could relate.

Francine was still in mid-love-song when I stuck a finger in. "What do you love most?"

She broke off, all bright-eyed, and said, "That's an interesting question. No one's ever asked me that."

"I'm just curious. When you're an English major, the sciences seem like another world. I've never known anyone high up in the sciences like you. What's the heart of it for you?"

Did I care? Or was I just trying to get on the good side of my savior?

"The heart of it?" She turned this way and that in her chair, with her knees together and her hands on them.

"Where does it make you most alive?" I asked. "What part gets you singing to yourself? Makes you bounce and shine?"

"Do I bounce and shine?"

"You do."

She turned the idea around in her head and smiled at it. "I suppose what I love is discovering things. I love discovering what's true."

"And as you discover things, you can help people," I said. "You can cure diseases. You must like having the power to help people."

I'd guessed wrong.

Shame crossed her face, like someone in a sexual abuse group honestly addressing a part of themselves that they don't want to look at. "I'm embarrassed to admit that I don't normally think about curing diseases. I guess I hope my work might help someone. But that's not what I do it for. All I think about is discovering the truth."

Honesty breeds honesty. "Francine," I said. "Do you know why I'm here? I'm here because I have brain cancer. Unless you discover how the immortality genes work and use your retroviruses to insert the genes into me, I will die. It all depends on you. I just wanted to tell you that."

Francine turned pale and scared and looked about to cry. She became so woebegone and sad that I felt awful and wanted to push the rewind button and make what I'd said go away. With no rewind button in sight, I blurted out a bunch more true things. "If it doesn't work, though, I'm fine with it. I don't care a lot about staying alive. After my father died … well, bad things happened to me, and later on, I compounded the matter by doing a lot of things I shouldn't have done. So really, it's no great loss to anyone, or even to me, if I kick off."

Now *that* was a strange way to try and cheer someone up.

"Me too," she said.

"You too, what?" The air in that Clean Room was so thin I could hardly breathe.

She licked her index finger and rubbed a stain on her pants. "Bad things happened to me when I was young, too."

So there I was, sitting with a science lady who could save my life and make people immortal and win the Nobel Prize, and we'd both been abused as children. At least, I thought that was what she meant.

"I got over it, though," she said.

"Oh really?" I said. "How?"

"I don't think about it. I work instead. If I start to feel it, I work harder."

I've been in sexual abuse groups all my life practically, and I can see denial even when someone doesn't hit me over the head with it. You're supposed to call people on it, not let it go. Only, if it was denial that kept her driven, maybe I better not screw with her dynamic until *after* she saved my life. Was that selfish? Yes.

And the air in that damn Clean Room was way too thin.

THE CLOCK WIDGET on Francine's computer steadily counted up toward 100. We held celebrations at every five percent. When the widget announced that the computer had figured out 45 percent of Blair's full DNA sequence, Lemon let me eat my first slice of pizza (homemade by Francine herself, who turned out to be quite a cook.) At 50 percent, Menniss made me a fiery Laotian dish that tasted damn good.

I left Lemon in the dust. Yes, we were both terminally ill, but he was old, and I was young, and I worked out every day in one of the subterranean gyms. It was a private one just for us lab people. The hafeems and a few mortals who were trickling into the larger underground had their own. Menniss gave me some pointers too, and after a month, I had to slow down so I wouldn't build too much definition.

At 75 percent, we had a big celebration. I drank too much wine and thought I should visit Blair right away. I imagined showing up in that pompous Illuminati rat hole, spicing up Blair's life with some handcuffs and rope, stroking that perfect body, touching that innocent, open heart, and kissing those wide, fluttery eyes. I didn't even bring up the idea because Saul would have said no. Anyway, I hadn't turned immortal yet, and I meant to meet Blair on level ground the next time I saw him.

Not going was a good thing for other reasons: cancer is weird. You can feel great, and at the same time, it's getting ready to kill you. I found that out the day after the clock reached 85 percent. First, I got a sick, aching headache that made me shove my thumb in my right eye so hard Lemon told me to quit or I'd detach a retina. Then I couldn't walk straight. I kept veering to the right and banging into the wall, and Saul got a wheelchair and wheeled me.

The tumor had come back. I asked Lemon why, and he said that's what cancer does. I wanted to know why I had brain cancer in the first place, but he said there's no reason; it just happens by bad luck.

It seemed to me that *some*thing must have caused it and that doctors should treat the causes of illnesses, not just the symptoms. (I was thinking of that Harry Boullard doctor in Santa Cruz and what he wrote in his brochure about how alternative medicine is better than conventional medicine.) But Lemon said the cause of illness is mortality, which I'd thought of too. Luckily, a certain friend of ours was trying to solve that.

Lemon pumped me full of prednisone, and I felt better.

But when the clock widget reached five percent, my brain decided to freak out again, even worse. I turned into a two-limbed person. By that I mean that the right side of my body felt stapled on, not part of me at all, and I wanted it taken off. In my head, I could remember I'd always owned a right arm and leg, but that was some other person. An Oliver Sacks thing.

Lemon explained that the brain is a computer that stores a map of the body, and my brain tumor had broken the map. I hated the idea that my brain was a computer because when you're about to die you want a soul, and computers don't have them.

Lemon upped my prednisone, and I turned back into a biped.

By then, I had my own bedroom, decorated exactly how I liked (courtesy of Baehl) with arty prints, matching houseplants, a big, ugly, soft sofa piled with books, and a bunch of the ugly, retro clothes I loved. I was lying on my bed, in a puke-green polyester shirt and blood-red cotton pants, reading Foucault's *History of Sexuality*, when Saul came in and told me that in about an hour, the computer would finish. Everyone was gathering around to watch, and did I want to join them?

I said probably not because I knew this wasn't the *real* moment of truth. Francine had told me many times that while the computer could write out Blair's DNA, it couldn't automatically figure out how Blair's DNA was different from a mortal's DNA because all the single-nuclear polyamories threw sand in its gears. ("Single-nucleotide polymorphisms," properly, but I like my version better.) Everyone's DNA is different, except for twins, and the challenge is identifying a *major*, world-shaking difference. That job took a person helping, namely Francine, and she didn't expect it to be super easy.

I understood that well enough, but I still felt the magnetic pull and ached to jump up and run to the Clean Room. However, I have a rule against being jerked around (except by guys who aren't good for me), so I fought the magnet. I put my arms behind my head and bent one leg so that my pants pulled up a little, and I invited Saul to sit on my bed and talk. I knew I looked hot, pretty much hotter than I'd ever looked because of all my working out. I also knew Saul didn't care, and I loved him for it. I loved him for it so much that I wanted to put my head in his lap and cry.

Do you think I *like* sexualizing every relationship? It's one of the things that happens when you've been abused, and I hate it. I treasured Saul for lots of things, but one of the big ones was that I could love him and not have to want to have sex with him. But putting your head in a male-type lap is iffy under the best of circumstances, so I didn't.

"So why haven't you gone to see Blair?" I asked. "What's kept you down here with me?"

"I'm looking after you."

"I appreciate that, but Lemon's here to look after me. Besides, you've been waiting to see Blair for a century."

"As I've said, I've become quite fond of you."

He looked like a dad now, but once he got the immortality genes, he'd turn young and probably gorgeous. And then ... I begged myself not to go there. "But aren't you worried about him? Those people are creepy."

"The Illuminati? Yes, they're somewhat disagreeable. However, for all that I might criticize their methods and manner, I don't doubt their competence, and they have a principled dedication to the well-being of True Immortals. Since I don't fear for Blair's safety, I don't feel a sense of urgency. Perhaps more to the point, they're not entirely taken with me, and I wouldn't be able to simply knock on the door and expect admittance."

I could tell that wasn't the whole story, and I might have been able to figure out the part beneath the surface, but the count-up clock ruined my focus. So I drew up my knees, pulled the covers over them as a little girl might, and asked, "How long have you known the Eldest?"

"It's a lengthy story," Saul said.

"Could you tell me some of it?"

"With pleasure, my dear. Let me reflect on where to begin."

That gave me a shiver because my history professor dad used to say almost the same thing when I asked about the past.

"When I was just over a century old, I migrated to Athens because, to use a current idiom, 'it was the place to be.' I made the acquaintance of Socrates and I joined his circle of students. He took a particular liking to me, and one afternoon he offered to introduce me to a friend of his named Diotima. She receives a favorable, if brief, mention in Plato's *Symposium*."

Saul sounded so professorial and familiar I could hardly stand it. I turned my head away in case any tears leaked out. "Isn't she the one Socrates goes to because he wants to learn about love?"

"Impressive," Saul said.

"I remember because it was so sexist," I added. "Socrates would never think to ask a woman about anything else."

Saul sighed. "He was a man of his time. But I can add a fact that Plato's rendition does not disclose because Socrates never told him: Diotima was, in fact, the Eldest."

"*Really?*"

"They were friends. Socrates, of course, revered the Eldest, and for her knowledge of many things beyond love. Indeed, he regarded her as a goddess."

"Literally?"

"Yes. Yet also his friend, for Socrates feared nothing, human or divine. Surprisingly, she admired him as well. Socrates, you see, possessed a power she did not: absolute equanimity regarding death. For this virtue, she was in awe of Socrates. Theirs was a remarkable friendship, between Immortal and mortal, or, as he thought of it, goddess and mortal, and yet also of true equality."

"Did Socrates introduce you to her because he figured out you're a hafeem?"

"He introduced us but not because he recognized my longevity, which I'd long since learned to hide. It was his daemon, his intuition. One afternoon, his daemon prodded him to take me at once to meet Diotima. I agreed. As we walked together to the temple where she lived, he told me what he knew about her. Socrates said she was '*deinos*,' a word in ancient Greek that lacks an English equivalent but can be roughly translated as both wonderful and terrible combined. Like an earthquake, perhaps; it is the root of the modern word 'dinosaur.' If it hadn't been for Socrates' skill at dealing with human frailty, I would have turned and run away."

"What did he say to calm you down?"

"Words to the following effect: 'Diotima, one might say, worships a deity even greater than herself: she is a devotee of chance. She bases all her most important decisions on the unpredictable and cherishes above all others those individuals who are to her by chance presented. And therefore, she will be most pleased to meet you.'"

"Well, that was reassuring, wasn't it?" I said.

"If he'd said no more, yes. But honest Socrates felt the need to complete his thought. 'Not only does she worship chance, but Diotima also practices its imitation. She is deliberately, masterfully and *dangerously* unpredictable. If the mood strikes her, she may feed us to her leopards. But it would do us honor as philosophers to die in such a manner, would it not?'"

"Oh, nice."

"I quailed. I quaked—literally. My legs shook and my knees knocked. But I'd fallen in love with the notion of being a philosopher, and so I followed Socrates up the hill to her temple.

"Diotima promptly engaged Socrates in pleasant conversation. She didn't speak to me for some while, and by the time she did, my robes were heavy with sweat. When at last she addressed me, what she said was, 'And what have you to confess?' I instantly admitted my overlong lifespan and threw myself on her mercy.

"Socrates stared at me with a certain disbelief. The Eldest, however, by means of pertinent questions, determined that my story was true. It pleased her greatly that Socrates had brought me to her without knowing my lifespan, which made the meeting a true accident. She talked to me for a long time, and Socrates, left out, turned somewhat dour."

"Well, poo on him," I said.

I could have stayed and listened to Saul's stories forever. But the lab's magnetic pull finally got to me, and I said we should go.

We gathered in a Last Supper tableau on stools around Francine's computer. Lemon sat beside her and pretty much dripped saliva on the screen. Menniss salivated too, but in a distracted way, and he sat one row back. Baehl took off his shoes, asked me for mine and juggled all four to pass the time. Saul, though, just looked like Saul.

And Francine? She was hunched over her computer and said she wished we'd go away. "I don't have any answers *yet*," she said. "You have to give me *time*. How can I work with all of you breathing down my neck? Go play Scrabble."

When no one moved, she pushed keys and made columns of letters move around. "It's not like comparing two Word documents to see what one has, and the other doesn't," she said. "Normal people have all kinds of DNA differences between them." She said a whole lot more, not only about single-nucleotide polymorphisms but other problems too, and only Lemon knew what she was talking about.

Menniss put his head close to Baehl and asked, "You're positive no one has her computer tapped?" He sounded a little cheered up compared to his normal gloomy self. "Because if someone's watching, they won't need us anymore the moment she figures out the secret, and they'll shut us down."

"We have nothing to fear," Baehl said. "We have protection."

"What protection?"

"Hush. You're disturbing Dr. Selis."

Francine was talking to Saul. "Are you *sure* it's not inheritable? That's a vital point. You're positive?"

"As I have previously mentioned," Saul said, "not one of my children digressed from the normal manner of aging."

"But they'd have to have lived till at least 30 or 40 for you to be sure," Lemon said. The sinews on his neck stuck out like cables tied tightly so his head wouldn't fall off. "People used to die quite young. Maybe they didn't live long enough for you to tell whether they'd aged?"

"As you say, people did quite frequently die at a young age, but they also showed their age more quickly. I can state with confidence that none of my offspring failed to age normally."

"What about miscarriages in your daughters?" Lemon asked. "Any departure from the norm there?"

"That would have been the province of women," Saul said.

"Late miscarriages. You were a doctor. Surely you'd notice."

Saul thought about it. "More than average, I would say. Certainly more, on consideration."

"More by how much?" Lemon asked.

"I didn't keep statistics."

"Ten percent more? Ten times more?"

"Perhaps two or three times the average."

The cables on Lemon's neck shifted, and his face turned back to Francine. "And that fits one and not the other," Lemon said.

"I see your point," Francine said.

Another hurricane of clicks, moving letters on the screen, a bunch of jargony jabber.

She clicked and jargobabbled forever. I left to go pee, ate lunch and came back hours later. Some considerate person must have pushed pause for me because the movie started up right where it had left off: the same jabberbabble, jargojababing, jububerjab. A lifetime of things like that.

We left. We came back. We slept. Not all at once. We brought Francine food that she hardly ate. This went on for days. It went on for weeks. You couldn't put a countdown clock to it because we were waiting on a person, not a machine. Lemon and I were getting nervous because if she didn't figure out how it worked soon, one of us would drop dead and then the other.

Maybe it wasn't even possible to figure out. Francine looked like her neck hurt, and I sat behind her, gave her a massage and told her not to worry.

"Oh my, that feels good," she said, but it didn't make her find the answer.

My brain kept shorting out, and Lemon kept increasing my prednisone. I hate prednisone. It gives you a pot belly and turns your face as round as a dinner plate.

One day, about three weeks after the sequencer finished, the right-hand side of the world disappeared. It was a lot like what happened before, except now I was a whole person in half a world instead of half a person in a whole world. I could see things to my right if I looked straight at them, but if I didn't look at them directly, they stopped existing. I tried to push Blair into the nonexistent right side of my imagination to make him go away, but he popped over into the left side, and I wanted him more than ever. I knew he'd never love a broken-brain girl like me, with prednisone fat everywhere. I had to give up on him, and I hated that.

Lemon stopped the prednisone and gave me new drugs that he said would kill me soon if I didn't turn immortal, but otherwise, they wouldn't have any side effects. The world turned whole again.

IN THE OLDEN days, when people did big things, you could see their bigness. Not anymore. Francine was a scientist, not an empress. She wasn't Queen Elizabeth or Catherine the Great. Or Alexander the Great, for that matter. When those guys remade history, the soundtrack spoke with trumpets, cellos and great soaring choirs. Now-adays, it's nerds like Steve Jobs and Francine who shake the world to pieces; at most, there's some ambient music in the background.

No storming of the Bastille. No 21-gun salutes. No people marching in the street. Just Francine excited.

"Hold on." She's talking to her computer. "Is that … yes, it is. Zoom in. Hurry up. What's taking you? Yes, yes, yes. Right there. Don't move. Don't go away. Oh, now we're getting somewhere. Oh yes. Oh, oh yes."

She sounded a lot like I sound when I get on the orgasm on-ramp, only I don't usually tell my vibrator things like "a set of three tri-nucleotide repeats with a histone structure effectively juxtaposing a start codon, aha."

Rumors spread fast when you have an immortality orgasm, and our Last Supper tableau filled out again in about half a minute. Not Last Supper—First Supper. Because this was eternal life, and we meant to sup on it the first chance we got.

"This segment, here. This is it." She had Lemon to talk to now, and not just her computer. "Do you see the pattern? Look here and here. Six, no, seven genetic loci."

He looked and nodded.

Where was the rainbow, the choir of angels, the comet? At least a drum roll. And *Encyclopedia Britannica* scribes, quills in hand, to write down history. It didn't seem right that immortality could slouch in so quietly.

"Congratulations, Dr. Selis." Dr. Lemon's head swiveled around on his poor, shriveled neck. Facing us, he pointed back at the screen with the bone he had for an index finger and said, "That's immortal-ity, right there. All we have to do is load those genes into a retrovirus and inject the virus into someone, and that person will become immortal. There's nothing to it. We already have the retrovirus made. We could do it tonight if we wanted."

"No, we couldn't," Francine protested. "First, it's not quite that easy. It might not work. The added genes might not be transcribed. Second, it's crazy. We can't just infect people with a gene-altering retrovirus based on conjecture. There could be any number of problems. Potentially lethal problems. We'd have to start with cell cultures, then try something analogous in animals … it will be *years* before it's ready for humans to try, if it's ever ready. As you perfectly well know."

"For two of us in this room," Lemon said solemnly, "years aren't an option. I, for one, am ready to take the chance. Janice, too. And about 50 hafeems and a few other mortals out there in the larger underground outside the walls are watching and waiting, too. I believe any or all of us would happily take the chance."

"Chance? Chance is a *wonderful* thing."

This was a new voice. A terrifying one.

SHE STOOD AT the door to the outer lab. So tiny and so terrifying. Silver-and-jade earrings, jade necklace, floral silk blouse, black silk pants, flat Tai chi shoes. And a miniature nuclear bomb attached to the silk belt around her waist.

No, she didn't have a bomb attached to the silk belt. But I saw one there. That was cancer manga, my brain tumor cartooning feelings as things.

But you couldn't help feeling the danger. She was in a mood.

She walked toward us in tiny steps, her presence so awesome that even the arrogant sequencer machines on their long empty benches got over their egos and turned into cheap stainless steel boxes. Lemon gave out a sighing groan. Menniss raised his hands like someone had a gun pointed at him. Baehl perspired buckets, sweat soaking his mustache and goatee, making a growing puddle at his feet.

Brain cancer manga again but that's how scared he looked.

Not Saul. I once saw a documentary where a guy standing on a beach looked up at a tidal wave coming straight for him, a tsunami rising to the sky, and he's calm because (the voiceover says) what else can you do when the whole ocean is coming to crash on your head but appreciate the chance to watch from close up? That was Saul looking at the Eldest. He looked more than calm. He looked *grateful*.

That's not how I felt. I felt something like thirst, hunger and lust mixed into one big desire to live. I wanted to live with no question marks, hedges or if-onlys. I'd never felt anything like that before. Apparently, I'm part normal. Who would've guessed?

And then there was Francine. She didn't even turn around in her chair, just looked over her shoulder in annoyance and asked, "And who are *you*?" That's not ordinarily how you respond when a goddess with a nuclear bomb strapped around her waist addresses you, but she was Francine and couldn't see the bomb.

Menniss and Lemon went white. Baehl pissed himself. (Well, not really, but almost.) Even Saul gulped. We were in deep, deep shit. But the Eldest didn't pull out a samurai sword and whip off Francine's head. Very politely, she said, "I am called Yavànna."

"I'm Francine." Francine sounded polite, but she kept her eyes glued to her screen.

I leaned forward and whispered the part Francine was missing. "You're talking to the oldest person on earth."

"I am?" Francine asked. "How old?"

"She was born before language was invented."

Francine finally turned away from her computer and upped and asked the Eldest exactly how old she was.

Saul hissed at her to be more respectful.

"But if she remembers the invention of language, that's one or two 100,000 years. I'm skeptical that even a True Immortal could live that long."

Francine was calling Yavànna a liar. What a cheeky lady.

"I remember the sky," Yavànna said, "and I remember where the man with three stars in his belt stood when I was young. He does not stand there now."

They had a quick conversation about constellations and where and when they appear in the sky.

Francine typed on her computer, then said, "No, I'm doing it wrong. It would have been in Africa." She typed some more, lit up with her eye-dazzled glow, innocent of what the rest of us knew— that the Eldest might kill us in five seconds.

But Yavànna looked entertained.

Francine cried, "Around 200,000 years!" Now she swiveled in her seat, a picture of joy. "I am so honored to meet you! And I have so many questions I don't know where to start. Were there other kinds of hominids? Things like people but not people?" Maybe figuring out immortality makes you a little full of yourself because I don't get how Francine managed to be so brave.

"Yes, there were others," Yavànna said. "They had fur, and they hunted us. Until we learned to talk. Then we hunted them, and they all died."

Francine's hands opened and closed several times quickly. "Oh, oh, oh. And you were there at the invention of speech. How did it happen? And when? How fast? What happened after? How did things change?"

But Yavànna didn't answer. She didn't refuse to answer; she just didn't. She stood calm, ordinary and silent. She closed her eyes and stayed that way for a long time. No one dared speak, not even Francine.

So we *wouldn't* just slouch our way toward Bethlehem to be reborn. Someone who'd been around for speech getting invented and the bow-and-arrow, too, and farms and cities and kings and war and Illuminati, was here to bear witness to when people invented immortal life.

Unless she put a stop to it.

YAVÀNNA OPENED HER eyes and stared at Francine. "I have questions to ask now. I shall ask and you shall answer."

Francine nodded and looked as scared as she should have been all along.

"I wish to know more of this creature that you possess."

"Creature?" Francine asked.

"This creature that can write on a scripture too small for the eyes to see, and, by writing, make men immortal."

Francine swallowed several times.

Lemon said, "She means retroviruses. I could explain."

Yavànna said, "But you shall not."

Francine swallowed again. "A retrovirus is a kind of virus that can rewrite DNA. It's called 'retro' because normally DNA is only read, not rewritten."

"I have had myself taught about this DNA," the Eldest said. "I have learned of these words inscribed on a scripture deep within the bodies of all beings. Words inscribed by some god or goddess who knew of writing four *billion* years before humans learned of it. Or do I have the years wrong?"

"You have the years right," Francine said. "DNA-based life began about four billion years ago."

"Yes. And this creature you possess shall on your instructions reinscribe this scripture? Is that not sacrilege? Can I permit it? Can I sanction offense to a god or goddess whom I do not know, and one so powerful?"

"But DNA wasn't written by a god," Francine said. "It's just information assembled mechanically by natural selection. And, anyway, there are natural viruses that write on DNA. The HIV virus, for example."

"Do you believe it pleads your case to give a plague as precedent? Or, worse, to demean the gods as mere machines? They who are jealous of immortal life, holding it for themselves alone except for that rare man and woman with whom they wish to share it? You would take from them this privilege? You would usurp the gods' power and, with your own hands, wield it?"

Yavànna, she was pissed. She was right on the edge. In two seconds or so, she might end this, and us.

"I don't want to die, Eldest." That was me talking. I didn't mean to say anything; it just came out.

Yavànna looked at me now but didn't burn me up with her eyes. She didn't even look angry.

"I, too, want you to live. And so I grow calm. I remember that I have asked a question of one who is here." She turned to Saul. "Have you sought an answer to what I asked you?"

"I have sought, Eldest. For half a century, I have studied, queried and thought."

"I am sorry I gave you so brief a time to answer so great a question, and yet now you see why I felt the need to hurry. For we are at the juncture. What is your wisdom? Have you an answer?"

"I have *an* answer," Saul said.

"You shall speak it, and I shall choose what I do."

"Perhaps you need not choose, Eldest. Perhaps that is not your burden to bear."

"And who does bear it if not I?"

"It falls to the world of mortals," Saul said. "Mortals shall make the choice, and they shall make it in only one way. They are doing so already, and not only here. Mortals are learning to regrow organs, Eldest, and to construct machines in lieu of organs. They are reading this DNA and will, in time, understand all its words. Whether today or in 10 centuries, all at once or in fits and starts, mortals will bring an end to death. Whether curse or blessing, immortality *shall* appear as fact. Mortals have the desire and shall soon have the power; they will learn to live forever and, regardless of any philosophy, they will choose to do so."

"This cannot be stopped?"

"No, Eldest. We mortal beings cannot help ourselves. Immortality calls to us. It drives us to have offspring; inspires us to achieve great deeds, discoveries and inventions; causes some to go mad with hunger; draws others into the love of that which lasts forever, whether God or gods or True Immortals. We are finite beings who yearn for infinity. The mortality that is and the immortality to be are neither curse nor blessing but mere fact."

She said nothing. We waited, afraid to breathe.

At last, she spoke. "There was a man who lived in high mountains and was wise; he was older even than me, although he is now no more. Writing then was not yet made, nor metal, but we could speak. This man called to me and said, 'A day shall come when all those who have lived to reach that day shall live forever.' And so I have been expecting. But not so soon. You say, Saul, it is soon?"

"It is soon."

"If it cannot be stopped tomorrow," she said, "then, by allowing it today, I do no dishonor to the god or goddess who writes in letters to small to be seen. But I shall not aid. From this time forward, I shall neither aid nor oppose."

And we breathed again.

YAVÀNNA TOUCHED ME. She put her finger next to my right eye and drew it down my cheek to my lips. "You wish to live?"

"I do."

She turned to Francine. "I ask you to save this one, for I am fond of her. I do not command. I ask. But I would honor you."

"I want to," Francine said. She twisted her hands against each other nervously. "But what if it hurts her?"

"You cannot hurt the dead," Yavànna says. "If you try, yet she does not live, I still shall honor you."

"I'll try. I promise."

Yavànna smiled. Then something startled her, and her eyes opened wide. "You have a secret."

Francine looked like she was about to say something.

"Do not tell me," the Eldest said. "I have released control." She turned to Baehl. She kissed him, lip to lip. "Lovely man. If you survive, you shall visit me."

Baehl was visibly ecstatic. "I will."

To Saul, she said, "Gather your things and come with me."

"I have no things," Saul said.

Menniss rose. He stood with his head bowed. "Please, Eldest, please give me your blessing, too."

"I have no power of blessing," she said. Still, she seemed pleased to have been asked. "You have built around yourself a trap and built no door to leave it. But it has a door you did not build. Can you find it? Now come to me. Come."

Menniss made his sluggish way around Baehl to Yavànna. She had him kneel—he was too tall otherwise—and kissed his forehead.

Then she turned to go. Saul followed her, and they left.

AFTER A PRIEST gives his benediction, there's silence. Also, after a bomb goes off.

Baehl had his eyes closed, and he was smiling. Menniss had his eyes closed, too, but he wasn't smiling. Francine wrung her hands. Lemon leaned his head on the bench, his face even more ashen than usual.

Francine broke out first. She turned back to her computer and went clickety-click. Lemon leaned over and said something technical to her in a low voice.

Baehl got up and walked with a wobbly gait across the Clean Room. He lifted a wall panel and went through it.

A long time later, maybe a minute, Mr. Depressed emerged from his trance. Eyes open, Menniss roared, "Baehl!" He wasn't depressed anymore. He was his old self again—pissed off, on a rampage and happy about it. "Where's that goddamn Baehl gone off to?"

CHAPTER 8

THE SAVIOR

"And an angel of the Lord came down from
Heaven and rolled away the stone."
MATTHEW 28:2

The pot begins to boil.
THE CHRONICLER

MENNISS

MENNISS OPENED HIMSELF to receive the power of her touch. He felt the Eldest's lips on his forehead. He waited for a revelation or at least clarity.

Nothing happened.

He was still half-dead, the way he'd been for months down here in this stifling underground with nothing to do but wait: a spy with no mission, third wheel to Francine and Lemon, a victim of a darkening mood that grew darker with each step toward the goal.

The Eldest left. The room gradually returned to life, but Menniss sat unmoving, trapped in torpor. And then the realization hit him. He jumped up and shouted for Baehl.

"Do you have to shout?" Francine asked.

"He went through the wall over there," Janice said.

Menniss ran to the panel she'd pointed at, pushed it open, and stepped into the orange hexagon outside.

A solitary man stood watching a large display screen. The display showed a split-screen image of the Clean Room, one view from each of the two cameras. The man was Cowper, a hafeem that Menniss had kidnapped several years earlier and delivered to the I-H. They'd become more pleasantly acquainted in the last several months, exploring Baehl's underground world together.

"It's getting close, isn't it?" Cowper said.

"You know as much as I do," Menniss said. "Francine's going to give the genes to Janice. If it doesn't kill her, then yes, we're close. Did Baehl walk through here?"

Cowper nodded. "He said he was going to his office. You'll let me know how it's coming along?"

"I don't know anything you don't."

"There aren't any cameras in your bedroom."

That was true; the ubiquitous cameras only showed public places. "If I learn anything from Francine directly, I'll tell you."

He excused himself and made his way to the pink hexagon. When he shoved open the door marked "Master Control Room," he found Baehl sitting in a velvet chair, smoking a cigarette in an idiotically elegant cigarette holder. Menniss yanked the holder from Baehl's hand and stubbed out the burning cigarette on the royal-red carpet. Dragging the unprotesting Baehl to his feet, he shoved him backward and kept shoving until Baehl was pinned against the wall. He grabbed Baehl by his goatee, intending to give it a painful twist, but the goatee was fake and came off. "Is anything about you real?" Menniss shouted.

"You could try my shoulders," Baehl said.

Menniss grabbed Baehl's shoulders and shook him ferociously. "What the hell did she mean?"

"That depends on which of her words you wish to divine. Her 'the,' her 'an,' or her 'of'?"

He slapped Baehl hard across the face. "Don't fuck with me. When she said, 'If you survive, come visit me.'"

"Oh, that." Baehl kept his smile turned on, but a hint of fear flickered around its edges.

"You said we had protection. That was the Eldest you meant, right? But now she's taken it away, and we're on our own."

"A cogent analysis."

"What's she been protecting you from?"

"'Whom' not 'what.' From a man and his plan. Though he has no canal." Baehl's hands began an amusing flourish that dissolved into nervous nothingness. "Alexandros. A difficult name to put in a palindrome. A difficult person, too. He's wanted to stop me all along. Up until now, she hasn't let him." He picked at his teeth with the nail of his little finger; the nail was longer than the rest and painted black. "I didn't think she'd let me get this far along and *then* stop protecting me."

"Please tell me this place has defenses," Menniss said.

"Defenses? Oh, sure. Whaddaya take me for? Let's see." Baehl tapped the long black nail against his upper lip, counting off. "There's nearsighted Joe on watch in the Crow's Nest. We've got a troupe of shock troops, butt naked, their underwear between their ankles. We have bright new pennies in all the fuse boxes and a brigade's worth of smoke alarms unplugged. In summary, we're screwed. Not that we ever stood a chance against Alexandros if he came after us."

Menniss gave Baehl one more vicious shake and stepped back. "You're unbelievable."

"Surely you can manage."

"Manage what?"

"To believe me."

Menniss swept a ridiculous vase off a ridiculous stand and took some relief in the resonant sound it made as it shattered. "Tell me about Alexandros. You can sit if you want."

Baehl reached above his head and patted the wall blindly until a compartment sprang open. He stuck his hand in and came out with a bottle of flavored water. "Would you like one?" When Menniss only glared, Baehl shrugged and sidled his way to the green silk couch. "Well, cheers, anyway." He found a straw somewhere in his clothes. "Alexandros is an old guy," he said, sipping from the bottle. "Two miles old. Ten thousand five hundred sixty years, approximately. A long second place after the Eldest, but still distinctly old."

He stretched out luxuriously on the couch. "The bar's over there if you'd like a real drink. As you've possibly heard by now, Alexandros runs a group of Immortals called the Illuminati. They're the Illuminati everyone who talks about the Illuminati would be talking about if they knew what they were talking about. Alexandros is the oldest, and Soraya, the number two, is just a couple of centuries younger. She runs a crew affectionately known as the blue&blacks. Jeremiah and Margaret, the third and fourth, are only five thousandish, just kids. They're not so bad. There are eight more, even younger, making a total of 12. Well, 13 if the Eldest would ever show up as Alexandros so fervently desires, but she's not interested. The Illuminati are Very Noble People. You know … civic minded, uncommonly brave, wise, farseeing, their word is their bond. And they can do great things on a horse. You'll like my scotch."

"Go on," Menniss said.

"Constrained by noblesse oblige, Alexandros and his Illuminati seek to graciously serve the common man. They're motivated only by compassion, so they feel awful when they have to kill people. If they had to kill everyone down here, they'd have bad dreams for a week."

"Kill everyone down here? What are you talking about?"

Baehl picked at his teeth again. "Just a guess. There aren't more than maybe 30 True Immortals in the world right now. At least so far as anyone *I* know knows about. I've got 800 or so hafeems on my mailing list, not to mention all the mortals like you that I've become good buddies with. Last time I checked, we had 445 people here in the Underground, and a few more arrive daily. If Francine turns us all immortal, Alexandros, Soraya and their bunch won't feel so special anymore. But they'd have higher reasons for killing us than to stay special. We'd learn about those reasons, too, because they like to get you to buy into their righteousness before they slaughter you."

Menniss said he'd take Baehl up on that scotch. Baehl pointed to a spot on the wall. When Menniss touched it, a door sprang open, revealing a liquor cabinet filled with bottles arranged in a horizontal pyramid. An expensive-looking single-malt scotch centered at the head of the pyramid wore a pink sticky note that read "For You." Menniss checked the label. It was the same rare vintage he'd ordered at The Catalyst when he'd made his move on Francine.

He poured himself a double. "So this place doesn't have any defenses?"

"It's a fallout shelter, not a fortress."

"A fallout shelter?"

"The Eldest's idea. When atomic bombs first came out, they made her nervous. She told Alexandros to take care of the True Immortals and gave me the job of building a shelter big enough to hold every hafeem in the world. She didn't say anything about defenses, only that I had to build it under a redwood forest in Santa Cruz and make it earthquake-proof. (My guess, by the way, is that the Illuminati underground is just a forest or two over.) Furthermore, and here I quote, she said, 'Do not make a cinderblock monstrosity, my Baehl. Build a home as amusing as you are. And if it makes me laugh, I may visit your bed.' You may have noticed amusing touches here and there, pink hexagons and whatnot."

Menniss choked on his scotch. "The Eldest came onto you, and you responded?"

"Of course. What else could I do?"

"You could turn and run."

"That would be rude."

"But she's a couple hundred thousand years old."

"She's a True Immortal, sir," Baehl said, offended. "She's 100,000 years hot."

"I didn't mean she's not beautiful. I meant she's terrifying."

"Yup."

"And the ridiculous features of this place are meant as a kind of erotic gesture to her?"

"Yup."

I change my mind, Menniss thought. He's no coward. In his way, this is the bravest man I've ever met.

He pulled up a chair and sat near Baehl. "Even a fallout shelter would need some defenses."

"We have a few crates of AK-47s to ward off the poorly bathed hordes. And with all our fancy cameras and video screens, linked by wireless these days, we could organize our resources properly to get them bathed."

"What are the cameras for?"

"So one group can find another in case of cave-ins, or whatever. And to build community. This is one of the best-designed fallout shelters in the world, even if I do say so myself. And for sure, it's the funniest. But it makes an awful fortress. An awful golf course, too."

He's not really what you would call an adult, Menniss thought. Maybe it takes longer for hafeems. "So you have AK-47s and your video camera system. Those are useful. What else?"

"Not much," Baehl said. "I had a guy named Lackman who worked on that kind of thing for me, but the Eldest got mad at him

10 years ago, and I haven't seen him since. We do have a few long-ish escape tunnels."

"I've found those. What else?"

Peevishly, Baehl said, "Well, Alexandros doesn't know where we *are*."

THE OTHER NIGHT, he'd dreamed of chasing Blair. He took incredible risks, racing his black Mercedes through traffic, tearing through police roadblocks and driving at heart-pounding speeds over roads encrusted with ice.

His Mercedes had a kind of harpoon built into it that could spear Blair's safe, fat Volvo. But he had to get close enough, and a convoy of National Guard trucks blocked his way. When he tried to bully through the convoy, soldiers rose from behind billowing camouflage nets pointing rifles, shoulder-fired missiles and laser target-spotters. Tanks on flatbed trucks swiveled their turrets, and fighter planes with 500-pound bombs banked and turned toward him.

Menniss took the hint and dropped back. The jets roared away. The tank turrets unswiveled, and the soldiers stood down. But Blair was already pulling far ahead of the slow-moving convoy. He had to catch Blair; everything depended on it.

The freeway grew a wide shoulder, and he swerved the Mercedes onto it. A light touch on the pedal, and he was doing 80. A hundred. A hundred and ten.

The shoulder ran along the edge of a cliff. Far below, concrete pilings and jagged granite reached up between waves of the Santa Cruz ocean, hoping to impale him. A few inches over, and he'd fall.

A hundred and twenty miles per hour. A hundred and thirty.

The Mercedes fishtails. A rear tire slips over the edge. The car tilts. He's seconds from tumbling over and feels incredibly alive. He jerks the steering wheel at precisely the right moment, turning *toward* the sea. The front end of the Mercedes bangs against a boulder, and the recoiling momentum pushes him back onto the road. All four wheels catch, and he pulls ahead of the convoy. A hundred and fifty miles per hour. Catching up with his prey.

A bundle of wood falls onto the road, its stacked sheaves tall enough to flip him over. He swerves, and half of the car leaves the ground, then rights itself. Two hundred miles an hour and only a dozen feet from Blair. Finger on the firing button.

A shrouded corpse falls from the sky. He drives straight over it, and a tire blows. He loses control. The Mercedes flips over, bouncing and rolling, battering and bruising him, taking him to the edge of death.

But he doesn't die.

He's bleeding from a gash on his face, blind in one eye, and his right leg is broken, but he moves his left leg over and floors the engine. He's never felt so alive.

Never more alive than when risking everything.

HE'D AWAKENED FROM the dream and thought: Once I'm immortal, I won't be able to take risks. What will I do with myself? Sip daiquiris on the beach? Take up the violin?

Francine wouldn't have any trouble with immortality. She could spend infinite millennia "discovering the truth." How quaint. How idealistic. And how utterly superior. Yet another way she transcended him. He should hate her for it, but he didn't.

Right now, though, he didn't have time to contemplate the drawbacks to immortality. Not when there was something to do that he was good at doing. He demanded maps of the Underground from Baehl and brought them to the Clean Room. He spread out the maps and convinced himself of what he already knew: He couldn't possibly make this underground city defensible. Not in a decade. It was too large and close to the surface; an enemy could dig down and break in anywhere. And how much time did he actually have? Weeks. Maybe days.

The best idea was to flee.

He could walk out whenever he wanted. But he'd never manage to get Francine out of there with him—not with Cowper and dozens of others like him hungrily watching her every move.

He heard a sound and jumped. The invasion already? No, just the fume hood turning on in the outer lab. Francine and Lemon were cooking up virus.

What about building a safe room, a place to hide, to wait out the attack?

The Underground had five primary tunnels that communicated with the world outside. Four were thoroughfares, in constant use by hafeems and mortals as they moved between living quarters, kitchens, game rooms and so on. But there was a fifth tunnel, too, one that was undeveloped and unused. It emerged from a hidden trap door in the Clean Room and penetrated a good distance without opening onto anything important.

Now that he knew it was there, Menniss found the entrance easily; it was centered in a video blind spot between two lab benches. Would he draw suspicion if he disappeared for a while? Not likely. All eyes were on Francine, not her useless boyfriend.

He opened the trap door. He put one foot down and felt the rungs of a ladder. He climbed further down and pulled the trap door back down. The ladder led him to a landing and a horizontal, stainless-steel-lined tunnel. According to the map, there were no video cameras here either; he was invisible.

He walked for perhaps a quarter of a mile before he reached a door. It opened onto a supply annex at least 50 feet across. Half was a workshop, supplied with machining tools, table saws, voltage meters and everything else one could want, along with stacks of plywood, wooden beams, sheet metal, pipes, rods, electronic parts and the like. The other half held food, medications, water and an enormous wine rack, all the essentials of life in a luxurious fallout shelter. But there were gaps in the wine rack; some bottles had been removed. Here and there, cases of water, soda and juice had been opened, too, and a third of the plywood was gone.

He wondered whether someone had broken in, then remembered that Baehl had built the original Underground in the 1950s; the Clean Room, Francine's lab and the rest of their private little world were recent additions. They must have used some of the supplies on hand to build it.

Menniss left the supply annex and continued further along the tunnel. After another half a mile, he passed several emergency exits, each leading to a small room stocked with basic supplies and connected via a vertical escape tunnel to the surface. But they were all well-marked on the map and therefore useless as hideouts.

He could walk out of here this moment and live out the remaining years of his natural life. But that wasn't an option. Apparently, he'd fallen in love.

USING TOOLS FROM the supply annex, he removed a panel from the tunnel wall. There was another wall about a foot behind the panel, and the airspace between them contained springs to moderate the effects of earthquakes. This place was designed to survive.

He removed a section of the second wall and forced a fiber-optic tube up to the surface to check for obstacles and also risks, such as a nearby road. All he saw was dense forest. He used a powered shovel to dig a 12-by-12 room and lined it with plywood supported by thick beams. When that was done, he dug a vertical tunnel to the surface, blocked at the top by a plywood square that he carefully covered with fern. He temporarily removed other panels from the tunnel wall and hid the dirt, springs and extra panel in the airspaces behind them. It took him four days to finish this part of the job, and Alexandros hadn't yet attacked.

Up above, Francine injected Janice with a retrovirus carrying the immortality genes, and everyone in the Underground waited anxiously to see whether it worked. Menniss kept at his self-appointed task. He destroyed all copies of maps that showed the fifth tunnel. He brought in water, food, blankets and computers. He installed video cameras at strategic places. These were off the grid, but he also installed display screens connected to the Underground's wireless so he could see everything anyone else saw. Still no sign of Alexandros.

Janice was feeling much better, and now everyone was waiting to see whether the scar on her knee would disappear.

Menniss rifled through the utility rooms and found old-fashioned air-powered alarms—klaxons, no less—and attached them to trip wires he installed near the end of the tunnel. He brought in AK-47s and plenty of ammunition.

Lemon pronounced Janice's scars smaller, and groups of hafeems and mortals throughout the Underground broke into cheers.

Francine gave Lemon the virus, but he became seriously ill. This spooked her; what if the virus killed people? Even after Lemon recovered, Francine remained fearful and wanted to postpone infecting anyone else. Baehl begged her to treat the sickest hafeems and mortals, the ones staring death in the face. Janice interceded, and Francine gave in. No one died.

Menniss was running out of things to do.

Baehl set up what he called the "Hexagon of Life," and Francine went there every day to dispense immortality. She was building a device to assemble virus in bulk, but until it was complete, she could only manufacture enough to treat 20 people a day. Since more than 100 needed it desperately, it was out of the question for Menniss to immortalize himself just yet. And that was a good thing; he could postpone deciding.

Lemon recovered his strength, gained weight, and began to look perceptibly healthier. Still no attack from Alexandros.

Mennis began to think Alexandros truly didn't know where Baehl's Underground was hidden. But that seemed unlikely. With so many people streaming in, the location would certainly leak. Could Baehl have managed that part competently? He could be competent when the mood struck him.

Menniss tweaked his cameras. He set up a proxy system so his tie-in to the network couldn't be traced. He was running out of tasks and sinking back into depression.

He couldn't ignore the symbolism of what he'd just built: a safe room. A place to hide. A foretaste of the endless years ahead that he'd spend shepherding his precious immortal life, taking no risks, scarcely living at all.

Flying from trap to trap, just as the Eldest had said, and this was the greatest trap of all. But she'd also said he could find a door.

Where was it?

He left his safe room and walked back up the tunnel. He paused at the trap door and checked a hidden camera he'd placed strategically; there was no one in the Clean Room above him, and he climbed up.

He sat by the virus assembler and listened to the click of robotic arms as they transferred liquid between yellow plastic squares. Clear droplets spurted into a stainless steel cylinder at the far end of the machine. It was a slow process. But once Francine had the bulk assembler working, there'd be enough immortality for everyone in Baehl's Underground. He'd have no excuse.

He felt like a man on death row marking down the dwindling days in a state of torpor and darkening gloom. How strange that immortality should feel like a death sentence.

FOOTSTEPS IN THE outer lab roused him: Francine was coming back. He sat straighter and faced the door. Despite his general depression, he knew he loved her.

But when the door opened, it was Janice, the first mortal being transformed into a True Immortal.

"Hey, Dennis the Menniss," Janice said. "I've been looking for you."

"Mission accomplished. Now you can leave."

"Stop being a dickhead and listen. I'm here to do you a favor."

"What's that?"

"To point out something that's right in front of your nose. Or it would be right in front of your nose if you didn't have your nose stuck so far up your ass. Your girl, Francine—you know who I mean, the one who's everyone's savior? Well, she's working herself up to a manic episode. I had a bipolar roommate once who refused to take her psych meds even though they worked perfectly for her, and every so often, we had to drag her to the ER. I recognize the signs. Your girl Francine's not there yet, but she's close."

"Manic?" His brain felt sluggish. "Bipolar?"

"She needs to be pumped full of drugs. Not that it's any of my business."

Menniss thought about it. People didn't sleep much when they were going manic. Did Francine sleep? He had no idea. He slept late, and she was never in bed when he awoke. And because of his depression, he'd been going to sleep early. For all he knew, she didn't go to bed at all.

"Have you talked to Lemon about it?" he asked.

"No. I have other things to do. She belongs to you, not to me."

"She doesn't belong to me."

"Fine. I just had to tell someone. Mission accomplished. Have a nice depression."

She was already halfway to the door when he said, "Wait. You're really worried about her?"

"I—Am—Really—Worried—About—Her. Got it? Good. Now, bye."

"Do you know where she is?"

Janice shrugged. "Somewhere around."

"Hold on. Let's go find her."

Janice gave a loud sigh, but she waited as he roused himself from the chair and made his body cross the room.

JANICE

I HAD TO tell *some*one. I owed Francine that much just for making me immortal. Besides, we have some similar problems, even if they work out differently in her than in me.

To explain how I got to the point of handing off that hot potato to her boyfriend, I have to back up a bit.

Remember when the Eldest showed up in the Underground with the imaginary nuclear bomb on her hip, outraged about retroviruses scribbling on some god's scripture? That was when I popped out with, "I don't want to die, Eldest," and for some crazy reason, she gave a damn. Saul supported me in his abstract and philosophical style, and the Eldest chilled and asked Francine to cram some genes in a retrovirus and shoot me up, come what may.

They kept close watch on me, checking my blood pressure, pulse and temperature every few minutes. Two hours after the shot, Lemon told me that my temperature was going up.

I shivered, which is what you do, weirdly enough, when you get a fever.

He laid heavy blankets over me. "I hope you don't get *too* terribly sick."

"Thank you," I said.

"Don't thank me. I was only worried about myself. Because if the retrovirus makes a young woman like you sick enough to notice, it might *kill* me."

Lemon went away, then came back. I told him to stay away from me because you usually tell old people to stay away when you have a fever and muscle aches so they don't catch it. But he explained that genetic therapy retroviruses aren't infectious like the flu. Gene-changing retroviruses are designed to be non-contagious. You can sneeze them on someone all you want, and nothing happens. They're meant to fix genetic illnesses like cystic fibrosis, and you don't want the virus to jump from person to person and fix cystic fibrosis in people who don't have it. You can't even spread retroviruses by sharing needles or having unprotected sex. Which is too bad because it would be cool if you could turn people immortal by having sex with them.

I felt way too dizzy to have sex with anyone.

My bed was soaking wet, and it smelled like pee. Lemon was sticking a needle in my arm. He said the infection itself wasn't so bad, but when you have brain cancer, even a low fever can give you seizures, and that was what just happened.

Menniss came in and carried me to a clean bed. *Menniss* did that. How embarrassing.

"When will my DNA start changing?" I asked. But they'd gone, and I was alone.

What kind of shivering do you have to do on your way up from death to immortality?

I listened inside my body to see whether I could hear the immortality genes turning themselves on. I listened for little pings. For cells saying, "You mean, I never have to die?"

I thought I heard a ping saying that, although I was probably imagining it.

After a few days, I wasn't shivering anymore. I felt great. In a week, my new surgical scar had disappeared, and the old one on my knee seemed to be fading. Francine was excited because that proved her "restoring to a template" theory, and she thought she was cool. Which she is, don't get me wrong. Restoring to a template means that the immortality genes not only cure illnesses and make people stop getting older, but they also turn people back to how they looked at about 24 or so, when they were fully mature but not yet starting to age.

Francine gave the virus to Dr. Lemon because he was about to drop dead from lung cancer, and she needed a doctor around to help her study the effect of the therapy. He got seriously sick because even plain flu is dangerous when you're almost dead. Also, it took a lot of energy to grow his wrecked lungs back.

For weeks even thinking about getting out of bed wore him out. I became his private assistant. I helped him get out of bed and into a wheelchair and even set him on the toilet. I also gave him sponge baths in bed, which weirded me out because he'd turn young again, and I'd have memories of him as old and shriveled. I brought him food, and sometimes I even cooked for him though Francine and Menniss were better cooks. Lemon and I became great friends.

And then he started to get better too. It would take him a while to turn younger, but his hair was already growing back.

Francine didn't want to treat anyone else until she made sure that Lemon and I wouldn't show up with late-breaking side effects, but Baehl pointed out that there were hafeems and mortals in the Underground just as sick as Lemon and me, and they'd die if she waited. He had tears in his eyes because there'd been a hafeem named Bonnie he'd wanted to save but hadn't been able to.

I threw in my two cents: "It's been weeks and my eyes haven't bugged."

She wasn't persuaded.

I promised Baehl I'd convince her.

I hung out with Francine in the Clean Room, and to break the ice, we talked about how I fell in love with Blair and she fell in love with Menniss. It was a great discussion, but it also made me miss Blair horribly. I felt I couldn't go another day without seeing my shallow lovely immortal narcissist; I needed him like water or food.

Then I changed the subject and reminded Francine that I felt perfect. I told her about the pings. I showed her my perfect knee. I lifted weights, heavier ones than she could lift, and I made up stories about hafeems who were about to die and didn't want to.

Francine, it turned out, was already convinced; she just needed a push. She yelled into one of the microphones for Baehl to come immediately, and he did. She had a tube full of virus and said she had to take it to the clinic to shove it into vials using an injection-vial-shoving machine and that Baehl should call 20 of the sickest folks to the blue hexagon to get treated, starting in about an hour.

Francine and Baehl left, but I stayed. I lifted one of the panels and peeked into the orange hexagon outside the clinic. It was empty—everyone was on their way to the blue hexagon.

I blame the call of the infinite for what I did next. Saul was right: mortals are drawn to immortality like lemmings to cliffs, moths to flames and astronauts to the moon.

I made my way to the room Baehl called his Master Control Room. No one saw me. I picked up the headset of his old-fashioned phone. I changed my mind and decided to leave. Then I changed my mind again. I dialed Blair's cell.

Apparently, they had cell service in the other Underground. Blair answered.

"I'm immortal now," I said. "I want you."

"I want you too," he said.

"Then let's meet somewhere. Where?"

"Hold on." He passed the phone to someone else.

"Janice? This is Maggie. Shall I bring you to Blair?"

"Yes, yes, as soon as you can!"

"I'll come get you in about a week. But this is important: don't tell anyone I'm coming. It will just be me. I'll find you and take you to meet Blair."

A week? Shit. I'd been putting off calling him all this time because I felt I should wait until I was immortal and we were equals. I had to wait another week? You can win awards for patience like that.

THE BLUE HEXAGON is the one next to the clinic. Baehl had dragged in some furniture from the clinic and was arranging it. He moved in his typical way, fancy with flourishes, but you could tell he'd waited a long time for this. People had died along the way, and his usual mock-seriousness was now almost real-seriousness.

In came Francine carrying a silver tray full of vials. She set the tray on a side table and fussed with her vials.

Baehl cleared his throat. "The Hexagon of Life is now in

session," he announced. "Soon, very soon, the first supplicant shall enter to receive communion. We wish to honor this day by—"

A nurse named Carol Denning told him to shut up and wheeled in an aged hafeem named Leyla.

Francine didn't look at Leyla. She attached a sterile needle to a syringe, looked confused, and moved things around. Carol said she had considerable experience giving injections and would be glad to help. Francine thanked her without making eye contact. She seemed nervous and rushed.

Carol used an alcohol wipe to clean the rubber top of a virus vial. She poked the needles through the rubber, pulled up the plunger, and filled the syringe with the virus. After tying a tourniquet on Leyla's arm, she patted a vein and stuck the needle in.

Where's Rembrandt when you need him? His paintings don't just show faces. They bring out what's behind the face: they show thoughts and feelings; they show souls. Other painters do that, too, but I think Rembrandt's the best, especially for old people. And Leyla was old, old. She had big white cataracts across both eyes, swollen legs and blue lips, but the main thing was the wrinkles. Sometimes they put an ancient person who got a lot of sun her whole life on the cover of *National Geographic*, and all you can do is stare at the wrinkles and see stories. Leyla had lived three and a half thousand years, give or take, and her wrinkles were deep enough to go backpacking in.

I wandered around inside those wrinkles. I got lost in them. I was still lost when Carol pushed the plunger.

The wrinkles filled up with enough gratitude to bathe in, but the gratitude was aimed at Francine, who didn't know how to let it in. She fussed with her vials some more, I guess pretending this was only a biology experiment, and never looked at the ancient lady she was saving. So Leyla turned toward me.

Her whited-out eyes had tiny black dots in the center, dots that shot out gratitude rays. I dove through the rays and looked inside.

I saw lots of things. The instant when a decrepit, hugely old person on the edge of death turned back from the edge. She'd been baptized by the virus, and her physical sins were washed away. It wouldn't show for a while, but it was starting.

And there was another thing I saw—it so entirely needed a Rembrandt. (Later, I asked around the Underground, hoping maybe Rembrandt had been a hafeem, but no luck.) You might think resurrection is pure joy, but it wasn't for Leyla. A sad part came along, too, and it surprised her. She wanted to live. That's why she was there. But another part of her had different ideas, and I thought I could see the two parts crashing.

Supposedly, old people come to accept death. Ordinary old people, I mean, when they get to be 80 or 90. Leyla had spent centuries working up to acceptance. She'd opened up to death, even embraced it. And now she had to let go of that acceptance and take up life again just when she thought she was done with it. It hurt. I could see how much it hurt in her whited-out eyes.

But she was also ecstatic. She was staring at me, and I supposed maybe I brought back memories of when she had been the loveliest lady in Athens. She was about to become that lovely lady again, whether she wanted to or not. So many emotions at once it would definitely take a Rembrandt to sort them out.

A WHOLE DAY passed with no Blair, and I passed the time in the Hexagon of Life. If you think that name sounds sappy, it shows you weren't there.

Like I said, Francine couldn't take it in at first. But she learned. Although Carol still helped out sometimes, Francine began doing her own injections, and after a couple of days, the magic started leaking through. She'd dart friendly glances at the box full of spare hypodermics or tap her fingers on the hazardous-waste bucket like you might tap on the back of someone you love. And when a supplicant's vein popped up nice and big, she would smile the way she does when she bakes pita bread and the bubbles come up.

Which meant Francine was connecting to the mood. But it took her longer to connect with the people. Jabbing a needle in someone's vein isn't the best way to touch soul to soul. Still, needles and all, Francine finally managed to do it.

The first person she made eye contact with was a young-looking red-haired hafeem dying of ovarian cancer. Francine only kept it up a second before she had to turn away. She smiled to herself instead of at the red-haired woman, but that was a start.

Little by little, she got better at it and began to take in the gratitude rays that the old and sick hafeems and mortals poured out when she saved them. When superpowered gratitude rays shine into you, it's hard to ignore them. Francine was a difficult case, but even she couldn't stay closed down in that kind of sunshine. She became less afraid and warmed up little by little. Her hard, dry, brilliant mind started to become a bit *juicy*.

I should have taken advantage of the change and invited her to my room for coffee or wine and to share gory childhood details. It might have helped her some; maybe she wouldn't have gone where she did. Maybe I thought I had plenty of time to get around to it. Anyhow, I missed the chance.

Francine's juiced-up phase lasted only about half a day. Then the juice caught fire. I probably couldn't have handled so much gratitude without it going to my head, either. Who could? The Dalai Lama? Saul, for sure. But no regular person. Francine was resurrecting about 20 people a day. If she'd been wearing one of those x-ray badges, it would have turned bright red from gratitude-radiation overdose.

And it wasn't just the rays. It was the speeches too.

I remember a speech delivered by a guy who looked about 99 and flimsier than a plastic bag, but he liked to talk. I'll set his words down like a prayer because that's what it was:

> *I thank you, Lord, that I have lived to see this day,*
> *That I have lived to pass through this gate*
> *and leave the curse behind: the promise given at*
> *birth that we shall grow old and die.*
> *Some believe in life after death,*
> *But those who do not have this comfort ask,*
> *"Why did You make us desire life yet give us death?"*
> *And You answered.*
> *You sent us one to lift the curse.*
> *One who has made for us a gateway that,*

once passed through,
Leaves the certainty of death behind.
For all who have lived unto this day and
Having lived thus far, need never die, I thank You.
For the one You sent, I thank You.

That speech and many more like it poured into Francine's poor head, and it made her crazy. But I didn't notice it immediately because everyone else was going a little crazy too.

Like Dr. Lemon. I walked in on him in the middle of a scene that weirded me out for weeks.

I'd made a tray full of scones for Lemon and knocked on his door. He told me to come in. I expected to find him propped up in bed, reading. I also expected a great big smile for the scones.

Lemon was propped up on a stack of pillows, all right, but he wasn't reading. He had the ugliest person in the world beside him and was fondling that ugly person's face. At first, I couldn't tell if Mr. Ugly was a him or a her because he was the kind of chubby guy who has smooth skin and breasts. His face didn't help a lot because he looked more like a parrot than a person; someone had drawn a line from his forehead to his chin and creased his face along it, making a beak. It was hard to look at him.

Lemon had a tray with two empty vials on it, the same kind of vials Francine used to hold the immortality virus. Two hypodermics were on the tray, one squeezed down with a droplet on the tip and the other half full. While I gaped, Lemon squeezed a few drops out onto his hand and, with retrovirus-wet fingers, lovingly fondled, rubbed and massaged Mr. Ugly's face. As if rubbing in the immortality virus would reshape it.

This scene needed Hieronymus Bosch, not Rembrandt.

I could tell that Lemon had already injected parrot-face with the virus—that's why there was an empty vial and a used hypodermic on the tray. This other part, this rubbing, was nuts. Worse than nuts—a waste of good immortality virus that could have saved someone's life.

"Meet my son, Gary." Lemon left off his fondling so Gary could look at me.

I had to fight with myself the way you do when you don't want to show that you're disgusted. But then I thought, he's just gotten a shot of the virus. Maybe it'll fix his deformity. So I kept that in mind and tried to see him as post-virus perfect.

"Hey, Gary," I said. "Good to meet you. I love your dad. He's totally great."

Only, I could tell Gary wasn't thinking, "My dad is totally great." He was thinking: "He's out of his mind."

I set the scones on a counter and sat on the bed beside Gary. "I used to have brain cancer, but the virus healed me. I used to have a big scar on my knee too, but it's gone." I lifted a pant leg and showed him my flawless knee. Not that the state of my gorgeous knee proved anything about the virus, since he and my knee weren't previously acquainted. "This virus has genes in it from my boyfriend, a True Immortal. He's about 300 years old and looks our age or even younger."

I almost added, Blair is beautiful and lovely, and pretty soon, you'll be beautiful and lovely, too, but I didn't know whether that was true. That's why the energy in the room felt so weird: Lemon wasn't sure either.

What if the immortality genes didn't fix Gary's appearance? What if he lived forever but as the world's ugliest person? Rubbing the virus onto his face couldn't possibly help, but I could understand why Lemon wanted to try. Still, it was a squirrelly thing to do.

I LIKED TO watch Francine give injections, but after that, she went back to her lab and worked on the machine that would make 100s of doses a day once it got going. To pass the time while waiting for Blair to get in touch, I wandered around the Underground and only returned to the Hexagon of Life when she was setting up shop.

It was getting crowded down below. Baehl's hafeems and mortals were flooding in the way people flooded in to stare at the King of China's granary during a famine. They would stare at me and point: that girl over there, she's Miss Immortality the First.

Most people nodded politely, but even the polite ones looked hungry, and some of them stared so hard it felt like they might bite me if I got too close. I understood then why Immortals and hafeems are so scared of hangers-on: it's more than the actual danger; it's the naked hunger. It's no fun when a toothy mouth drips saliva all over you even if it doesn't bite. I got pretty sick of it, and I might have completely stopped going out and about in the Underground if it hadn't been for the mask fetish.

The oldest hafeems and mortals started wearing masks first. Someone downloaded one of those apps that shows you what you'd look like at a different age. They took selfies of their old, wrecked faces and rolled back the years to what they looked like when they were 24. They'd paste the photo on a face mask and walk around looking young. Within a few days, everyone was doing it. It was like a fetish ball but with everyone looking perfect instead of weird.

When someone wears a mask, you can't tell whether they're licking their lips. Still, even the prettiest face looks weird when ancient eyes gnaw at you through the eyeholes, and I wished Francine would finish building her bulk virus-maker and treat all of them.

FIVE DAYS PASSED, and it still wasn't a week. Not that five days usually adds up to a week, but I didn't see why this time they shouldn't make an exception. I had to wait two more days to see Blair, and I couldn't stand it.

I got in a pretty stinky mood. I started smoking again and smoked three packs in a day. Then I stopped smoking because it's no fun when it can't hurt you. So I walked and walked and walked and walked.

The Underground was full of long corridors, and the corridors were full of rooms, like a hotel. At the end of each corridor, you came to a huge cave—a dug cave, not a real one with stalactites. They used the caves to store cots, bottled water and canned food, stacked on shelves that reached the ceiling and went on in rows forever. It reminded me of the library at Bennington College.

Sometimes old people in young masks wandered around the shelves too. If I saw one in my way, I'd walk faster, like it was a game of chicken, and they always stepped back and let me through because I'm Miss Immortality Lady the First, but it feels creepy passing so close to someone who wants to eat you.

Day seven at last. But Maggie had said "about a week," and no one showed up on day seven. I couldn't use the phone to call him again because there were too many people around, which made me shy. No one showed up on day eight either, and I was going crazy with waiting. Which meant I fit in.

By now, there must have been a thousand hafeems and mortals down below, and they were all impatient. A few times, I got pulled aside and questioned by folks who wanted to know what the wait was about. To get away from them, I'd go deeper into the stacks.

I was running my finger along a shelf lined with amber bottles full of antibiotics, wiping off dust, when it happened. I saw someone ahead blocking my way, and as usual, I walked faster to intimidate her. But when I got close, I realized she was wearing Maggie clothes and that she had on a Maggie mask. I screeched to a halt.

She lifted her mask, and though she wasn't the real Maggie, she was practically a twin of the True Immortal who'd made me her pet project. How typical of that lady to say, "I'll come get you," and then send someone else.

"Come with me," the Maggie said. "It's time to see Blair." She started walking, and I followed her for a few steps before I stopped.

Considering how long I'd been waiting, I know it sounds strange that I didn't just run right along, but two things held me back. First, Saul had left me presents to give to Blair, and I wanted to get them from my room. Second, I wasn't a stray cat anymore. I was a True Immortal, Maggie's equal, and it bugged me to get bossed around, especially by someone who was only a Maggie copy.

The truth is, if she'd acted even a teensy bit displeased, I'd have crumbled. But she didn't. When I told her I needed to run back to my room, she said no problem, just make sure to get back in an hour.

I ran off. I ran as fast as I could, but the closer I came to Downtown, the more crowded the corridors got, and I slowed to a walk. ("Downtown" was one of the names they used for our special private quarters around the lab.) The last quarter mile or so, the corridors were packed solid and smelled like the armpits of corpses. I wormed my way through whatever spaces I could find. The hafeems and mortals with the most seniority got the closest places to Francine's Resurrection Show, and they were also the people who showed the most respect to Miss Immortal the First, so the spaces that opened up most easily led me straight to the Hexagon of Life with Miss Messiah presiding, which wouldn't have been my preference.

At the beginning, onlookers stayed at the entrances leading to the hexagon and watched from there. But now the hexagon was jammed. The folks nearest the walls stood, while the rest sat on the floor, silent and reverent as Francine did her thing. Each time she pushed the plunger, she erased sickness, old age and death. She was an anti-Buddha.

I glanced her way while she was working on a supplicant with Stephen Hawking's disease (Lou Gehrig had it first, but Hawking stole it). The woman presented a problem: she was too folded up in her wheelchair to show a vein. I thought maybe I could squeeze past unnoticed, but no such luck. Francine lit up with a face full of floodlights and cried, "Janice!" like she hadn't seen me in a million years. She jabbed the needle in and said, "Janice, sweetie, would you walk with me? I'm out of virus, and I have things to talk about. Let's go together. Okay?"

No, it wasn't okay, but I said, "Sure."

WE WALKED ARM in arm. The last time we'd walked that way, she'd practically held me up, but I wasn't broken-brain girl anymore: I was a True Immortal and had all the energy in the world. And this time, it was Francine who needed her arm held. Not to hold her up, but to hold her down, to keep her from flying away to la-la land.

She was halfway to la-la land already, motor-mouthing away about some wild, braniac new version of Christianity that included immortal aliens from space sticking the Tree of Life in our genome. Her words came out full of pressure like water from a fire hose, as if she had to get this stuff out or the world would burn down.

That's when I flashed on Suzie, my roommate who'd go manic every few months because she didn't believe in drugs. The doctors called it pressured speech. The way Francine looked reminded me of Suzie, too. Out-of-control brain chemicals give your face a Santa Claus shine. I'd been seeing the signs for days without paying attention, but now it came together. Francine was having a manic episode.

Shit.

Shit, shit, shit. I didn't have time for this. I'd already wasted who knows how long wiggling my way through the crowds in the corridors, and I'd have to wiggle my way back too. I'd told the Maggie I'd be back in an hour. What if I took too long, she turned into a pumpkin and I lost my chance?

But Francine was out of her gourd. My roommate thought she could walk through walls and tried it on second-floor windows. I owed Francine too much to duck out on her right now. *Shit, shit, shit.*

She hurried me through Lemon's clinic and into the corridor. We passed the kitchen; the door was open, but no one was there. Menniss, that's who I wanted.

"Francine," I said. "Have you told all this interesting stuff to Richard?"

She gave me a smile like everything bad in the world had come to an end. "I haven't told anyone else. You're the first."

"That's so sweet," I said. "I'm in a bit of a hurry just now, so I thought maybe you should tell Richard the story and then tell me when I finish up what I have to do."

"But why are you in a hurry?" Francine asked. "There's nothing to hurry about down here. This place is the opposite of hurry."

I should have said I had diarrhea. Or that I'd promised a hafeem lady I'd do up her hair, and you should see her hair; it really needs it.

When my roommate went manic, her mind worked so fast that she turned something like psychic. And, unlike Francine, Suzie didn't start life as a genius. It wasn't easy to lie to super-Francine, a genius amped up on the upside of bipolarism. I got confused and my lying tongue stalled out while Francine's mind zoomed ahead at hyperspeed.

"You're going to meet your lover. Your lover Blair. Oh, that's so sweet."

How the hell did she know?

It was her mind on steroids, I guess.

Francine turned conspiratorial. She made me wait while she checked the corridor ahead and behind. There was no one around but the bust of Baehl. She pulled me a little farther down the corridor so the bust couldn't spy on us, fumbled around in the pockets of her jeans and brought out a chunk of folded up aluminum foil. After checking both ways down the corridor again, she shushed me silently with her finger on her lips, unfolded the aluminum foil and showed me a blue and white capsule inside. She made silent faces to show me that this was a very important capsule, a really big deal. She made the shush sign again and refolded the foil. Putting the packet in my hand and wrapping my fingers around it, she said, "Just before you go outside, swallow this."

When a crazy lady hands you a pill, you don't ordinarily trust her. "What does it do?" I asked.

If she'd kept on talking like a maniac, I'd have thrown the capsule away the first chance I got. But her voice turned into scientist Francine again, super-objective and trustworthy.

"You could call it a booster," she said. "Technically, it stabilizes the immortality segment by linking it to citric acid cycle genes. Once this booster is in your system, you're safe against genetic drift. Without it, your immortality might slip away."

I'd had no idea my immortality could slip away. I needed my immortality to stick around, not only so I wouldn't die but also so I could meet Blair as an equal. The idea that I might lose it scared me so much I mostly forgot that I shouldn't necessarily believe what Francine was telling me. Still, I couldn't help asking, "Doesn't everyone else need the same booster?"

"Of course they do. And they'll get it. Just not yet. The virus has to unwrap the histones and complete its initial pass; the booster won't work until sufficient messenger RNA has been transcribed off the gene segment. You're the only one who's gone that far."

I had no idea what she was talking about, so I was totally convinced. I crammed the aluminum packet into the pocket of my tight pants. No way I could lose it.

Then Francine clapped her hands on her head. "But why am I going to the lab? I came out to get more immortality virus, and that's in the clinic, not the lab." She took my hand. "You go. Go to your lover, sweetheart."

"I'm going in a second. But we need to see Richard first. Do you know where he is?"

"He's in the Clean Room, I'm sure. He's always there." She giggled. "Don't let him cut off your ear, now."

"Why don't you come with me?" I said. "I want you to tell Richard all your interesting new ideas."

But she let go of my hand, waived gaily, and jogged down the corridor away from me. And there I was, alone.

I hurried down the corridor to my room and stuffed Saul's presents into a duffel bag. I also stuffed in a couple of days' worth of clothes and all the other items you need to pack when you have no idea where you're going.

I showered at light speed and changed my clothes even faster. According to my nagging watch, I only had 20 minutes to go. Where was that aluminum packet? I dug around in the pockets of the pants I'd taken off, but I couldn't find it. I got frantic and searched all around my room. I checked under the bed, in the bathroom, and back in all my pockets again. Then, it finally showed up, caught in a fold of my bedspread.

Christ. I could have joined Blair and then turned non-immortal all over again. I unrolled the foil and swallowed the pill right then and there.

Which reminded me how much I owed Francine. So even though I only had 15 minutes, I ran off to the Clean Room to tell Menniss.

FRANCINE

HER MIND HAD never worked so well. People often called her a genius, but she'd met geniuses and knew she wasn't one of them. A genius didn't have to struggle constantly against so many obstacles.

Gray Fog, her constant affliction, resembled a dense liquid heaviness, a mental humidity that scattered thoughts like drizzle. She'd go for fast walks to clear her brain, to reach a patch of road where she could see ahead. Every so often, it would work. The fog would part for an instant, and she'd get answers to problems she'd been struggling with for months. Her most important ideas came to her during moments like that. But Gray Fog always closed in again and dimmed her mind.

Not now. Today, her brain was filled with bright sun.

Siren Lullaby probably came from her fibromyalgia. Her doctor said people with fibromyalgia woke up in the morning exhausted and sore, as if someone had spent the night beating them with a plastic baseball bat, and that was a good description of how she normally felt. She was always tired. Siren Lullaby sang a constant invitation to sleep, a lullaby that cajoled her thoughts to yawn, curl up and go back to bed.

No more Siren Lullaby. Today, her brain zipped along like an athlete in top form, its thoughts too vibrant and vigorous for sleep.

Gray Fog and Siren Lullaby interfered with work, but *Blocking Monster* interfered with life. When she tried to see into people, Blocking Monster plopped down in her way—ten tons of opacity, an ugly old man carved in sandstone with his arms stubbornly folded. Don't even try, he'd say. You'll never understand people. I won't let you.

She'd been walking down the corridor with Janice, having an interesting conversation. As usual, Blocking Monster glided between them, his sandstone feet scraping the floor, making sure that she had no idea what Janice could be thinking. And then a miracle happened.

It happened when Janice said she was in a bit of a hurry and she should talk to Richard. Right then, Blocking Monster gave a big rocky wink and vanished.

Vanished! Gone.

He'd never done that before. He sometimes briefly stepped to the side, but he never disappeared.

She could see straight into Janice's mind. Not with telepathy but deduction. She could identify what Janice was thinking from how she moved, the tone of her voice and little hints she'd accidentally dropped.

She's had recent contact with her lover, the True Immortal Blair she's told me about. That's why she's so happy. She talked to him. And now she's in a hurry because she's on her way to meet him. She's about to leave the Underground.

She imagined Janice in the arms of an incredibly handsome young man with a missing ear. She saw it as if it were happening now and cried out with happiness for Janice as if it were her own happiness.

Then her mind showed her a new image: behind Blair stood a shadow, a tall, dark shadow.

A man in a toga. A man named Alexandros.

YOU SHOULDN'T HATE people you'd never met, but she hated Alexandros.

Janice had told everyone about her visit to the Illuminati underground. She paraphrased and sometimes recited almost verbatim Alexandros' grand, poetic and horrifying speeches, including one in which he claimed that the Illuminati had put Hitler in power on purpose because they thought it would work out best for the world that way.

What arrogance! As if he could predict the future. As if he had a right to control things. As if he were God.

He wasn't God (not that there was a God). He was a fascist like Hitler himself. Even worse: an immortal Hitler. Alexandros and the Illuminati, the multinational corporations, the fossil fuel companies, the CIA and the creationists were all working together and bent on taking control.

If Janice could go to Blair, Alexandros could come here.

Alexandros was already on his way.

FRANCINE HAD COMPLETED all these thoughts before Janice got out another sentence. And she knew exactly what to do.

She'd known what to do for months, long before the constant sun dawned, back when lightning flashes of insight were the best she could manage. Even in that relative darkness, she'd seen ahead to the problem, and the solution too. Weeks ago, she'd secretly prepared a batch of a second retrovirus. This one you could take as a pill. She had one with her right now.

Alexandros coming made the radical solution necessary, and Janice leaving provided the perfect means. Game-theory puzzle solved; Alexandros frustrated and thwarted. Alexandros helpless and gnashing his teeth. How elegant: the cause and solution combined.

She pulled the folded aluminum foil out of her pocket and put it in Janice's hands. "This is a booster, Janice." Total nonsense. But Janice would believe it.

Janice would go to Blair. And Blair had a dyed-in-the-wool instinct to run; Janice had told everyone about that. Everything would work out perfectly.

A chess problem solved. Her mind had never been so clear.

FRANCINE HURRIED BACK to the clinic and prepared 10 vials of normal virus. She arranged them neatly on the silver tray. Grabbing a pile of hypodermics, she put them on the tray, too. Like a communion plate.

She hurried out into the Hexagon of Life and that sea of masks. Young-person masks. A little bizarre, that habit, but no matter.

Baehl brought up another supplicant. Male or female? The mask was male.

She stuck the plunger into a bulging vein. She drew back first, proper technique to make sure you hadn't hit an artery by mistake. Blood swirled into the syringe and mixed with the virus. Blood and virus. The transubstantiation fluid. The blood of the new and everlasting covenant.

And delivered by my own hand.

Did Jesus feel the same when he healed with a touch?

Don't be silly. Jesus never healed anyone. The gospels were a fabricated myth. Jesus had been a wonderful man, an ethical teacher, another Gandhi. But he didn't have magical powers.

Unlike him, I really *can* heal the sick. Except it's science, not magic. Two thousand years from now, if people tell stories about me, *they'll be true.*

FRANCINE INJECTED 10 people and returned to the lab to make more virus. Usually, she stopped at 20, but today she didn't want to stop healing people. She wanted to heal everyone.

She'd finished her bulk virus assembler, and it was working away. But it laboriously constructed viruses in parallel; it didn't finish one batch and then make another. She'd have thousands of completed doses in another day, but now she had none.

And Alexandros was coming.

What about handing out doses of retrovirus2? She'd been holding off. Why? Because it was such a huge step. But now that she'd given a dose to Janice, she'd taken the step.

Francine checked her pockets and panicked when she couldn't find the capsule. Then she remembered: that was the one she'd given to Janice. Obviously. She had to go back to her lab to get more.

In fact, she was already on the way back to the lab. Her body seemed to move as fast as her mind. How would she explain the capsules? She'd say she was working on an oral delivery system.

Hurry, Francine. Run. Alexandros might show up any minute now.

She ran through the outer lab. It took an awfully long time to get there, time enough for her mind to brim over with new thoughts.

"It's my theory," she said aloud, "that every religion has a true intuition at its core. The superstructure is superstition, but the center is real. For example, my friend Paul in the physics department says the Buddhist version of reality fits beautifully with quantum mechanics. I don't think it's an accident. And I've figured out the intuition that underlies Christianity."

Yet another discovery. She'd write this up and publish it in *Science*. To be followed by how many other major breakthroughs? What happiness! An infinity of time to do research. Pure bliss.

She'd reached the Clean Room door. Before she could open it, it opened by itself, and Janice was standing there. Richard was standing just behind her. Francine hugged Janice then Richard. He felt good, but no time for that now.

"I'm so glad the two of you are here. I have so much to tell you."

"Oh? About what?"

His voice sounded odd, but she didn't have the leisure to analyze his tone because a thousand words were piling up inside her mouth, and it took all her strength to wrestle them into proper order.

She grabbed the first strand of thoughts and said, "You remember the Bible story of the Tree of Life? Where Adam and Eve ate of the Tree of Knowledge? God caught them. And here's what he said when he caught them: 'Now that you've eaten of the Tree of Knowledge, you might eat of the Tree of Life and become immortal like one of us.' And God didn't like that. So he drove Adam and Eve out of the Garden of Eden."

"I thought you were an atheist," Richard said.

"Of course I am! It's not literally true. It's a metaphor."

"A metaphor for what?" Richard asked.

How could anyone be so dense? But she had to make allowances. "It's a metaphor for what we've done here. Think about it. What allows us to eat of the Tree of Knowledge? Science. We've been plucking fruits right off that tree for centuries, starting with Galileo, I guess. Or Francis Bacon. And now, at last, we have enough knowledge to do exactly what God didn't want Adam and Eve to do. You see? We can eat of the Tree of Life at last. Just like God worried we might."

She looked triumphantly at the two of them. They looked suitably impressed. She hugged them both again.

"Then you're in trouble," Janice said. "Because if God didn't want anyone to eat from that tree of his, he's going to be almighty pissed."

It was hysterically funny! Francine hugged them both again. After a while, she realized she was hugging just Richard. Richard had turned remarkably romantic and lifted her up in his arms. She felt so happy she wanted to dance. So she did, even though her feet didn't touch the ground. She was air-dancing.

Janice tagged along with them as they air-danced down the corridor to Dr. Lemon's room. He was sitting up in bed, staring at them.

She wriggled out of Richard's arms and ran to Lemon's bedside. "How are you doing, dear Doctor Lemon? Are you starting to feel better?

"My pulmonary function has reached 80 percent of normal." He sounded so doctorly, she kissed him.

Behind her, Richard said, "Excuse us for barging in, Dr. Lemon. But I need your help. I think—Janice thinks too—that Francine's having a manic episode."

Her brain filled with rage. The *bastard*. What a cruel thing to say!

Manic? Bipolar? Like her brother or her aunt?

"How dare you say that? I should slap you!" Then, she slapped him.

But that wasn't the right way to go about things. Better to prove she was sane. She made herself stiff and formal and put on her most rational voice. "I am not at all manic. I'm just excited."

"She's figured out the true meaning of the Garden of Eden story," Janice said.

"Yes, that's right." That traffic jam built up in her mouth again. She made the ideas come out one by one. "The Tree of Life is encoded in our genes. And do you know how it got there? Not from God. From immortal aliens. The universe is full of immortal beings. It has to be. About 100,000 years ago, they came here and rearranged our DNA so a few of us would turn immortal. Then they left. But they knew we'd eventually eat of the Tree of Knowledge and find the genes they put there."

"Well then," Janice said. "Are we squared away? All agreed? Good. Well, I've got things to do. See you later."

Francine winked at Janice conspiratorially because she knew exactly what "things" Janice had to do. But Janice was already gone.

"And how did the aliens get here?" Lemon asked. He sat up on the edge of his bed. "There's still the problem of distance. The speed of light, and all."

Francine waved her hand—a single wave of the hand and the objection disappeared. She liked how that felt and waved her hand again. "Once you're immortal, the speed of light is immaterial. If you can live a billion years, the piddly 10 thousand years it takes to fly at sublight speed to another planet hardly matters."

Lemon crossed the room to one of his cupboards. He walked with difficulty; she could almost hear his joints grind. It made her angry. She'd given him the virus weeks ago. Her virus. He ought to feel perfect already.

Maybe retrovirus2 would work faster, better. Only, as she perfectly well knew, that made no sense, and Lemon's recovery was proceeding as expected.

Lemon was filling a syringe. He meant to give *her* a shot of the immortality virus. Good thinking. Her mind would work even better once she had the blood of the new covenant in her veins.

But after Lemon stuck the needle in her arm, she realized it wasn't the immortality virus. She looked at him in horror; this needle wasn't like the needles she'd been sticking in people. This syringe didn't heal. It was full of some awful drug that brought back Gray Fog, Siren Lullaby and Blocking Monster. It took away all her confidence. It made her tiny, small and human again.

It made her afraid.

Because now she remembered something awful.

Now she remembered that she could make *mistakes*.

CHAPTER 9

THE ANGEL

"All at once, there was a violent earthquake as
an angel of the Lord descended from Heaven.
His face was like lightning and his robe
was white as snow."

MATTHEW 28:2-3

This chapter may cause you to feel desperate fear for my
well-being. Don't worry: I had the last laugh.

THE CHRONICLER

JANICE

I HAD 10 minutes left to meet the Maggie. Francine had talked like a crazy person in full view of half a dozen cameras, and if I ran into anyone, I'd never make five feet an hour for all the questions I'd get about the state of mind of our Savior. So I took the most private way out I knew: the broom closet. I pushed my way through swiffers, buckets, and vacuum cleaners, opened the little panel at the back, and peeked into the violet hexagon. Few people went in there because it didn't have any display screens. It was empty now, and I stepped in.

Better than empty. I spotted someone's mask lying on the ground and thank goodness or I don't know how I'd have gotten anywhere. That first day I landed in the Underground, I asked Baehl if he lived in a beehive. Now it was a hornet's nest.

I had a friend who raised bees, and once, when I was visiting, he trapped a swarm in a cardboard box and then accidentally dropped it while carrying it across a slope. The underground sounded a lot like the box did after it came to rest, only lower-pitched, a scary grumble from behind the masks of hafeems and mortals milling around in a mood and sometimes throwing off their masks, which is how I got mine.

I put it on and circled around to the corridor painted with bawdy pictures, the corridor I'd tried not to laugh at when I'd just had chemotherapy and laughing made my organs jostle. I pushed between streams of people going my way, the opposite way, or nowhere. I heard a worried voice fretting about how Francine seemed to have lost her mind, and I stumbled over the speaker, a middle-aged (looking) lady sitting on the floor beneath a mural of a circus poodle standing on a circus lion's nose and trying to have sex with a circus elephant. I apologized and tried to skoodle off, but my mask slipped.

She saw who I was, grabbed me and cried out, "Here's Janice!"

I struggled to get away because I only had minutes left. Still, I was a healthy True Immortal, and she was an oldish lady. I remembered a judo move Maurice taught me to make someone let go of you if they didn't want their wrists broken. The worried lady wanted to keep her wrists as they were, and I got out of there running. After that, I kept my mask on tight.

The hornet buzz in the supply cave reminded me too damn much of a riot about to start, and when I found the Maggie where I'd left her in the stacks, I begged her to get me out of there fast. As people behind us yelled out my name, we marched out like ladies on a mission. We walked fast through a long corridor that had bedrooms in it. People stood in some of the doorways talking loudly.

The Maggie opened a closed door, and I popped in behind her. We pushed dressers and the bed up against the door without discussing it.

There was a long pole on the ground where the bed had been before we pushed it. It had a hooked end that she used to unlock a trap door in the ceiling. The trap door fell open, and lots of wet muck came through the hole. Then just light and water.

"What the heck?" I said. "There's a tunnel to get out?"

"There are several," the Maggie said excitedly. "We found this one with radar. It was quite a project—I'll tell you about it once we're away."

A rope ladder dropped down from above, and I didn't need any convincing to climb it. Near the top, arms covered in saffron grabbed me and pulled me up, and there I was in the outside world for the first time in I don't know how long, surrounded by saffron folks holding umbrellas and bowing to me.

Or *trying* to hold umbrellas; the real world had a huge storm going on, with sheets of rain and hurricane-strong wing and lightning crashes. My Maggie came up from the ground after me, shaded her eyes and yelled, "Where's the helicopter?"

"Can't fly in this storm," one of them shouted. "We have to drive."

The saffrons shepherded me over as best they could, but in wind like that, umbrellas are weapons. To make sure they didn't impale me, they let me get soaked.

We ran through a clearing at the edge of a redwood forest, and I watched those stiff giant trees bow and genuflect in the wind like I didn't think they could. Most of them did okay except for one gigantic monstrous tree that tilted down, then tilted further until, with a rumble like an earthquake, it flew toward us, redwood needles shooting everywhere, branches flailing back and throwing wind. A cluster of saffrons yanked me away, and the tree hit the ground. It missed me but not by much. I told you redwoods hate me.

And then we got in the Humvee and drove to find Blair.

FRANCINE

SHE WOKE STICKY with sweat beneath heavy covers. Her eyelids felt like leaden blankets, and she couldn't open them. Why was she so sweaty? She felt for her nightgown but felt the buttons of a dress shirt. She must have been exhausted to fall asleep fully dressed.

She needed to take a shower. But she felt too sick and exhausted to move. She turned her head to face the shower and worked on opening her eyes. They opened, finally, and for a disorienting moment, she thought someone had walled up the door that led to the bathroom. Then she realized this wasn't her bedroom. She was in a tiny, bare room she'd never seen before, built like a prison with walls made of concrete and only one door. A chair was next to the door, and Richard sat in it, snoring.

She tried to call out to him, but she couldn't make her voice work. She tried again, and this time she must have squeezed out a sound because Richard stirred. He scratched his groin and under his arms, the way he often did when he woke up. Crude, yet oddly comforting.

"You're up?" He scratched his neck, yawned, and stood up.

She persuaded her thick tongue to form words. "What exactly happened?"

"You sound plastered," he said. "What have you been doing, sleep-drinking? That's a terrible habit. Shame on you."

"What are you talking about?"

He stretched like a bear. "It's the drugs, sweetheart. Lemon pumped you full of them. You can't remember?"

"I'm not sure." She made herself sit up and tried to focus.

He ambled over and sat beside her on the bed. "You had a manic episode. Lemon called it a 'classic, full-blown bipolar switch.' He gave you some drugs to bring you down."

Francine knew he was speaking English, but she couldn't understand a word of it. She pulled her hand free and plucked at the sleeve of her shirt, a nice formal shirt all wrinkled. "That's not possible. I don't have bipolar disease. You're thinking of my brother. Or my aunt. The family curse. But I escaped it."

Except, now she remembered all the nights she hadn't needed to sleep, and the week of boundless energy, her mind clearer than ever before.

And filled with crazy ideas.

A dead calm came over her. "I've been afraid of this all my life. My brother—he's a wreck. He's been in and out of mental hospitals since childhood. And my aunt once tried to burn down my mother's house. They live in chaos. But my life hasn't gone that way. I've done things, accomplished things."

He put his bear-like arms around her, and she realized he needed a shower even more than she did. But his Richard odor comforted her, too. She brought her knees up to her chest to make herself a smaller bundle and let him surround her.

"It might never happen again," he said. "According to Lemon, mania isn't entirely brain chemicals. Life has something to do with it, too, and for Christ's sake, Francine, you were bringing back the dead. Playing savior. That could go to anyone's head."

More memories now. Thinking of herself as Jesus. Feeling that she had magical powers.

"And besides," he added, "you'd only just started your manic episode. With any luck, the drugs will knock you right out of it. How insane do you feel at the moment?"

He said it with such gentle affection that she wanted to cry. "I don't think the Bible is a symbolic representation of cell biology." She said this very soberly. "Or that I've been busy growing the Tree of Life in my orchard."

It sounded funny, but it wasn't funny at all. Especially not if she'd inserted the immortality genes into a full dose of retrovirus2 and kept it in something as insecure as folded aluminum foil.

It felt like one of those dreams where you've murdered someone, but the police don't know you're the one who did it. You know you should confess. You know that if you confess voluntarily, you won't get as long a jail term; also, it's the right thing to do. But you're afraid. If you keep it secret, maybe no one will ever find out, and even though you'll carry the guilt with you for the rest of your life, you wouldn't go to jail. She always chickened out in those dreams and didn't confess.

She remembered too many details for it to have been a dream. She saw herself standing under the fume hood, filling the capsule above a bowl of nitric acid to catch any virus that might fall. Wiping the capsule with a greased cloth and dropping the cloth into the bowl of acid. Cleaning the outside of the capsule with proteinases and RNases to ensure it was absolutely safe. Setting the capsule in a dish. Removing her latex-free gloves and dropping them into the acid too. Putting on new gloves, lifting the capsule out of the dish, setting it in a strip of aluminum foil, folding the foil.

There was no pretending it didn't happen. While insane, she'd gone ahead and given Janice a loaded capsule of retrovirus2.

"It's okay, Francine," Richard said. "It's okay."

"No, it's not." She wanted to sob but felt too tranquilized to sob.

She wanted to tell him what she'd done, but a stubborn part of her wouldn't let her. "I'm completely terrified of being bipolar," she said, "terrified to death." This was true, though not to the point.

She pushed herself against his chest and let him caress her.

Maybe Janice just threw away the pill. She knew I was crazy. Why would she take a pill a crazy person gave her?

Because that crazy person told a diabolically clever lie, claiming that the pill was a booster and she had to take it or her immortality would slip away.

Maybe her True Immortal immune system will throw off the infection. True Immortals never got sick, did they?

But that was a vain hope. True Immortals *did* get sick. Just not *very* sick.

Oh, dear God.

Maybe Janice will stay safely in Alexandros' underground, and it will never get out. But, according to Janice, there were mortals down there who went to and fro. And what if she was going to meet Blair somewhere out in the world?

She knew from the beginning, long before she went manic, that she might have to use retrovirus2. But only as a last resort. And only after she knew it was safe. Instead, she'd given it to Janice like it was candy.

"You're trembling," Richard said. "You're shaking. But Francine, bipolar disease can be controlled."

"I know. I know, Richard. There's something else."

"Tell me." He stroked her hair.

She covered up the lie by telling a related truth. "I think Janice just left the underground to meet Blair."

"To meet Blair? How do you know?"

"I figured it out. And then she confirmed it."

"To meet him where? *Where?*"

"I don't know. Inside, outside. She didn't say. But unless she walked out of the redwoods on foot, doesn't that mean someone came to get her? And Blair was staying with Alexandros."

Once, while she was on a seminar cruise around the Galapagos Islands with Richard Dawkins, a storm came up in the middle of the night. She remembered gripping the mattress with all her strength to avoid getting thrown across the cabin. That's how her Richard looked now: gripping the mattress so hard his fingers dug deep in.

"Do you think Alexandros might come?" she asked.

"Oh yes," Richard whispered. "He'll come. He might be here already."

How terrible.

And what a relief.

MENNISS

VERY GENTLY, HE said, "What do you say to getting out of here as fast as we can? I know a place we can hide."

It pleased him greatly that she didn't argue or ask questions, just set about putting on her shoes and tucking in her clothes. "I should have told you sooner," she said.

"Don't worry about it. I already knew Alexandros was coming; I just didn't know when. He always opposed Baehl's project, but the Eldest was keeping Baehl under her protection. Since no one dares go against the Eldest, Alexandros did nothing. And then came that moment in the Clean Room. Remember what she said? 'I shall neither aid nor oppose.' At that moment, she withdrew her protection."

"But that was more than a month ago."

"True. The only explanation I can think of for why Alexandros hasn't attacked already is that he didn't know where to find us. But obviously he does. He and his friends must just have been preparing. Oh, and they needed Janice out of here, because the Eldest likes her."

"So what can we do?" Francine asked. She was brushing her hair as if they were getting ready to go out on a date. Why wasn't she frightened? Because she was filled with tranquilizers, that's why.

Menniss patted his pockets and felt three bottles. He was supposed to give her one of each every four hours. But not now. She seemed OK, and at that moment, he needed her wide awake.

He told her the place was defenseless and explained how he'd found the fifth tunnel and built a hidden safe room.

"You did all that without me noticing?" she said.

435

"You were too busy being Jesus."

"But why did you keep it from me?"

"I already cried wolf once before. I didn't want to look like a fool again."

"Oh, Richard, taking precautions doesn't make you a fool. But I'm ready. Let's get out of here. This room is like a prison cell."

"Sorry. I picked it because it doesn't have any panels people can stand behind and listen through. Just a few more things: we have to be careful. If you're spotted leaving, we'd make it about two feet before 100s of hafeems jumped us."

"Why?" Still in that excessively calm voice.

"You're their savior. They'd never let you leave before you turned them immortal too. I'm counting on Alexandros to create enough chaos when he attacks that we can get away during the confusion. Let's go to the Clean Room and wait for the right moment. You can look busy making viruses or something."

"I can do that," she said.

"Keep in mind that the moment we step outside of this room, we'll be under surveillance. Act normal. Walk, don't run. Ready?"

Menniss opened the door and looked both ways. He was exhilarated and excited, and his heart was pumping hard.

Yet another reminder, as if he needed one, that he felt most alive when risking everything.

THEY WALKED PLACIDLY down the corridor. Several hafeems approached, worried about their savior's condition. Menniss explained that Francine had suffered a small nervous breakdown from overwork, but she was fine now. Would they give her a little space? He made frequent comforting gestures toward Francine, lightly rubbing her back or squeezing her hand, as one would naturally do for someone who'd just come through a crisis. The story and her appearance reassured people, and they stepped away to spread the story.

They passed the clinic and the living areas. They paused at Baehl's bust. Menniss reminded Francine about that time early on when she made the hafeem donate a piece of flesh though all she needed was a scraping from the inside of his cheeks.

"I guess he rubbed me the wrong way," she said. "But it was mean of me. I wish I hadn't done it."

If Baehl were here, he'd say something amusing to lighten the mood. Menniss tried to play the role himself but hadn't yet thought of anything when a violent shout came from outside the walls. No one *ever* shouted down here.

Another shout. More voices joining in.

"Alexandros?" Francine whispered.

Menniss nodded. He took her hand, and they ran. They threw open the door of the outer lab and raced through it. More yells and shouts from outside the walls. They reached the Clean Room.

Menniss listened to the shouting outside the room. It was either Alexandros or a riot. Maybe both. It was time to go.

He opened the trap door and helped her down. He followed, shut the door above him, and led her quickly down the corridor. When they reached his secret room, he woke the computer and viewed the nearby tunnel through his hidden cameras. Nothing but an empty tunnel; no one had followed them.

Francine was squatting on her heels on the bare dirt floor, catching her breath. Menniss arranged the folding chairs he'd brought down and invited Francine to sit beside him. She didn't move. The display screen continued to show an empty tunnel. He connected to the Underground's Wi-Fi and flipped from camera to camera. People were running. And in the background, faintly at first and then growing louder, he heard a repeated chant. It sounded like, "Luh. Luh. Luh."

"What's that?" Francine asked. She leaned her head on his shoulder.

They heard sounds of clashing gear and stamping feet, and three columns of soldiers in riot gear came into view. Light blue tassels waved from the edges of black Kevlar shields, and a blue fleur-de-lis marked each soldier's black body armor. Menniss counted at least 200 marching past. They moved with an archaic solemnity, like one might imagine Roman soldiers marching; they even carried standards, tall poles topped by the letter "S" in bronze.

The Illuminati were here.

SWITCHING FROM CAMERA to camera, they watched blue&blacks round up everyone in the underground. The costumed figures marched along every corridor and into each hexagon. There was some resistance, but it rapidly folded. The blue&blacks were competent, armed and armored.

Within an hour, everyone had been herded into the supply caverns, where a different uniformed group took over. Military police? If so, they were the gaudiest military police Menniss had ever seen, wearing bright red uniforms, white berets, white sashes around their necks and white armbands emblazoned with the letter "L."

The red&whites, as Menniss mentally dubbed them, unpacked folding chairs and cots from the stored supplies. Hafeems who were too aged, sick or injured to sit were allowed to stretch out on the cots, restrained by leg- and handcuffs. The others were restrained in chairs.

This act of mass imprisonment took some time, but once it was done, the red&whites stepped back, and a new group entered, this one dressed in white clothing inlaid with strings of white pearls. They were medical staff, apparently, for they moved among the prisoners providing water and food and tending to wounds.

In the Clean Room, a crew in orange biohazard uniforms were sealing equipment in what looked like heavy, orange garbage bags and carting them off. They removed everything: viral assemblers, DNA sequencers, and, finally, lab benches and stools. Once the room was empty, they scrubbed it with bleach.

Francine had watched all this silently, but now she sat up and asked, "What's with the uniforms? It's like a graphic novel."

"Isn't it?" Menniss asked. "Very strange. Although, now that I think of it, the only True Immortal I've met other than the Eldest sees himself as a superhero in a comic book. She does too, in her own way. Maybe that's just how they are."

They were followed by a group wearing yellow jackets and trousers with black-beaded trim and a fanciful letter "B" embroidered in black on the backs of their jackets. They carried electronic devices and ladders. After using their devices to check the walls and the floor, they climbed the ladders and checked the ceiling. They examined the two cameras but didn't disconnect them.

"Do they know we're watching?" Francine said.

"They know someone could be watching."

"Can they trace us back?"

"No, I made sure of that."

The yellows departed, and a crew in silver and orange took their place. They pulled up the vinyl floor, leaving only bare concrete, and poured some kind of white liquid plastic on it that rapidly hardened. They carried in heavy plastic panels and constructed an inner wall over the drywall panels, retaining only a single opening into the orange hexagon beyond, which they covered with a swinging door of white plastic. They removed the acoustic tiles on the ceiling and cut and sealed all the ductwork and piping. They thoroughly caulked the edges and corners of these new walls and departed, leaving the room a sealed, featureless compartment, white plastic over everything but the ceiling, which was now bare stainless steel.

What happened next didn't seem real, partly because the tiny microphones of the Clean Room cameras were ludicrously inadequate to convey the sound. On the screen, an enormous, hollow metal rectangle could be seen punching clear through the ceiling of the Clean Room. Menniss took it for CGI until, after a delay of a second or two, the ground shook with the force of a minor earthquake.

It would take enormous power, not to mention a great deal of equipment, to drive so huge a shaft through a dozen feet of earth and a plate of stainless steel in one unbroken motion. Why? Drama for the sake of drama?

A group of silver&oranges returned and sprayed rubbery white sealant over the ceiling, taking care to spare the lenses of the two video cameras. Then they vacuumed debris from the floor, mostly dirt and redwood needles. They wiped down the ceiling, walls and floor again and used hot air blowers to dry each surface. Then they withdrew, leaving the stage empty, a white room dominated by a huge metal shaft.

Two men dressed in gold-and-green livery carried a small desk through the remaining opening in the wall. Another arrived with a computer's hard drive and placed it on the desk, followed by two backup drives.

An exceedingly dignified gold&green now entered carrying a stain-less steel cylinder as reverently as if it were a piece of the True Cross. He set the cylinder on the desk, polished it with a cloth and brushed it with a feather duster. Then he turned and faced the intruding rectan-gular mass of metal. Menniss thought he stood and moved like a butler.

"What's that?" Menniss asked.

"It's the cylinder from my bulk assembler. It's probably full of active virus by now. It was almost finished last time I checked."

The outer surface of the rectangle slid upward, exposing an inner layer of brass smudged with dirt. A team of yellows rushed in and polished the brass surface clean. Once they'd done this, the but-ler, who had been standing at attention all the while, turned around slowly, examining the room. He stepped to the desk and shifted it slightly. He stood back and studied the arrangement again. Then he left.

A line appeared on the brass shaft. The line widened as two doors drew apart. The shaft was an elevator. A man stepped out.

HE WAS TALL and silver-haired. He wore a white robe. His face was young, unscarred by time, but he radiated the serenity and wisdom of great age. A painted triangle framed the upper half of his face and, rather than looking ludicrous, it enhanced his dignity.

He turned and faced the cylinder full of virus. "I, Alexandros, salute you," he said.

As if to a king or a great hero. Or a respected enemy.

Alexandros turned from the cylinder and clasped his hands behind his back. He moved his lips as if he were speaking. But even with the volume turned all the way up, Menniss couldn't hear anything. He zoomed in and spotted the Bluetooth earpiece, incon-gruous for a man wearing a long white robe.

Francine stood up and stretched. "I'm afraid to ask what kind of food you have down here."

Menniss tore his eyes from the screen with difficulty. But they'd been watching for hours, and he was hungry too. "It may surprise you."

He dug around in the boxes and brought out a few treasures he'd stored away specifically to please her: shrink-wrapped smoked tilapia, roasted red bell peppers, tarragon mayonnaise and Armenian flatbread crackers. She clapped her hands, laughed, and arranged the food on a silver tray. A flash of normalcy. But only a flash. There was nothing to look at but the screen, and things were happening again.

The elevator door opened, and a woman in a long violet robe stepped out. Someone still hidden in the elevator handed her a cylindrical white chair or stool. She carried it over to Alexandros and gestured to him to sit. He did, and she stood behind him, her hands at her sides.

The elevator came and went 11 more times, each time giving forth a violet-robed attendant and a chair; no two of the chairs were alike. The violet robes arranged the chairs in a semicircle facing the stainless steel cylinder. The elevator made another 11 circuits, bringing down one person each time. Their faces were ancient and young; they were each conducted to a specific chair by a specific violet-robed assistant. Each person's chair matched the clothes of the person who sat in it. Those clothes, in turn, invoked the gaudy uniforms they'd been watching since the invasion had begun.

Menniss began to explain this to Francine, but she'd already noticed.

"It's such a comic book," she said. "All they need is capes."

Alexandros rose. "The Illuminati are assembled in expedition," he said. "We leave no chair empty for the Eldest, as our presence itself embodies her will. We shall proceed."

The Illuminati remained motionless except for their lips.

Francine giggled. "I bet they love their earpieces. Do you think they're pretending to control their troops by telepathy?"

Menniss thought, Yes, it's a comic book. But it also draws me in. I can't mock them like Francine does.

The elevator door opened again, and a small balding man came out, pushing a wheeled office chair with a laptop on its seat.

Francine laughed out loud. "That's Martin! Martin Stockman. Oh my God. Is that the best they could do?"

"Who's Martin Stockman?"

"We sit on the same NIH study section. I told you about him

before. He's an idiot. Well, not an idiot, actually, but he's not much of a scientist. He looks good on paper, with his long list of credentials and publications and committee chairmanships, but he's never done any creative work in his life. How funny that they picked *him*."

The balding man set his laptop on the desk and connected it to one of the external hard drives, and Francine huffed with an outrage so wholehearted and familiar that life felt normal for a moment.

"Do you think he'll figure it out?" Menniss asked.

"With all my data?" Francine said. "Of course he'll figure it out. I already told you—he's not *actually* an idiot."

The elevator door remained closed. Martin worked at his computer. The Immortals sat motionless, speaking into their headsets. Menniss rummaged around his boxes and found a bottle of good wine, much to Francine's approval. They clinked glasses and drank but skipped the toast because neither could think of one. Francine cleaned up the remnants of their lunch. They drank a second glass of wine. They tried to talk but couldn't find anything to say.

The elevator door opened again. Yet another woman in a violet robe stepped out. Someone they couldn't see handed her a simple wooden chair that wouldn't have been out of place in a classroom. She carried it across the room and set it beside the cylinder, facing the circle of Illuminati. She returned to the elevator and waited for its doors to open. When they did, Baehl was standing there.

BAEHL WALKED WITH a limp and slightly bent forward, his right arm cramped to his side. He had a deep scratch along his face and the beginnings of a black eye, but he didn't look seriously injured.

"Hiya," he said with an incongruous sense of cheer that made Menniss and Francine laugh.

"Please, my friend, be seated," Alexandros said.

Baehl pretended to misunderstand and offered the chair to his personal violet-robed attendant. When she protested, Baehl scratched his head, said, "You mean me?" and sat cross-legged in it.

"I am sorry to see you are injured," Alexandros said. "How did it happen?"

"A slight fracas among the hafeems," Baehl said, "whose moods were lightly fricasseed. Truth be told, they'd gotten a little edgy there at the end. We had a wrinkle, a production problem, and some thought they wouldn't ever be made immortal. Honestly, if you hadn't come, there might have been a riot, and not the funny kind. I got punched. t could have been hurt worse if your gaudy troopers hadn't pulled me out in the nick of time, but I was only nicked."

While Baehl talked, Menniss could see the Illuminati as cartoonish, the way Francine did. But when Alexandros spoke, he fell back under their spell.

"I am sorry that you came to harm," Alexandros said. "It was unsafe to gather so many in so tight a spot and face them with the object of their desire. Had we been free to do so, we would have intervened before you gathered so many. But a greater power stayed our hand for months, and even after releasing the stay, demanded that we hold off until we had transported to safety a certain young woman recently turned immortal. So that wound on your face is not from our servants?"

"From my crew," Baehl said. "Damn tricky business trying to help people, have you noticed?"

"I have noticed little else for many thousands of years," Alexandros said and made a sound like a tired chuckle. "But you must forgive your friends. Is it not accepted by law and instinct that when a child's life is threatened, that child's parents will do anything necessary to protect the child's life? More than accepted, for we would regard as cowardly, or worse, any parent who failed to do so. And what is a child to a parent? Nothing but an image of immortality. How much more excusable must we regard it when a man or woman attempts to protect a potential immortality rather than the image? The truest child of an immortal being is his own future life, and, therefore, your followers were compelled by ethics, morality and instinct to do whatever they could to give life to those future selves."

Baehl jumped to his feet and applauded. "Bravo!" he said. "Truly a grand speech. Bravo again! How properly famed for their eloquence are the Illuminati. Oh, please drench me with more words, and more words still, so shapely, so abstract and deeply thought, so marvelously pompous. Bravo. Bravo."

"A riot?" Francine asked.

"I was worried about that," Menniss said. "Everyone down there was becoming like me, a hanger-on, hungering to be made perfect."

"I would have had enough virus for everyone in about a day," Francine said. "But I guess I didn't tell anyone."

Menniss stroked her.

"Words truly are not enough." Alexandros sounded sad and burdened. "Those who, unlike yourself, know the true weight of life, and with whole heart seek to lift it, must do more than speak. And so we shall, using whatever wisdom we possess."

He rose. He closed his eyes. He opened them. With enormous gravitas, he crossed to the stainless steel cylinder, took it in his hands and held it high. Turning to the assembled Illuminati, he said, "In all responsibility, what should we do with this great and poisonous gift?"

MENNISS TURNED FROM the screen to look at Francine. She'd begun to rock to and fro beside him, a strange behavior that reminded him of the repetitive mechanical motions of an autistic child. "What's wrong?" he asked.

"They created Hitler," she said. "You know that, don't you?"

"What are you talking about?"

"Weren't you there when Janice told that story? She visited the Illuminati once, remember?"

"I know, but I don't remember hearing that particular story."

"Alexandros bragged about putting Hitler in power. Stalin too. On purpose."

"Why would they do that?"

"Because they thought it would prevent something worse."

She repeated the words but with altered emphasis. "Because they *thought* it would prevent something worse." She resumed her rocking.

Alexandros had returned to his seat and held the cylinder in his lap. "Expand for us your vision," he said, addressing Baehl.

"Pardon?" Baehl said.

"Your plan. Your intentions. What you meant to achieve by making mortals immortal."

"I meant to help my hafeems and my mortals. Heal the sick, you know. Keep my friends around longer."

"Yes, of course. And beyond that? Surely you analyzed what would follow?"

Baehl shrugged. "That farseeing thing, it's your style, not mine. I'm not a control freak. You keep your mortals from talking to the tabloids by monitoring their every move and threatening spontaneous combustion if they step an inch out of line. If one of my hangers-on sold his story to the *National Enquirer*, then I guess we'd be outed. I don't believe in trying to predict the stock market. I expect that life will do what it wills. It usually does, anyway."

"Indeed, that is a philosophy," Alexandros said. "Do not overstep the mandate of the moment. Never lean forward into the future but let the rightness of the day suffice. Life will indeed do as it wills, and therefore, your people grow mad with lust for longer life. You are content with this?"

"I could say something earnest," Baehl said. "For example, I might point out that your thoughtful compositions often hurt the world a lot more than my crazy improvisations. But that would be out of character. I don't believe in being earnest. How about you ask me next Tuesday? I'm sure I'll think of something funny by then."

A flash of anger passed over Alexandros' face. Anger, then sadness, and then both dissolving into a great serenity. "Guiding the future is difficult. And yet, when one has the perception to see beyond the immediate moment, one can hardly set aside that which one has seen. If there were before you a man beating a woman, surely you would intervene. If the man drew her out of sight around a corner before beginning the beating, still you would feel so inclined. And what if he did not beat her in the present but promised to beat her that evening in their home? Would you then feel relieved of all responsibility? Soraya, would you be so kind as to see tomorrow for us?"

A woman beside him rose. She wore a black gown with iridescent blue flecks, and her face shone with outrage and intelligence.

"You wish me to calculate the consequences, Alexandros?" Soraya asked. "To foresee? To enlighten this man who does not see?"

"Not for him, Soraya," Alexandros said serenely.

"For the scientist?" Soraya said. "Is she watching? I am pleased and honored to speak to her." She turned slightly and faced the camera, in a startling illusion of direct conversation. "If you are watching, I ask you to think on this: What shall come after a thousand hafeems and mortals are made immortal? Will they keep the secret of immortality hidden? Of course they will not. There are too many of them. The miracle will become known, and everyone in the world will want *this* for themselves and their families." She tapped the cylinder.

"The most powerful and the wealthiest will transform first, but the rest will follow. Will these newly made Immortals decline to bear children? Of course not. Their children will not be born as True Immortals, but they will soon be made so by their True Immortal parents. When everyone lives forever, each birth is an addition rather than a substitution, and the human population will grow with unbearable speed. If this growth is left unchecked, how long before 100 billion humans burden this planet? A century? And yet the earth cannot bear so many. It will be a disaster worse than climate change, and there will also be climate change.

"Mortals value their lives, but Immortals value their lives still more. The most farseeing of the newly made Immortals will realize that they must act quickly to prevent the becoming of so many. Can you foresee what actions they will take to forestall a world choked with hungry Immortals?"

Baehl put his hand to his forehead and circled his thumb and forefinger between his eyes. "I am very stupid, as you know. I could not possibly have imagined the population issue. But now that you mention the problem, I foresee a brilliant and strange device to solve it. And what shall we call this marvelous creation that can save the newly immortal world? I dub thee birth control."

Francine broke into peals of laughter.

"You didn't use to like him," Menniss said.

"I do now," she said. "I like him extremely."

The female Immortal was not amused. To Alexandros, she said, "He does not feel the bite. He does not think; he plays."

"It's only that I'm tired," Baehl said. "I can't think on my feet so great when my feet hurt; otherwise, I'd say something funny enough to knock your socks off. But I shall be serious." He put on a clownish frown. "The population of the world has doubled twice in the last century. Why has it doubled? Because nice doctors figured out how to reduce infant mortality. Population doubling twice in a century is a Very Bad Thing. So according to your thinking, someone should have stopped those crummy docs from saving those awful babies. Righty-oh?"

Soraya scowled. "The other audience," Alexandros reminded her. She nodded.

"No children at all? That is a grim image. Think of a world composed only of adults made wise, cynical and pessimistic by experience, never enlivened by hopeful springs of newly born life. We would sink into despair. To avoid that fate, perhaps we would ration innocence? Perhaps one child shall be allotted to every 100 households, and those dreamers moved like pawns of delight from home to home.

"How sad this image of a world with no new young. And yet, it is not a likely outcome. The world is not an organized institution controlled by technocrats but a wild and anarchic jungle controlled to a limited extent by the strong. Violence is more likely than a carefully managed lifestyle. Consider this: the first newly made Immortals after your hafeems will be wealthy and powerful. Won't some of them foresee the threat as clearly as I do? And won't some find it wise to thin the numbers of the world and thereby forestall starvation? If they act quickly after becoming immortal, they could release a plague that kills many of those who have not yet transformed. How difficult would it be, oh scientist, to engineer such a counter-plague? Not hard. You could do it yourself in days."

"Could you do that?" Menniss asked.

Francine looked worried. "It would be trivial. I've often worried that some angry graduate student might act out young adult annoyance by assembling a modified smallpox virus."

Baehl was trying to say something, but Soraya overrode him. "You may say that no one would do such a terrible thing. Surely, we Illuminati would never countenance the release of such a plague.

But do you trust the wealthy and powerful of the above-ground world to show restraint? They will be young, unseasoned and even more arrogant than they are now. Are you sure they would hold back? There is a self-fulfilling, self-escalating nature to all such scenarios. If I foresee that a billionaire or a dictator will commit so great a crime, am I not bound to act first and prevent the crime? Foreseeing my foresight, will not some billionaire or dictator attack me first? And won't I, foreseeing their foresight into my foresight, attack *them* first?

"I have described these events as if they occur in sequence, but such visions unfold all at once in self-catalyzing calculation. Each group sees what *could* occur and takes steps to ensure it does not. This has happened often in the history of mortals. As the great Thucydides taught us, Sparta and Athens were each compelled to attack the other to forestall attack, and out of that whirlwind tautology, a disaster even greater than what had been foreseen by either befell both sides. If mortals, with such short lives at stake, can lose them by striving so hard to save them, how much more unstable would be a world of new Immortals with infinity at stake?"

"Oh, such visions!" Baehl said. "But you've left out one part: Immortals are chicken-shits. What I'm more afraid of than your Thucydides trap is that the world will turn into a passel of sober, scared-shitless Immortals living in holes." He brought out a file and rasped at his fingernails.

He performed this simple act with such theatrical sobriety that Francine burst into laughter again. This time, though, Menniss thought he heard a hysterical edge.

Soraya turned to Alexandros. "I shall stop now, shall I not?" Her manner had lost all its bite; she was a picture of equanimity.

"Thank you, Soraya," Alexandros said. He remained silent for some time, tapping gently on the stainless steel cylinder still cradled in his lap. Then he said, "Thank you for your part, too, Mr. Baehl." His voice was gentle and poised. "You may go now."

"Go? Where do you want me to go?"

"Into the elevator, friend, and up. We shall take you to the other, grander underground and keep you safely there."

Baehl rose obediently and ambled to the elevator. He paused at its door, and though he didn't stage a backflip, he did turn around and twirl his mustache. "Sometimes you win, and sometimes you lose. Sometimes you win after losing. Check my sleeves—I might have something up them." He stepped inside, and the elevator doors closed upon him.

"What a beautiful exit," Francine said.

"What did he mean about having something up his sleeves?" Menniss asked.

"Maybe he sent a copy of my data to someone outside? I don't know. I'd never count Baehl out."

ALEXANDROS SPOKE TO the bald man at the computer, the one Francine despised, Martin Stockman. "How have you progressed, sir?" Alexandros said. "Have you discovered how it was done? Can you reproduce it?"

"Easily," Stockman said. "It's just a short genetic sequence. She inserted it into a standard gene therapy retrovirus. It's trivial."

Francine huffed again.

"Very, very good," Alexandros said. "I have one additional question: must we fear that any of our people who have entered here could carry the infection out with them by accident?"

"Not at all," Martin said. "Retroviruses used for gene therapy are engineered so they can't survive in the open air. They have to be injected. So there's no risk at all."

"This is a great relief," Alexandros said. "Thank you. One must, at times, sacrifice the few to save the many, but it always breaks one's heart to do so. What you have said limits the size of the necessary holocaust, and I thank you for it."

"Holocaust?" Francine cried. "*What* holocaust? What's he talking about? Richard, do you know what he's talking about?"

BACK IN THE early days of his career, Menniss had loved small sports cars—Datsun 240Zs and Toyota AE86s. He'd redline them and enjoy the engine's snarl as it rose from gear to gear. Then someone gave him a Mercedes. At first, he wasn't impressed: no gears to shift, no growling engine, no drama. It took a while for him to learn that real power surges silently and forges forward without a sound.

The Illuminati didn't strut or fret as they calculated the means of slaughter. They didn't grow excited. They spoke quietly, a solemn conversation without excess words.

The scene unfolded on the screen like a nightmare remembered in advance.

They choose poison gas as their method. Which type? They chose a type. Soraya had anticipated this and already had the means at hand.

Further discussion. The necessity of supplementary corrosive gases to penetrate walled-off areas. Small explosives to be strategically placed. The sealing of the tunnels, the collapse of the caverns, the burying of a thousand hafeems and mortals.

A nightmare made more horrific because so gravely, so responsibly, so *compassionately* discussed.

"BUT WHY?" FRANCINE moaned. "Why?"

Alexandros was giving a speech. "To Yavànna, the Eldest, we must give tribute. For, as always, she has shown that her vision surpasses ours. We would have prevented this discovery. She, in her farseeing wisdom, allowed it. Why? Because mortal science would on its own, and surely in no more than a century's time, have attained this same power. And released it far and wide, wisdomless. Yavànna protected a gifted half-immortal and allowed him to speed the discovery forward. We, in our ignorance, protested; in her wisdom, she ignored our protest. She protected him from us until he succeeded, and then—oh, how magnificently conceived—at the final moment, she allowed us to step in and receive the fruits of his work. With this work her wisdom wrought, we can safely manage its introduction to the world."

Alexandros is a great man, Menniss thought. *If he were to lead me, I would follow. But he's leading me to my death.*

"To you, oh gods," Alexandros said, "we offer this holocaust. We ask your blessing as we commit, in the service of a greater good, this crime so terrible it bursts the heart. After this cruel act is accomplished, we pray for wisdom so that we can create institutions and powers that will allow the world to safely assimilate so great and dangerous a gift. For this, we pray."

Menniss imagined it: the Illuminati and their servants would withdraw, leaving a thousand hafeems and hangers-on in those caverns. Then, 100s of pipes would snake in and fill the underground with gas.

The poison would seep through the safe room's cracks and wisp lazily toward his skin. Poison gases and corrosive gases too. These would sear him, dissolve his living flesh.

He'd always believed in life after death; he just wanted to avoid it. But now, he would avoid nothing. He would sit motionless through the pain. Like his Sensei burning to death with dignity and strength, Menniss would stare without flinching into the next life. As the gas suffocated him and the corrosives burned, he would pass through.

The doorway he hadn't built—the always available escape from the trap—he'd found it at last. And he would go through.

He would let go of everything. Gladly, for his life had been a constant struggle without purpose, a tale of sound and fury signifying nothing. A foolish life lived by a fool.

No more. No more struggle. No more fear. No effort. Just great peace.

And then he heard someone calling.

FRANCINE

"RICHARD, LISTEN TO me." She shook him. "Richard, I can stop him. Can you hear me? Richard?"

"Yes, I hear you. What is it?" He began to scratch himself like he did when he woke up. But he couldn't have fallen asleep.

"I can stop him," she said again. "I can make him not do that—that horrible thing."

"No, Francine," he said, "you cannot."

How could she get him to take her seriously about this? "Yes, I can. That first night here, you said you needed me to protect you. Remember? I paid attention, and I did something to protect you. It will protect everyone else down here too."

Richard looked at his watch. "Damn. I was supposed to give your medications hours ago." He fumbled around in his pockets.

"What I'm saying isn't crazy," she protested, but she knew how that must sound. He'd found the pill bottles; she could hear them rattle in his pocket. He wouldn't ever believe her. She had to do it on her own.

She lunged for the door's handle and pulled it a few inches aside. "We're in here!" she shouted. "Come here and get us."

But he'd grabbed her ankles. He was too strong, and she'd never escape. She felt his grip tighten.

And then he let go. "Go on," he said.

She opened the door the rest of the way and jumped through it.

SHE ROLLED ONTO one shoulder on the metal floor of the corridor. She picked herself up and ran toward the Clean Room. It was hard

453

to think while she ran, but she had to think because the two impera-
tives pushed in opposite directions. Blair and Janice needed time to
get away, which meant she should keep the secret as long as possible.
But she had to give up the secret soon enough to prevent mass murder. What was the right balance? She lacked sufficient data.

She estimated viral replication speed and counted back the hours.
She turned the possibilities up and down, but she hadn't solved the
problem by the time she reached the tunnel's end. She climbed the
ladder and pounded on the plastic above it. She pounded hard.

After several minutes, a saw appeared and cut a hole in the
plastic floor. Moments later, several blue&blacks pointed guns at her.
"Francine Selis?" one of them asked. They took her arms and pulled
her up.

She was now in the room she'd been watching on the display.
She'd been watching the scene on a screen for so long that when she
walked in, she felt like she was stepping onto a stage. Here were all
the Illuminati, plus a new contingent of blue&blacks. They pointed
guns at her. She'd never faced a gun before. She felt no physical fear,
only detachment, as if she were watching a movie with the sound off.

Richard appeared from behind with his hands raised above his
head, just like in the movies. He gestured for Francine to do the same.

"We're unarmed," Richard said.

She missed the mental clarity of mania. She couldn't think half
so clearly now. All her usual mental obstacles made their presence
known, and she wasn't getting anywhere with the problem.

It was a *really* clean room now. No, not perfectly clean. She spotted a few flecks of dirt on the concrete floor and a few blades of grass,
probably from the Illuminati's boots. You'd have to vacuum a room
like this constantly because everything would show.

Watching him on the little screen, she'd found Alexandros pompous and silly, but in person, he made her legs tremble. Richard took
her hand.

"Dr. Selis," Alexandros said. "I am honored to meet you."

This terrible but great man: how could she possibly stall *him*?
Manipulate *him*?

"We have a great deal to talk about," he said. "But I must beg your patience. I have a few arrangements to complete. If you would indulge me one or two minutes … you shall then have my full attention."

He turned partly away and spoke into his headset. The other Immortals in the room spoke into their headsets too. Were they giving orders to begin the holocaust?

A red-haired Immortal, a woman, smiled at Francine and nodded reassuringly.

Reassuring about what? That I won't be killed along with the rest? As if I care about that.

"Alexandros," she burst out. "Listen to me. Your plan doesn't make any sense. It's completely wrong."

"Of course, it is wrong, child." He remained standing, angled away from her. "The murder of innocents is always wrong, even when intended to save a far greater number of other innocents."

"That's not what I'm talking about," she said. "I'm trying to tell you that your calculations are totally off base. You're missing a key piece of information."

He gave her his full attention now, and it was a crushing weight. A weight of what? Not of power only. A weight of sadness. Of nobility and sadness.

"There's something you don't know," she said. "But before I tell you, you must promise—you must give your word—not to harm Richard."

"Little one," Alexandros said, "from the moment you and your lover arrived in this room, you were both saved."

She'd promised herself to save Richard, and now that was done. The mental click of a task completed. Onto the next. "What about Dr. Lemon? Is he okay?"

"The doctor is safely recuperating with his son," Alexandros said. "He's agreed to work with me and shall not be harmed."

Work for Alexandros? The coward. "What about protection for everyone else down here? Can't you—I don't know—take everyone into captivity? Why do you have to kill them?"

"Dear child. I do not wish to recreate in life those fables where the father says, 'All things thou can do but open this box.' My servants are loyal, but some temptations transcend all loyalty, and immortality is the greatest temptation of all. We have no choice; we must prevent death with death."

In person, he was overwhelming. Everything he said seemed *true*.

Baehl had pushed back their power. But Baehl wasn't here, only Alexandros and Soraya, and their vision filled her. She saw it coming: the free gift of immortality leading inevitably to anarchy and war and mass slaughter.

Which meant everything she'd thought up till now was backward.

What if that horrible thing Alexandros intended to do was *right?* That was so awful she couldn't bear it.

"Child," Alexandros said, "Do not hold yourself to blame. Science is a force of nature. Those who carry it forward are servants, not actors. You are not responsible."

You think I was only a servant. What you do not know is that I took a step further.

I made the final choice while manic. But I conceived it while sane. My own free choice, and perhaps it was utterly wrong.

"I will explain now, and you will have to listen."

Soraya's eyes bored into her and Alexandros', too, and behind them, the other Immortals clustered like ravens.

"Was I wrong?" Alexandros said. "Are you other than innocent? Have you acted? Have you made a choice?"

Francine ignored him and tried to think. If Soraya's vision was accurate, she should admit everything. Perhaps they could stop Janice, pull her back.

But the instant Alexandros had Janice under his control, he would feel free—feel obliged—to carry out his holocaust.

Allow Janice to escape, and possibly World War Three would follow. Bring Janice back, and certain death for everyone underground would follow. The choice—the trigger—was in her hands.

Francine sank to the floor. She wrapped her arms around her stomach.

Soraya's voice followed her down. "What have you *done*, child? *Tell me, what have you done?*"

I will burst. This abscess inside me will explode.

SHE FELT RICHARD'S touch on her shoulder and came back from the brink. She put out her hands to push herself up.

Hands on a cold plastic floor. On the floor of a prison cell, a gulag, a concentration camp. The answer, when it came, flowed up through her hands—her mind had nothing to do with it. Perhaps she was shallow. Perhaps she hadn't looked at the whole picture as she should have. But she would take Baehl's path and choose the present over the future. She wouldn't let Alexandros kill everyone down here.

RICHARD HELPED HER to her feet.

She didn't meet the eyes of Alexandros or Soraya, for she knew they could overpower her with a glance. "Do you understand how retroviruses work?" she asked. "They reverse engineer DNA." Because the point now was to delay, at least a little longer.

"Yes, I have heard of this," Alexandros said.

He sounded so friendly and interested that Francine looked up at him directly. And that was the end. She couldn't possibly deceive this man.

She could only try. "My first hypothesis," she said, "was as follows—"

But she was a beginner playing against a grandmaster. Alexandros put up his hand. "No more. Your purpose is only to delay me." He tapped his earpiece. "We shall begin now."

"No, you won't," she said.

She said it with absolute certainty. Because the logic of the circumstance now took away all other options. If Alexandros had decided to go forward, she had only one choice. "You think of yourself as noble. And maybe you are. But the justification you think you have for your mass murder isn't correct. You mean to kill everyone down here to stop immortality from escaping. But it won't work. It won't stop a thing." She paused. Even giving Janice an extra second might help. "Because I gave Janice an infectious form of the virus."

"You did what?" Martin Stockman shouted. He pounded on the table. He jumped up, red-faced, furious. He advanced on her, enraged, but Richard stepped between them. "You've set an infectious retrovirus loose? A virus that changes DNA? How could you dare?"

"I don't know," she said.

A hand lifted her chin. It was Alexandros, pouring his gaze into her. "Explain yourself," he said.

"Just before Janice left, I gave her a different kind of retrovirus. It carries the immortality genes, and it alters DNA, just like the regular one. But it's extremely communicable, about as infectious as measles. It's active enough to make even a True Immortal sneeze, and whoever gets it should remain contagious for a week or more. Many people she passes by will catch the disease, and in turn, they'll give it to many of those they pass by. I've set an immortality plague loose, and it will percolate into the entire population of the world. Killing your captives won't do a thing."

"But you must have prepared this long before I arrived," Alexandros murmured. "Why?"

"To stop someone like you," she said.

Silence. Deep breathing. "Oh, my child," he said.

To her immense surprise, he took her in his arms.

ALEXANDROS HELD HER close. Like a father. Like a brother. "So great a burden," he said.

The warmth of his multimillennial life filled her.

"Oh, child, so great a burden." He stepped away. "I must do what I have promised never to do. I must take on a burden perhaps too great."

He faced the other Illuminati. "I choose to defy the Eldest and capture this mortal. Those who do not wish to join me, leave now."

Shock, disbelief. Rebellion. Against all rules, all history and established tradition. Violating the absolute rule of seniority. Impossible. Impious.

"I do not ask any of you to join me," Alexandros said. "You can all go. But go now."

Horror. Anger. One by one, they entered the elevator and left. All except Soraya.

Five in this blank room: the two tall Immortals bearing a weight heavier than hers. Martin and Richard, relatively weightless. Standing together.

Alexandros said, "Will the Eldest accept it, Soraya?"

"She may take it as part of nature. But she will not accept it."

"Can we personally escape her power after we violate her will?"

"I have spent 10 years preparing. I think we can."

"You have a little time," Martin said. "This Janice person won't become infectious immediately. It typically takes 36 to 72 hours to become contagious. Unless Dr. Selis tweaked the virus."

"Of course I did." Francine looked directly at Alexandros so he'd see she wasn't lying. "Janice will become infectious no more than 12 hours after taking it. And I told her to swallow the pill the moment she made it outside."

"Eight hours from now, then," said Soraya.

"She's under Jeremiah's care," Alexandros said, "and he will do whatever she asks."

"But she is with the child-Immortal Blair, and before he left the underground world to meet the first artificial Immortal, I caused a transmitting chip to be placed beneath his skin. We shall have them."

"This shall break the Illuminati."

"Leaving only us," Soraya said. "As has happened before."

"Though never also in defiance of the Eldest. But so it must be. Send out your blue&blacks, Soraya. Once in range, they must kill her from a distance. They must incinerate her and everyone with her. I, Alexandros, take responsibility."

"I, too, take responsibility," Soraya said.

Francine thought, *I'm no less a criminal or hero than they.*

"I, too," she murmured. Then louder, "I too."

CHAPTER 10
REUNION

"To maladapt a fine bombastic phrase, one might
call it 'the sneeze heard round the world.'"

MY EARLY YEARS, VOL.1.
BY HOWARD EZEKIAL IVANOVICH BAEHL,
AKA, THE CHRONICLER.

BLAIR

STANDING ALONE ON the small beach, Blair watched two boats criss-cross the ocean before him, their white sails beautiful against the deep blue of the sea and the lighter blue of the sky. The boats carried protectors, he knew, guards against threats by water. On the cliff above, two men in saffron suits sat in a white Pontiac. There were others nearby as well. Jeremiah had guaranteed him a dozen guards, enough to keep him safe from any hanger-on. So why did he still feel vulnerable?

Blair touched the deep red rock and ran his hand down it to the phone number inscribed at its base, the phone number that had led him to Saul.

Or rather, led *Janice* to Saul. He still hadn't seen his old mentor. Janice and Saul had been on their way when they found Richard Menniss and kidnapped him.

The thought of Menniss made him shiver as if the hanger-on were crouched somewhere nearby, ready to seize him. But it didn't make sense. What would Menniss want from him now? He's already taken his ounce of flesh. Literally.

Blair fingered his ear, once a stump but now fully grown back. Janice said she had become immortal, which meant that Menniss had succeeded in what he'd set out to do. Amazing enough. And shared it with Janice. Even more amazing.

Turned immortal, Menniss would be a friend, not a threat. There was nothing to worry about, so why did he feel so anxious?

He wished Saul were here. Saul was a person. So was Janice.

And he was not. He'd been dancing around the idea for a while, but now he fully admitted it to himself: he was a nobody. A zero. A shaving of pretty wood curled around a central emptiness.

Take those 12 bodyguards around him: he'd never even dared have bodyguards because he was afraid that if a hanger-on found him, he'd turn his bodyguards into hangers-on too. Those followers of Jeremiah knew he was an Immortal, yet they didn't act like hangers-on. Why? Because Jeremiah had charisma; he had personal power; he was a great being; he could trust his followers because they worshipped him.

He was nothing like Jeremiah. Nowhere close. He didn't even exist.

But that didn't explain why he was so frightened. Back before all this happened, he walked in the open. He lived a normal life in Australia, Micronesia and Brazil. He took reasonable precautions, but he wasn't afraid of living his life. He hiked and swam and sunbathed; he shopped in open markets; he sailed in boats no larger than those two offshore.

He didn't have anyone to protect him then. So why, at this moment, was he terrified merely to stand on this beach?

Twelve bodyguards. Far more than necessary. He had nothing to fear—unless an earthquake tossed the cliff down or a terrorist dropped a nuclear bomb on Santa Cruz. But impersonal disasters like that could happen to him anywhere.

Was it living underground that had done it? Had those months of safety taken away what little ability to face the world he used to have? Was he like a man who'd been carried on a litter and had to learn to walk again?

Those months in the Illuminati catacombs. Profound security and equally profound humiliation. He quivered with shame to think of the days when he thought of himself as the crown of creation. Down below, he'd never been allowed into the council halls of the Illuminati, seldom even seen an Illuminatus except to receive instruction. He'd been forced to find companionship among hafeems and mortals, who played a lot of Scrabble.

He'd found it novel to move among mortals who knew his status as a True Immortal. But they didn't worship him. More the opposite: they served high Illuminati and treated him like an infant.

Where was Janice? He'd been waiting on this beach for most of a day.

Hours passed, and the sun dropped toward the ocean. Blair closed his eyes and listened to the sounds—the frothy noises of the water's curling upper edge, the hollow warning as the underwave pulled back, the shaking thud of tons pounding the sand, the confident racing forward of wave over sand, the genteel hiss of the water's hem as it drew back, the pop of bubbles parting over the open breathing tubes of crabs.

Blair teased apart the ocean's tang and separated its perfumes and flavors. He opened his eyes and watched the sunset reds overtake the sky's blue. *This is life*, he thought. *Underground I wasn't alive.*

Someone waved to him from the clifftop. Someone was racing down the stairs (no longer rickety, they'd been repaired for this meeting). *It was her.*

She jumped off the bottom stair onto the sand, stumbled, laughed, recovered, and ran toward him. She stopped a few feet away. Neither smiling nor frowning, just looking.

Looking at him like an equal. He could feel the change. In the past, despite all their games, he'd been superior, an Immortal dating a mortal, his body alone able to dazzle and overwhelm. But now she was an Immortal, too. Now she could dazzle *him*.

"Hey, Blair." She gave him the smallest of kisses. She kicked off her shoes and walked past him to the water's edge. She let a wavelet run over her feet. "They put me through all kinds of tests. This nerdy scientist, Martin, who was in a real hurry to get somewhere else, wanted proof that I'd become immortal. I've lost the scar on my knee, but he'd never seen me when I had the scar, so that didn't help. I was afraid he'd have to cut off one of my toes or something to prove it. Luckily, he found what he wanted in my mouth—I'm growing a new tooth to replace the one with a crown. That got him excited.

"After he finished up, someone else put me through all kinds of tests to make sure I didn't have any electronic bugs in my body. That's why it took so long. Sorry."

A wave larger than the others slapped water up to her waist, and she shrieked playfully.

He joined her by the water and put his arm around her, but he couldn't think of anything to say.

"So, are my teeth going to fall out every so often when they get dull?" she asked. "I hope it doesn't happen all at once."

"Just one at a time." Involuntarily, Blair turned to look back up at the clifftop. He saw a movement there and thought again of Menniss. "What about that hanger-on?" he asked. "The one who cut off my ear."

"Menniss? Dennis the Menniss. We're friends. He's down there in Baehl's underground getting ready to become immortal as soon as Francine makes enough virus for everyone. The idea seems to depress him. Poor guy. To get what you want and not want it—that just sucks."

Janice was still staring out to sea. Blair wondered whether she was feeling what he used to feel when he looked at the ocean: a sense of kinship, of infinity joining infinity. He touched her shoulder and asked her what she was thinking.

"Before you touched me, or after? Before you touched me, I was thinking that the world looked new, like someone had just made it. I was sick for a long time, so sick I almost died. Probably anyone who gets well after being seriously ill feels reborn. But after you touched me?"

He took her in his arms, hoping to sense the immortality in her body. She trembled.

"Why me?" he asked. "There's nothing special about me. I'm nobody."

"Let's go find a motel," she said. "*Now.*"

They tried to hold hands as they walked up the stairs, but the stairs weren't broad enough. At the top, she pulled him across the street and into Lighthouse Park. They passed behind windblown cedars and completely out of sight of the boats. But Jeremiah's body-guards would be spreading out around them on foot and by car.

They stepped over fallen branches and skipped around mud pits. They reached the other side of the park and the street that ran along it. A Porsche coupe pulled up alongside them.

In sudden terror, Blair froze, his legs tense and ready to run.

The car's window rolled down. "I wonder whether I could prevail upon you to join me," the driver said.

A white car with saffron highlights came speeding toward them from the connecting street. Undoubtedly his bodyguards. Blair waved at them to leave him alone, and that car stopped and parked 100 yards away.

Saul climbed out of his Porsche; they were embracing, thumping each other on the back. "More than 100 years," Saul said.

"I'm so sorry," Blair said.

"Never mind. To continue flogging oneself over a transgression for which one has been absolved suggests poor breeding and ill manners." Saul turned to Janice and kissed her on the forehead. "And what about you? It hasn't been a century since we last spoke, but it feels as though it's been that long. You were terribly sick when I left you. Now, you look well."

"I'm perfectly well," Janice said. Feeling shy and proud simultaneously, she added, "I'm immortal, too."

"Wonderful!" Saul smiled broadly.

They know each other better than I know either of them, Blair thought. He was jealous, though of which one he wasn't sure.

"But Saul, *you're* not immortal yet." Janice sounded distressed. "Let's go back to Baehl's underground and get you one of those shots."

"Perhaps not just at the moment," Saul said. "There's a pressing concern we really must attend to first. Also, I've developed certain philosophical objections to immortality."

"But you have to," she said. "For me. I want you around forever."

"That's extremely kind of you."

"Give me a chance, and I'll talk you out of all your objections," Janice hugged Saul again, and in the middle of the hug, gave a great sneeze.

"Oh my goodness. Sorry."

Saul handed her a silk handkerchief. "My dears, I deeply regret that I must taint our reunion with a hint of pressure. And yet I fear I have no choice. We—that is to say, you two—are at risk. However, if I can persuade you to trust me, I can assure you that, after a brief interval of unpleasantness, this urgency will be replaced with deep repose."

"But I'm not in any danger," Blair said. "You don't know about this, but I have protection." He pointed to the car full of bodyguards.

"Based on their coloration, they're servants of Jeremiah," Saul said. "And he's perhaps the only Illuminatus of whom I've heard good things. Not surprisingly, Jeremiah remains your friend. But a severe alteration in the plan has occurred at a higher level where more power is wielded, and Jeremiah, good soul that he is, can't protect you. However, there's one being who can, and she's charged me with carrying you to safety. There will be certain forms of assistance, delicately given, I am sure, and ..." Saul broke off and looked at the distant sky, shading his eyes.

Blair followed his gaze and saw a dark, rapidly moving cloud. The cloud seemed to alarm Saul greatly. He hurriedly opened the back door of his car. "Please, my friends, do get in."

Blair hesitated. "Who are you talking about? The one who wants to protect me, I mean."

"The Eldest, Blair. Now let's go."

The Eldest? But from what he'd heard in the Illuminati underground, the Eldest was capricious at best. "Where does she want us to go?"

"Into invisibility. Into the anonymous safety of the great cities of the world. We'll travel together, just as in the old days."

Blair still hesitated.

"I would go so far as to beg you," Saul said.

Blair felt his arm rising; it wanted to beckon the watching bodyguards. But Janice shoved him through the open door. "If Saul says we should go, we should go, and that's that," she said.

Saul drove at a measured speed. Blair's bodyguards pulled away from the curb and followed at a discreet distance. Saul continued to drive slowly, but when he turned left on a loop road that ran along the ocean, the natural flow of traffic placed three cars between them and their friendly pursuers.

"Excellent," Saul said. And then, with sudden alarm, he said, "Blair, you're transmitting."

"I am? What do you mean?"

"Sending a signal. And we are intended to leave the car. This is a wrinkle in our plans."

A tracker! He felt polluted. And his body was sheltering it. For the first time in his life, his body was the enemy. Or at least colluding with the enemy.

"Can't you call the Eldest," Janice said, "and ask her what to do?"

"Alas, I cannot. And she does like to leave things balanced on a knife's edge."

A fearful silence. This is it, Blair thought, what I've been worrying about all day. It's happening now, and not even Saul can protect me.

"Speaking of knives," Janice said, "you waved something over Menniss to locate his transmitter. Do you still have it?"

"The detector?" Saul reached into his glove compartment, came out with something that looked to Blair like a big cell phone, and handed it back.

"How does it work?" Janice asked. "Oh, I get it." She ran it over Blair's arms and his legs. She made him lean forward and slid it down his neck. "Here it is," she said. "Saul, give me a knife."

"But my dear, you're not a surgeon, and I don't have a knife."

"Or a razor blade. Shit, I have one."

She opened her purse and removed a disposable razor she used for her legs. She cracked the plastic, and the blade came off. "A towel, Saul," she said, "or a napkin?"

He handed her a wad of napkins.

Blair felt a sudden sharp pain, a blazing burn. "Damn it," Janice said. "Where *is* this thing? Oh here. Blair, push down on these napkins."

She showed Saul a small piece of plastic. Her hands were bloody. She put the transmitter in her mouth and bit down. "Are we still transmitting?"

Saul gave a deep sigh. "No, we are not. Thank you, child. Now please, if you can, remove the signs of blood. We shall have to move in public without attracting notice." He handed her a first aid kit.

They came to a street where the stoplights had malfunctioned, and masses of cars were piled up at intersections. A policeman walked into the street to direct traffic; the first lane he allowed to move forward was theirs.

As Saul glided through, Blair looked up the street and saw half a dozen SUVs racing toward them. They were all identical, painted in colors of blue and black, but they were obstructed by the traffic jam.

"Who are those people?" Blair asked.

"The ones who do not wish us well." Saul looked up. The dark cloud resolved into a handful of blue and black helicopters. They were coming dangerously close. Then dozens of much larger, double-rotor helicopters approached from another direction, and the blue and black ones veered off.

When they came to the next street, the SUVs again raced toward them, but just as they did, police cars and fire engines cut them off. Saul drove through two more intersections, similarly blocked on both sides. He pulled to the curb and said, "May I suggest that we abandon the car and dash through the doors of that restaurant? Again, sorry about the urgency."

Saul led them at a fast walk through the restaurant's lobby and into its bar. The room was full of people, and Janice was embarrassed when she had a sneezing fit.

Above rows of brightly colored bottles, a television mounted on the wall displayed a news announcer. "We have just been told that Homeland Security is conducting a drill in the greater Santa Cruz area. We are assured this is only a drill. There has *not* been any terrorist threat to the area. We repeat, there is *no* real threat. This is only a drill." The image switched to a group of helicopter commuters unsparing in complaints regarding the temporary closure of Santa Cruz's airspace.

Leaving the bar through a door marked "Employees Only," they passed along a service corridor to a covered loading area. An empty yellow taxi was parked there. They got in, with Saul behind the wheel.

After driving for a little while, they switched cars again and drove on. After two more car switches, they got into a Jeep. Saul turned into the parking lot of a convenience store and drove behind the store into a redwood forest. In near-total darkness, he navigated between giant trees, the tires occasionally slipping on the redwood mulch.

They stopped at a small clearing where a waiting pilot removed the camouflage cover from a helicopter. Cruising just above the tree line, they crossed mountains. They landed in another clearing, got in another Jeep, drove to a municipal airport and took off from the airport in a Learjet. Saul led them to the jet's private bedroom, kissed them goodnight, and closed the door.

"Where are we going?" Janice asked, stifling another sneeze.

"A large and diverse city with little surveillance," Saul said. "Crowds are best when one wants to hide."

Suddenly alone in a bedroom with Janice, Blair was overcome by shyness. Janice, however, demonstrated a considerable absence of shyness. They made love, the lovemaking of two Immortals, as the jet burrowed them deep into the night, into invisibility, into the anonymous safety of the great crowded world.

EPILOGUE

To set your mind at ease.
THE CHRONICLER

YOU MAY ALREADY have noticed that you feel a little healthier, a bit more energetic, than you used to, and that you look better, too. But what about Francine and Richard? Soraya and Alexandros?

Francine, Richard and the rest of us walked out of the Underground feeling profoundly disappointed we hadn't become immortal (haha) but otherwise unharmed. The two Illuminati aren't malicious, and when Janice escaped their net, they merely fled—no one knows where to. Saul believes that they are working to ease the world's transition to immortality, according to their own views on what that means. And as for Janice and Blair ... well, as I hope you expected to hear, she grew out of him pretty soon.

And what will happen to this world? *Much of it is up to chance.* Just wait and watch. We'll all know soon enough. A lot of it isn't going to be pretty. But when was it ever? We'll muddle through.

Check that childhood scar on your knee again. Is it getting harder to see?

Made in the USA
Middletown, DE
14 May 2023

30186042R00265